CHRISTIAN'S HOPE

Advance Praise for *Christian's Hope*

"The story of the Hochstetler family is shot through with threads of brutality, murder, kidnapping, and separation. In *Christian's Hope*, the long-lost son returns, and two worlds (Amish and Native American) collide. The golden strands of forgiveness unmerited, mercy triumphant, sweetest redemption, and amazing grace weave a tapestry of hope for us all."
—**Rhonda Schrock, writer, blogger, and columnist**

"Once again, Stutzman has drawn us in and makes us feel the angst of being forced to choose between these two cultures. He keeps us wondering how it will turn out in the end."
—**Becky Gochnauer, director, 1719 Hans Herr House & Museum**

"Stutzman employs honesty and sensitivity in fictionalizing the story of a young man striving to understand and mend his divided heart. A remarkable retelling of an extraordinary life."
—**Janice Dick, author of the Crossings of Promise series**

Praise for the Return to Northkill series:

"An evocative and gripping story. . . . Stunningly depicted Amish life and history."
   —**Sherry Gore, coauthor of the Pinecraft Pie Shop series**

"An intriguing exploration of a little-known true story of the French and Indian War."
   —**Marta Perry, author of the Keepers of the Promise series of Amish novels**

"Beneath Stutzman's spare prose runs a river of loyalty, faith, and emotion. A tour de force of research that serves to make these characters as real as memory."
   —**Adina Senft, author of the Healing Grace trilogy of Amish novels**

"A rich and authentic recounting of the perils faced by the Lenape nation and white settlers. A must read."
   —**Emma Miller, author of *A Match for Addie* and *Plain Killing***

"Written with honesty and grace. . . . A must read for all of us who strive to live out our faith."
   —**Becky Gochenaur, director, 1719 Hans Herr House & Museum**

"An incisive historical novel. . . . A truly edifying and rewarding read."
—**William Unrau, distinguished professor emeritus of history, Wichita State University**

"A great story about an Indian mother and her adopted Amish son who became an Indian: a young white man who crossed the cultural barrier that separated two very different peoples."
—**C. Rusty Sherrick, interpreter of Delaware Indian history**

"An intimately imaginative entrée into the most famous Amish experience in colonial America."
—**John L. Ruth, author of *The Earth Is the Lord's***

"A beautiful narration of nonresistant Amish life."
—**Sam Stoltzfus, Old Order Amish historian**

"Allows us to imagine the joys, tears, doubts, and religious devotion of the earliest Amish immigrants."
—**Karen Johnson-Weiner, coauthor of *The Amish***

"A dramatic and accessible tale. . . a searing virtual experience that challenges us to see how extraordinarily difficult it is to follow Jesus Christ and love our enemies."
—**Susan Schultz Huxman, president, Eastern Mennonite University**

CHRISTIAN'S HOPE

Return to Northkill, BOOK 3

ERVIN R. STUTZMAN

HERALD
PRESS

Harrisonburg, Virginia

Herald Press
PO Box 866, Harrisonburg, Virginia 22803
www.HeraldPress.com

Library of Congress Cataloging-in-Publication Data
Names: Stutzman, Ervin R., 1953- author.
Title: Christian's hope / Ervin R. Stutzman.
Description: Harrisonburg, Virginia : Herald Press, [2016] | Series: Return
   to Northkill ; book 3
Identifiers: LCCN 2016025313| ISBN 9780836199420 (softcover : acid-
free paper) | ISBN 9781513801285 (hardcover : acid-free paper)
Subjects: LCSH: Amish--Fiction. | Domestic fiction. | GSAFD:
Biographical fiction. | Historical fiction. | Christian fiction.
Classification: LCC PS3619.T88 C48 2016 | DDC 813/.6--dc23 LC record
available at https://lccn.loc.gov/2016025313

CHRISTIAN'S HOPE
© 2016 by Herald Press, Harrisonburg, Virginia 22802. 800-245-7894.
   All rights reserved.
Library of Congress Control Number: 2016025313
International Standard Book Number: 978-0-8361-9942-0 (paperback)
   978-1-5138-0128-5 (hardcover)
Printed in United States of America
Cover design by Dugan Design Group

Unless otherwise noted, Scripture text is quoted with permission from the
King James Version.

26 25 24 23   14 13 12 11 10 9 8 7 6

To Shirley Hershey Showalter and Gloria Yoder Diener, members of my monthly writers' group, whose patient and creative feedback at every milestone of the writing journey has made this book so much better than it would have been without their touch.

Contents

Author's Note

The story of Jacob Hochstetler of the Northkill is well known. Many of his descendants regard him as a hero of faith because he stood firm on his pacifist convictions during the French and Indian War. The story of the attack on his family has been recounted through various media over many generations. Yet little has been written to interpret the meaning of the Indian captivity experienced by Jacob and his sons Joseph and Christian. I attempt to address that gap by recounting the story of the attack and its long-term consequences in the Return to Northkill series. *Jacob's Choice* tells the story from Amish points of view—those of Jacob and his daughter Barbara. *Joseph's Dilemma* takes up the story from a very different point of view—that of Jacob's son Joseph and Joseph's adoptive mother, a Native American named Touching Sky.

In *Christian's Hope*, the third and final story in the series, I explore the meaning of a return to a settler's life for Jacob's son Christian, who had also been adopted by Native Americans. The clash of cultural perspectives between the Amish, the Shawnees, and even the Dunkers is writ large in these pages.

The Shawnees were Algonquin people who shared many traits with the Delawares; the war party that captured Christian during the Indian attack comprised both tribes. Both had conflicts with the white colonists who settled on their native lands.

The Dunkers had their origins in Europe in the early 1700s. While they preferred the name Brethren, their peculiar mode of baptism led them to be known in America as German Baptists, Tunkers, Dunkers, or even Dunkards—the most derisive of those terms. To avoid confusion, I've used Dunkers throughout.

Eighteenth-century colonists thought of Native Americans as descendants of the Lost Tribes of Israel. Thus, some white doctors claimed curative Indian powers using ancient Native American patent remedies with pretensions of biblical roots. Other purported healers combined traditional botanical medicines with *Braucherei* (powwowing), practices with ancient European roots generally involving a magical transfer of an illness into an object or the earth. Although *Braucherei* was very popular among German Pennsylvanians, English colonists viewed it as witchcraft. In this book, Anna depends on the healing power of herbal remedies, not *Braucherei*.

As much as possible, I used the known names of the people in this story—the protagonist Christian Hochstetler and the members of his Amish family, as well as Elder George Klein of the Dunkers. There are three exceptions—Orpha Rupp's name in real life was Barbara, and Sarah Blank's name was Anna. I changed their first names in this story to avoid confusion with Anna Hochstetler and Barbara Stutzman. I also changed Fanny Stutzman's name to Ruth, to distinguish her from her deceased aunt Franey, a character mentioned here and in *Jacob's Choice*.

I should also note that Christian Frederick Post of the Moravians was sometimes called Frederick Christian Post. The name order was less important in his day than ours. Post and other Moravian missionaries such as John Heckewelder did groundbreaking ethnography and language study among Native Americans. Later on, some Christian missionaries forced the Natives to adapt to white culture and religion via residential schools, leading to one of the saddest chapters in Native American history.

I used my imagination to put the flesh of this story on the bones of the few known facts of Christian Hochstetler's life during the period between 1757 and 1767 to create a plausible account of what may have happened. Better known is Christian's later life, including his land purchases, his work as a minister among the Dunkers, his final will and testament, and an inventory of his goods at the time of his death in 1814. I relied on scholarly research to assure an accurate portrait of the history and culture of that time. Any errors or conflicts with known facts are mine.

—Ervin R. Stutzman

-Prologue-

"The thing long expected takes the form of the unexpected when it finally comes."
—*Amish proverb*

December 10, 1764

Several figures slipped quietly past the cabin window, casting momentary shadows from the setting sun onto Anna's face. A few moments later, she was startled by a shout at the door. She paused in the middle of a mending stitch to glance nervously at her husband, Jacob, as he rose from his rocking chair. Who would be paying a visit at this time of evening in December?

Jacob lifted the clunky iron latch and swung open the oaken door to reveal a young Indian silhouetted in the doorway. Anna shrank back from the sight of a tomahawk and a knife in his belt, and a heavy necklace strung with large bear claws. A leather bag embroidered with beads hung at his side, and he wore brightly beaded moccasins. She shivered as two other Indians—a man and a woman—stepped to the side of the young man at the threshold. What had brought the dreaded Indians to their door? Had they come in peace?

Perhaps they were hungry. Should she offer them the pie she had baked the day before? She wasn't about to deny whatever they'd demand.

All she could think about was the story. More than seven years ago, before she was married to Jacob, several Indians had scribed a charcoal *X* on Jacob's cabin door. Jacob's first wife, Lizzie, had shooed them off empty-handed rather than sharing the peach pie they'd requested. Later, Lizzie was stabbed to death when a French and Indian war party surprised the family in a predawn raid. They also killed two of Jacob and Lizzie's children and kidnapped Jacob and his sons Joseph and Christian. Then they departed, leaving the Hochstetler house and barn in ashes.

By God's grace or good fortune, Jacob had escaped after eight months in the Seneca village of Buckaloons. Anna married him four years later. His sons, however, remained captive with the Indians. Jacob's persistent nighttime prayers and his written appeals to the British authorities were in vain. His longing for his lost sons had always hung like a cloud over their home.

A cold breeze from the open doorway now swept across Anna's feet as Jacob surveyed the visitors from head to toe. Was he about to invite them in, she wondered, or would he step through the doorway to speak to them outside, as she hoped?

As Jacob stood there wordless, the youngest Indian uttered one simple and hesitant word.

"*Dat*?"

Anna took a quick breath. Why was this young Indian calling her husband *Dat*? She laid aside the trousers she was mending for Jacob and leaned forward to scan the young visitor's expression, noticing his narrow nose and green eyes.

Jacob's face wrinkled in disbelief. "Jo–Joseph?"

"*Jah.*" The young man nodded.

The young man watched Jacob's face, as if looking for a sign. The silence stretched into discomfort as the young man waited.

Amish men did not show physical affection in public. But Anna could see disbelief and pent-up joy in Jacob's inability to speak.

At last, Jacob extended his hand. "My son." Jacob paused again, his voice breaking. "Come in." A tear coursed down his cheek as Jacob gripped Joseph's hand in his strong and calloused right hand, and tenderly enfolded it with his left.

It was a gesture Jacob reserved for the most intimate of greetings; she had seen him use it only once before, when a visitor brought greetings from Jacob's extended family in the Old Country. Father and son stood, clasping hands, their eyes wet with tears.

Joseph turned away from Jacob and reached out with affection to touch the woman with russet skin who stood at his left side. "*Mein mutter,*" he said. And then he nodded at the warrior who stood on his right. "*Mein mütterlicher Onkel.*"

Who would have expected Joseph to bring his adoptive Indian mother and uncle to their door? Anna and Jacob had heard rumors of captives being adopted by their captors, but hadn't imagined it happening to Jacob's sons. Did this mean they'd only come for a visit, or was Joseph intending to stay? She trembled as she rose from her chair to greet Joseph and his Indian family. He was no longer the athletic thirteen-year-old neighbor boy with the impish face as she'd known him years before.

As she reached out to shake Joseph's hand, she noticed yet another visitor who stood behind them—a tall young man dressed in a British uniform and wearing a ponytail.

"I will assume this is your son, then?" the soldier asked.

"*Jah,*" Jacob said, his voice breaking a bit. "Thank you for bringing him home to us."

"It is our responsibility, according to the treaty," the soldier replied. "Now I'll be on my way."

"Won't you stay for supper?" Jacob asked, with a questioning glance at Anna.

"No, thank you, sir," the soldier said. "You'll have your hands full with the company you have."

Anna thought she saw the hint of a smile on the soldier's face as he bowed, turned, and strode into the gathering darkness that hinted of snow.

Jacob motioned the remaining guests into the room. The man wore a ring in his nose and silver earrings that dangled from loops of skin on the bottom of his ears. The woman wore a red blanket around her shoulders, and her long black hair was tied back in a braid with a red cloth. They stepped in hesitantly and shook their heads when Jacob pulled back chairs from the table for them. Expressionless, Joseph sat cross-legged onto the floor, and his uncle followed suit. The woman hesitated for a moment before squatting on the other side of him.

These people must be famished, Anna thought. What could she add to the meager fare she'd prepared for supper? Perhaps she could fetch a couple of cabbages and red beets or turnips from the underground storage barrel in the garden, or onions from the attic. And where was she to bed down the guests for the night?

She had often prayed with Jacob for Joseph's return. But this was so different than they'd envisioned it. Despair washed over her as the reality of the moment began to sink in. Somehow, Jacob and she had always imagined that his two sons would be released at the same time and come home together. Where was Christian? Had he not survived the captivity?

If only his companions had gone with the young soldier. She hoped Jacob would find a way to dismiss them without incident—the sooner the better. She was afraid of Indians, so she was terrified at the thought of having them stay. Being a stepmother to a son who'd lived among the Indians was frightening enough; it was even worse to think about offering hospitality to his adoptive family. How would they occupy themselves all day? What kind of food would she need to prepare? And what would Joseph think of her—his father's new wife?

Even if his Indian friends left and Joseph remained alone with them in the house, how could she feel safe, not knowing what lay in the depths of his heart after his long exposure to the untamed habits of the Native people? She'd heard too many accounts of stealth killings in the colony, acts of violence

that severed the fragile cord of trust between the whites and
the Indians.

How could her stepson, this lanky young man who carried
himself with the stony-faced demeanor of a Delaware warrior,
ever earn her trust, let alone her love?

And how could she ever earn his?

PART I

-1-

August 1, 1765

Christian reluctantly forced one foot ahead of the other as he walked the road toward the Hochstetler farm—his childhood home. He shifted his bag on his shoulder and smoothed his scalp lock.

The fields of wheat, spelt, and rye were mostly stubble on the rolling hills of northern Berks County, Pennsylvania. The sound of the soft ripple of the Northkill Creek flowing over the rocks permeated the air. He reached down to adjust the tomahawk dangling from the belt that secured his breech-cloth at the waist. This hardly looked like the place he'd left many moons ago.

At long last Christian knew that his father was alive. Sir William Johnson, the Superintendent of Indian Affairs, had told him so when he arrived at Johnson Hall in Johnstown, New York, with other captives who were being returned. Even though the British had signed peace treaties with the French and Indians, the war still raged in his heart and soul. Against his wishes, he would now be expected to live on land that had been taken from the Indians, the people he had come to love. He would be forced to live with the people of his childhood, who thought of the Shawnees as uncivilized heathen.

On most of the trip to Berks County from Johnstown, he'd been escorted by Esquire Samuel Weiser, who lived a half day's walk from the Hochstetler farm. Weiser had lived among the Indians as a child and understood their ways. He said he trusted Christian to walk the final leg to his home by himself. Despite his unwillingness to leave the Shawnees, his eagerness to see his father after eight years of separation kept him walking homeward.

23

Christian pressed his way through a few brambles to get to the brook for a cool drink of water. He'd often romped in this water as a boy, or so it seemed as he scanned the creek, gazing toward the place where it made a small bend. He hoped to detect a familiar landmark, perhaps a large tree that he had known before he was taken from the area by the Shawnees as a boy.

He drank, then wiped his mouth on his arm and pressed his way back toward the path. When he had first been taken, he had desperately plotted to escape from the Shawnees to return to the family farm by the Northkill Creek. But now, having been forced by treaty to leave the Indian village, it brought him no delight. After years of carefree living in the woods among the Shawnees, how could he be content in the disciplined life of his Amish family? How could he return to the ways of his childhood, the ways of the Amish that he could now hardly remember?

Christian took a deep breath and followed the path framed by two large chestnut trees. They cast their leafy arms over the split-rail fence—much as they had on the day when the house was burned to the ground by the raiding party.

A different house stood in the place his childhood home had once occupied, or so it seemed. Yes, it must be the place, since on a gentle rise behind the house stood *der Backoffe*, the domed oven made of limestone with a sheltering tile roof.

He rehearsed a few Swiss-German phrases as he stepped onto the cobbled path that led to the two-story log house with a small curl of smoke rising from the chimney. It brought some comfort that the door stood open.

"Ho!" he said loudly, according to Indian custom. He stepped cautiously into the doorway. A man's hat hung on a wooden peg near the doorway. Bundles of herbs hung from the ceiling. A set of redware dishes and a few glass bottles were stacked on a shelf behind the table. Storage baskets lined one of the walls. A man and a woman sat at a wooden table eating their supper. They looked up in alarm.

"*Kann ich dich helfa*? (Can I help you?)" the man asked. The words sounded both strange and familiar to Christian, like the call of the wood thrush when it returned to the forest as the weather warmed.

Is that Dat? Christian sought desperately for something to say. All of the phrases he had dreamed of using when he met his family vanished from his mind. Overwhelmed, he stood silent.

The man's eyes swept him from the crown of his head down to the brightly beaded moccasins on his feet. "I'll be with you as soon as I'm finished with supper," he said in German. He took another spoonful of *Kalte Schale* (cold soup)—toasted spelt bread crumbs soaked in milk topped with fresh blueberries.

Christian hesitated for a moment before turning from the door. He sat on a large stump not far from the house.

His father had the same broad forehead and his untrimmed beard had the same shape, although it was a light shade of gray. His voice sounded the same. But who was the woman at the table with fear in her eyes?

I wish I was back home, with the Shawnees, Christian thought. His eyes roamed around the farm. Over there, a split-rail fence. Not far from that, the stone pile, the springhouse. His eyes shifted toward the corral where a horse neighed. It sounded like Blitz, the gelding that he'd last heard screaming in terror and running from the burning barn that the raiding party had set on fire. He shook his head to clear away that awful memory and sat with his head in his hands in the dimming light of the sun. Why had he come back? His chest ached with the force of all that had happened here. Staying here, in this place, was impossible.

I don't want to be stuck on a farm. I want to roam free the way my adoptive people do. Perhaps I'll sleep in the nearby woods tonight, and then head back home tomorrow.

He looked up as his father came toward him. He forced himself to his feet, breathing hard.

The man looked at him with expectancy. *"Vu bishsh du? Kann ich dich helfa?* (Who are you? Can I help you?)"

Christian gazed into the settler's eyes. He knew now that this man was his father. Drawing from the deep well of memory, Christian formed the words he had been practicing. *"Mei noma is Christlich Hochstetla,"* he managed to say.

The man's eyes flashed open with surprise. In two strides he was in front of him. He grabbed Christian's chin and tipped it up.

Christian stood, unflinching, as the man's eyes filled with tears.

Suddenly, the man wrapped his arms around him. *"Christlich! Ich bin da Dat!* (Christian! I am your father!)" Christian stood rigid in the man's arms. His father stepped back and wiped his eyes.

Dat motioned toward the house. "Please come inside. We'll get you something to eat."

Christian hesitated. It had been years since he'd sat on a kitchen chair or eaten at a white man's table. He sat back down on the stump, overwhelmed.

The slender woman with the large gray-green eyes appeared at the doorway. She had fine-textured skin, strong cheekbones, and features that weren't at all displeasing. Her honey-brown hair was mostly covered by a linen cap. She said something to *Dat* which Christian strained to understand.

Dat took a couple of steps toward the house and motioned for Christian to follow. Christian shook his head and stayed seated on the stump, fingering the tomahawk at his side. He wasn't ready to eat at a white man's table, even *Dat's*.

The woman stepped back into the house but soon reappeared with a cup in her hand. As she held it out, Christian took notice of her smooth, relatively uncalloused hands. He took the cup, which smelled of mint. It reminded him of his Indian home, where the women prepared teas from various plants they gleaned in the woods. They believed that the Great Creator had provided everything they needed to be healthy.

He took a little sip and peered at the woman over the top of his cup. She looked back at him. Her eyes seemed sympathetic. He drank the tea slowly, glancing between *Dat* and the woman as he drank.

"*Meg-wich* (Thank you)," he said, handing the cup back to her. Remembering that they didn't speak Shawnee, he added, "*Danka*," the word he'd been taught to use as a boy.

The woman smiled. She motioned for him to follow her and moved toward the house, disappearing inside. Christian held back. In a few moments she reappeared with another full cup of tea and held it out to him. Eagerly, he took the cup and gulped it down. The woman smiled.

"Her name is Anna," *Dat* said, reaching out to take her arm. "We married several years ago."

Anna beamed and nodded.

Christian blinked, trying to comprehend what it meant to have a stepmother.

"Is Joseph here?" Christian asked. The language of his childhood sounded odd in his ears. The question had been on his mind during much of the journey back to Northkill, and he asked it now, a bit haltingly.

The woman shook her head. "He went to Morgantown to visit a friend."

Christian's shoulders sagged in disappointment. No one could understand his situation better than Joseph. He hadn't seen his older brother since a chance meeting shortly after their capture years before.

Again Anna motioned him toward the house, silhouetted against the setting sun. This time, Christian followed. He paused for a moment at the doorway to let his eyes adjust to the dim light. Anna lit a candle and set it on the wooden table.

"Would you like something to eat?" she asked.

Christian wasn't sure he understood. Seeing his confusion, Anna made eating motions with her hands and mouth.

He nodded.

Dat pulled out a chair. "Sit," he said.

Christian hesitated and then shook his head. He gracefully sat down cross-legged on the wooden floor, his back against the kitchen wall.

He looked around the room in silence, taking in the details. Through an open doorway into another room he could see a low-posted rope bed with a striped blue-and-white cotton cover with a bolster and pillows to match. A wooden chest stood at the foot. *What would it be like to live in a white man's house again?*

Anna stirred some endives and parsnips into a spider pot that stood over the hearth fire. She scooped some of the contents of the pot into a wooden dish and offered it to Christian with a wooden spoon. The familiar smell of cooked corn reminded him of his hunger. He began to eat, slowly at first and then downing the rest of the contents in a few large bites.

"More?" Anna asked, motioning with her hands.

Christian nodded. The food was good enough, but it was saltier than anything the Shawnees served. Anna scooped another generous helping from the pot.

Christian finished his meal, then rose to leave. As he moved toward the door, *Dat* stepped in front of him. "We have a bed waiting for you," he said, pointing toward the steps that led to the upstairs bedrooms.

Christian shook his head. Grandfather Sun had gone to bed, but it was the time of the Grain Moon, and the house was hot and stuffy. At least there'd be a slight breeze outside. He'd sleep in the woods near the house. There the bubbling sound of the Northkill Creek and the chirping of the crickets would remind him of his home in the Indian village.

Christian bowed slightly toward the woman called Anna and went outside. He took in a deep breath of the evening air. He longed for his bed in the wigwam back in the village, a platform made of strong saplings lashed to one another to form a solid surface to keep his body straight and lean. Who would want to be cooped up in the house all night, especially in a soft feather bed? A soft bed could only lead to a soft body, unfit for the hardships of woods and weather.

If he were ever to call this place home, it would need to feel more like a Shawnee village. Maybe he could build a wigwam next to the creek and hang a hammock nearby.

If only Joseph were here, he could ask him about such things. Being with Joseph might make it tolerable to stay on the farm. Perhaps they could live together near the creek, where things felt more familiar.

Anna toyed with the edges of her apron as she stood beside Jacob, watching Christian head for the creek.

"Anna will have breakfast for you in the morning," Jacob called to his son. He turned toward Anna, and she saw he had tears in his eyes.

"I can't believe that I didn't recognize him," he said. "His looks changed more than Joseph's did. And he must use some kind of stain on his skin and hair. He's so dark."

"Maybe so," Anna replied. "Joseph was older when he was taken."

"But I still should have recognized him." Jacob swallowed hard.

"Don't be too hard on yourself. We would have known it was Christian if a British soldier had accompanied him, as they did Joseph."

"He's my own flesh and blood. Now he won't even stay in our house."

Anna patted Jacob on the arm. "It was the same when Joseph came back. He didn't want to sleep in the house, even though it was wintertime. Now it's summer, and he probably wants to sleep in the woods where it's cooler."

"I hope he won't leave us," Jacob said, then sank into a rocking chair and buried his face in his hands.

Anna rubbed Jacob's shoulders. "I can't imagine that he's going very far," she said. "Let's give him some time by himself. That's what Joseph wanted when he first came back."

Jacob looked at her. "That was different. He brought two Indians with him, and he wanted to sleep in the same place with them. They were happy to sleep in the barn."

Anna stroked Jacob's neck. "This is a big change for Christian. He doesn't even know me. He probably wants to sleep outside, like he's been doing for the last few weeks."

"I hope you're right," Jacob said. He flinched as Anna massaged a sore spot on his shoulder.

Anna wasn't worried Christian would leave, although she felt bad that neither she nor Jacob had recognized him. If they had, they certainly wouldn't have let him wait outside until they had finished eating. Perhaps Christian's feelings were hurt? She hoped it hadn't put him off so badly that he'd leave for good.

"In all the years I prayed for his return, I never imagined him looking like this," Jacob said. "He doesn't even seem to understand what I'm saying." His voice was husky with grief.

Anna continued to rub Jacob's back and shoulders. "I'm sure it won't take long for him to learn German again. It will come back to him, like it has for Joseph."

"He seems so wild, so different from Joseph . . ."

"Let's not worry too much. I'm going to make some peach cobbler so that if he comes back, I'll have some to offer him. I remember how much he liked it that time I brought it to your house, not so long before the Indian attack. How old was he then?"

Jacob paused. "Lizzie remembered those dates better than I do. But I believe Christian was born in '46. The Indians took him from us in the fall of '57. He would have been eleven years old then, and nineteen now. He won't be of age for a couple more years."

Anna considered this. In the Amish community, youth usually lived under their parents' authority until they were

twenty-one years old. "I suppose that means you'll want him
to work on the farm," she said.

"Of course. What else would he do?"

"If he's like Joseph, it will take some time for him to get
used to being back home. Joseph would still rather fish or
hunt than anything else."

"He's twenty-one, so he can make his own decisions."

"Maybe Christian will think he can do what he wants to.
Wouldn't he have been on his own among the Indians?"

"Yes, when I was held at Buckaloons, the young men his
age would play a lot of games, and go hunting and fishing.
Most of them went on the warpath, trying to prove they were
warriors."

"You don't suppose . . ." Anna hesitated, remembering that
Christian's forehead was shaved and his long black hair was
braided into a traditional pigtail, known as the queue. He
wore a tomahawk at his side. Had he ever put on war paint?

"Those young Indians did whatever they liked. They could
decide whether to go to war or not. They had too much freedom—more than I gave John or Jakey when they were that
age," Jacob said.

"It might be hard for Christian to be tied down here. He's
spent almost half his life with the Indians. I'm sure he's used
to doing many things that are different from the way we do it."

Jacob rocked, considering. "Of course, we'll need to give
him a week or two to get used to being back home. But the
sooner he starts working the farm, the better off he'll be."

"I'll do the best I can with the cooking."

Jacob sat quietly. "Thank you, dear. I hope he'll be here in
the morning."

The two of them got ready for bed in silence, hanging their
clothing onto the peg board mounted on the bedroom wall.
Anna put on her nightcap and crawled into the rope bed beside Jacob. She lay on top of the linen sheet that covered the
tow-chaff bag filled with chopped straw, scrunched her body
into the familiar hollow, and laid her head against her feather

pillow. She turned her face toward Jacob, who gave her a peck on the cheek and then turned his back.

It was late in the rye harvest season, and Jacob usually fell asleep within a few moments after going to bed. Not this time. Anna listened to his troubled breathing. *If only we had known that it was Christian, we would have invited him into the house right away, rather than leaving him outside by himself,* she thought. *But how could we have known? If Joseph had been here, it might have gone differently. If only . . .*

No use thinking of what could have been. Sunday was only a couple of days away, and she could invite Jacob's son John and daughter Barbara and their families to celebrate Christian's return. No Sunday service was planned, so she'd invite Bishop Jake and his wife, Catharine. They had been good friends to Jacob through the years the boys were missing.

It would need to be a carry-in, since she didn't have the food on hand for a large group. Mulling over the details in her mind, she turned over and fell into a troubled sleep.

-2-

Anna woke early the next morning and padded to the window to look for any sign of Christian in the dim morning light. She was wearing the bleached linen shift that served as an undershirt during the day and a nightgown at night. Disappointed at not seeing Christian, she decided to get dressed for the day. It would be hard to go back to sleep anyway. She quietly pulled on her stockings in the near-darkness of the bedroom, hoping not to wake Jacob.

I hope Joseph gets back soon. Maybe he'll be able to get Christian to stay. She fastened her long underpetticoat and then put on her outer clothing—a petticoat skirt that hung near the bottom of her calves and a shortgown that hung down to the bottom of her hips, fastened in the front with straight pins made of thorns.

I wonder what Christian wants for breakfast. She folded a kerchief into a triangle and pinned it in front of her neck, then tied on a large fabric pocket that hung from the front of her waist, covering it with an apron that hung to midcalf.

Anna listened to Jacob's light snoring as she took off her nightcap and combed back her wavy hair. Then she wound it into a tight bun, securing it with small combs poked into the twisted coils. *He must not have slept well. He's usually awake by this time.* She fitted on her head covering, tied the wide strings under her chin, and then sat on a chair to tie on her black leather shoes.

When Jacob awoke, he still seemed upset that he'd failed to provide the best welcome for Christian, wondering aloud to Anna where Christian had spent the night. To cheer him, she brewed some spearmint tea.

Anna sat down at the table across from Jacob. She fidgeted
with a couple of loose threads in the unbleached linen table-
cloth as she sipped her tea, trying to remember Christian as a
young boy. As a young widow at that time, living on the neighboring farm, Anna had at times benefited from the Hochstetler
family's generosity. One day during the tense years of the
British war against the French and Indians, she recalled, Jacob's
family helped her clean up the branches after a thunderstorm.
She had offered them spearmint tea. Eleven-year-old Christian
had drunk at least three cups, she remembered, and asked her
to show him the garden where the spearmint grew. *So much
has changed since then*, she thought now.

Although the Amish didn't participate in the war, Indians
had attacked the Hochstetler farm a few months later. Jacob,
Joseph, and Christian had been taken, and she hadn't seen the
boy since. Fearing more raids as the French and Indian war
came to a formal end, some members of the Swiss-German
colony had moved away. She would have moved away too if
she'd had the means. And then, a few years later, after Jacob
had escaped from captivity and rebuilt his farm, she had consented to marry him. Ever since, she had waited and prayed
with him for his sons' return.

Joseph had been home for nearly eight months now, and
he seemed to be adjusting well. The Indians he'd brought with
him hadn't stayed more than a few days. Joseph didn't turn
out to be as wild as she'd imagined he might be. Gradually,
he was assimilating into their household. He still disappeared
from time to time without notice—likely to be alone in the
woods—but Anna and Jacob were no longer alarmed by his
absences. If Christian learned to fit in as well as Joseph, she'd
be able to manage.

Jacob drained his cup and set it on the table. "Thanks,
Anna," he said as he put on his hat to go outside. "It does my
heart good to see you caring for my sons. Let me know if you
see Christian."

"I'll do that." She took comfort in his tenderness.

Anna thought ahead to the day's work. She checked the almanac, suspended by a heavy string from a nail in the wall. Their almanac was Christopher Sauer's popular German version, an annual calendar supplemented by dozens of closely printed pages of religious and practical advice. Anna and Jacob relied on it to show the phases of the moon, the Sabbath, and holy days of the church. Anna's father had always quoted the biblical writer of Ecclesiastes, who declared, "To everything there is a season, and a time to every purpose under heaven . . . a time to plant, and a time to pluck up that which is planted." The best time to plant anything was in the sign of Gemini—the twins—since it could double the yield. *Looks like it's supposed to be a good day to plant root crops*, she thought.

The world and everything in it was in God's good hands. They could trust the hand of Providence to bring about God's good purpose in his chosen time, from the appointed years of one's life to the growth of plants in the soil. The almanac recommended rhythms of planting and harvesting that corresponded with the cycles of the heavens, like the rhythms of her body reflected the rhythms of the moon.

Anna thought of her faith as she put on the flat straw hat that would shield her face from the sun's harsh rays. Her beliefs turned to habit in the way she cared for her kitchen garden—her own garden of Eden. She kept it weed free. In turn, it was productive each season. Jacob called it the "woman's garden," since it was entirely her province. He only set foot in it at her request, usually to deliver a wheelbarrow full of dung for fertilizer. However, she relied on Jacob to plow the field patch that lay farther to the south. There she grew long rows of turnips and cabbages next to her potatoes and corn.

She picked up her hoe and started to clear an area in one of the four raised garden beds. "Something is wrong with this hoe," she said aloud. She looked closely at the blade. Sure enough, there was a crack. *I must ask Jacob to fix it before it gets worse.*

She spread the seeds for the season's second planting of radishes and turnips, pausing to wipe her brow with the kerchief around her neck. When she finished planting the seeds, she picked up a jar and headed to the creek for water. A deep soil soaking would get her seeds off to a good start for a fall crop.

Before she returned to the house, she hitched up her petticoat and knelt next to her lavender plants, her bare knees pressing slender hollows into the moist soil. She stroked the light purple flowers that sprouted from the dusty-green plants. She closed her eyes to savor the fragrance—a balm for the soul. She took her paring knife and cut enough sprigs for a small bundle.

Then she rose, brushed off her knees, and carried the lavender into the house and laid it on the fireplace mantel. Once it dried, she'd stuff it into a small linen sachet and tuck it into the pillowcase that lay at the head of the rope bed she shared with Jacob. The fragrance would help dissipate the musty smell of the room and ward off the insects that sometimes plagued them at night.

Mixed with the fragrance of dill and other herbs, the scent of lavender reminded her of the goodness of God's creation, irrefutable signs of divine favor etched in the flora that sprang up in Penn's Woods. The least she could do was have the lovely scent of lavender in the house to give Christian the best welcome.

Assuming he would come home.

Christian woke up with a start at the sound of a rooster crowing. He looked around in the early-morning light. *Where am I?*

As the grogginess in his head cleared, he remembered the events of the previous evening. *I'm not going to go back into that house if I can help it,* he decided. *I wonder when Joseph will come back. He'll understand me.*

Christian walked to the creek and splashed water on his face, rubbing the sleep out of his eyes. The familiar routine gave him a small sense of comfort. But still, he felt depressed. *I wish I were back home in my Indian village.* His stomach growled. *This is a good time of the year to pick berries,* he thought, and he headed for the woods. It wasn't long before he found a patch of blackberries, so he ate himself full, the purple juice staining his hands.

He wandered around the farmstead, looking for signs that he'd once lived there. How was he to call this home without some reminder of his childhood? If he was ever to feel at home, he'd need to feel a sense of comfort and security, like he felt when he slept in the wigwam back in the Shawnee village. Now he was a stranger. Even his father hadn't recognized him. If *Mam* were alive, she would surely have known him! Instead he'd need to get accustomed to a stepmother who seemed half-afraid of him.

He walked through the meadow dotted with stumps from trees felled to make way for the farm. Didn't *Dat* realize that trees were sacred, designed by the Great Creator to shelter and protect the earth? When would this madness stop? The surrounding hills would soon be strewn by dead wood, riven by ditches gouged by torrential rains.

He strolled toward a horse grazing quietly in the tall grass, hobbled by a leather thong. He walked up to the gelding, who snorted and swung his head at him. It *was* Blitz! The horse he had loved as a child looked older now, with a crop of gray hairs sprouting around his muzzle. Christian reached into his bag and pulled out the few remaining grains of ground corn from his journey back to Northkill.

"Blitz," he said as he offered the corn with arm outstretched and open palm, "I'm sorry *Dat* makes you work so hard. If you were mine, we'd have lots of fun together." The Shawnees would never think of forcing a horse to cultivate the fields.

Blitz chuffed as he scraped the corn off Christian's hand with his long scratchy tongue.

"Good boy," Christian said as he wiped the wetness off his palm onto Blitz's mane. Whether or not Blitz recognized him, he seemed friendly enough.

He turned to walk through the large field patch that produced many of the vegetables for the household. There were dozens of hills of corn intertwined by bean stalks and vines of squash—the familiar three sisters inspired by Indian custom. There were long rows of cabbage next to potatoes, turnips, and parsnips. A scrawny scarecrow stood in the middle of the garden, waving strips of linens to scare away birds.

A plump groundhog waddled out of the patch as Christian approached, strands of greenery trailing from its jaws. Christian bent down to pull a couple of turnips and then strode toward the creek. He rinsed the turnips, then took a bite. As he savored the tangy flavor, Christian listened to the sounds of children playing on the farm on the far side of the creek. Did his older brother John still live there? If so, they might be his nieces and nephews. *Would they remember me? Probably not.*

Still hungry, Christian ambled through a yellow patch of dandelions near the grape arbor that stood not far from *Dat's* cabin. The clusters of grapes that hung heavily from the vines were still green. *These should be ripe in another half moon.*

Christian remembered the sweet grape juice he'd loved as a child. *"Don't wipe your hands on your shirt,"* *Mam* had always said when they squeezed the juice from the purple-skinned fruit. Now that he was a bare-chested Indian, that would not be a problem!

Christian thoughtfully considered his clothing—and lack of it. No one in the Amish community worked bare-chested in public, even in the fields. He didn't mind standing out, as long as he had a good reason, which he did. But still.

"Ho!" someone shouted from the farm lane. Christian wheeled around to look. A tall Indian was striding toward him. Could it be Joseph?

He strode eagerly toward the figure, who picked up his pace as they neared each other.

"Christian, is that you?"

"Joseph!" Christian ran toward his brother with arms outstretched. The two of them met on the path and threw their arms around each other. Christian hugged his brother tightly. "I was afraid I'd never see you again." He stepped back and looked at his brother, admiring the lithe yet muscular frame that made him an excellent runner. "Do they still call you Swift Foot?"

"I was Swift Foot among the Indians, but I'm Joseph around here," his brother responded. "I'm sorry I wasn't here when you arrived. Do the Shawnees still call you Stargazer?"

"Always." Christian was pleased that he could understand Joseph so easily, even though he spoke in the Delaware idiom. It was a close cousin to the Shawnee tongue, as both were expressions of the Algonquin language.

"When did you leave the Delaware village?" Christian asked.

"I arrived back here last winter in the Full Cold Moon."

"What made you decide to come back here?"

"I would have stayed at Custaloga's Town when the war ended, but Colonel Bouquet forced the chiefs to return all their British subjects. I had no choice."

"Do you ever think of going back to your village?"

"Yes. I'd like to visit my adoptive mother. I hated to leave her. She needs me."

"I hated to leave too," Christian said. "Everything has changed around here. I don't recognize much except *Dat*'s orchard."

Joseph nodded. "That reminds me—the plums are ripe. Let's go pick some. Then we can go fishing."

Christian's face brightened. As they headed for a pair of plum trees, he asked, "Where do you sleep at night?"

"In Anna's little house. She left it empty when she married *Dat*. If you want, you can live there with me."

Christian pondered the invitation. Living with Joseph would certainly be better than living in the house with *Dat* and Anna. But what about the vow he'd made to Little Bear, his Shawnee brother? He wasn't ready to explain it to Joseph at the moment; nor was he ready to ignore it. "I think I'll sleep outside for now," he said.

When they reached the orchard, Joseph pulled a ripe plum and held it out to Christian.

The plum reminded him of the thrill of the early fruit harvest as a child. *Dat* had let him climb to the tops of the trees to pick fruit, which seemed to favor the uppermost branches.

"Thank you," Christian said as he bit into the tender fruit. "How do you get along with *Dat* and Anna?"

"Good enough. It's best not to get sideways with *Dat*. He's the chief."

"Does he make you work on the farm?"

"Not too much, since I've seen twenty-one winters and can live on my own. But I help *Dat* with some things. He and our brother John work all the time. Never any games or fun."

"How about Anna? What's she like?"

"She's scared of Indians like *Mam* was, but she's friendly to me. Barbara says she worries too much and wants everything to be perfect, especially her garden. *Dat* thinks her flowers aren't necessary, but he lets her have her way."

"Does Barbara still live around here?" Christian asked.

"Yes, her family lives on a farm close by, and so does John's. Both families had several babies while we were gone. John farms *Dat*'s land on the other side of the creek. *Dat* recently bought a new piece of land in the township not far south of here."

"Why did he do that? Doesn't he know when he has enough?"

"He bought that land so you and I have a place to farm. Eventually, it can be ours, the way John has his own land."

Christian scowled. "I don't want my own land to farm."

The two were silent for a few moments, thinking about that. Christian shook himself and changed the subject. "I feel like I need a good long run. Want to go with me?"

In response, Joseph took off running. Christian laughed and followed at a fast pace.

Joseph ran out front, with Christian close behind. Together they turned onto the trail that wound up and into the Blue Mountains north of the farm.

They had not gone far when Christian spotted a deer crossing the path not far ahead. Joseph slowed to a walk and Christian caught up, breathing hard.

They stood for a moment, catching their breath.

"Did they let you hunt for deer at the village?" Joseph asked, watching the deer.

"Not at first," Christian said. "It took a while for them to trust me with a gun."

"Same with me."

"Did they treat you well?" Christian asked.

"Yes, really well. A woman named Touching Sky adopted me to take the place of her husband and son, who were both killed during the war. I didn't want to leave her alone. That's why I didn't want to come back to Northkill." He sat down on a large log that had fallen beside the path.

Christian sat down on the log with him. "I didn't want to come home either."

"Have you told *Dat*?"

"No. I doubt I will. What good would that do?"

Joseph shrugged. "I'm sure it would hurt his feelings. He wouldn't be able to understand why we'd want to stay in Indian villages and not be back at home with him."

"But he was at Buckaloons for a while."

"Yes, but he always wanted to get away, like I did at first. I couldn't stand it—the food, the bed, everything. After a while, I got used to everything and learned to fit in with the Indians. I don't believe *Dat* ever did that. All he could think about was how they killed *Mam* and our brother and sister, and the farm and family back home."

"What did you like most about being with the Indians?" Christian asked.

"Most things—except for the war-making. I hated that."

"Me too. Did you get to know any girls?"

Joseph had a faraway look in his eyes. "Yes, there was one I thought about marrying. She had dark eyes like a doe. She made these moccasins."

Christian's eyes widened in admiration as he examined Joseph's footwear. "She's really good with a needle. Are you planning to go back to see her?"

Joseph paused for a moment, looking away. "No, she died of smallpox, about the same time as my adoptive little sister." His voice broke as he spoke.

"Smallpox?" Christian was silent for a moment as memories pressed close. "That's one of the worst things that can happen to you."

Joseph nodded. "A lot of people in our village died at the same time." He picked up a fallen leaf and twirled the stem between his thumb and forefinger.

Christian's throat turned sour. He hoped Joseph wouldn't say more about death. It conjured up memories he took pains to dismiss. There was no good reason to recall the cruel attack that robbed him of *Mam* and two siblings or revisit the loss of his adoptive Indian father, whom he'd come to love as his own. He didn't even want to think about the dreadful effect of smallpox in the Shawnee village about the time of Pontiac's War, when several young men his age succumbed to the white man's disease. His stomach twisted at the memory of fluid oozing from the pustules blanketing the face and arms of a dear friend days before he died.

Christian longed for a life free of care, where neither toil nor tears usurped the Great Creator's intent for life on earth. His heart throbbed for Joseph's loss, but talking about it would only increase the pain.

Joseph quit twirling the leaf and looked at Christian. "Sometime I'd like to visit a white captive named Summer Rain. She was sent back home the same time I was. She lived near Fort Harris."

"I'll go with you," Christian said eagerly. "We could stop by on the way back to the Ohio Territory."

"Did you have a girl you liked?" Joseph asked.

Christian smiled. "Yes. Her name is Morning Dew. I plan to go back to see her soon."

Joseph looked around as though to make sure no one was listening, and then he said, "I have my eyes on Sarah Blank now."

"Does she know you like her?"

"Oh yes, we've talked about getting married."

"What do you like about her?"

"She asks me about my time with the Indians. She's fun to be around. And she has a pretty smile."

"That's what I like about Morning Dew too. She's beautiful, especially when she dances. But *Dat* will probably want us to marry women of our own kind and take up farming."

Joseph nodded. "I don't enjoy working on the farm. The Indians know best—the women do the farming and the men do the hunting. The Indian women are pretty good farmers too!"

"I agree," Christian said. Suddenly, he felt an intense longing for the life he had left. "Let's go back to our villages right now." Impetuously, he got up from the log and started to follow the path that led away from the farm.

"We can't do that," Joseph said, alarm showing in his face.

"Why not? I don't want to live where nobody knows me. *Dat* didn't even recognize me when I came home. I had to tell him who I was."

Joseph looked at him and shrugged.

"You can't blame him. Your looks have really changed. We both changed a lot in the years we were gone."

"That's why I want to go back to the village," Christian said, a tinge of desperation in his voice. "Let's go now."

Joseph shook his head. "You've got to at least stay around long enough to see Barbara and John and their families. This morning Anna told me she's planning for a special dinner on Sunday. That's the day after tomorrow."

Christian and Joseph walked in silence until they came to a small brook. The warm autumn air was thick with the buzz of bees and the scent of goldenrod. Christian's long hair swished forward when he bent down to get a drink. He wiped his mouth and looked at Joseph. "When did you cut your hair?"

"Several moons after I got back—after I started working in the fields this spring. The people around here didn't understand why I liked it long. Even Sarah said she likes it shorter."

Christian shook his head. "I'm going to keep mine like it is, regardless of what people say."

"Up to you." Joseph took a drink and changed the subject. "I'll race you."

Like a shot, he was off. Christian ran in pursuit, jumping over logs that had fallen across the trail, dodging sumac, and ducking under low branches. Joseph reached the top of the Blue Mountain pass a few steps ahead of Christian. He drew to a stop in front of a large rock at the top of the ridge. Exhausted, he collapsed onto the stone, pulling himself into a cross-legged position. Christian joined him.

"I wonder if they still call this Indian Territory," Joseph said. "It's not far from the farm at all. When we were boys, it seemed like a long way off. Lot of things seem different when you get older."

"Things not only *seem* different; they *are* different," Christian said. "How can you stand being back home?"

"It was hard at first," Joseph said. "*Dat* doesn't say much, but I'm sure he's glad we're both back home."

"How about his new wife?"

"I like Anna. She's good for *Dat*," Joseph said.

"She can't take *Mam*'s place."

"I agree, but she's kind. She helped me get adjusted to being back home."

"More than *Dat*?"

"Yes, way more. I didn't want to sleep in the house so she helped me set up a nice place in the barn. It was like my own wigwam with the hay all around. It stayed pretty cozy when it was really cold outside."

They sat for a while, watching a hawk turn lazy circles in the sky. Then, by mutual unspoken consent, they rose and dusted themselves off. Joseph turned toward the path that led to the farm.

Christian followed reluctantly. *Joseph is probably right,* he thought. *I should stay a few more days. Maybe after I've met the rest of the family, Joseph will change his mind and go back to the Ohio Territory with me.*

-3-

Anna stirred several handfuls of lentils into a large pot of stew, worried that Christian wasn't going to show up for the carry-in meal she'd planned as a celebration of his return to the Northkill. It was a Sunday when there was no worship service, and the extended family would have plenty of time to visit with him. That is, if he stayed around for more than the few minutes she'd seen him over the past couple of days.

She looked up to see Bishop Jake and his wife, Catharine, arriving in the wagon. He was tall and thin, his dark-brown hair showing patches of gray strands. Catharine was a large-boned women who carried herself with dignity and grace. Her large brown eyes spoke of sympathy as she came to the door.

Anna bade Catharine come inside while Jake went to tie the horse. It was a hot August day, so Jake tethered him in the shade of a large oak tree.

"Can I help with something?" Catharine asked as soon as she stepped through the door. She was carrying a basket of elderberry shoots and lovage greens, as well as a cooked dish of dumplings made of chopped liver and onions boiled in savory beef broth.

Anna set the food dishes on the table and then shook Catharine's hand warmly and nodded, "You can slice the bread."

"You must have baked yesterday," Catharine said as she picked up a loaf. "This feels really soft and fresh."

"Yes, I used the last of the wheat."

"Are the boys here? I don't see them."

"Joseph and Christian both went fishing this morning. They said they'd be back in time to eat with us."

Not long after, John and his wife, Katie—the daughter of Jake and Catharine—arrived with their six barefoot children. Katie set a fresh cabbage salad on the table, along with a large dish of green beans and chunks of potatoes cooked with ham.

Barbara and Cristy arrived at almost the same time with their brood of seven. The children quickly ran off to wade in the creek while Barbara handed Anna a basket of bread and Cristy set an earthenware dish with stewed rabbit on the table.

"Where is my brother?" asked John. Barbara chimed in, "I can't believe Christian is home! I've missed my little brother." Barbara and John were Jacob's oldest children; both had been married with children and living away from the home farm at the time of the Indian attack. This was their first time to see Christian in nearly eight years.

Anna was talking to Barbara outside the house when Joseph and Christian entered the clearing, carrying a string of fish. The children abruptly left the creek and crowded around the two brothers, admiring the fish they had caught and gawking at Christian's hair.

"May I touch your hair?" nine-year-old Mary asked, her eyes wide with wonder.

Anna smiled as Christian tipped his head forward to accommodate his niece. Mary stroked the long hair that emanated from the crown of Christian's head and hung down over his shoulders. She fussed with the brown cloth that tied it together at the back of his neck, and stroked the stubbles on the perimeter of his scalp where he shaved off his hair.

"You look funny," Mary said. "Men don't wear their hair that way around here."

Christian grinned. "But *I* do."

"I'll take the fish," Anna said. "I can fry it while you meet your family again." The fish were good-sized bass and catfish, a nice addition to the meal. She glanced at Jacob, who frowned and then nodded. He had always discouraged fishing on the Sabbath, but the boys made no distinction between the days of the week. Anna looked at the bishop out of the corner of her eye and was relieved to see that he was looking the other way.

She was grateful when Christian reached out to shake the proffered hands of his siblings and in-laws.

"Let me give you a hug," Barbara said to her brother, who stepped into her warm embrace. Barbara had her mother Lizzie's ample frame, with the same wide forehead and beautifully expressive eyes that dominated her otherwise plain face. She said a few words to Christian, and then all the men went outside.

Anna filleted the fish and laid the boneless strips into a frying pan on the hearth. The smell of frying fish soon filled the house.

"Look outside," Catharine said.

Anna saw Joseph and Christian, each with a child on his shoulders, bouncing around the farmyard like young colts turned out to pasture. They looped around the far side of the orchard, all the way to her bee skeps and back.

The other children ran after them, clapping and giggling. "I want to be next," one of them shouted. The two brothers obliged, giving one child after another a ride on their shoulders. Anna looked at Catharine and smiled.

The boys were still giving the children rides when Anna rang a cowbell to indicate that the meal was ready. In addition to what her guests had brought, Anna laid out two watermelons and three muskmelons fresh from her field patch, a large dish of boiled cabbage flavored with chives, and a large bowl of boiled asparagus soaked in vinegar and served with butter and pepper. Finally, she set out three pies made with red raspberries that she'd gathered in the wild.

They all gathered in a large circle around a table placed in the shade and spread with food. Jacob bowed his head in a silent prayer, and the rest joined him. When the prayer was over, Anna and the other women helped the younger children dish out food while the older ones served themselves. The adults sat on chairs or makeshift seats under the trees, and the children found places on the ground.

Anna smiled as several of the children crowded next to Christian. He was playing a game of sorts, pointing at something and saying words in his Indian language. The children responded in German. Was he trying to teach them his language? Or was he trying to relearn his native tongue? Either way, the children were shouting out words that Anna had never heard.

Christian and the children soon finished their food. And then they were back at games again, this time on the far side of the kitchen garden.

"It seems that our grandchildren really want to learn about the Indians," Catharine said.

Anna nodded. "I suppose they're learning a lot today. Christian acts more like an Indian than a white man."

As Anna visited with Catharine, she kept a close watch on Christian. She didn't see anything to cause concern. Until Christian got his knife out. She half-stood, watching. He threw the knife at a dead tree near the edge of the orchard.

This could be dangerous. Catharine joined her as they walked to the edge of the orchard. What was he doing?

Anna had noticed that both Joseph and Christian carried knives in their belts, but she'd never seen them use them. Jacob always carried a small pocket knife, but this knife was a wicked-looking weapon.

Christian and Joseph stood behind a line some six paces away from the tree, and took turns throwing their knife at an X they had scribed on the bark. She marveled at how accurate they were, sending their knife spinning through the air and slicing into the tree. Anna shivered. Was this something they had been taught to do to an enemy? The children shouldn't be watching! They might try to imitate these young uncles of theirs. Someone might get hurt!

Anna looked at Catharine. Her face was sober. "Do you think we should ask the children to do something else?"

"Let's let the parents decide that," Catharine said. But Barbara didn't seem too concerned, other than making the children stand behind the line.

The game didn't end with the knife throwing. Christian soon started whooping and throwing his tomahawk instead of his knife. Joseph joined him, whooping even louder and waving his tomahawk each time before he threw it at the tree.

"They must've practiced this many times," she said to Catharine as she watched the boys hit the target time after time with their tomahawks. Were these really Jacob's sons? Should it be allowed?

Barbara must have grown concerned too. Soon after, she spoke a word to her brothers. Anna couldn't hear what it was, but she saw Christian and Joseph put their weapons into their belts and head to the creek. The children shouted and chased after them, splashing into the water with their bare feet.

Anna and Catharine walked toward them, laughing as Joseph and Christian splashed water on each other and then on the children. The mid-August day was one of the hottest of the year, and no one seemed to mind getting wet.

"It looks as though Joseph is wearing the shirt that Barbara made for him," Catharine commented. "I'm sure it means a lot to her to see him wearing it."

"Yes, Jacob told me about it," Anna replied. "He gave it to Chief Custaloga's emissary at the treaty conference in Lancaster several years ago, but Joseph said it wasn't passed on to him until last fall, about the time he left there to come home. For a long time, his Indian mother didn't want him to know that she had it."

"Didn't Barbara make one for Christian too? I wonder what happened to it."

"Maybe the chief kept it for himself," Anna replied. "Now I'm minded to make one for him myself. Barbara hardly has the time, with all her children. I hope I have enough linen for a shirt. If not, I think we'll have enough flax this year to make a shirt for him next year."

"I'm so glad to see Joseph and Christian playing with the children," Catharine commented on the delighted shrieks coming from the creek. "Our grandchildren are really enjoying it."

"I'm glad too," Anna said, "but I'm a little worried about what they might learn from them. I know Joseph is having some trouble getting back into the farmwork, and Jacob is worried about Christian too. It seems as though the Indians like to hunt and fish and play games more than they like to work."

Catharine looked serious. "I guess time will tell how it works out."

Anna watched the children leave the creek and come running toward them, sopping wet.

"We're having lots of fun, Anna," said Barbara's daughter Mary as they approached. "We're soaked!" The girl's linen dress clung to her slender body and dripped water onto the ground.

Anna smiled and nodded. "Yes, you are. Go play in the sunshine. You'll soon dry off."

When the children wandered off to play, Catharine turned to Anna. "So . . . they don't call you '*Mammi*'?"

Anna's lips quavered. "John's children do, but not Barbara's."

Catharine was quiet for a moment. "Everything takes time. Jake says it will take time for Joseph and Christian to adjust back to our way of living. I suppose Jacob will have patience with them, because he lived with the Indians for a little while too."

Anna wrinkled her brow. "I hope so."

She knew that it taxed Jacob's patience to watch Christian cavorting with their grandchildren, looking so much like an Indian. He had struggled with Joseph's appearance upon his return. Christian was the same. Rings in his ears! Long hair! And a tomahawk! It was a bad example for the youngsters. But it would grieve her if the way Christian dressed or wore his hair caused a rift between Jacob and the son who'd been missing for so long.

There must be a way to keep that from happening. But how?

After the family gathering was over, Christian settled in for the night near the creek, where the ripple of the water reminded him of home—among the Shawnees. Fireflies twinkled all around, and a whip-poor-will sang its rhythmic, endless chant. Christian breathed deeply of the moist night air, filled with its earthy scent, as he thought about the events of the day.

It felt good to see his sister, Barbara, and his brother John again, even though they knew so little about the Indian way of life. Being with nieces and nephews was the most fun. They didn't mind that he looked like an Indian.

He wasn't about to move into the house with *Dat* and Anna. To truly stay happy and healthy on the farm, he'd need a familiar dwelling—like the wigwam he'd slept in back home. It would be cooler than *Dat*'s house on hot days and serve as a shelter when it rained. If his Indian friends ever came to visit, they'd feel right at home.

He lay awake, going over various locations in his mind. Before he fell asleep, he had decided on the ideal place.

The next morning he woke up with the sun, eager to get started. After washing down a few bites of Anna's cornmeal with water from the spring, Christian picked up his tomahawk and went into the woods. The first thing to do was find some tall saplings that could serve as supports. The wigwam wouldn't have to be large, so it wouldn't be difficult to carry the cut saplings back to the building site.

Christian spent the morning in the woods on the far side of the creek, cutting down saplings about the size of his wrist. He cut them off at the roots and then trimmed off the branches and tossed them onto a pile. By the time the sun was high in the sky, he had a pile of sixteen poles. *That should be sufficient.*

He walked back to the place where he had decided to build the wigwam and found Anna standing there.

"Would you like something to eat?"

He nodded. He was famished and followed her back to the house. Joseph was already waiting. Together, the three of them finished a loaf of bread, leaving only crumbs.

"Thank you, Anna," said Joseph, and Christian tardily echoed his words.

Anna nodded and began tidying up the table. The boys turned and left the house.

"I heard you chopping in the woods this morning," Joseph said. "What are you doing?"

"I'm building a wigwam. Will you help me?"

Joseph considered this for a moment.

"Why don't you stay with me in the cabin that Anna used to live in before she married *Dat*?"

"I don't want to stay in a house. It's too hot and stuffy."

Joseph snorted. "When winter comes, you'll be glad to have four strong walls and a roof."

"I'd rather build my own house, like the one I had back in the Ohio Territory."

Joseph shrugged. "Do it your way. But *Dat* won't be happy about it."

"Why should he care what kind of house I build?"

Joseph looked incredulous. "Christian, look around. Do you see any wigwams?"

"No." Christian paused. "Why do I have to be like everyone else?"

Joseph looked at him with pity. "Okay, do it your way. But it will mean trouble."

"So will you help me carry the poles?"

"If you're sure that's what you want to do."

The two brothers carried the sapling poles out of the woods and onto the site where Christian was building his wigwam. He drew a circle on the ground that would mark the circumference. The two lost track of time, immersed in their work.

"I'm building this wigwam like one I first lived in," Christian said, "along with the old man who adopted me. I came to love him very much."

"Why was that?" Joseph asked as he put a pole in the ground. "Did he take good care of you?"

"Yes, but it was my job to care for him. He was too old to do much hunting, so he might have starved if I hadn't been there. But once when game was scarce and I came back empty-handed, he found some game and made a stew for us. It was like a feast."

A twig snapped. Christian looked up to see *Dat* coming.

Jacob approached the building site and stood, mute. He looked at the faces of the two boys, and then at the emerging frame. His face was expressionless. The three of them stood looking at one another in uncomfortable silence.

After a long time, *Dat* said, "It looks like you're building something."

Christian nodded. "I'm building a wigwam."

"You don't need to live by yourself. We have a room with a bed for you upstairs in the house."

Christian crossed his arms. "Thank you, but I'd rather live out here."

There was a long pause. Joseph looked uncomfortable.

"That's up to you," Jacob said. He turned and walked back to the field where he had been cutting hay.

Christian looked at Joseph. "I know I'll feel more at home if I live in a wigwam by myself. I won't get in *Dat*'s way."

Joseph nodded. "It's hard for me to live in a house. But I'm getting used to it now that nearly nine moons have gone by." He paused. "You have to give yourself time to get adjusted."

"I didn't choose to come back here," Christian said, his voice uneven. "I want to be like a Shawnee, at least in some ways."

"I understand," Joseph said. He clapped Christian on the back. "Come on, let's build your wigwam. I'll fetch *Dat*'s shovel from the barn."

The two of them took turns digging holes around the perimeter of the circle. By the end of the day, they had dug sixteen holes around the circumference, each one about two feet from the other, except for one wider spot where Christian planned for a doorway. It would face east, since it was a Native custom to have the door opening face the rising sun.

Although Christian was hot and sweaty, he was elated with the progress they had made. "Let's go swimming," he told Joseph. He sighed with satisfaction. By noon the next day, they should have the framework in place, ready for the bark covering.

Christian was comforted as he splashed in the creek, rinsing off the wood chips and shavings that stuck to his sweaty skin. It would feel good to live in his own house, no matter what *Dat* or anyone else thought.

-4-

"What are you going to say when *Dat* asks you to help with the rye harvest?" Joseph asked Christian as they were hanging the last piece of bark on the wigwam. The rye in the fields was ripe and past ready to harvest. The heads of grain waved in the slight breeze. *Dat* was expecting a dozen neighbors to show up as harvest hands that day.

Christian winked at Joseph. "I'm going fishing before he has a chance to ask me."

Joseph threw back his head and laughed. Then he turned serious. "*Dat* won't stand for that. Since there are people coming to help, he'll want you to be there too."

As a child, Christian had seen large groups of harvesters come around with scythes to help each season. "If lots of people come, why should they need me?" Christian asked, picking up his fishing pole.

"There'll be trouble," Joseph warned as Christian turned toward the creek.

Christian stabbed an earthworm onto the fishhook and tossed it into the water. It didn't really matter whether or not he caught anything. Being in the woods near the water was enough.

Not less than an hour later, people began arriving. All were carrying scythes. A few looked familiar—maybe neighbors—but he couldn't remember their names. He recalled that it was common for neighbors to help each other with the harvest. And some of them would expect *Dat* to serve spirits—fruit of the previous rye harvest—as a reward.

He had caught one small fish when *Dat* appeared at the edge of the woods, motioning for him to come.

Christian drew a sharp breath. Why must *Dat* expect him to help with the harvest? He paused and then laid down his pole and walked toward the clearing. He wasn't about to spend the whole day sweating in the hot sun.

"I'd like for you to meet the people who have come to help us with the harvest," *Dat* said. "I'll give you a scythe so you can help too."

Christian hesitated. Why should he expose himself to all these people? Already some of them were gawking at him.

"Come on," *Dat* said. "Henry wants to talk to you. He's been our neighbor for a long time and he'll remember you."

Christian shrugged and followed *Dat*, who led him over to a heavily-muscled man with an untrimmed beard.

"Henry," *Dat* said, "This is my son Christian. A few days ago, he came home from a Shawnee village, where he was a captive ever since the Indians attacked our farm in '57."

"Welcome back," the man said, extending his hand. "I'm sure you're mighty glad to get away from them varmints."

Christian drew back his hand and looked at the ground. Why should he shake a man's hand who spoke of his people as pests to be eradicated, like the rats that nibbled at *Dat*'s stored corn?

"You came back at the right time," Henry went on. "You can help your dad with the harvest and then help us all celebrate with a little rum. I'm sure you learned to enjoy rum when you lived among the Indians. They're crazy for firewater."

Christian turned away without answering. Would he have to put up with this kind of talk all day? There were more than a dozen people standing nearby. More were still coming up the path toward the farm.

"Let's get started," *Dat* said, pointing to the rye field on the far side of the meadow. "Christian, here's a scythe for you to use."

Christian shook his head and headed for the outhouse. He could feel his *Dat*'s eyes watching him go.

It was the first time he'd used the privy since he'd been taken from the farm. He shrank back as he swung open the door. Had it always smelled this strong? How could people stand it? Quickly, he finished and cracked open the door. Everyone was gone. He headed back to the place where he'd been fishing and picked up his pole. He wanted to stay as far away from Henry as possible.

Not wanting to fish where the harvesters could see him, he turned his face to the north, following the creek toward its source. He swatted at several persistent mosquitoes as he made his way through a low place where the ground was wet. Hoping to keep his moccasins dry, he stepped carefully on rocks and sticks as he walked. *Ouch!* Whack! One mosquito down. A blotch of blood remained on his arm. *That was a really big one*, he thought. *I need some bear grease. I wonder if Anna has some.*

He swatted several more of the pesky insects that swarmed around him. Soon he had dozen large welts on his arms. He paused for a moment. Should he go back and ask Anna for some kind of repellent? She seemed to have plenty of concoctions. He thought of Henry, and his resolve hardened. No! He wasn't going to get near those harvesters again.

He pressed on into the woods and came to a meadow. The mosquitoes thinned out, driven away by the heat of the sun. Christian kept going until he came to a place where the creek ran through a farm clearing. He found a place in the shade of a tree that stood right next to the creek, its twisted bare roots reaching hungrily into the water.

Rigging his line, he tossed off his moccasins and soaked his bare feet in the creek. A few minnows darted around his line. *At last. Peace. And quiet.*

A dog barking broke the silence. Christian looked up. He could see a man working the nearby clearing full of grain, swinging his scythe. Christian moved a little closer to the tree so that the trunk would block him from the man's view.

He fished for much of the day without catching much—only a couple of bass and a pickerel—but that would be enough for a tasty meal.

Christian gathered enough wood to make a cooking fire. He lit some tinder with a spark from the striker and flint he kept in the leather bag he always kept at his side. Then, he filleted the fish while the fire got hot. He speared the pieces on a stick and held them over the hot coals until they were tender and ready to eat.

It grew late. Christian tossed more wood onto the fire and sat next to it for a long time. When it was dark, he cleared a circle on the ground and lay down for the night.

Gazing at the glow of the fire, Christian thought about the harvesters who'd worked hard all day. No one should have to work that hard. At least not all day long.

He was about to go to sleep when a mosquito buzzed next to his ear. He whacked at it and then scratched at a few of the places where he'd been bitten earlier in the day. Another buzz. Whack! He slept fitfully that night.

The fire was still smoldering when he rose early. Christian stirred it back to life with a stick. The mosquitoes didn't seem to mind the smoke. He continued swatting them until the sun's first rays illuminated the horizon.

Christian went back to the creek with his fishing pole. He splashed water on his face. *Ahh.* He felt more awake. He put his pole into the water. Then he heard the sound of someone walking through the brush. It was the man he'd seen the day before, with a dog trotting at his side. Seeing Christian, the dog began a frenzied barking.

"What are you doing on my land?" the man demanded in German. The dog was growling now.

Christian couldn't think of the right German words to say, so he blurted out his answer in Shawnee.

"Get off my property!" the man said, waving him away. "I saw your fire this morning and thought for sure you'd burn down my woods. Now get out of here!"

"I'm sorry," Christian said as he scrambled to his feet and backed away with his fishing pole in his hand. But not fast enough.

"Sic him!" the man yelled at his dog. Christian turned and ran. He skirted a pile of stones that had been pulled out of the fields. The dog came rushing after him, growling ferociously.

Christian turned and faced the dog. His heart pounded as he walked backward on the path, keeping the dog at bay with his fishing pole.

The dog growled and circled Christian.

"Get him, boy!" the man yelled again. The dog lunged, its jaws wide open and drooling. Christian reached for his tomahawk and faced the dog as it leapt toward his throat. Almost by instinct, Christian swung his tomahawk at the dog's head, slicing its right ear. The dog yipped but leaped toward him again. Christian brought the flat side of his tomahawk down hard on the dog's skull, knocking it to the ground.

The canine lay silent with his feet splayed and blood draining from his ear.

"Hey! *Hey!* You killed my dog!" shouted the man. Christian turned and ran toward home. "I'll get you for this!"

Christian's chest tightened as he ran. Was the man following him? He didn't dare turn around to find out. Fear of the dog and what he might have done made him tremble. Finally Christian stopped to catch his breath. Between gasps, he listened. There were no sounds of pursuit. Had the man given up the chase? Christian started walking again, listening for any signs the man was coming. Nothing. *I must get back to the farm . . .*

When he arrived, he saw more than a dozen men and boys helping to harvest the rye. They'd made good progress the previous day, and there were many sheaves standing around the field.

Christian shrank into the woods so that he could observe the workers but remain out of sight. He watched as they worked in the hot sun, swinging their scythes and laying the golden-brown stalks onto the ground. Others came behind the reapers and gathered up the stalks, tying them into bundles and stacking them into sheaves.

That will make some good bread, Christian thought, *and some good whiskey too.* Years before, Christian remembered, Jacob had turned some of the rye crop into spirits that served as medicine for the family and as goods to sell.

Exhausted, Christian was about to doze off when he heard a shout. The man who'd sicced his dog came striding through the woods. "There you are," the man yelled, running toward Christian with his rifle in hand.

Christian jumped up and ran toward the harvesters for safety. He dashed up to *Dat* with the angry neighbor in pursuit.

"That Indian was fishing on my property," the man yelled, "and he nearly killed my dog." He looked from Christian to Jacob and pulled up short.

Jacob took in the situation with a glance. He motioned for Christian to step behind him. Then he looked the man straight in the eyes. "I'm sorry, Adam," he said calmly. "This is my son. He just came back from living with the Indians. I don't suppose he knew it was your property, since he's used to fishing wherever he wants."

The harvesters quit swinging their scythes and watched. Christian's hand rested on his tomahawk. He hadn't caught all the words in the exchange, but the neighbor's tone warned of imminent danger.

The man's face relaxed. "I heard your boys were back, but didn't know this was one of them." Then his anger flashed again. "He'd better quit dressing like an Indian or he's likely to get shot. He doesn't look civilized. I don't want no varmints on my property."

Jacob nodded. "I'll make sure that he doesn't fish there again."

"You'd better keep your word," the man blustered. "Let him roam around and you'll find one of your hogs dead in the woods one of these days. Or worse."

"Again, I'm sorry. Can I get you a cool drink before you head back home?"

The man scowled. "I don't want anything from any Indian lovers." As the man began to walk away he pointed his finger at Christian. "Don't let me ever see you on my property again."

Christian took a deep breath and nodded. His stomach hurt. He looked at *Dat*, who stood watching the man go.

"You best keep away from that man, Christian. He has no patience."

Jacob stood silently while the other men talked softly among themselves. Christian walked slowly past the house to the edge of the woods. He needed to be alone.

Anna knew that Christian was upset the moment she stepped out of the house and saw him walking toward his wigwam. "Christian!" she called. "Can I get you something to eat?"

Christian didn't change his pace. He continued across the yard to the woods without looking at her.

She stood for a moment. *I wonder what has upset him.* She saw a small knot of harvesters standing around Jacob, so she walked to them to find out.

Jacob explained what had happened. "Adam's angry enough that he might do some harm. I don't think it's good for Christian to sleep out there by himself in his wigwam at night."

"He's probably hungry," Anna said. "I'll bring him something to eat."

Jacob stepped close to Anna and lowered his voice. "See if you can get him to help with the harvest. There are a lot of neighbors here, and many of them are wondering why he's not helping too."

She nodded and turned toward the outdoor oven, where she was about to bake a dozen loaves for the harvesters. Surely Christian would appreciate some fresh-baked bread.

She kept her eye on the woods as she slid the lumps of dough into the oven. The harvesters went back to work as she waited for the bread to bake.

Bread baking took work, but it was one of the simplest ways to feed people and win their hearts at the same time. Everyone loved fresh-baked bread. She used the last of their rye flour, anticipating the new crop. Wheat brought a better price at market, so the family ate rye. Wheat bread was only for special occasions.

She had finished pulling the last loaf of bread out of the oven when Christian stepped out of the woods and began walking toward the house. She waved at him and pointed to a fresh loaf of bread.

He nodded. She quickly cut a couple of slices from the end of the loaf and spread butter and jam on them as he approached.

Christian smiled tentatively and took the bread in his hands.

"You have some bad mosquito bites," Anna said as he stood there wolfing down the fresh bread. She reached out to touch a cluster of welts on his arm.

"They itch," he said, scratching his arm with his free hand.

"Let me put something on it," she said, motioning him toward the house. "First, help me carry these loaves into the house."

Christian helped her load the loaves into a basket and followed her to the house. There, Anna searched through her collection of health potions and brought out a small bottle of lotion.

"Let me rub these onto the bites," she said. "It will keep them from itching. But they will heal faster if you don't scratch them."

Christian nodded. "Back home among the Indians, we used bear grease to keep from getting bitten by mosquitoes. Do we have any here?"

She shook her head. "No, there aren't many bears around here. Maybe you can shoot one this winter. If you do, I'll render the lard for you."

He nodded and moved toward the door.

"Wait," she said. "Do you want another piece of fresh bread?" She sliced another piece of bread and slathered butter and jam on it.

Christian took his time savoring each bite. Anna watched him. When he was almost finished, she put a hand on his shoulder. "Christian. Would you like to help with the harvest today?"

He frowned. "I don't like all those people watching me."

She nodded. "I understand." But privately she thought that she couldn't blame the neighbors for staring at his long hair, bare chest, and dangling earrings.

Like Jacob, many of the neighbors were still grieving the death of family members at the hands of Indians. Why should they take kindly to Christian's appearance?

She knew it took all the forbearance in Jacob's soul for him not to demand an instant change on Christian's part. She knew, too, Jacob was worried that if he acted too harshly, the boy might leave and never come back. *He would never forgive himself if he drove Christian away,* thought Anna.

"Maybe there's something else you could do today," Anna thought out loud. "Something away from the crowd."

Christian shrugged. "I want to fish."

Anna's mind raced. What could she find for Christian to do that could give him the dignity of work yet spare him the condemning gaze of curious neighbors? Perhaps he could fish for food for the whole family and its guests.

"I know where there is a pond with a lot of fish," she said. "Would you mind getting fish for everyone and frying them for the harvesters?"

Christian's eyes brightened. "I could do that."

"Come, let *Dat* tell you how to get there."

The two of them went to find Jacob. In quiet tones, Anna explained what she'd suggested that Christian do. Jacob looked at Christian and nodded. Christian, with a lighter heart, headed down the lane toward Peter Hiestand's pond.

Anna breathed a sigh of relief. Peter was a good man who knew about Christian's and Joseph's experiences. Anna mouthed a quiet prayer for God to give Christian success. If only he could come back with enough fish for all! It would compensate for what had happened that morning.

In the late afternoon, Anna built a fire in preparation for a fish fry. By the time Christian returned with more than two dozen good-sized fish, she was ready. She helped him fillet the fish and fry them over the embers.

Anna served the fish with horseradish sauce and fresh bread as people held out their plates. When all had finished eating, they headed back to their homes. Christian stood alone with Jacob and Anna.

"Thanks for the fish," Jacob said to Anna, and then nodded at Christian as well. "The people really liked it."

"I'm so glad there are some good places to fish around here," Anna replied. "And I'm glad that Christian is such a good fisherman."

Christian frowned. "I wish I could have fished in the creek. I don't know why that man sicced his dog on me. He'd have bitten me bad if I wouldn't have hit him with my tomahawk."

"That man hates Indians," Jacob said. "Please don't go near his place again."

"He shouldn't be able to tell me where to fish," Christian said. "The creek doesn't belong to him. Why can't I fish wherever I want?"

Anna struggled to understand Christian's German words, spoken with the accent of his Indian language. Jacob didn't have any problem, however.

"Around here, people have property lines," Jacob said. "They don't want you trespassing onto their land."

Christian shrugged his shoulders. "I'm sorry."

Anna breathed a silent prayer. She wanted to broach the idea of Christian coming to church with them. Might this be a good time? *Maybe I should ask him.* She took a deep breath. "Christian, this Sunday we will be going to the church fellowship. Would you like to come with us?"

Christian's shoulders sagged. "Must I?"

Jacob spoke slowly. "Anna and I would very much like for you to come with us. There are many people who have been praying for years that you would be freed from captivity, and they will be eager to see you."

Christian stood silently. Then he spoke. "I'm afraid that everyone will stare at me."

Anna paused, considering how to respond. Today's gathering had proved Christian's point. No matter where he went, people turned to look at him. But why wouldn't they?

Jacob looked at Anna and then at Christian. "I would like for you to worship with us so that people can meet you," he said.

Christian fingered the tomahawk at his side. "Yes, I'll come one time."

Anna's heart leaped. "Good," she said, wondering if she should ask him to take the rings out of his ears. Or cut his hair. No, that would make him less likely to come. Better to let him decide for himself rather than try to force it. When he met the people whom he'd known as a youth and felt their love, he might eventually make those changes on his own.

Aloud, she said, "You'll want to meet Joseph's friend Sarah. She'll likely be there." Anna lifted the pan, which had a small amount of fish left in it. "Do you want it?" she asked, holding it out to him.

He nodded and silently finished the last scraps, thanking her as he ate. When he finished, he gave her back the pan with a small smile.

Anna sighed. It seemed as though Christian liked her—at least a little bit. If only he'd come around for more meals, perhaps she could win his heart with her cooking. He surely wouldn't be able to resist a freshly baked pie. There were still ripe peaches in the orchard, and the oven was still hot enough to bake it before she went to bed.

-5-

A few days later, Christian woke to the sound of a barking dog. He sat up with a start and looked around. Was the angry neighbor coming after him again? Perhaps he should stop sleeping outside.

He listened. The barking stopped. Warily, he went to the creek and washed his face. What would *Dat* ask him to do today? All the grain was harvested, so at least there'd be no harvesters coming around.

His stomach was rumbling, so he wandered over to the blueberry bushes *Dat* maintained with pride. The blueberries were ripe and would make a good breakfast. Bees and wasps buzzed around him in the early-morning sun, seeking the sugary sustenance of the ripe fruit. He picked them by the handful, stuffing them into his mouth until he was sated.

Christian was getting ready to go fishing when Joseph came sauntering up to the wigwam. "Anna says that you're going to church with us today."

"Oh no! Is this Sunday?" Christian asked with surprise. "I had hoped we could go fishing together. Do we have time to go before we leave for the service?"

"I'd have to look at the clock in *Dat*'s house. But if we go fishing, we won't know when it is time to leave."

Christian sighed. "You're right." *I don't want to live by clocks*, he thought. He wished he hadn't committed himself to go to church. But he dreaded the look of disappointment he'd see on *Dat*'s face if he told him he had changed his mind. *Better to do it now and get it over with.*

The sun had risen over the top of the trees when he strolled over to *Dat* and Anna's cabin. Smoke rose lazily from the chimney at the center of the house. This meant that Anna was cooking. Maybe there would be something good to eat.

"Ho," he said, and stepped through the doorway.

"Come in," Anna said in a cheerful voice. "Would you like something to eat before we go to the church service?" Without waiting for an answer, she motioned for him to sit at the table, and then dipped some mush onto a wooden plate. She put it in front of him and gave him a spoon. When Christian finished the mush, she held up the peach pie. He smiled as she cut a piece.

Christian ate the pie in silence, glancing over at *Dat*, who was reading a well-worn copy of *The Wandering Soul*. Watching *Dat's* finger move from one side of the page to the other made Christian wonder how many of the words he'd recognize after years of not holding a book in his hand. Not long before the Indian raid, *Mam* had told him he would soon be the best reader in the family. Now books were a thing of the past for him, with no practical use.

Christian went into the living room to pull on the clothing Anna had given him—a linen shirt and linen trousers. He put aside the old pair of leather shoes she'd found. Why should he bind his feet when he could have the freedom of his moccasins? He stroked back his long hair and tied it with the small brown cloth he'd carried from the Shawnee village.

When the mantel clock struck nine, *Dat* laid down his book. "It's time to go." He rose from his chair and took his hat from its peg on the wall. Without a word, Anna retrieved the empty plate from Christian. She wiped it with a wet cloth and then set it on a shelf.

Christian reluctantly followed *Dat* and Anna out the door. *Such an echo of the past!* When *Dat* said it was time to go, it was indeed time to go—without lingering or argument. To dally or protest would mean trouble. He hadn't forgotten *that*!

Dat and Anna walked beside each other on the path toward the Zug home where the church fellowship was meeting that day. The sky was clear blue overhead, not the usual sultry

August haze. A few clouds scudded across the sky, throwing an occasional shadow on the path. A rabbit hopped in front of them and then darted into the woods.

When they arrived at the Zug home, Anna left them to walk into the house. Christian accompanied *Dat* to the gathering of men and boys, who remained outside, and followed his lead, shaking hands with each one before taking his place in the circle. He was the only one not wearing a wide-brimmed yellow straw hat. He mostly looked down, glancing at the feet of those around him. All the younger boys were barefoot, while most of the men had shoes. He was the only one who wore moccasins. When he dared to glance into the faces of those nearby, their eyes darted away.

Why had he agreed to come? He hated having people stare at him.

A few moments later, Bishop Jake joined the circle, shaking hands all around. When he came to Christian, he stopped.

"I'm so glad to see you here, Christian," he said. "I'm sure you know that we prayed many times for your release. We rejoice with your father that you have been able to come home."

Christian nodded and took a deep breath. How he wished he was back home with the Shawnees, where everything was familiar! After a few more awkward moments, Bishop Jake turned to walk toward the house. Two older men joined him, followed by the married men and their boys. Christian took a step to follow *Dat* as he'd always done at worship services, then realized that the young men his age sat by themselves. He waited until all the young men had started to walk in and then followed, last in the line.

He paused for a moment as those in front of him disappeared inside. Perhaps he could remain outside, listening through a door or window.

Just then Bishop Jake appeared at the doorway and motioned him in with a friendly smile. Christian sucked in his breath and stepped inside. The men and women sat on opposite sides of the room, with small children divided between them. Every eye was on him as he made his way to a place at the very back of the room. All the chairs and benches were full, so he sat on the floor, his back against the wall of the cabin.

As *Dat* often did, he started off the service by calling out a hymn number from the small, thick songbook they called the *Ausbund*, and then led out by singing the first line alone: "*Ich weiss wer Gottes Wort bekennt, Dass der sich viel musz leiden* (I know that whoever confesses God's Word must endure much suffering)." The congregation joined in the slow, undulating chant, singing the beloved tune from memory, since the songbook contained no musical notes.

And then, following long custom, they followed with a second hymn: "*O Gott Vater, wir loben dich* (Our Father God, Thy Name We Praise)." Both words and tune sounded familiar, but Christian wondered if they'd always sung the hymn that slowly.

Christian looked around the room while the rest of the congregation sang. He wondered why, as a child, he'd never noticed the suffocating sameness of his people's dress and manner. All of the married men sported untrimmed beards and clean upper lips. All wore unbleached linen shirts cut on the same pattern, with broadfall linen breeches that met their stockings at the knees.

The women dressed alike too—with linen shortgowns, linen skirts, and aprons over petticoats, and little variety in color. Their heads were all covered by traditional white coverings with strings tied under their chins, sewn in the style they'd brought with them from Switzerland. They sat quietly with their skirts spread smoothly across their laps, their heads bowed slightly, and their eyes cast down in quiet submission. They clung to their whiteness, hiding all but their hands and faces from the sun even in the stifling heat of summer.

He yearned for the life-giving diversity of his adoptive people—men's chestnut bodies painted with colorful strokes and tattooed with creative images. And women with hair arranged to suit personal taste, sporting jewelry from head to toe, and wearing brightly beaded leather or colored fabrics from the trading posts.

As he watched the minute hand on the Zugs' mantel clock sweep nearly a quarter of its face while the congregation sang one hymn, he ached for the lively music and movement of Indian gatherings—the chants and shouts of Native dances accompanied by flutes, drums, and rattles and accented by the noisy bangles on women's wrists and ankles.

After they had finished singing the two songs, Deacon Stephen Zug rose and read from Psalm 19: "The heavens declare the glory of God; and the firmament sheweth his handywork. Day unto day uttereth speech, and night unto night sheweth knowledge. There is no speech nor language, where their voice is not heard. Their line is gone out through all the earth, and their words to the end of the world."

The words about the heavens declaring the glory of God sounded a little familiar. *Dat* had always said "the heavens" meant the sun, the moon, and the stars. The Shawnees saw it that way too.

Christian looked over at Anna, sitting on the women's side of the room. She seemed distracted by her granddaughter Ruth playing on her lap. Had she heard the deacon's words?

The deacon finished reading the Scripture and made a few comments. "When we look at the skies at night," he said, "we can see the greatness of God. He is far beyond our understanding."

That's right, Christian thought. His curiosity was always roused by watching the heavenly bodies move around at night. He wondered how the Big Dipper rotated around the North Star and what made up the band of light *Dat* called the Milky Way.

After the meditation was over, the congregation turned in their seats and knelt to pray. Christian's knees soon protested the hardness of the wooden floor, but the deacon went on and on. How could people stand it? He shifted restlessly on his knees and looked over the backs of the congregation, all hunched over the seats. He wondered how the deacon could think of so many things to pray about. How much better to pray outdoors in the manner of the Shawnees, raising one's hands toward the sky in honor of the Great Creator.

When the prayer finally ended and the congregation was seated again, Bishop Jake rose to speak. He was tall and thin; his dark-brown hair showed only a few gray strands. "We are so grateful to God for answering our prayers," he said. "Some months ago God brought Joseph Hochstetler back to our congregation, and now he has brought his brother Christian back to us also." He motioned toward Christian. Not that he would have needed to. Everyone had looked in his direction a number of times. The little children stared at his long hair, hanging in a queue in back of his head.

"It reminds us of God's goodness," Bishop Jake said. "Let us remember the words of Jesus to love our enemies, even the Indians who attacked the Hochstetler home. And let us be faithful to the words of the apostle Paul in the book of Romans. 'Recompense to no man evil for evil. . . . Therefore if thine enemy hunger, feed him; if he thirst, give him drink: for in so doing thou shalt heap coals of fire on his head. Be not overcome of evil, but overcome evil with good.'"

Christian admired Jake's ability to quote the Scriptures. Perhaps he was like *Dat*, who rose early each day to read the Bible before doing his farm chores.

Christian's mind wandered off as Jake spoke. The Shawnees never memorized words from books. They had to be on guard when the white man came around with words on paper, which often meant they were about to take away the Natives' ancestral lands.

The Shawnees read the heavens instead, which told them about the desires of the Great Spirit, the Creator of all good things. They read the signs in the skies, the shifting directions of the wind, the movements of the clouds, and the changing colors on the horizon. They were far better than the whites at reading the signs on the earth; even the faintest clues left by humans and animals in the woods, on the trails, and in the watercourses. Since the Shawnees were superior to the white man at reading what God had written in creation, why should they pay attention to what the white man wrote with pen and ink?

Christian didn't comprehend much of Jake's sermon, or even the final hymn and the benediction. His stomach growled. He looked forward to the simple meal afterward—the usual bean soup and bread—but he didn't look forward to conversing with others. They spoke Pennsylvania German faster than he could comprehend it, and it was difficult to put his Shawnee thoughts into their words. It helped a little that Joseph was available to translate some of the German words into Delaware for him.

"It was several moons after I got back home that I was able to understand most things people were saying," Joseph told Christian after the service. "I still don't understand everything Bishop Jake says in his sermon."

Christian wondered if they'd understood it all as boys. "When we were taken as captives," he told Joseph, "*Dat* told us to recite the Lord's Prayer in German every day. I didn't remember to do that. Did you?"

"No," Joseph said. "Maybe if we'd have done that, we wouldn't have forgotten so much of the German."

Christian and Joseph sat with the other men at the tables where the meal was to be served. A young woman came up to Christian with a smile. She tucked a few wayward wisps of brown hair under her white linen cap.

"This is Sarah Blank," Joseph said, "the prettiest of all the girls at church."

Sarah blushed, her rosy cheeks complementing her full lips. Christian offered an awkward half smile in response. So this was Joseph's special friend. She'd look even prettier if she had olive skin like Morning Dew, or wore earrings or bracelets.

An older man leaned toward Christian as he was about to take his first bite. "Aren't you glad to be home again?" he asked. "Free from the Indians at last!"

After Joseph confirmed the meaning of the man's words, Christian paused and nodded. "I'm glad to see *Dat* again. And to meet Anna."

That was the truth. But he wasn't about to comment on leaving the Indians. How could they comprehend that he'd much rather be back in the Shawnee village than in the church service today?

If anyone tried to force him to attend another church service soon, it would hasten the day he'd leave the Northkill. And never come back.

After walking home with Jacob after the service, Anna headed for Catharine Hertzler's house. She'd promised to bring Catharine a bottle of her cough syrup, and she hoped to talk to her about ways to help Christian fit in at home. Although he hadn't breathed a word to her about the church service, she could tell he felt awkward and uncomfortable.

As the bishop's wife, Catharine might know how to deal with his reluctance to identify with his own people. She could trust Catharine to speak her mind. And besides—Catharine knew what it was like to raise stepchildren.

Anna was halfway to the Hertzler home when she spied a familiar figure striding toward her on the path. Her heart sank. It was Silas Burkholder. Once, before she had married Jacob, Silas called on her, supposedly to find healing for chest pain. But he was overly familiar with her, standing a little too close, touching her hair. When he asked for a massage of his feet and shoulders, she demurred, hoping to avoid his touch. When she offered an herbal remedy from her herb book instead, he called it a handbook for witchcraft.

Worse, when she turned to show him to the door, he grabbed her from behind and pressed himself against her. She screamed and kicked his shins, then, as he cried out in pain, she turned and kneed him in the groin. She ran for the neighbor's house as he shouted out threats.

A week later the deacon came calling, reporting that Silas had accused Anna of giving him a witch's brew to drink, and of being too familiar with her touch as she massaged his back and shoulders. *A witch!* Anna's anger rose at the injustice of Silas's attempt to discredit her as a way to cover his own wrongs.

Silas was a liar, and she told the deacon so. But things had never been the same for her since. Silas was a respected member of a neighboring church, and people seemed to take him at his word. She had told Jacob the truth about her run-in with Silas after Jacob had expressed interest in her, but mostly she kept the story to herself. Who else would believe her?

Ever since, she had succeeded in avoiding Silas, slipping away quickly the few times when she spied him at the local market. But now there seemed to be no way to avoid him.

Silas was grinning as he strode toward her. She could see his bent nose and his straggly beard. Soon their paths would intersect, and there'd be no easy way to get away from him. If only there were someone else around! *What shall I do?* she wondered. *Should I turn around and run toward home?*

No, to run from him in broad daylight would only invite his scorn. Anna gritted her teeth. *I'll ignore him,* she decided. She slowed her pace, feigning interest in a hawk that soared overhead.

Silas was but a few steps away. "Hello, Anna." He leered at her.

She ignored him and walked as close to the edge of the path as possible.

He stepped in front of her. "I want to talk to you."

"Leave me alone!" She stepped to the other side of the footpath and held her basket between them.

Silas moved sideways to block her path. "Have you made more of your witch's brew for that stepson of yours?" he asked.

"Now that Jacob's sons are back from the Indians, you can learn more magic from them."

"I've never made witch's brew, and I don't want to talk to you. Now move out of my way."

"Of course I'll move," he said with a smirk on his face as he stepped aside. "Why should I talk to someone as rude as you?" As she passed, he reached around her carrying basket and swatted her on the backside of her skirt.

Her cheeks flushed hot as she sped up her pace.

"I hope you're not late to wherever you're going in such a hurry," he shouted and then laughed.

She walked as fast as she could without running. She glanced back twice to make sure he wasn't pursuing her. Only when he was completely out of sight did she slow down to her usual pace. Hot tears welled up in her eyes and spilled down her cheeks. She was trembling. Should she tell Catharine what had happened? Or Jacob? Anna suspected that Catharine believed Silas's rumors rather than Anna's explanation of what had happened. Maybe, if it seemed right in the course of their conversation, she could bring it up. Otherwise, she'd keep it to herself and maybe not even tell Jacob. He had enough on his mind, with the two boys.

She arrived at Catharine's home and stood for a moment, wiping her face free of tears and settling her nerves. Then she walked up the path and knocked.

Catharine answered the door with a welcoming smile. "Anna! Come in, come in."

Anna fanned her face with her handkerchief. "It's so hot. Would you mind if we sit outside in the shade?" She didn't want anyone else to overhear their conversation, and that would be a simple way to have privacy.

"Of course. I would enjoy that." Catharine left for a moment and came back carrying a quilt. She handed the quilt to Anna, and went back for a jug of water and two glasses. Anna led the way into the yard and spread the quilt in the shade of a large elm tree. They both made themselves comfortable as

Catharine poured them a cool drink of water from the jug. "How is Christian doing?" she asked.

"That's what I've come to talk to you about," Anna replied. "I'm afraid it's not going very well. He's not adjusting in the way that we had hoped."

Catharine nodded. "I'm sure it will take some time."

"I didn't expect it to be this way. Jacob and I have been praying for Christian to come home for years. Somehow it seems harder with Christian than it was with Joseph, which was difficult enough."

"What makes it so hard?"

"He rarely sits at our table! He wants to live outside by himself. Like the Indians do, I guess."

"I always liked Christian as he was growing up," Catharine said. "He was such a curious boy, so quick to ask questions. I remember Lizzie getting tired of trying to answer all of them."

"I remember him that way too. One day when their family helped me clean up some fallen branches after a storm, he took an interest in my herb bed. He even asked me about the names of the plants and how I use them. And I remember how much he liked my peach pie."

Catharine nodded. "That was years ago. He's mostly been with the Indians since that time."

"I had hoped I could really make him feel at home. It doesn't seem to be working." Anna's voice broke as she spoke. "I wonder what I'm doing wrong."

Catharine patted Anna's knee. "Maybe you're not doing anything wrong at all. Remember, you're a stepmother, and he'll need some time to get used to you. At least that's how it was with me."

Anna considered this. "But Catharine, your stepchildren all seem to treat you like their own mother. I wish Jacob's children would treat me that way—especially Barbara."

Catharine paused. "That might be too much to expect. My stepchildren were young when Jake and I got married. If they'd been married with several children—like Barbara was

when you married her father—they might never have seen me
as their mother."

Anna took another drink of water, hoping to steady the
tremor in her voice. "I want so much to be a mother. I had
hoped Jacob and I would be able to have children, but . . ." Her
voice trailed off a bit. "I guess there's something wrong with
me."

Catharine nodded sympathetically. "Maybe it's not God's
will right now," she said. "But you're young enough that it
could still happen."

"I pray every day that it will."

The women were quiet for a moment. "Maybe you've
prayed enough that God knows what you want," Catharine
said softly. "Now might be the time to let it rest and pray for
something else."

A tinge of anger welled up inside Anna, and an awkward
silence followed. Catharine could be so sympathetic at times,
and so contradictory at others. Hadn't the bishop encouraged
the congregation to pray without ceasing?

"How then shall I pray?"

"Pray for God's will to be done, whether you bear your own
child or help Christian—the one you already have—to fit in
back at home."

"I already pray that way. But Christian barely talks to me
and he won't even sleep in our house."

"How does he get along with Jacob?"

"That's part of the problem. Jacob wanted so much for
Christian to come home for years, but now that he's back,
they don't seem to get along with each other."

"Oh?" Catharine paused, looking curious.

Anna paused. Should she tell Catharine about her disappointment with Jacob? She wouldn't want her to tell the bishop.
But unless Jacob softened his approach, he'd be butting heads
with Christian for a long time. She gathered her courage and
said, "I think it really bothers Christian that Jacob didn't recognize him when he got back. And Jacob blames himself for

that, even though I didn't recognize him either. The two of them hardly talk to each other."

"Maybe Christian didn't want to come back to the Northkill, and he's looking for excuses to go back."

"If that's true, what can we do about it?" At times she felt like telling Christian that if it was so bad at their home, he should go back to live with the Indians.

Catharine paused. "Well, the Indians love the out-of-doors. Maybe you need to spend time with him outside the house. Have you shown him your garden?"

Anna shrugged. "I'm sure he saw it. It's not far from the house."

"Maybe you should show him around in it. It might remind him of the good times as a child."

"I hadn't thought of that."

They both sipped their water, thinking.

"Has he visited his mother's grave?"

"I doubt he knows where it is." Anna had only seen it once herself. Why should she remind herself of Lizzie, whose absence had left a hole in Jacob's heart that she now struggled to fill? Why remind Christian or Joseph of the terrible attack, with all that ensued? On the other hand, maybe if he were reminded of what the Indians had done to their family, he wouldn't be so enamored with Native ways.

Catharine spoke slowly, "If I were you, I would do what I could to remind him of good times from his childhood. And I would learn from him about the Indians."

"How would that help?" If she were frank with Catharine, she'd tell her that she was repulsed by Native American habits. The sooner that Christian put aside his Indian identity, the better it would be. Even the way that Christian carried his tomahawk at his side frightened her.

"If you're going to win the boy's love, you'll have to show interest in the things that interest him, not try to persuade him to like the things you care about."

Anna paused, considering. Catharine's words seemed wise, like proverbs. But it would not be easy to put them into practice. She wiped the sweat from her face with her handkerchief. Then, brushing off her skirt, she stood up. "I guess I'll be going now. Jacob will soon wonder why I've been gone so long."

Catharine stood next to her and put her arm around Anna's shoulder. "I'm glad you came by. Remember, we're friends! You can talk to me anytime."

"Thanks for your good advice. You help me think more clearly." With that, Anna turned and headed back toward home, pondering Catharine's words. How was she going to put them into practice? What should she say to Jacob about it?

-6-

When Christian got back from the church service, he stepped back into his wigwam to get his fishing pole before heading for the pond where he'd fished for the harvesters. On the way past the field patch, he pulled a small head of cabbage to assuage his hunger. When he got to the pond, he sat in the shade of a tree and threw a hook into the water.

It was a hot day with hardly any wind. The water was placid except for the occasional turtle that poked its head above the surface. A blue jay scolded a squirrel overhead.

Christian pondered what had happened at the church fellowship that morning in the crowded house. *I'm not going back there,* he resolved. How could *Dat* enjoy this way of worship? It was so different from worship among the Shawnees. The ways of the Amish, deeply familiar to him as a child, now seemed strange and uncomfortable.

A beaver dove into the pond at the far end, swimming with a large stick in his jaws. He disappeared under the surface for a time. *Perhaps I can get that beaver this winter,* Christian thought. Back at the Shawnee village, he had often hunted for beaver and traded the pelts with the white man for ammunition and other supplies. He'd need to hunt some deer too, and perhaps a bear. Or maybe it would be better to go back to the Indian village for the winter, where everything seemed more familiar.

Dat seemed satisfied to sit inside to sing songs from the *Ausbund* and listen to the bishop speak. Anna seemed satisfied too, or at least she pretended to be. As a child, he had endured it, but now it suffocated him. He thrived in the unwalled sanctuary of the Great Creator, surrounded by trees and animals. Sitting on the bank with the fishing pole gave

83

him a much greater sense of inner peace than sitting in a congregation with people staring at him.

He soon dozed off. Waking, abruptly, he realized his pole hadn't moved. *The fish sure aren't biting today.* He decided to leave the pond and try the creek.

Christian followed the creek to the north as he had done before, passing through the property of the man who'd been so angry at him. He walked deeper into the woods as he went through the man's property, making sure that the dog wouldn't see him. He kept walking beside the creek, hoping to find a good place to stay for the night.

There were a number of settlers in the area, and it appeared there were fewer woods than there had been when he was a child. At least *Dat* cultivated an orchard, which was better than clearing the ground for crops of wheat, rye, or barley.

What would happen to all the wild animals if the white man kept clearing the land? Where would does cavort with their fawns or she bears find sanctuary for their cubs? Where were the foxes and coyotes to make their dens? Was there something in the holy book they used at church that demanded they cut down trees?

The white man tamed his fellow creatures—horses, cattle, sheep—building fences to keep the animals in and the neighbors out. The Shawnees let their animals run free as the wind that carries the winter from the north and brings the summer from the south.

Christian gave up fishing and headed toward the ridge of the Blue Mountains. As a child, he had seen it as a dangerous place for white boys. Now he saw it as a place of refuge from the thrust of the whites to subdue the land. No one would ever farm the rocky soil atop the ridge that ran for miles, as far as he could see. It would be an ideal place to stay for the night, to watch the moon crossing the sky, and to witness the stars twinkling in their places.

As he hiked toward the top of the ridge, he found some huckleberries, which were wont to grow on the rocky hillsides where pine trees drop their needles. He stopped and ate the tiny blue berries hungrily, staining his hands with the juice.

Christian crossed the ridge and found an open place. He pulled together a pile of leaves to soften the ground for his bed, and then started a fire nearby. If a bear was in the area, it was better to have a fire.

He sat on a log for a long time, contemplating the things that had happened during the day. Night fell. Stars began to come out. He lay in a small clearing with an unobstructed view of the sky. It gave him a peaceful feeling inside to see the sky lit with stars. He sought out the Big Dipper and the Little Dipper. By watching the Big Dipper each night, he discovered that the constellation rotated around the North Star, which seemed to be fixed in place.

Christian grew sleepy. Dreams mingled with reality.

He was running, the angry white neighbor in pursuit, accompanied by the short-haired cur who had attacked him several days earlier. He tried to scream, to call them off, but the sound stuck in his throat. He dodged in and out among the trees in the dim moonlight, shielding his eyes from the branches that swept hard against his face as he ran. Twice he tripped and fell as he ran down the sloped path, deeper into Indian Territory. Both times, the dog nipped at his moccasins and the angry neighbor shouted curses at him.

Christian was panting with fatigue when he came to a cabin in the woods. A place of refuge! He yanked on the latchstring and the door opened. He quickly slipped inside and slammed it behind him. The dog barked madly on the outside. A minute later, someone banged on the door and shouted, "I know who you are. Let me in or I'll burn your house down!"

Christian's heart beat wildly. What was he to do? He surveyed the small cabin, but it was too dark to make out anything except the outline of two small windows. He peered outside to see several shadowy figures. One of them had a firebrand. He lit the dried leaves that lay outside the window. The man added sticks to the fire until it burned bright and crackled loud enough that Christian could hear it from the inside of the house. By its light, Christian could make out the faces of several angry-looking settlers not far off in the trees.

"Come on out," one shouted. "We have bullets waiting for you."

Christian stepped to the side of the window, pondering what to do. "Your best friend is surprise," the Shawnees used to say. "Always act in ways your enemy would not predict."

He fingered the tomahawk at his side, and then his knife. Perhaps he could catch the men off guard by swinging open the door and throwing his knife, or even his tomahawk, before the enemy could fire a gun.

No. There were too many of them, and they might all have guns. Perhaps there was another way out of the cabin. He sniffed the air. The cabin wall was smoldering—he would bet on it. There wasn't much time.

Just then there was a heavy thud against the cabin door. As it crashed open, Christian swung his tomahawk at the figures that darted into the room. He met only air. Something hit him hard from the rear, throwing him onto the cabin floor. A heavy boot pressed down hard on his neck as someone else tied his hands tightly behind his back and bound his feet.

"His Indian people burned down our houses," a voice shouted as the smoke from the fire drifted through the doorway. "Now let him burn with his cabin."

In a few moments, the attackers left, and all was quiet except for the sound of the fire crackling. The cabin wall was soon aflame. Christian wiggled his wrists, trying to free himself. He scooted across the floor on his chest, moving away from the fire toward the back of the room. The fire illuminated a rectangular hole in the floor at the back on the room. He got to it and peered into the blackness. A cool, damp smell wafted up. Was it a root cellar? Perhaps it would have an opening to the outside. Should he take a chance and go down the stairs? No, it was too risky. What if he got trapped there?

He scooted farther forward as the front wall collapsed under the flames. It was only a matter of time before the roof would fall in.

"Help!" he shouted. "Let me out of here."

"This will teach you," someone shouted, followed by boisterous laughter.

I should never have left the Indian village, Christian told himself. *If I get away from here, I'm going back as soon as I can.*

A burning rafter fell with a thud, showering sparks onto Christian's bound legs. When he jerked forward, it threw him off balance and into the hole.

He fell headfirst with his hands behind his back, so he had no way to break his fall. He landed heavily on his shoulder, and then all went black.

Christian woke with a start and looked around the place on the ridge where he had fallen asleep. His heart was beating wildly and sweat was pouring from his body. It was the first time in several years that he'd had such a terrible nightmare. At least he hadn't walked in his sleep as he'd done as a boy.

Christian watched the faint flicker of the fire. He stoked the flames to ensure that a wildcat or some other creature didn't wander too close. He took several deep breaths, grateful that his vivid dream hadn't been true.

Christian lay back down and looked into the sky, wondering what would have happened to his spirit had the dream been true and he had died in the fire. He wondered if *Mam* or Jakey or Franey could see him as he lay there. He had nearly forgotten them when he lived at the Shawnee village. But now that he was back at the Northkill, he thought of them often.

He thought of *Mam*, stuck in the small window in the root cellar of their burning cabin on that fateful morning years before, when *Dat* worked desperately to get the family out of the smoke-filled room. They'd all gotten out moments before the burning floor above them caved in, only to fall into the hands of the enemy, who grabbed *Mam* and . . .

Christian swallowed hard and shoved the memory out of his mind. There was no good reason to dwell on the painful memories of what the Indians had done to his family that day.

After all, he was an Indian now.

The next morning Anna walked down to Christian's wigwam to see how he was doing. Christian had looked so miserable in the Sunday service that she almost wished she hadn't invited him to attend. Judging his love for ground cherry pie by the way he'd eaten it at the family gathering, she carried the sole remaining piece on a wooden dish as a treat.

Anna peered into the bark-enclosed hovel. Empty! Had Christian gone fishing? Or had he disappeared for good?

Worried, she stepped inside the wigwam. The domed structure had no windows; the only light came through the doorway and a smoke hole at the top. There was a large gap between the bark siding and the ground, which would help the air circulate through the dwelling on hot nights. But what about the cold days to come as winter approached? There was no way Christian could keep the wigwam as warm and cozy as their cabin. Why would he want to live in such a crude dwelling when there was plenty of room upstairs in the house?

After his escape from the Indians, Jacob had rebuilt the house with three small bedrooms upstairs, each with a window. The rooms were cold in the wintertime, but nothing like the frigid air and snow that would drift into Christian's wigwam. The Pennsylvania winters could be brutal, especially when the north winds blew.

She smiled to remember a saying from her father: *Winter is the season when we keep the house as hot as it was last summer when we complained about how hot it was.* He didn't like to hear people complaining about the weather.

She was turning to leave when she heard the sound of voices near the creek. Were John's children playing there? She cocked her ear to listen. No, these were unfamiliar voices, likely those of young boys. She saw a flash of clothing and heard splashing in the creek as she scanned the area. "Who's there?" she called out.

The sounds stopped. She stood still for a few moments. Hearing nothing more, she sighed and left.

As Anna walked toward the orchard, she mused about the way that Joseph had fit in upon his return. Like Christian, he'd resisted living in the house. And when she'd suggested that he could live in the small cabin she'd called her own before she got married to Jacob, he took up the offer right away. It wasn't far from the farm, but far enough that he didn't clash with Jacob the way that Christian did. Joseph had only been home a few months when Sarah Blank caught his eye. That's when things really changed for the better. Although Jacob didn't say much about it, she could tell he was very happy about Joseph's interest in the girl. Neither Joseph nor Sarah had joined the church—yet. They would need to do so if they wanted Bishop Jake to marry them.

Getting married often helped young men to settle down in the Amish neighborhood, and it would certainly be true of Joseph. As soon as Joseph got married, Jacob would give him a piece of the farm. And if God blessed the new couple with children, it would surely rid Joseph's mind of thoughts about going back to the Delawares.

Anna blinked back tears. She was one of the few women her age in the congregation who had no children of her own. At times, sitting in a church service with empty arms, surrounded by children, was almost more than she could bear. It brought some relief when one of John's or Barbara's children came to sit on her lap. "At least you have grandchildren," she chided herself.

It still stung when she thought of Catharine's words about needing to love the stepchildren she already had, rather than praying incessantly for her own. *If only God will grant me both.*

When Anna arrived at the orchard, Joseph was there, gathering peaches from the uppermost branches. They worked beside each other in silence for a little while. Then Anna asked. "Do you know where Christian went?"

"No. He doesn't tell me what he's doing."

"I'm sure he'd like these peaches."

"Yeah, probably would. But he has other things on his mind."

Anna tipped her head, waiting, but Joseph said nothing more.

"He doesn't seem happy," Anna said, hoping to get Joseph to speak.

Joseph nodded. "He misses his Indian family very much."

Anna flicked a bee off a peach. "How can I help him feel more at home here? I'd like to do whatever I can."

Joseph paused. "The best thing to do is to leave him alone. Give him time to adjust."

Anna sighed. "But there must surely be something I can do," she said.

Joseph shook his head. "If you try too hard to help him, it will do more harm than good."

That's something Jacob would say, Anna thought. She filled the rest of her basket in silence and carried the peaches back to the house.

Anna's mind was in a whirl as she considered Joseph's advice. Would Catharine agree? Why shouldn't Christian want someone to show he was truly loved? That's what she was determined to do. But now that she'd talked to Joseph, she realized it might be harder than she had thought.

Christian was loath to go back to the farm. He was eager to fish with Little Bear again. He thought about heading back to his Shawnee village. Even more, he hoped to see Morning Dew, who occupied his mind most days.

If he disappeared for a time, *Dat* would likely send Joseph after him. If so, he should probably travel with Joseph in the first place. Besides, it would be safer to travel as a pair. *That's what I'll do—ask Joseph to come with me to Indian Territory—the sooner the better.*

After another day and night away, Christian headed back to the farm with some fish on his string. As he approached the property owned by the angry man *Dat* called Adam, he heard the man's dog barking. Christian left the path and walked farther from the property's edge, pressing through a dense part of the woods. The nightmare had been too vivid for him to take any chances of being followed or attacked.

The sun was setting as he reached the clearing where he had built his wigwam.

The wigwam was gone. In its place lay a pile of ashes. Someone had burned his wigwam! Who would do such a thing? And why?

Christian held his hand over the ash heap. It was only slightly warm. *Someone must've done this last night,* he thought. *Maybe that's what my dream was about!*

The more he thought about it, the more agitated he became. *That man, Adam, saw me passing through his property a couple days ago. I bet he burned it down!*

Christian mused over what his Shawnee family would do if something like this happened to them. Revenge was both necessary and sweet. As an Indian, to do nothing would reflect badly on his character.

I'm going back there to burn down one of his buildings, Christian thought. *Maybe his outhouse.* He laughed bitterly at the thought of seeing the outhouse in flames.

Christian paced around the spot where his wigwam had been. Where was he going to sleep? If Adam had indeed burned down his wigwam, he might well be in the woods watching him right now, planning for more harm.

Perhaps he could sleep in the barn, or some other place that would be safe.

He looked up to see Joseph walking toward him. "I wondered when you were coming back," Joseph said. They both stood, looking at the ashes of the wigwam. "I'm sorry, Christian. *Dat* woke up and saw the fire, but it was too late to save anything."

"Who do you think did it?" Christian asked, his voice laced with anger.

"Anna said she saw some young boys playing down by the creek yesterday. They might have been playing a prank."

"There's nothing funny about this," Christian said. "I'm going to get back at them. I bet it was that old man who sicced his dog on me and chased me off his property."

"I thought of him too, but *Dat* thinks not. He knows that man and doesn't think he'd do that."

Christian pulled the tomahawk from his belt and slammed it into the ground. "He's not going to get away with this."

Joseph reached out and put his hand on Christian's shoulder. "You better make sure you know who did it before you do something you'll regret."

Christian's eyes flashed. "Who else would have done it?"

"As I said, Anna saw some young boys playing down by the creek."

"If they come down here again, they'll be in trouble. In the morning, I'm going to follow their tracks."

Joseph put his hand on his brother's arm. "Don't go, Christian."

Christian wrestled with his anger.

"Come on," Joseph said. "It can wait."

"Okay. I'll think about it. But will you help me build another wigwam?"

"Sure, I'll help you. We'll get it back up soon."

With that assurance, Joseph left. Christian tossed some old dry leaves onto the ash heap and fanned the embers with a piece of bark. Before long, the leaves burst into flame and he built up the fire. He fell asleep by the fire, still nursing his anger.

He wondered about the meaning of the dream he'd had two nights ago. Although he'd been among the Shawnees for more than seven years, he didn't try as hard as they did to make sense of every dream. Nevertheless, it seemed like a bad omen.

He worried about the motives of those who had destroyed his wigwam. Plenty of people had given him hard looks because he dressed like an Indian. *Might it have been one of those people who burned my wigwam?*

If it was young boys, as Joseph would have him believe, what prompted them to do it? *Dat* said that "the apple doesn't fall far from the tree." Were the boys acting out their parents' wishes?

He could rebuild the wigwam with Joseph's help, but what if something more sinister were at stake? If an irate man was willing to sic his dog on him or burn down his wigwam, what might he be willing to do next?

How come they'd never done something like this to Joseph? Was it because he no longer wore his hair like the Indians? Was it because Joseph had quit wearing his medicine bundle?

"I'm not going to let them scare me into becoming like the rest of the settlers," he mumbled as he was drifting into a troubled sleep. "If they do anything more like this, I'm going to teach them a lesson they'll never forget."

The next morning, Christian woke with the sun. All thoughts of fishing with Joseph were gone. All he could think about was revenge.

As he studied the tracks, he soon determined that there were four or five people involved. They were indeed young boys. The footprints indicated midsized bare feet, not the heavy-soled leather shoes that the grown settlers wore.

Christian traced the footprints to the creek, where they disappeared. Had they actually been smart enough to hide their tracks from him as part of their plot? Or had they been wading in the creek and happened to come upon his wigwam?

He was puzzling over the tracks when Joseph came with his fishing pole.

"What are you doing?" Joseph asked. "I thought you were going fishing with me."

"I'm following these tracks."

Joseph sighed. "Christian, give it up. Come fishing with me."

Christian spat on the ground. "I'm going to find out who did this. They'll be sorry they ever got close to my wigwam."

-7-

A couple of weeks later, Christian decided to rebuild his wigwam, a little larger this time. He was finishing the platform for the bed on the inside when *Dat* approached him to help gather in the hay.

"Not today. I'm finishing up my bed so I can sleep better," he said. It was partly true. He also didn't care to handle the scratchy hay or to sweat on a warm September day.

Dat seemed to read his mind. "Well, if you don't want to help with the hay," he said, "I'd like to have you take Anna's big hoe to the smithy to have it welded. It has a crack in it."

Christian shrugged. "I guess I can do that."

"Do you remember where he has his shop?" *Dat* asked. Christian shook his head.

"Go up this road until you get to the large oak tree where the path forks. Then go right until you see the smithy's place on the left. Anna's been wanting to get this hoe fixed for several weeks already."

Christian shrugged and nodded. He headed up the path, carrying the cracked hoe over his shoulder.

The sun was high in the sky when he arrived at the smithy's place. The shop had an air of familiarity about it, since he'd been there on occasion as a child with *Dat*. The forge was housed inside a log cabin with doors wide enough to let a wagon inside. They stood open now, admitting the bright sunlight from the east into the dark interior of the workplace. The sounds of the smithy's hammer echoed from inside the shop, ringing against Christian's ears. The smoke from the forge hung heavily in the air, and the smell of sulfur burned his nose.

Two men stood near the anvil, watching the smithy do his work. They took a long look at Christian as he stood in the doorway and then looked at each other in a way that made him shrink back.

A horse was tied under a maple tree, stamping its feet and swishing its tail to drive off the horseflies. A dog lolled in the shade nearby. Christian looked at him, and the dog growled.

The smithy ceased his pounding. He thrust a piece of metal into the forge's hot coals while his assistant cranked the handle. Air was forced to the coals, turning them red-hot.

The metal turned orange with heat. The smithy pulled it out of the fire with his tongs, then laid it on the anvil. He beat the glowing metal flat, alternating a rhythm of tapping on the anvil and the metal. In a few moments, the orange color faded and the metal turned hard. The smithy put it back into the forge and then pulled it out to shape it some more.

There were no smithies among the Shawnees that Christian could recall. They always took broken metal to the trader's shop. He thought of the smithy's job and shuddered. Who would want to smell sulfur and hot metal all day long?

One of the men looked at Christian with suspicion. "Where are you from?"

"I live on a farm a few miles down the road from here." Despite himself, Christian's voice quavered.

"What are you doing there?"

"I grew up on that farm," Christian said more confidently.

The smithy stopped his hammering. "Aren't you one of Jacob Hochstetler's sons?" The smithy turned to the two men. "Jacob is that Amish man with the long beard. One of them folks that don't believe in guns."

Christian was motionless, silent.

The smithy looked hard at Christian. "I asked you a question. Are you one of Jacob's sons?"

Christian nodded. He hadn't expected to be interrogated.

"You and a couple others were taken by the Indians a few years ago, right? The time when a soldier from the Northkill fort was tomahawked and scalped by them fiends."

Christian bristled at the reference. "I don't know about the man from the fort. Three of our family were taken to Fort Presque Isle."

"It was Indians, though, that took you. What were they: Delawares, Shawnees, or some other kind?"

"Delawares and Shawnees."

"I talked to your father after he escaped. He come near to starving to death in the woods."

He took a long look at Christian. "So you was held by the Indians too. When did you get away?"

"I came back several weeks ago—with other white captives through Johnson Hall in New York."

"I bet that was the happiest day of your life, when you set your feet back on this soil a free man."

Christian took a deep breath but said nothing. He held out the hoe. "Will you be able to weld this? My *Dat* wants you to fix it."

The smithy shrugged. "I'll look at that after I get finished with the project that Silas brought in." He nodded to his assistant, who cranked the fan on the forge as the smithy buried a piece of metal in the coals.

Silas looked at Christian. "I'm wondering why you're wearing your hair like an Indian."

"I like it. I've worn it this way for years."

"You better be careful. You could get shot walking the paths in these parts with hair like that. We've had enough of them Indian devils around here. We're likely to shoot first and ask questions afterward."

Anger flashed like a knife in Christian's chest. "The Indians were here before us. What does it hurt if some Indian wants to visit the places where he used to live?"

The smithy smashed his hammer down hard on the anvil and glared at Christian.

"You better watch your tongue, young man. I don't want to hear any talk of this being Indian land. William Penn bought this land from them Indians fair and square. I can prove it by the deed I have for my property."

"There's not an honest man among them Indians," Silas said. "All they do is steal or burn down settlers' cabins. Someone should burn down their houses."

The smithy nodded his head vigorously. "That's why you'd best get rid of your long hair before someone takes it from you."

Christian fidgeted with the tomahawk that hung from his waist. Did Silas know about his burnt wigwam?

"What does your father say about you dressing like an Indian? If I was your father, I wouldn't stand for it," the smithy said. "I'd take you down and cut that hair to a decent length."

Christian's face flushed red. "Will you please fix my hoe?" He hoped he was using the right German words to say what he meant.

"Not when you're talking the way you do."

Christian's heart was in his throat. He pivoted and quickly left through the open door.

He had taken only a few steps away from the shop when a man with a long untrimmed beard and a prominent mustache rode up on his horse. He swung his leg over his horse's rump and down to the ground. He stepped toward Christian, his round cheeks glowing in the sunshine. "Good day to you."

Christian nodded, still scowling.

"My name's George Klein," the man said. "I'm the elder at the Dunker congregation down the way in Jefferson Township. Looks to me as though not everything is going the way you had hoped today."

Christian nodded. "Those men don't like me dressing like an Indian," he replied in a low voice. "The smithy isn't going to repair this hoe, even though it's for *Dat*."

"What's your father's name?"

"Jacob Hochstetler. He lives only a few miles down the road here."

"I know him." The man paused with a twinkle in his eye. "Tell me why you're dressed like an Indian. Your blue eyes tell me that you've got white blood."

Christian generally shrunk back from talking to strangers, but the kindly elder's gentle manner gave him courage to speak. "I lived with the Shawnees for some years. Just got back to these parts a few weeks ago."

The man's eyes showed sympathy. "You've had an unusual experience—living among Indians."

"I was taken in a raid when I was eleven. The British treaty forced me to come back home."

"So you'd rather have stayed with the Indians?"

Christian cast down his eyes for a moment, and then looked into the kindly man's eyes. "Coming home has been hard for me. Nobody understands me." He spoke so quietly that the man took a step closer.

"I can see why the smithy's not happy with you. His brother was killed by Indians, and he'll never forgive them for that."

"I'm sorry," Christian said. "I don't mean to make trouble for anyone."

"I'm sure that's true," the man said. "I hope things go well for you in your adjustment back to this neighborhood." He paused for a moment. "You know we live not far upstream from the farm your *Dat* bought in Heidelberg Township, right near the Northkill Creek. Our church meets there on Sundays. You'd be welcome any time."

"Thanks for inviting me," Christian said, wishing he could mean it. After his experience at the Amish church fellowship a few weeks earlier, he had no interest in attending church again. But he warmed to this man, more than anyone since his arrival. Maybe this man could understand how important it was for him to look the part of an Indian, and to assure that farmwork didn't displace his love for hunting and fishing.

They talked for a few minutes, and then Christian started for home. *Dat* wasn't going to be happy that the hoe wasn't repaired. Not in the least. But he wasn't about to go back to the smithy's place again. Ever.

Christian walked slowly toward home. *How am I going to explain to Dat why this hoe is not welded?* He found his father cutting hay in the meadow.

"He couldn't weld it today," he said as he handed the hoe back to him.

Dat looked up, surprise evident on his face.

"He must have had a lot of people waiting for him."

"Yes, a few men were there. One had a broken shovel and another man came to shoe his horse."

Dat searched Christian's face. "Why didn't you leave it there? We could have gone back tomorrow to fetch it."

Christian looked down. "I don't think he wants to weld it."

Jacob paused and wiped his face with the kerchief that hung around his neck. "That's strange. Is that what he said?"

Christian held out the hoe to *Dat*. "I think you better take it to him."

"What difference would that make?"

Christian fished for words, but the stream of German words that had flowed so easily for him as a child had nearly run dry. How could he explain the pain he felt about the smithy's rejection?

"Did he tell you he won't do it for you?"

Christian nodded. "That man hates Indians."

Dat took off his hat and scratched the top of his head. "Didn't you tell him you were my son?"

Christian nodded. "Yes, but he doesn't like me dressing like an Indian."

Jacob nodded slowly as he looked at the ground. "The smithy lost a brother in an Indian raid."

"We lost *Mam* and Franey and Jakey. But now I see a different side of the Indians. Why can't I dress like them if I want to?"

The muscles on *Dat's* neck tightened. "Son, you'll have to decide whether you're going to be an Indian or a member of our family. You can't keep sitting on the fence." He put a hand on Christian's shoulder.

Christian winced and drew back. "I like being an Indian."

"My son," Jacob said, raising his voice, "you are my own flesh and blood. The Indians stole you from *Mam* and me. Can't you understand that?" Jacob's voice broke and tears sprang to his eyes. "If the Indians hadn't taken you from us, we could have taught you not to be so stubborn. The sooner you forget about the Indians, the better it will be for you. And for the whole neighborhood."

Christian drew back in surprise and panic. "I'm not going back to that shop," he said. He threw the hoe to the ground and turned his back on Jacob, almost running in his haste to get away from his father. *If* Dat *believes that people are supposed to love their enemies, then why did he mind me standing up for the Indians?*

He could feel his *Dat's* eyes on him as he reached the ash pile that marked the spot where his wigwam had been. If only others had lived among the Indians, like he and Joseph had, they could see for themselves how loving they were. And maybe—just maybe—they could see how wrongly they had treated the Indians.

If only the people at the Northkill could get to know his adoptive brother among the Shawnees, they might change their minds about the Indians. If they could sit in on their councils, and see how hard they tried to make peace with their enemies, they might think differently of them. Surely the smithy would act every bit as savagely as the Indians if he had been treated like them.

He looked over at *Dat*, who had returned to swinging his scythe through the stems of hay. It's true that *Dat* had gotten to know the Indians, but in a different way. He had lived among the Seneca for only eight months, too short a time to come to love them. He had never become part of an Indian family. That would be too hard a thing to tell *Dat*, especially now that Joseph was starting to fit back into life at home.

Why must *Dat* push him into a corner, rushing him to fit back into a way of life he had nearly forgotten? Christian saw with relief that *Dat* had moved to a different part of the meadow. Now he'd have a little more space to think—without his father's watchful gaze.

Not sure where to go, Christian walked, deep in thought, until he found himself at Anna's garden. It reminded him of the Shawnee gardens, except for the fence. The ground sloped gently from one end of the garden to the other, providing the drainage that kept water from standing in the paths. It was divided into four large squares—beds of soil raised a hand's width or more with a cross-shaped path running between them. Paths ran around the perimeter of the garden as well, with dozens of flowers, herbs, and woody perennials planted in the space between the path and the fence.

He picked a sprig of fresh peppermint. He bruised the leaves between his thumb and forefinger, savoring the minty fragrance. As he chewed a few leaves, he pondered his next move. He'd had enough of *Dat* begging him to work on the farm. It was time to get away. Joseph and he could go back to the Ohio Territory to stay with their Indian families, or at least visit for a while until he could figure out what to do.

He longed to see Morning Dew again. He might even decide to marry her. She'd cook the Indian food he loved. She would welcome the way he dressed and wore his hair. They would raise a family. An Indian family.

He'd hung around the Northkill long enough to find out that he didn't like it. Now was the time to leave.

If only Joseph would agree to go with him.

PART II

-8-

Christian spent a restless night rehearsing the painful events of the day at the smithy's shop. When he awoke, he decided to find Joseph and convince him to leave the Northkill with him.

Joseph was cutting hay. He put down his scythe as Christian approached. "I thought *Dat* asked you to work in the orchard today."

"He wanted me to, but I said no. I don't want him to tell me what to do." Christian was silent for a moment, then blurted, "I've got to get away from here."

Joseph looked at him thoughtfully. "What's the matter?"

"*Dat* yelled at me."

Joseph tilted his head. "*Dat* doesn't yell at people."

"He raised his voice, anyway. He was angry at me for respecting Indians. I have to get out of here! And I want you to go with me."

Joseph let out a low whistle. "We'd better think that over. Come, let's sit in the shade." Joseph moved toward a tree and sat down in the grass. Christian sat beside him.

Joseph took off his hat and wiped his brow. "Where do you want to go?"

"Back to the Indian villages. I'd like to visit my Shawnee family." He paused. "Don't you want to visit the Delaware?"

"It would be dangerous." Joseph's face took on a worried look.

"That's why we should go together."

"But what will *Dat* do without us at home?"

Christian sighed. "He managed for all the winters we were gone. Besides, the farmwork will soon be done for the season."

Joseph thought for a few moments. "I wouldn't mind seeing Summer Rain again."

Christian vaguely remembered Joseph mentioning that name. "Who's she?"

"A white captive who now lives near Fort Harris. I knew her at Custaloga's Town. When I left, I told her I would try and find her again."

"What will Sarah think about that?"

Joseph frowned. "There's no need to tell Sarah about it. Summer Rain is just a friend. I want to see if she made it back home, and how she's doing."

"Okay. When can we leave?" The words tumbled out of Christian's mouth.

"Not so fast. It will take a little time to make plans."

Christian scowled. "What's so hard about this? We'll go to Fort Harris first, and then we'll visit our villages. Maybe we'll stay only a few days at each one." It would be such a welcome thing to get away from the farm. Back in the village, he wouldn't have to think about going to the fields every day. And he wouldn't face the pressure of deciding whether he was Indian or white.

Joseph looked dubious. "It will take several weeks to get there."

"If it's only the two of us, we can travel quickly. We'll be back before the heavy snows."

Joseph got a faraway look in his eyes. "I'd love to see Touching Sky again. I haven't seen her since she came back to the Northkill with me. I told her I could build a wigwam here on the farm for her, but she wanted to go back to the village. I really miss her."

"Then what are we waiting for? Let's leave this afternoon."

Joseph stood up. "Let me think a little more about it."

Christian jumped up. "I'll ask Anna for some rations. She's been drying apple slices. And we could take a rifle for game."

"If she gives you food without asking lots of questions, I'll go," Joseph said. "But I can tell you, *Dat* won't be happy about it. Think of all the peaches and apples that need to be picked."

"There are plenty of other people who can help. I'll tell Anna we won't be gone long."

"Anna will tell *Dat*, and then there'll be trouble." Joseph picked up his scythe and moved back toward the tall grass.

Christian headed for the house to talk to Anna. *Dat* wouldn't need to know about it until they were gone. *I hope Joseph doesn't say anything to him.*

Already he could taste freedom! He would decide each morning whether to go fishing or hunting or spend time with his friends. He might even decide to stay with the Indians for good. Yes, there would be the hard times when the game was scarce, with hardly enough food to eat. But at least he would be back home with the familiar rhythms of the Indian village.

This has to work out. It just has to.

Anna saw the troubled look on Jacob's face when he came in for the noon meal. "I'm sorry your hoe isn't fixed yet," he said. "Can you do without it for another day or two?"

"Yes, I can manage. Was the smithy not able to fix it?"

"Christian ran into trouble with the smithy. He wouldn't fix it for him because he was dressed like an Indian."

Anna was shocked. "That's not fair! Let me take it over there myself."

"No, no." Jacob's voice was soothing. "I'll send Joseph tomorrow. He has more sense than Christian these days."

The edge in Jacob's voice told her that he had more to say about it, but he turned the conversation to talk about the work to be done in the orchard.

Later that day, Anna was pulling the honey from one of her bee skeps when Christian approached.

"I'm sorry I couldn't get your hoe welded," he said.

Anna looked serious. "Jacob told me you had some trouble with the smithy. He said he'll send Joseph tomorrow."

"It wasn't only the smithy that gave me trouble. A fellow called Silas was just as bad. They both said cruel things about Indians."

Anna's pulse quickened. "Silas?"

"That's what the smithy called him. He has a bent nose. I felt like bending it some more."

Anna quickly looked away, lest Christian notice the apprehension in her eyes. She quickly turned back to her bee skep. They were both silent for a few moments as she worked on the honey extraction.

"We didn't have bees when I was growing up," Christian said, "but we got honeycombs from a neighbor."

"My father taught me about bees," Anna said. "And I've always liked honey." She lifted the round rye-straw dome and overturned it to show Christian the crossed sticks where the bees hung their honeycombs. "Looks like there's lots of good honey here."

"Aren't you worried about getting stung?"

"I smoke out the bees, so it's not too bad. Besides, honey is too expensive to buy. I like it better than molasses."

"Me too," Christian said. "But how do you get the honey out of there?"

"I break the honeycomb into pieces. Then, I'll put it into a bag and hang it in the attic with a pot under it. The honey drips through the cloth and leaves the larva and egg cells inside."

"*Mam* used to do that too. We boys would sneak into the attic to get a lick from the pot. *Mam* didn't like it. She said if we kept snitching it, they're be none left for the rest of the family."

Anna laughed, grateful that Christian could admit to his mischief. "If you help me carry these honeycombs back to the house, you can have some honey now," she said. She handed him several honeycombs stacked in a pan.

"Okay," Christian agreed, his face breaking into a smile. They started walking toward the house.

"Joseph and I are planning to go on a short trip," he said.

Anna tensed as he spoke. "Where you going?" she asked.

"Joseph would like to visit a young woman who lives near Fort Harris. She was a captive in the Delaware village who was released at the same time he was."

"How long will you be gone?" Anna tried to hide the anxiety she felt.

"It's only a few days away."

Anna nodded. "Must you go? This is a very busy time of the year." *Doesn't he realize how much this will upset Jacob? What can I do to change his mind?*

Christian nodded. Wordless, Anna continued toward the house and opened the door.

"Just set that pan on the table and I'll squeeze a little honey out of it for you. And I have a piece of bread you can eat."

Christian wolfed down the treat. While he ate, Anna thought of the wampum bracelet that Jacob had gotten from Scar Face years before. Maybe if Christian heard Jacob tell that story, he'd have more respect for him.

"I have something to show you," Anna said, heading for the bedroom. She opened the wooden chest and found the little wampum belt. It had played a big part in her decision to marry Jacob.

"Have you heard about this wampum?" she asked. "*Dat* got it from an Indian at the treaty conference in Lancaster back in '62. He expected you and Joseph to be there. He was terribly disappointed, but he brought this wampum back."

Christian stuffed the last of the honeyed bread in his mouth.

Anna continued, "You should ask Jacob to tell you about it. It's quite the story."

Christian stood up, resolute. "Maybe when we get back."

Disappointed, Anna realized his mind was made up. "Can I send some dried food with you? Maybe some apples? A little corn or beef?"

Christian smiled. "I would really like that. And we might shoot a little game along the way."

Anna's mind raced. *They won't need to hunt on such a short trip.* "It's harvest time. Have you talked to *Dat* about this?"

Christian looked down. "Joseph said he'd talk to him this afternoon."

Anna paused. "Joseph has been spending time with Sarah Blank. I'm surprised that he wants to visit another girl."

"They have been friends for a long time."

Anna was silent, hoping her face reflected curiosity rather than the skepticism she felt. "So Joseph's the one who planned this visit? You don't have anyone to visit?" She found it hard to believe that Joseph was the instigator for the trip. He seemed much happier on the farm then Christian.

"Who knows?" Christian said. "We may be able to visit some of my friends as well."

Anna felt sick to her stomach. *Oh, the trouble this will cause.* "It will take me a little while to get things ready for you. I'll have to see what *Dat* says."

"Okay." Christian turned and walked away.

Anna sighed and wiped her hands on her apron. How could the boys expect to earn a place on the farm if they ran off during a time when Jacob needed them the most? Why couldn't they wait until winter, when the harvest was finished?

Intuition told her that the boys were looking for something that Jacob wasn't prepared to give them. Something beyond the farm or food on the table. The whole family carried a deep and festering wound from the days of the Indian attack. Perhaps if they talked about it together, they could find healing.

Jacob and his sons simply didn't talk to each other that way. At least she'd never heard them speak in such depth in her hearing. Perhaps they didn't know how to do it. Rather than talk about their pain, they acted it out in a multitude of ways. Why couldn't they admit their grief? Cry?

Anna gathered a few handfuls of dried peach slices and a few fresh pears. She added strips of dried beef left from last winter's butchering. There was still a little dried corn. If the boys would only wait for a couple more months, there'd be plenty of food for them to take! But then they might not want to face the vagaries of winter weather.

She put the provisions on the table and headed back to the garden. There weren't many weeds to pull, but she needed the solace that the garden always gave her. The earthy scent of the damp soil and the star-shaped flowers of the sedum cheered her soul.

The squeak of the garden gate caused her to turn around. There was Christian in full Indian regalia, from head to toe. He wore his medicine bundle around his neck and carried a large embroidered bag at his side. His hatchet and his knife were on the belt that held his breechcloth. On his legs were leather leggings to guard against thorns and rough branches.

She doubted that he was simply going on a short trip to visit Joseph's woman friend. What white woman would welcome someone with Christian's appearance? She held back the words she wanted to say.

"I have some food for you inside the house." She wiped her hands on her apron and moved toward the garden gate. "I wish I had more beef jerky, but we had very little left."

"I don't mind," Christian said. "I'm sure we'll find some food on the way."

They went into the house together, where Anna indicated the provisions she had for Joseph and Christian. She watched Christian stuff the food into his bag. "What did your *Dat* say when you asked him about the trip?"

"I didn't talk to him. Joseph is going to do that."

Anna waited a few moments. "When shall we expect you to be back?" She kept her voice casual. *I must not press too hard.* If the boys were like their father, they wouldn't welcome lots of questions once they had their mind made up to do something.

"I'm not sure. That depends on what Joseph wants to do." Christian avoided her eyes as he spoke. "Thank you for the food."

She longed to bid him stay, but an invisible hand stayed her lips. Instead, she said, "May God protect you. *Dat* and I will look forward to seeing you back home in a few days." She turned quickly to pull the worn twelve-patch coverlet from the back of the rocking chair. She held it out to Christian. "You might need this. It gets chilly at night."

Christian paused for a moment and then shook his head. "Thank you, but we'll do without."

Tears sprang to Anna's eyes as Christian walked out of the house. Did he really intend to return, or was this short trip a ruse to leave for good?

Perhaps Christian himself did not know. Only time would tell.

-9-

A flood of relief washed over Christian as he left the farm the next morning with Joseph at his side. Each wore a linen shirt and a deerskin breechcloth, with fringed leather leggings and moccasins. In addition, both wore their medicine bundles and an embroidered bag for supplies. Joseph wore his heavy bear-claw necklace. As for weapons, each carried a hunting knife and a tomahawk. Joseph carried his rifle with a supply of bullets and powder.

Christian's excitement rose as he relished his full Indian vesture. Now he was free from the backbreaking work of the fields—plowing and planting, harvesting and thrashing. Free to hunt and fish and hike as he liked. Why couldn't the white man learn from the Indians, who left the fieldwork to the women so the men could pursue the manly work of hunting?

"What do you think *Dat* will do when he finds out that we're gone?" Christian asked Joseph when they paused to get a drink at the creek.

"He's going to be upset. I'm sure of that."

"I hope he doesn't take it out on Anna for giving us food to eat on the way."

"Maybe she won't tell him she knew we were leaving," Joseph said.

Christian shook his head. "She's too honest for that. She lets *Dat* know what's on her mind in a way that *Mam* never did."

Joseph laughed. "Really? Maybe she's like the Delaware women. If one of them is unhappy with her husband, she puts his things outside the wigwam, and that's the end of it. He has to find another place to live."

113

"That is true among the Shawnees too. That's why the men try not to get their wives upset. If they get kicked out of the wigwam, they have to find another woman to live with."

Joseph grinned. "Can you see *Dat* being afraid of Anna putting him out of the house?"

Christian chuckled. "Of course not." He paused for a moment. "I wonder if she's happy being married to him."

"What difference does it make?" Joseph asked. "Once you're married in the Amish church, you have to stay together for the rest of your life, whether you're happy or not." He waved his hand forward and started back onto the path.

Christian followed close behind him, pondering Joseph's words. Were the Shawnees happier than the Amish? Anna seemed happy enough, although he sometimes saw tears in her eyes. She was sensitive. But that was true of the Shawnees as well; the women were more likely than men to cry. He couldn't remember seeing a Shawnee man cry. *Dat* didn't cry much either, when Christian arrived home or was about to leave. It wasn't a manly thing to do.

The two brothers walked until it was nearly dark before they stopped for the night. After they built a fire, they sat down to talk.

"We should make it to Fort Harris tomorrow," Joseph said. "I hope we're able to find Summer Rain."

"Why don't we wait to see her until we come back?" Christian asked.

"But we told Anna the reason we're leaving is to see Summer Rain," Joseph said. "Besides, I'm looking forward to it."

"Of course you want to see her. But if you wait, you can tell her about our visit to Custaloga's Town. I'm sure she'll be interested to know how her Indian family is doing. Who else but you could tell her?"

"That's true," Joseph said.

After further conversation, they decided to go to the Shawnee village first because Christian was so eager to see Morning Dew.

Christian and Joseph pressed westward for more than three weeks to get to the Tuscarawas Valley. They chose familiar paths, trodden by generations of Delawares and Shawnees, Senecas and Mohawks, Cuyugas and the Onandagos. They forded narrows and streams and rivers, stumbling over roots and logs and sloshing through ferns in marshes and bogs. They hiked up steep mountains through thick stands of spruce and fir, and down through narrow valleys lined with oak and hickory, marveling at the changing colors of red maples and yellow birch, of white ash and hemlock.

It was the time of the Full Hunter's Moon—which the whites called October—when the air was crisp and clear under an azure sky. The days were mostly cool and pleasant, with only an occasional rain that drove them to seek shelter. Flocks of geese flew south, heading for warmer climate. They were nearing the Shawnee village when a cloud of pigeons passed overhead.

"Must be passenger pigeons," Christian commented as the flock blocked out the sun. "I've never seen so many birds."

"I wish they'd land here," Joseph said. "I'm hungry for some meat."

Christian was hungry too, and tired of living off the forest. The food Anna had sent was long gone, except for the peach slices that he intended to give to Little Bear. He wasn't about to eat those. "It can't be too far," he told Joseph. "We might make it before nightfall."

It was nearly evening when several familiar landmarks came into view. Christian quickened his pace. "We're getting close," he said.

When they passed a large outcrop of rock, Christian thought about the time he'd been there with Morning Dew.

What an appropriate name. Her smile was like the morning sun that softened the hoarfrost clinging to blades of grass on cold mornings. He mused about the afternoon they'd spent together gathering fruit.

"I promised to pick some berries for my mother," Morning Dew had said as she walked past Christian's wigwam toward the edge of the woods.

"I'll help you. I'm good at picking berries," Christian replied.

She paused and then nodded. "I want to get back before Grandfather Sun lies down to rest."

"I know where there's a thicket of raspberries," Christian said. "Or were you looking for blackberries?"

"Either one is fine for me."

Christian led the way toward a patch of raspberries he'd seen several days earlier. "I hope the bears haven't gotten them. They were nearly ripe the other day."

"I'd like to fill this basket and give some to my neighbors," she said.

"I like your basket. Did you make it?"

She nodded, looking shy. "An aunt who lives with us taught me how to make baskets. Sometimes she makes them for the trader. She uses the money to buy jewelry and beads for us."

"Like the beads on your jacket? And your moccasins?"

She nodded again. "Yes, my mother taught me how to use beads for decoration."

"They look very nice. You are good with a needle."

"I am very lucky that my mother and my aunt are such creative people. The spirit of the Creator lives in them."

They picked berries for a while in silence. Christian stole looks at Morning Dew but felt at a loss to know what to say. Finally he asked, "How did they come to call you Morning Dew?"

"They gave me that name when I became a woman two winters ago. As a child, I was called Dark Waters. But now I love to wake up in the morning and walk through the dew on the grass. It brightens my day."

"You brighten my day," Christian said.

She blushed. There was an awkward pause. Then she said, "I think we've gotten the better part of these berries. Let's go to another spot."

The beams from the late-afternoon sun streamed through the openings in the trees, casting long shadows on the path as they walked through the forest. "Let's take this trail to the left," Christian said as they came to a fork. "I'm sure I saw some berries near here a few days ago when I came with Little Bear."

They headed off. Morning Dew easily kept pace with him.

Presently the path wove through a heavy thicket. "The berries are over there," Christian said, pointing to the spot. Morning Dew stepped back as he pulled out his tomahawk and hacked his way through the brambles that blocked their way to the berries.

"We are lucky," he said as he got to the thicket. "The berries are still here. They are ripe for picking."

Morning Dew's face lit up. "Oh, there are lots of them. There'll be enough for all of my neighbors." She set down the basket and started picking with both hands.

Christian picked too, occasionally popping one into his mouth. Soon his fingers were stained purple with raspberry juice. They picked until the basket was heaping full. There were still some raspberries hanging on the vines.

"I can put some berries in my bag," Christian said.

"No, let's leave them for our friends—the deer and bear. They deserve to eat as much as we do."

"Let me carry the basket," Christian said, taking it from her hand. The two of them made their way back through the thicket.

"Oh no," Morning Dew said. "My blanket got caught."

"Here, let me help you." As Christian turned to free her, a bramble snared the lip of the basket, dumping a third of its contents.

"I'm sorry." He set the basket on the ground in front of him and turned to free Morning Dew.

Once she got free, they gathered up most of the spilled raspberries and put them back into the basket.

"Let's leave the rest for the ants and insects," Morning Dew said. She laughed as she tossed a berry into the bushes. "That one's for our friend the blacksnake."

Christian could have walked on air. He'd never seen a more winsome smile. The trip to the village was much too short. As they entered the clearing where the village stood, Morning Dew stopped. "Here, you take some berries for yourself and I'll share the rest with my family and neighbors. I won't tell them you helped to pick them. If they find out, they might not let me go into the woods with you again."

Christian nodded and put a handful of the berries into his bag. "You go ahead. I'll wait to come into the village until you're in your wigwam." He reached out to touch her arm. "I enjoyed picking berries with you. I'm sorry I spilled some of them."

She laughed. "You picked a lot more than you spilled. Now I must be going."

As he remembered his time with the girl, Christian glanced sideways at Joseph. Now, as he neared the village, his pulse quickened. He must see Morning Dew. He loved everything about her. Not only her pleasant manner but her long silver earrings and the bright-yellow cloth tied into her jet-black hair. Would she want to spend time with him?

"Here we are," he told Joseph as they rounded a bend and the village was plainly in sight.

A dog barked. Children stopped playing and watched open-mouthed as the two brothers walked by. One ran ahead and into the wigwam where Christian had once lived.

There seemed to be little change in the village in the moons he'd been gone. A woman who sat by the fire nodded to him as he approached the wigwam in the middle of the village. Little Bear stepped out and grasped Christian's arm.

"My brother!" he said. "It has been too long."

"Little Bear," Christian replied as he pulled him into an embrace. His voice was husky with emotion. "This is my brother Swift Foot."

Little Bear nodded to Joseph.

Christian exulted in the presence and affection of Little Bear and others who came by. He reveled in the sight of their brown skin and deer hide, the bright calico garments and silver jewelry. The familiar scents of family and wigwam spoke of home.

After a meal, Little Bear asked Christian, "Have you kept the promise you made to me?"

"Yes," Christian replied. "Can't you see that I still have my scalp lock?" He glanced at Joseph, who looked curious. He didn't care to discuss the matter any further with Joseph present.

Christian rummaged around in his bag. "I picked some peaches in the orchard. Here, I brought a couple of dried slices for you to eat." He pulled out three wrinkled slices he'd saved for the occasion.

Little Bear put one in his mouth and chewed it. "Thank you. I like peaches."

"My father's trees are full of them."

"That's good."

That night, they sat around the fire talking until late. Christian went to bed in his old sleeping spot—the place where he'd last slept before returning to the Northkill. Joseph lay on the floor beside him.

Crickets chirped in the shadows. Christian smelled the familiar scent of the logs burning in the center of the wigwam. From time to time, the quiet snoring of Little Bear in the bed next to him interrupted the sound of the crickets. From time to time, he heard the howling of a wolf to the north. The moonlight shone dimly through the smoke hole at the top of the wigwam, and sent a thin stream of light past the flap in the doorway.

Perhaps he would stay. Joseph could go home by himself. Tomorrow he would go looking for Morning Dew.

The next day, friends came to share their happiness about Christian's return. The women served venison and hominy with bear oil and maple sugar for the guests. The Indians went from one house to the other, visiting, smoking, and sampling the food. Christian looked anxiously at every face. But he didn't see the person he most wanted to see. Christian began to worry. Where was Morning Dew?

That night, the men gathered around the campfire to tell stories and play dice. Christian felt again the contentment of his time spent with his Native American family. But still—no Morning Dew. Finally, he nerved himself to ask Little Bear, "Where is Morning Dew?"

Little Bear paused for a moment, as though to consider his answer. "I heard someone say she went to another village for a few days. I'm sorry that you won't get to see her."

Christian swallowed his disappointment. *I must persuade Joseph to stay until she returns,* he thought. *Or else set out to find her.*

Despite his disappointment, Christian was happy to be back in the village. The next morning, he ate mush with Little Bear, savoring each bite. He shared a little bit about *Dat* and Anna, and the reception the whites had given him on his return to Northkill. Little Bear listened, occasionally asking a question. He was especially interested in the orchard, and Christian spent almost an hour describing to him the various fruit trees and how they were cared for, with Joseph throwing in an occasional aside.

Morning Dew, however, remained on his mind. Casually, he broached the subject. "Where did you say that Morning Dew went? I may stay a few extra days until she returns."

Little Bear looked down at his mush. Joseph looked from Little Bear to Christian but said nothing.

Christian kept pressing. "Do you know when she'll be back?" He wasn't about to return to the Northkill without seeing her.

"I don't know where she is," Little Bear said, hesitantly.

"Come on, Little Bear. What do you mean—you don't know where she is?" Christian tried to be as nonchalant as possible, but his words had an edge. "Can't we ask her parents?"

"It would be best if I did that, rather than you."

"I understand." Of course Little Bear was right. For him to ask Morning Dew's parents about her whereabouts would alert them to keep a watch on him. It would be difficult to get her alone. He tried again. "Can you do that for me this morning?"

"I prefer to wait until evening. I was hoping that we could fish together this morning. Like we used to do."

"Yes, let's go fishing." Christian tried to hide his impatience. From long years of being with Little Bear, he knew that nothing he could do would make him quicken his pace or change his mind.

Joseph joined them as they made their way to the river, where they fished in a quiet eddy under a willow tree. On almost any other morning, Christian would have enjoyed their time together. The chilly morning had warmed up quite pleasantly. Small beams of light streamed through the branches of the willow. Everything was perfect except that Little Bear was hiding something. Surely he knew something about Morning Dew that he wasn't willing to say.

Which probably meant it was bad news. *Maybe she's ill.* The suspense took the joy out of fishing with his Indian brother.

In spite of his preoccupation, Christian caught three wall-eyes and a sunfish. He added them to his stringer. When he grew tired of using his pole, Christian and Little Bear waded into the water, suspended a seine between them, and soon had several more fish.

Grandfather Sun had climbed to the top of his arched dome when the three of them brought back their catch. Christian savored the aroma as they cooked them over the fire.

As they ate, he resisted the urge to mention Morning Dew's name again. To say anything to Little Bear would show a lack of trust, and might slow things down even more. He tried to enjoy the fish but his mind was wandering around the villages upriver, imagining where Morning Dew might be. Perhaps she'd gone to help a relative with a new baby or to take care of a sick friend. If it was either of those things, she might be gone for a while. But neither of those things made sense, as he thought about it. Her relatives and friends were here in the village.

Little Bear finished his meal and stood up. "I'll go talk to Morning Dew's mother now. Do you want to wait here until I return, or do you want to go fishing again?"

"I'll wait here," Christian said. Why wait any longer than necessary?

Christian and Joseph lay under the shadow of an oak tree and napped. He was deep into a dream when he realized someone was shaking him. "Wake up, Stargazer," he heard Little Bear say.

Christian sat upright with a start and looked around. No Morning Dew.

"What did you find out?"

Joseph, next to him, yawned and stretched. They both looked at Little Bear expectantly.

Little Bear played with the fringe on his leggings. "Morning Dew is not ready to receive your visit."

"Why not?"

Little Bear hesitated. "They say . . ." He stopped.

Christian looked at him, worried. "They say what?"

Little Bear bit his lip. "They say . . . she has found another man."

Christian groaned. He jumped to his feet and turned in circles. *No, it can't be true. It just can't.*

He had missed his opportunity. If only he'd promised her that he'd come back! Little Bear looked sympathetic. Christian covered his face with his hands. "She should have waited for me! It hasn't been that long since I left. Why couldn't she have waited?"

Joseph looked embarrassed by Christian's display of emotion. Little Bear waited a few moments, then slapped Christian on the back.

"Come on, Stargazer. There are plenty of other women in the world."

"Not like Morning Dew," Christian wanted to say, but he was silent. His hopes for a future among the Shawnees had vanished in an instant.

"Let's go for a hike in the woods," said Little Bear. "You'll feel better doing something."

Christian nodded. Walking would certainly be better than sitting around thinking of Morning Dew.

Joseph eyed them both. "I'm going to stay here," Joseph said. "The two of you can go by yourselves."

Christian looked at him and frowned. "Why don't you want to come with us?"

"The two of you need time together."

Christian shrugged and followed Little Bear. Together they headed into the woods.

The two of them walked the path for a time, with Little Bear in the lead. At any other time, Christian would have reveled in the sights and sounds of the woods. The maple leaves were turning from dark green to hues of yellow and red. The sumac was fiery red, and the oak leaves were turning brown. This time, what he noticed were the gusts of wind that stripped the leaves from the trees, leaving the branches as bare as his soul.

A buck peered at them from the undergrowth and then bounded away. Mating season had begun, and deer were moving freely in the woods.

"We could be hunting," Christian said. "Why didn't we bring a gun?"

"This is a day to enjoy the woods," Little Bear said, sitting down on a large log that had fallen across the path. "Perhaps we can hunt tomorrow."

Christian nodded and sat down beside him. Ever since they'd become brothers by mixing their blood in a loyalty oath, they'd gone hunting together. Little Bear was as close to him as Joseph. Sitting together in silence with this brother was as comfortable as talking.

The sound of a woodpecker hammering on a dead tree echoed through the woods. A flock of geese honked overhead on their way south. A long-legged spider crawled up the side of the log and across Christian's bare leg. He scooped it up in his hand and watched it scamper back and forth on his upheld palms. He held it out to Little Bear, who let it run down the side of his body all the way to the ground. Back in the Northkill, his family would have smashed the spider, but not here, in Indian country, where every living creature was respected.

Little Bear turned to him. "I'm sorry that Morning Dew was taken by someone else," he said. "I know you admire her."

Christian nodded. "She has such a pretty smile."

"Are there girls your age back at your other home?"

"A few. But their skin is pale and their noses are sharp. And the women do not wear beautiful jewelry like the ones here. No earrings, necklaces, or wristbands. They are very plain."

Little Bear looked puzzled. "No nose rings? Or bells on their ankles when they dance?"

"No, they don't wear any of those things. And they don't dance. At least not to the beat of the drums like the women do here."

"Who would want to marry someone like that?"

"Not me. That's why I was hoping to see Morning Dew."

"There are several other pretty girls in this village. And you can always look in other villages as well."

Christian sighed. "I never had my eye on anyone else."

Little Bear's face was sympathetic. "I can't blame you for being disappointed. She is a fine woman."

"It was the main reason I came back to the village."

Little Bear's eyes twinkled. "I thought you came to see me." He punched Christian's shoulder in a friendly way. "Come, let's head back home. Swift Foot will be waiting for us."

Christian nodded and followed. Now he needed to make a decision. With Morning Dew gone from the village, how much longer should he stay? Did he still want to stay?

It was late afternoon when they got back to the village. A friend of Little Bear walked up to them. "Come join us. We decided to have some running games while you're here. We hear that Swift Foot is a very fast runner and we'd like to give him a chance to prove himself."

Colorful leaves fell in the cool breeze as the village gathered for outdoor games. Joseph had told Christian that he'd often won races with other boys during his stay at Custaloga's Town, and he walked with a stride that showed his confidence.

The men ran races in several heats, starting with the youngest. Christian noticed that there were no white captives in the group. The British had forced them all—like him—to go home.

When it was the time for his age group to race, Christian reluctantly moved toward the starting line. He would compete against Little Bear, Joseph, and three others their age. He was not much of a runner, which would make Joseph look good.

As he crouched at the starting line, Christian glanced at the gathering crowd and was startled to see Morning Dew among the others. He gasped and looked down, and then stole another glance. She looked so beautiful, and she was looking his way. So her first look at him would be as he lagged behind in a race! Christian looked at his feet again. What did it matter? He'd already lost the chance to win her hand.

Someone shouted "Go" and they were off. Joseph was out front from the start, and he easily beat the rest to the finish line. Christian finished next to last and was relieved to drop out. He would leave the racing to Joseph. He watched with pride as Joseph won twice more.

The village moved from races to an archery contest, a sport in which Christian had more confidence. Little Bear lent Christian his bow and several arrows for the event. Three other men shot arrows before it was Christian's turn. Each one put their arrow within a finger's width of the center of the target.

Christian stepped to the line and nocked an arrow onto the bowstring. Had he lost his touch?

Zing! The arrow struck in the center of the target—inside the smaller circle made by the other arrows. Twice more he hit the very center. He breathed deeply of the autumn air. This was one of the reasons why he loved the Indian village. One could shoot arrows without worrying about working the fields. If only Joseph would cooperate, Christian could practice shooting arrows for a whole week. And fish. And sit with the men and talk. No more farming!

The rest of the evening went by quickly. Christian didn't have time to look for Morning Dew among the people, and he wasn't sure that he wanted to. Whenever he caught a glimpse of her face through the crowd, his chest tightened. He didn't do as well with the tomahawk- and knife-throwing contests, but he loved the sense of belonging he felt. Unless he thought about Morning Dew. Why had she disowned him? The longer he stayed in the village, the more he'd be reminded of her.

When Joseph suggested that they head for Custaloga's Town the next day, Christian was relieved, in a way. At least he didn't need to be reminded of Morning Dew. Losing her made the village feel less like home. As he settled down for his last night in the village, he tried to erase her face from his mind. After a few hours of restlessness, he fell into a dreamless sleep.

-10-

A nna headed for her kitchen garden with her repaired hoe and a basket in hand. *I must find a quiet place to pray,* she thought as she shooed away a chicken that pecked at the dirt in front of the garden gate. She walked slowly through the paths of her garden, pulling a stray weed here and there. After bending down to cut some sprigs of mint, Anna crushed a leaf between her fingers. The fragrance was a balm for the soul.

She continued weeding and putting a few herbs in her basket. The recent rain had encouraged the weeds, and she was determined to stay ahead of them.

Anna chased away a hog that rooted outside the garden fence. Perhaps Jacob should put their three hogs into the corral for the next few weeks, rather than letting them run loose in the woods. Their neighbor Adam might take vengeance against Christian by harming them. *Maybe he's the one who burned down the wigwam,* she mused.

Why did Christian insist on having a wigwam? Couldn't he see that building a wigwam and dressing like an Indian was causing lots of trouble? Several of the neighbors had lost loved ones or acquaintances to Indian raids during the war with the French. To them, the wigwam was a real threat.

And what about Jacob? He rarely spoke of his own captivity in the Indian village at Buckaloons, but she could sense his pain in the words he mumbled during his sleep, and the way he set his jaw when he looked at Christian's scalp lock. If only there were an ointment to apply to his hidden hurts, some balm for his soul.

Twice Jacob had mumbled something about the wigwam in his sleep. Something about Buckaloons. Did the wigwam remind him of something that had happened there? Couldn't Christian see the pain he was causing his father?

Anna hacked at the weeds with her hoe, wondering how they sprouted so quickly after the rain. A few days before, the garden had been free of weeds. The seeds must have been lying right below the surface, waiting for a little moisture to make them sprout.

In a way, they were like Christian's feelings, lying under the surface, hard to see or understand. Confused thoughts tumbled through her mind. How could he carry a tomahawk and a knife in his belt without thinking about the way the warriors had killed Jakey or Franey? Didn't his long hair and his wigwam remind him of the cruelty the Indians had shown to his mother? Why would he want anything to do with the Indians after what they'd done to his family? Surely he couldn't have forgotten those things. So how could he go back to the Shawnees after he'd had the chance to get away? Would he ever come back to the Northkill?

Anna wished she knew what Catharine would have to say about it. Maybe she'd have some wisdom to contribute, an insight that might help her understand Christian's frame of mind. But all this wouldn't matter if Christian didn't return at all. Already three weeks had passed since he and Joseph had left. If he did come back, it would take a long time to earn his trust.

Anna sighed. She thought of Jacob again. Even now, after several years of marriage, it was hard for her to read Jacob's mind. He guarded his feelings, so she had to guess what he was thinking.

I shouldn't be surprised, she thought to herself. That's the way it was with all the men she'd ever known. There was little she could do about it except pray for God's will to be done. But she wasn't satisfied that praying was enough. She must do something more.

It was a warm afternoon in early October. Anna dropped by to see Barbara, who was working in the garden. They exchanged a few pleasantries as Barbara pulled weeds.

"Where are the children?" Anna asked.

"Mother Stutzman is watching them," Barbara told her. Perhaps this was a good time to have a deeper conversation. Anna hesitated, and then ventured a few words to get to her point. "It seems like I don't get to see you very often," she said.

"I see you in church every other Sunday," Barbara said, refusing to meet her eyes.

"I mean in the times between the church services." Anna struggled on. "I know I'm just a stepmother, but I expected that I'd spend more time with you and the children."

Barbara continued pulling weeds with uncharacteristic vigor. At last she sighed and stood up. She brushed off her clothes and looked Anna in the eye.

"It seems as though you're trying to take the place of my mother," Barbara said. "And I really don't want that. I think that *Dat* is the one who needs you the most."

Anna flushed. "*Dat* says that your children need a grandmother. I can help with them."

"That's true. But they have Mother Stutzman, who's their *real* grandmother."

Anna flinched.

Barbara saw the expression on Anna's face and quickly added, "The most important thing you can do is to keep *Dat* happy. It's really good for him to have you."

Anna bent down to pull a weed poking out between two rows of lettuce. Barbara's words had hurt, and she didn't trust herself to say anything.

Barbara's face softened. "*Dat* would be so lonely without you. After he got back from the Indian village, he was not well. It was good to have him live with us until he was healthy enough to live by himself again. He missed *Mam* terribly. They had always worked together without any problems." Barbara paused. "One time he told me that he felt like only half a person when he was living by himself. He's not much of a cook so he didn't eat very well. He didn't have anyone to talk to." She smiled at Anna. "He seems much happier now."

"I'm glad to be married to him," Anna said, nodding. "After my husband, Ulrich, died, I lived alone for a few years. Your family helped me out from time to time, especially in the orchard."

"I remember *Mam* talking about that," Barbara said. "She felt sorry for you when you lost the baby, and then your husband not long after that."

A deep sadness gripped Anna as Barbara spoke. The years that had gone by since those deaths had hardly erased their sting. "A lot of church people helped me out during that time. I had hoped to remarry and have a child of my own." Her voice trembled. "That is, until Silas Burkholder started spreading lies about me. Then people pulled back and started treating me as though I had done something wrong."

Barbara's face changed as Anna spoke. "You can be glad that *Dat* believed you," she said. She raised her eyebrows and smirked. "He likes the way you rub his feet."

Anna smiled a bit. "I've given foot rubs to people since I was sixteen years old." Then she sobered. "I never had any trouble until Silas came to see me. He was looking for something more than a foot rub, and I wasn't about to give it to him." She spat out the words.

Barbara looked quizzical. "What did he do to you?"

Anna wondered how much to tell Barbara. It wasn't easy to talk about this. She finally spoke, a bit haltingly. "He grabbed me . . . and, well, he pressed himself against me." Anna paused, and her voice fell. "I was so afraid! Who knows what all he had in mind? I pushed him away and ran out of the house. I explained to the deacon what happened, but he thought I must have done something to provoke him. I did no such thing." She was silent for a few moments. "Why can't people believe me?"

"*Dat* believes you. He wouldn't have married you if he didn't."

Anna took courage and asked the question she'd been pondering for a long time. "How about your mother? She wasn't as friendly to me after Silas started spreading rumors."

Barbara paused, as though pondering her response. "Do you really want to know?"

Anna swallowed. "Yes, I want people to tell me the truth. At least I think I do."

"*Mam* pulled back from you after that time you came to their house with the peach pie. She didn't like the way that you rubbed *Dat*'s feet."

Anna's mind flew back to the incident. It seemed so long ago. She had visited Jacob and Lizzie one evening after they had helped her clean up after a storm. Foot massages were a common healing practice in their church, as were herbal remedies. "I don't think I did anything unusual when I rubbed his feet," Anna said. "He seemed to appreciate it."

"*Mam* said that you massaged *Dat*'s back and shoulders too. She thought you were a little too free with your hands, and that *Dat* enjoyed it a little too much."

The knot in Anna's stomach tightened again. "Your mother was standing right there. I certainly didn't mean to do anything wrong. I even offered to rub her feet."

Barbara nodded. "She liked having her feet rubbed, but she was upset at both you and *Dat*."

Anna paused. "Is that why you weren't happy when your *Dat* wanted to marry me?"

Barbara nodded again. "That's why I needed to ask your forgiveness, especially after you were so kind and helped us with my baby when he had an earache."

"That made such a difference to me. I wouldn't have married *Dat* otherwise," said Anna.

Barbara's face softened. "I'm glad for all you're doing for *Dat*. But I still miss *Mam* very much. I don't want anyone else to try to take her place."

Anna nodded. "I can understand that. No one could ever take the place of my mother in my heart, even if she tried."

"I still can't understand why God let her get killed by the Indians," Barbara said, her voice wavering. "And it doesn't make sense that Joseph and Christian still want to be Indians after those warriors killed *Mam.* Sometimes I can hardly stand it. It's hard on *Dat* too."

Anna pondered what she might say. She wanted to sympathize with Barbara. "Catharine helped me to see the whole thing in a different way," she began. "Because of her advice, I tried hard to listen to Christian, to try to understand what was going on in his mind. Now he's gone. I wonder if he's coming back."

Barbara frowned. "I wonder too. Sometimes I think he should stay with the Indians if he loves them so much, and not bother us with his tomahawk, his crazy hair, and all the rest. But then I feel guilty for feeling that way. After all, he is my brother, and he couldn't help what the Indians did to *Mam.*"

Anna thought for a moment. "Because of what Silas did to me, I know what it's like to be misunderstood and spoken against. It makes me feel more sympathetic to Christian. He doesn't deserve everything that is said about him."

Barbara nodded. "I've had a bad attitude toward both of you. I'll try to do better."

Anna felt lighter. "Thank you. And I'll try to understand the way you feel about your mother, and not try to impose myself. I don't mean to interfere where I'm not needed. I'll help where I can."

"That's good," Barbara replied in a gentle voice. "I know you love my children too, so I'll try to let you take care of them more often. You are a part of our family, and I want to act that way."

Anna went home, thinking about the next conversation she'd have with Barbara. Perhaps she could speak about her longing to have a child of her own. Might it help her step-daughter to understand the emptiness in her heart, and her longing to fill it with the love of Jacob's grandchildren, even if she never bore another child of her own?

Anna felt comforted that Barbara was a loving daughter, despite her sharp tongue. And she was willing to change her attitude. What more could she ask for?

-11-

Christian followed Joseph as he quickened his pace; Custaloga's Town was now within sight. He was glad to be farther from his Shawnee village, farther from the memories of Morning Dew and the dreams he had held onto about their future. The grief of losing her to another man loosened just a bit with each step between the village and Custaloga's Town. Christian straightened his shoulders and once again erased her face from his mind.

As they rounded a bend in the path by the river and saw smoke rising not far ahead, Christian recalled a few stories that Joseph had told about Touching Sky, Joseph's adoptive mother. It would be exciting to meet her in person. Would she be short or tall? Stout or slim? Would she be smiling and beautiful like Morning Dew? Or ill natured, like the Shawnee woman who had put her husband out of the wigwam and forced him to sleep in the snow? How would Joseph be received in the village—with coolness as a deserter who had left, or with warmth like a son returning home?

Joseph picked up his pace as they neared the village, and Christian lengthened his strides to keep up with him. "I built this wigwam," Joseph said with pride as they walked up to one of the first houses at the edge of the village.

"It's bigger than most of the others," Christian said with surprise as he looked over the structure. "How come?" The wigwam was a rectangle with walls on four sides and a ridge pole on top; not round with a domed top like the one Christian had built back in the Northkill.

"I wanted to have plenty of room," Joseph said.

"Ho!" Joseph called as they approached the house. A woman appeared at the doorway. "Touching Sky," Joseph said with affection.

Touching Sky stepped through the door flap and threw her arms around Joseph in a warm embrace. "Swift Foot! I am so glad you have come back to see us." She looked at Christian and stepped back. "Who is the young man that you brought with you?"

"This is my brother, Stargazer," Joseph said as Christian offered his hand to Touching Sky. "He was with the Shawnees for many years, and was made to return to our family at the Northkill not long after me."

"You are welcome here," Touching Sky said warmly, folding his hand in hers. "Your face tells me that you are a brother to Swift Foot. Your nose is shaped like his, and you have the same thin lips."

Christian listened carefully, hoping he was understanding her Delaware words. Her black hair framed her smiling face and was tied back with a bright-red ribbon. *She looks too young to be Swift Foot's adoptive mother,* he thought.

"Silver Sage will be very happy to see you," Touching Sky said to Joseph. "Let me fetch her." She turned and stepped back into the wigwam, emerging a few moments later with a woman at her side. "Look who came to visit us," she said to the silver-haired woman who looked old enough to be her mother.

Silver Sage stepped forward and greeted Joseph warmly. "We have missed you," she said. "Is your family well back home?"

"Yes, I have several new nieces and nephews. And my father has married a woman to take the place of the one he lost."

Her eyes twinkled. "That is good to hear. Touching Sky has found another man to care for her since you left. He has gone hunting, but he should be back home soon."

"Ah, my mother! I am eager to meet your new companion," Joseph said. "Is he someone I know?"

Touching Sky had a mischievous glint in her eyes. "Yes, you met him more than once, but you must wait to find out who he is until he returns. He said he'd be back home before dark."

"Perhaps we can visit Miquon and Tamaqua," Joseph suggested. "Then we can return here to eat."

"Please invite them to join us for food tonight," Touching Sky said. "They can help to celebrate your visit."

"Tamaqua is Touching Sky's brother, and Miquon is his son, who's my age," Joseph explained to Christian as they set out. "Tamaqua was like a father to me; he showed me how to hunt and find my way in the woods."

They had not gone far from Touching Sky's home when two young children came running to Joseph. "Swift Foot!" they shouted. "Give us a ride on your shoulders!"

Joseph grinned at Christian. "Let's do it," he said.

Christian smiled in return. Each of the brothers knelt down and let one of the children climb onto his shoulders, and then they both pranced like horses as they made their way through the village. The excited shouts of the children soon drew more children and their parents to join the two brothers on a march through the village.

Christian helped Joseph give rides to the children, large and small, until everyone had at least one turn. *These people love Joseph as much as I love the people from my village,* Christian thought.

Joseph learned that Miquon was fishing. They bade goodbye to the children and walked beside the riverbank until they found him.

"Swift Foot!" Miquon shouted when he saw him. "You've come back home!" Joyfully, he embraced Joseph. "I hope you can stay with us for a while."

"I've brought my brother Stargazer with me," Joseph said. "He lived with the Shawnees when I was with you."

"Come with me to my house," Miquon said, "and I will show you the most precious thing in the world."

What could that be? Christian trailed Joseph to Miquon's wigwam. Miquon disappeared inside and reappeared a moment later with his wife, Autumn Leaves, who was carrying a baby in her arms.

"A . . . a baby?" Joseph asked with excitement in his voice.

Christian stepped up beside Joseph to look into the child's face.

"Does he—she—have a name?" Christian asked in Shawnee, hoping Miquon would understand.

Miquon knit his eyebrows. "Not yet. She was born only two moons ago."

I shouldn't have asked such a question, Christian thought to himself. *Being back at the Northkill is making me forget how Indians do things.* He listened as Joseph and Miquon spoke of old times and then met Tamaqua and his wife as well.

Not long before supper, an Indian strolled up to the door. "That man looks familiar," Joseph said, "but I can't remember his name."

At that moment, Touching Sky stepped out of the wigwam and said, "I want you to meet my husband, Black Elk. He is the healer from the Shawnee village whom you fetched for Runs Free and later for Nunschetto."

Christian looked at the man in surprise. "I know you! We lived in the same Shawnee village."

Black Elk reached out to grasp his hand. "Yes," he said, "I remember you, Stargazer, but I didn't know that you were Swift Foot's brother."

Christian looked down at the ground. "I didn't tell you because I was afraid the chief might try to keep us apart. That was many moons ago, when I first lived in the village."

"I understand," Black Elk said. "I liked the way that Swift Foot helped Touching Sky. Had Swift Foot not come to my village, I would never have met her." He smiled. "And now she is my companion." Black Elk gazed at Touching Sky with endearment.

Blushing, she stared at the ground.

The group sat in a circle around the fire while Touching Sky and Silver Sage made the meal. Christian ate with gusto when offered Joseph's favorite food—venison seasoned with savory spices ground from the dried herbs that hung in clusters in Touching Sky's wigwam.

Through that pleasant evening, Christian looked around the circle of his brother's adoptive family. As their faces glowed in the firelight, a feeling of peace settled on Christian's shoulders.

Several days passed, and Christian and Joseph lingered in the village with Touching Sky and Black Elk. They had many conversations that filled in missing information for Joseph and Christian.

One night over dinner, Joseph talked with Black Elk about his futile attempt to heal Joseph's little sister, Runs Free, of the spotting disease—the affliction the white man called smallpox.

"The spirits of the white man's disease were too strong," Black Elk commented. "They were evil beyond our powers to heal."

"The spotting disease is a terrible thing," Joseph said. He chewed his lip as he paused and looked down. "I understand it is gone from the village now. I hope it never comes back."

"We must not anger the Great Spirit again," Black Elk said sadly.

"More food?" Touching Sky asked, looking around the circle.

Christian handed her his wooden plate. He studied the woman who was Joseph's adoptive mother. Her long black hair was gathered in a knot on top of her head, and a pair of silver earrings dangled from her ears.

Touching Sky filled the plate, and he dug in eagerly. How good it was to eat Indian-cooked food again, a corn stew with a pumpkin dish seasoned with Touching Sky's favorite blend of herbs. The settlers couldn't match it.

When the three men were finished eating, Silver Sage and Touching Sky joined the little circle. Silver strands accented Silver Sage's dark hair, pulled together by a piece of red fabric and hanging down her back. She moved with the easy grace and confidence of a woman who knew herself and her place in life.

"We have missed you, Swift Foot," Silver Sage said, her eyes shining in the firelight. "How has it been for you to live among the white man again?"

Christian turned to hear Joseph's response. "I had forgotten how many differences there are between the white man and the Indian," he said.

Touching Sky joined the conversation. Christian leaned in to make sure he caught every sentence. He'd learned many words from a Delaware friend who'd lived in the Shawnee village, but they didn't sound the same when Touching Sky spoke them.

"When Tamaqua and I accompanied Joseph to his home," she said, "I learned a lot about the ways of the white man for myself. Joseph's father invited me to stay, but that would have been too hard."

Christian looked at Joseph. Why had Joseph never told him? It would be a relief to have Touching Sky live in the wigwam close to *Dat* and Anna's cabin. Maybe Joseph or he could get married to an Indian woman and bring her back to the Northkill. If *Dat* was willing to have Touching Sky live on the farm, he should be willing to let him live there with an Indian wife.

"The white man has strange ways," Touching Sky continued. "I could not stand to live among them, cooped up in cabins and sleeping in their straw beds with large pillows. I could not live with the way the men treat their wives like servants. The worst is that they lay claim to property that belongs to the Creator alone, and they build fences and walls to keep God's creatures in or out. They are tied down by crops and animals, and are not free to roam as the Delawares do."

"All of these things are true," Christian murmured under his breath, wondering if she had said those things to *Dat*. He would not be happy to hear Touching Sky or anyone else speak this way.

"From what I have seen of the white man," Silver Sage said softly, "he treats the earth as though it belongs to him rather than the Great Spirit who created it. He cannot even see the spirits that live everywhere around us. He treats the plants and animals as though they were an inferior race to be subjected and tamed, and he slaughters us Indians as though we were less than human."

Christian swallowed hard and looked at Joseph, who was fingering the medicine bundle that hung around his neck. What was he going to say?

"As I said before," Joseph began, "there are many differences between the white man and the Indian. During my years in Touching Sky's home, I learned much about the Delaware ways that I shall never forget." His face was pensive.

"Has the white man accepted your Delaware ways?" Silver Sage asked.

Christian wanted to shout out his own answer, to say "No!" with all the strength in his body. He wanted to tell them of his frustration with the smithy, who would not even fix his hoe because he wore a scalp lock. He wanted to tell them about *Dat*'s wishes that he fit back into the world of the white people by shedding all the vestiges of his Indian appearances. He longed to blurt out his hatred for farmwork, with so little time for hunting and fishing.

But Silver Sage had addressed the question to Joseph, and he must be the one to respond. Joseph looked at Touching Sky and then shifted his eyes toward Silver Sage. "Do you remember the time when I first learned to speak the Delaware language?"

"Of course I remember," Silver Sage commented. "Touching Sky's little daughter helped you learn new Delaware words. And you tried to teach her some of your German words."

Joseph nodded. "Living back home in the Northkill is like learning a new language, except that the people around you think you already know the words."

Christian took in a sharp breath as his brother spoke. Yes, that's how it was for him too.

"They think they know who I am because they knew me as a child," Joseph continued. "They treat me as though I have only grown older, not realizing that I have become a different person." He sighed and looked down into the fire.

Tears welled in Christian's eyes as Joseph spoke. Silver Sage had drawn Joseph to say something he'd never heard him say before, full of honesty and candor.

The night had come to drape the village in darkness, and the wind that stirred in the trees drove the chill through Christian's clothing. He pulled a blanket over his shoulders and leaned closer to the fire.

"Is it not true," Silver Sage continued, "that you are living with two different voices inside you—the voice of the white man and the voice of the red man? Both are trying to tell you how you should live. They do not follow the Delaware custom of waiting on each other when they wish to speak. Instead, they rush in with words that vie for your heart, interrupting each other and filling your mind with confusion."

Silver Sage paused, and the silence felt deep and full around them. "Your body is like a wigwam, which only has room for one of these men to live," she said. "He will be like the chief of the tribe. The other must be content to trail behind."

Christian took a deep breath. Even now, the two "men" pushed and shoved each other inside the wigwam of his heart, vying for the place of honor. He had so hoped that these men could live in peace with each other, but instead they argued with each other in his mind and tugged at his soul. Here in the Delaware village, the red man stood ready to win the contest. But when he was in the Northkill, the advantage shifted to the white man. The folks there didn't even want the red man in the neighborhood.

He should have known it would be this way. Over the past decade, the white man had driven the Delaware people before them from the Atlantic Ocean to the forks of the Muskingum, and the Shawnee people from the Carolinas to the Ohio Territory. Why would they want the red men to have any room in his heart?

"Ever since the white chief brought his army to the forks of the Muskingum," Silver Sage said, "the army sends spies to walk among us, looking for British subjects who are hiding among us because they did not wish to return home."

Black Elk nodded. "The same is true among the Shawnees. They have taken away our dearest captives, who truly love our way of life. They bound one white woman hand and foot as they took her away from her husband, a man who loved her as much as her own family ever did. Had they not bound her, she would have fled back to our village."

Christian sat silently, despair growing inside. Was Silver Sage implying that he would not be able to stay among the Indians, even if he declared himself to have a red heart and pledged his loyalty? His hope to stay in a Native village was slowly being crushed under the weight of Silver Sage's words. His plan to live like an Indian among the white man was fading like a nighttime dream at dawn.

Am I a white man or an Indian? Christian thought. *How can I know for sure? Dat* claimed him as his own flesh and blood, believing that his Indian identity was only a passing whim. How could he help *Dat* understand that his long hair was but the outward sign of his inner being? *I am a Shawnee and they're trying to make me into something else, something I don't want to be.*

Maybe it was impossible to live like an Indian among the settlers in the Northkill as he had hoped. He wondered how Joseph would take Silver Sage's advice.

When he was alone with Joseph, he'd find out.

-12-

Anna studied the calendar before scooping a second help-ing of thick breakfast porridge onto Jacob's plate. Joseph and Christian had now been gone for five weeks.

"I thought the boys would have been back by now," she said to Jacob. He picked up his mug of apple cider and drained it, then wiped his mouth.

"Give them a couple more weeks," he replied. "It takes a long time to get to the Ohio Territory and back."

"I thought they were going to Fort Harris. That's only a few days' walk from here."

Jacob shook his head. "They might have said that, but I know better. They wanted to see their Indian friends again."

Anna paused. "Christian didn't feel at home here. He wants to live like the Indians do. He doesn't even want to live in our house." She wrung her hands on her apron. "I must be doing something wrong."

Jacob made a shushing sound. "Don't talk that way. You're not doing anything wrong. Give him some time to get used to being Amish again."

Anna began clearing the dishes, talking as she worked. "Maybe I should try cooking Indian food."

Jacob snorted. "I don't want to eat Indian food. I had enough Indian food for a lifetime when I was at Buckaloons."

"I'm talking about what Christian likes," Anna said, glanc-ing at her husband out of the corner of her eye.

Jacob looked stubborn. "You don't have to cook special food for him. Joseph got used to our food soon enough."

Anna thought about this. "I think Christian is different than Joseph. We shouldn't treat them both the same way."

"Why not? It wouldn't be fair otherwise."

Anna thought about this. How could she convey her concern that Jacob didn't understand Christian's needs? The two boys were not the same. How could she help Jacob see this? She sighed.

"Do you want more cider?"

"No." He spoke sharply.

She poured another cup for herself and took a deep breath. "Have you ever asked the boys to tell you about their time in the Indian village?"

"No, I figure they can tell me when they have something to say about it. I don't want to go digging for it."

Anna waited a few moments, then said, "What if they are waiting to be asked?"

"I know that when I came back from Buckaloons, I got tired of answering people's questions. I knew they wouldn't understand it anyway."

"Maybe it's different for them. Maybe they want to know that you're interested in their experience," she said.

"If they want to talk about it, I'm ready to listen." His lips were in a firm line.

"Maybe they don't talk about their experience because they're not sure what you want for them. What is your wish for the boys?" she asked.

Jacob folded his arms and frowned. "I want them to join the church and become good farmers. I want them to marry good wives and have godly children so they can earn a good inheritance. I want them to be prosperous and faithful to God. I pray for them every day."

Anna nodded. "I want all those things for them too."

His voice rose. "I'm working as hard as I can to help them get those things. That's why I bought the farm in North Heidelberg Township—to make sure they each have enough land."

Anna sat down across from him and sipped her cider. To say more would only make him more defensive. It was obvious that he wanted the very best for his boys. Who was she to tell him that he was going about it the wrong way?

"Well?" Jacob asked after a moment. "Is there something else you think I should do?"

Anna thought for a moment. Did he really want to hear what was on her heart? She might as well try. She plunged in.

"If Christian were my son, I'd quit trying to change him."

Jacob raised his eyebrows. "Women are different than men. Lizzie often reminded me of that."

"What do you think Lizzie would say if she were here now?" Anna hadn't known Lizzie well, but she was confident that she had spoken to the boys differently than Jacob.

"Lizzie's not here now, so it won't do much good to act as though she was."

"I always thought that Lizzie was good with the boys. I'm sure they miss her very much. I wish I could be more like her, for their sake."

Jacob got up from the table. It was obvious he had done all the listening he would do for now. "I have work to do. I'll be back in at noon."

Anna nodded, disappointed. There was so much they needed to talk about. She cleared the mugs from the table and sat down to weave a strip of linen tape to replace the torn string that secured the large cloth pocket in place under her skirt.

Anna counted off eleven flax threads and tied them onto the doorknob to the bedroom. Then she passed the other end of the threads through a set of slots and eyelets in a heddle, a wide, thin board she held between her knees as she sat on a chair. She tied the ends of the threads into a knot and began to weave a piece of tape about a half-inch wide. She used her legs to raise and lower the warp threads with the heddle, passing a small shuttle from one side to the other with a woolen thread to serve as weft. When she finished weaving the tape, she sewed it onto the pocket and headed for her garden. A little time with her beloved plants would clear her mind and soothe her soul.

She cut some kale and bundled it into a basket. It was one of the plants that yielded a harvest all winter long if she kept a little straw around it. Then she looked up into the trees, which would soon be at the height of their color. Nothing inspired her in the fall of the year more than the changing colors of the leaves. Winter was on the way, and it would make travel more difficult for the boys.

What if an early snow blocked the paths that led toward home? What if they could not find sufficient food—a fate that Jacob escaped only by the providence of God and the goodness of a British soldier? What if the boys came back even more reluctant to settle into the Amish way of life? Her questions went on and on. *What if? What if?*

If the boys ever came back, she'd ask them what they really liked to eat. Maybe she'd need to cook different meals for Christian than for Jacob. But if it helped him get adjusted, it would be worth it. She hoped to find some bear grease for him. Perhaps someone in the neighborhood could shoot a bear, although there hadn't been many sightings of late.

And if only Christian could find a young woman he liked, that would make a difference. At least it had for Joseph. His affection for Sarah Blank seemed to help him adjust more quickly. It gave her hope. Unless, of course, Joseph had gone to the Indian village to see a girl . . .

A gust of wind carried a bevy of leaves into her garden. The falling leaves marked a change of season, a time of rest when the garden was nearly dormant. Maybe Christian was in a new season too, a time of adjustment back to the life he'd left as a child. Perhaps she shouldn't expect him to do it quickly, any more than she should expect the arrival of spring before the worst of the winter had come and gone.

Anna sighed. It might be easier to be a stepmother if God gave her the pleasure of bearing her own child again. It's not that they hadn't tried. Jacob was older, true, but still capable.

Even bountiful servings of parsnips, claimed by herbalist Christopher Sauer to increase the chances of pregnancy, had not helped her to conceive.

Even if I never have a child, I'm going to do the best I can with my stepchildren, Anna resolved. *If Christian returns, I'm going to do some things to make him feel special. Perhaps we can get him a woolen blanket to keep him warm. And a pair of winter moccasins.*

She turned and left the garden, latching the gate behind her. Anna was satisfied that she had done all she could for now. If in God's providence Christian and Joseph returned, she was ready to do much more to make them want to stay.

-13-

Christian and Joseph had been in Custaloga's Town for four days when Joseph insisted that they go back to the Northkill. "I want to leave—soon," he said.

Christian looked at him with surprise. "Why? We've only been here for a short time."

"Why should we stay here any longer?" Joseph asked.

Christian thought. What was he to say? He had hoped to stay at least until another moon went by. "What's your hurry? I'd like to do some hunting and fishing before we go."

"We have to get back before winter. Anna will worry herself sick if we aren't back by then."

"She has *Dat* to take care of her." Christian's voice rose. "We might never come back here again, so we should make the best of it while we can."

"Silver Sage already told us that we shouldn't stay here long. We might as well go now."

"You must have Sarah on your mind," Christian taunted. "Why else would you be so eager to go back?"

Joseph gave Christian a friendly punch on the shoulder. "If you had a girl back in the Northkill, you'd be the one begging to go back. Come on, admit it!"

"Let's stay here until we get a deer or two for the village," said Christian, trying a different tack.

Joseph stood firm. "I'm leaving the day after tomorrow, whether you come with me or not."

Christian sighed. Why was he in such a hurry? Had he forgotten what it meant to live on "Indian time," where the most important thing was to enjoy the company of friends? Already Joseph seemed to be on white man's time, where you were always looking ahead to the next thing to be done.

Christian shrugged. What was he to say to his older brother, who had suddenly gotten bossy? Joseph wasn't likely to back down. He had Sarah on his mind, and nothing was going to change it.

Two days later, upon Joseph's insistence, they set out for the Northkill. Christian acted as though he was upset, but part of him was beginning to realize that he'd never be able to live in the Indian village as he had before. It seemed as though Joseph knew it too. It was one thing to visit, but it would be quite another to live there. Sadness gripped him as he realized that even in Little Bear's home, he had been more a guest than a brother.

They hadn't gone far when Joseph turned to Christian and asked, "What promise was Little Bear talking to you about?"

Christian looked down. "Something between the two of us."

"Can't you tell me about it?"

Christian paused, considering whether Joseph would understand. "When I became a blood brother to Little Bear, I made a pact with him that I would never go back to the white man's ways. As I was leaving the Shawnees this summer, he reminded me of my vow, and I promised I would always keep it."

"What does that mean?"

"It means I'm not going to live like the whites. I won't dress like them or take up a religion that makes people whack down trees and plow fields that were taken from the Indians by deceit."

Joseph whistled. "Good luck keeping that promise. There's not much land in these parts that wasn't taken from the Natives by force or fraud. Why did you promise all that?"

"When Little Bear asked me, it seemed like the right thing to do. I wanted to make him feel good."

"He'll never know if you keep that promise or not," Joseph said. "I wouldn't tell *Dat* about that if I were you."

Christian was troubled by Joseph's answer. How could he go back on his word? He wished Joseph hadn't heard Little Bear ask him about it.

"Do you still want to try to find Summer Rain?" Christian asked. "Or are you in such a big hurry to see Sarah that you don't want to take the time to look for her?"

"Of course I want to see her," Joseph said. "It won't be far out of the way when we head home."

After several weeks of steady walking, the brothers neared Fort Harris. "Summer Rain's folks lived south of Fort Harris by Penn's Creek," Joseph said. "Let's hike down there a little ways and then ask somebody if they know her."

"But you said her parents were killed. Why would she come back here?" Christian asked.

"She probably lives with some white relatives here." Joseph paused. "Unless . . . Maybe they have moved away."

Just ahead, an older white man came toward them. He looked at them fearfully and fingered his gun. Christian tried to look as friendly as possible.

"Hello. We're looking for a German woman named Elizabeth," Joseph said. "She recently returned from a Delaware village at the forks of the Muskingum. Do you have any idea where she lives?"

The man looked suspicious. "What is your business with her?"

"I was a captive with her in the same village. We left about the same time."

The man looked at them more closely. "Ah, you're white. Couldn't tell with all that Indian garb on you." He thought for a moment. "I believe a young woman was brought back here from Fort Pitt a few months ago. She lives near Penn's Creek. But be careful. Folks are on the lookout for Indians here, and might shoot at you before you have a chance to explain who you are."

Christian looked at Joseph. "Are you sure you want to go?" Joseph nodded.

The two boys walked rapidly until they came to a creek with a cabin nearby. At the edge of the creek, a woman was washing clothes. Joseph squinted for a moment, then he broke into a run. "Summer Rain!" Joseph shouted out in Delaware.

The girl turned. She saw Joseph and smiled. "Swift Foot! Can it really be you?"

Joseph picked her up and twirled her around. They were both laughing and talking at the same time.

Christian listened as Joseph and Summer Rain conversed excitedly for a few minutes. They seemed oblivious to Christian. He felt a surge of jealousy. If only Morning Dew hadn't been snatched away from him.

They were interrupted by a man who stepped out of the cabin and glared at Christian. "Hey! What are you doing here?" he asked in German.

Summer Rain turned. "Uncle John, this is my friend Swift Foot, who was a captive with me in the Delaware Village. He has come to visit me with his brother."

"Indians aren't welcome here," the man said gruffly.

Summer Rain's face fell. "But, Uncle, he's my friend."

"Then why does he dress like an Indian?" He looked squarely at Joseph. "Where are you from?"

"The Northkill, a few days walk from here. My brother and I were born there, on a farm. We're part of the Hochstetler family in the Amish community."

"You don't look Amish to me," the man said suspiciously. "Looks like the two of you haven't settled down to farming or any other kind of honest living. Why are you still dressed like Indians?"

Christian stood beside Joseph and Summer Rain, not sure what to say.

"Summer Rain's father wouldn't have wanted an Indian hanging around with his daughter, and I won't allow it either," the man growled.

Christian swallowed hard. Did whites everywhere hate Indians?

Summer Rain looked into Joseph's eyes and spoke a few words in the Delaware tongue.

Joseph grimaced. The man scowled and made a shooing motion with his hands.

"I'm so glad I got to see you," Joseph said to Summer Rain. She nodded sadly. Joseph and Christian turned to leave.

As they were heading back to the path, the man shouted at Summer Rain: "I don't want you hanging around with those men, do you hear? If they ever come around again, there'll be trouble."

Christian waited until they came to a bend in the road and then commented to Joseph, "I can see why you wanted to visit her. She's a beautiful woman."

Joseph kept walking, deep in thought. Finally he said, "I needed to see her this once, to make sure she's not the one for me. And now I'm sure."

"What makes you so sure?"

"Even though our time together was brief, I realized she was only a friend. I love Sarah. My feelings for her are different than they are for Summer Rain."

"Really?"

"Yes," Joseph said simply.

"But Sarah has never lived among the Indians. How will she understand what your life has been like?"

"She understands, in her own way." Joseph was quiet for a moment. "I'm ready to leave that life behind."

Christian pondered what he'd just heard. *Is Joseph losing his senses?* How could Sarah cause Joseph to forsake his life among the Indians so quickly? Summer Rain was much more attractive than Sarah. But that was up to Joseph. Still . . .

"I'd like to marry someone who understands Indians," Christian said. "I doubt most women back home would relate to my life with them."

"Maybe Summer Rain is the woman for you, then."

Christian suppressed a smile. "So you wouldn't mind if I call on her?"

"Not at all. When I heard that Morning Dew was married to someone else, I immediately thought of Summer Rain for you."

"Really? Maybe I'll go back to visit her sometime."

"You'll have to get past her Indian-hating uncle. That might not be easy to do."

Christian snorted. "If I decide she's the one for me, I won't let him stand in my way."

-14-

The moons that passed after their return from the Indian village were filled with misery for Christian. Although Anna reached out to welcome Christian back home, *Dat* said little. Gone was his dream of a Shawnee home, and his arms went limp when he thought of farming for the rest of his life.

The worst thing was that Joseph seemed to be slipping away. Drawn by his love for Sarah Blank, he moved steadily toward adopting the life of a white settler. He dressed just like the white man and no longer wore his earrings. Soon after their return from the Indian villages in the Frosty Moon, Joseph joined the church and announced his engagement to Sarah Blank. They were to be married as soon as the harvest was in store.

Joseph invited him to share his cabin, but Christian stayed in his wigwam. It was unbearably cold at times, but he clung to it like an anchor. Without it, he feared, he would be like an unmanned canoe, adrift on the current of a white settler's life. *I must find a different way,* he thought to himself over and over again.

"I wish you could serve as a witness at my wedding," Joseph told Christian one day as they trudged through an early snow to check their muskrat traps.

"Is there a reason why I can't?" Christian asked.

"The bishop says you have to dress like a full member of the church. Are you willing to cut your hair?"

"No, this is the way I want to keep it. Always."

"Then I'll ask John. Sarah chose a friend named Esther."

On a day in early December, Christian walked with Joseph to the home of Hans Blank for the wedding. It was a cold morning, with a layer of snow on the ground. Christian rubbed his hands together to keep them warm.

"Aren't you a little scared to get married?" Christian asked. "Now you have to live by all the church's rules."

"It will be worth it," Joseph replied. "I want to spend the rest of my life with Sarah."

"She's very different than the girls back in the Indian village. She doesn't even wear any jewelry."

"She's beautiful on the inside," Joseph countered. "There's more to a woman than the clothes she wears, Christian. Like *Dat* says, 'The most beautiful garb is a smile.'"

"What do you like about her?"

"She's a lot like Barbara, but without the bad moods. Sarah knows how to have fun."

"I still like the Indian girls best." Christian hit him lightly on the shoulder. "I'd be with them now, if you hadn't been in such a hurry to come back home."

Joseph laughed. "Don't worry. You'll soon find a girl around here that you like, and then you'll change your mind."

Christian sighed. "I'm sure I won't find anyone I like as much as Morning Dew."

"If you keep looking, someone will show up," Joseph said.

"You got lucky." Christian felt sorry for himself. "Things never turn out that well for me."

"It's not luck," Joseph said. "You have to be willing to do something. I introduced you to Summer Rain, but you never went back to see her."

"I couldn't make up my mind to go," Christian said lamely.

"That's my point," Joseph said, a bit sharply. "Now don't ruin my wedding day by complaining."

They walked in silence, but Christian's mind was busy. He *had* thought about Summer Rain often but worried that she was interested in Joseph, not him. Besides, her foster father, the uncle, clearly didn't want him to come around.

Christian and Joseph soon arrived at the Blanks' home. Sarah's father, Hans, opened the door at their knock and welcomed them. There were more than a dozen people in the room. Christian felt hemmed in. He slipped over to a quiet corner where he wouldn't be noticed.

He sat there watching the women bustle with food preparation. The men sat, talking. Joseph had said it wouldn't be a large wedding. *What a relief.*

Christian looked around the house, taking in the shape of the room and the crafting of the woodwork. He noticed that the logs were joined differently in the corner than in *Dat's* house. Instead of each log overlapping another, the ends were thrust into a corner pole. He stroked the joints with his fingers, wondering why it was built that way.

Sarah's father seemed to read his mind and came over to him. "I see you noticed that the corners are made differently in my house," he said.

Christian nodded. "*Dat* didn't build his house that way."

"This is the way they make the corners in France," Hans said. "So we decided to build our house that way here."

"Did you live in France?" Christian asked.

"We speak French, because we lived in Montbeliard for a time," Hans said. "It's a French-speaking county not far west of the borders of Switzerland and Germany. We fled there from our beloved Switzerland when some men from the popish group raided our house one dreadful night. I was away, and my wife, Magdalena, had to flee in the midst of a snowstorm. She followed mountain paths across the border, and some friends found a place for her to stay until I could join her."

"Was Sarah with her?"

"Yes, she was only two weeks old. Magdalena had to carry her a long way."

Bishop Jake and Catharine arrived, so Hans left Christian's side to greet them. Soon after, Bishop Jake invited everyone to sit facing the front of the living room, which was heated by a stove. Hans and Magdalena sat on chairs in the front row, as did Jacob and Anna. Other adult relatives and friends sat nearby on chairs or makeshift seats, such as crocks or heavy baskets. The children sat on the floor.

The bishop presented a message on marriage, drawing a lesson from the wedding story of Tobias and Sarah in the apocryphal book of Tobit. When he had finished speaking, he drew out a small black book from his pocket and invited Joseph and Sarah to stand in front of the group. John rose to stand beside Joseph as a witness, and Esther took her place beside Sarah. The couple repeated their wedding vows, and then the bishop led in a prayer of blessing.

It was the first time Christian had attended a wedding since his capture by the Shawnees. As far as he knew, Shawnee couples lived together without the benefit of wedding vows. If they had taken solemn vows like the Amish, would they have been more likely to stay together for a lifetime? From what he had seen, men often moved from one woman's wigwam to another.

As soon as the ceremony was over, the women rose to finish meal preparations. When the food was ready, a few pale-faced girls stood by nervously, each waiting for an invitation from a boy to join him at the table laden with food. Christian wasn't interested in choosing a girl but sat down close to Joseph.

Christian relished the ample fare, eating lustily of the cooked turnips drenched with butter and a large helping of roast turkey. He enjoyed stewed apples and shredded cabbage flavored with vinegar and sugar.

As he ate, Christian kept glancing at a young woman who sat near Sarah. She had wavy, dark-brown hair, and hazel eyes that twinkled when she laughed.

"What's her name?" he asked Joseph quietly, hoping to conceal his budding interest in the young woman.

"That's Orpha Rupp," Joseph said. "She's Sarah's friend, who lives not far from here. She's part of a Dunker church."

The Dunker Church? I didn't think the Amish had much to do with them, Christian mused. He tried not to be too obvious, but he kept stealing glances toward Orpha the rest of the afternoon. He thought she was lovely. She reminded him of Morning Dew, who was always the center of attention in the Shawnee village—not because she sought it, but because people sought her. Orpha brimmed with the same life and happiness.

It was midafternoon when everyone finished the meal, crowned with cakes, fruit pies, and cookies. Bishop Jake and many of the married couples left, while the young people continued to converse around the table. That's when Orpha looked at Christian and said, "I'd like to hear about your time with the Indians."

All eyes turned toward Christian. He hadn't expected to be singled out. It was difficult to know what to say. But for the sake of this girl, he would try. He cleared his throat.

"I guess you know that Joseph and I both lived with Indians for a long time," Christian began, a bit haltingly. "We were taken into their families as though we belonged to them." He paused. "I returned a few moons ago."

"Do you mean months?" she asked.

"No, moons aren't quite the same as months on the calendar. Indians tell time by the phase of the moon, not by an almanac the way settlers do. They name most of the moons by the weather, plants, or animals—the Wolf Moon, the Snow Moon, the Worm Moon, the Flower Moon, the Corn Moon, the Beaver Moon, and so on."

"That's very interesting," Orpha said. She leaned forward with an open expression on her face that bade him keep going.

"The most important things I learned from the Indians have to do with the outdoors. I learned how to track and hunt all kinds of animals, and how to find my way in the woods. I learned about plants too, and how to use them for healing."

"I'm sure there's lots of other things that Indians do differently than we do," Orpha said. "I heard a Moravian missionary tell about his work among the Indians. It was very interesting."

Christian leaned forward to hear more. "What was that missionary's name?" he asked. "I never heard of missionaries to the Indians."

"I don't remember his name," Orpha said. "But he talked about living with the Indians and learning their language. He listened to the words they spoke and wrote them down in a journal. That's the way he learned to speak their language, which I think was Delaware."

Christian opened his eyes wide. "I'd like to meet that man sometime."

"The elder at our church could tell you his name," Orpha replied. "He is interested in the Indians."

Shortly after that, the conversation turned back to the newlyweds, leaving Christian on the edge of the conversation. But when he walked home by himself that evening, he couldn't get the young woman Orpha out of his mind. *I'm going to get to know her*, he resolved as he breathed in the night air.

The following Sunday, Christian trudged the path to the church fellowship. He wasn't looking forward to being in the service. But he had promised Joseph he'd be there with him on this first Sunday after he was married. A vow of marriage was a pledge to the church, so Joseph and Sarah would be expected to attend on a regular basis. *A good reason not to get married to an Amish woman*, he thought.

To his surprise and delight, however, Christian saw Orpha sitting next to Sarah on the women's side of the gathering. He wondered what had brought her to the Amish fellowship. *I must go talk to her after the service.*

It was a cold morning, and the fireplace blazed hot inside the house. People were packed in. It soon was warm and stuffy, and the service seemed longer than usual. Christian dozed off during Bishop Jake's sermon. He sneaked a few looks at Orpha, but she seemed absorbed in the message.

As was the custom, when the service concluded Christian went to the barn with three other young men his age. They chatted about the events of the past week and commented about the presence of Sarah's two guests.

"I wonder who they are," one of them asked. "We should go back in to meet them."

"One of them is Orpha Rupp," Christian said. "I met her at Joseph and Sarah's wedding. She belongs to the Dunker church."

"I wonder what she's doing here," another commented. "My father says we shouldn't mingle with Dunkers."

"Why not?" Christian asked. "What's wrong with Dunkers?"

"They teach you can't be saved without being dunked under the water in a stream," the boy replied. "Think what it would be like to be baptized in the creek on a day like this. You might freeze to death!"

"I've taken a bath in the water on a day as cold as this," Christian said.

"Naw, you haven't. Why would anybody get into the water when it's so cold?"

"Some Indians take a bath every day regardless of the weather," Christian replied. "It makes you tough if you go swimming when it's really cold."

"That's not why Dunkers do it," the other boy replied. "They do it because they think it's the only right way."

Christian shrugged. "Maybe so." Why should he argue with these boys about baptism when his interest was in Orpha? He excused himself and slipped back inside the house. He spotted Orpha helping Sarah set the food on tables for the noon meal. Since the men and women ate separately, he wondered how he might get into a conversation with her without drawing undue attention to himself.

Ah, there stood Joseph at the corner of the room. *Maybe he can get Orpha's attention for me.* Nonchalantly, Christian walked up to Joseph.

"I'd like to get to know Sarah's friend Orpha today. Can you help me figure out a way to do that?"

Joseph smiled. "Sure." He winked and went to Sarah. The two of them conversed for a few moments. Joseph smiled and whispered to Sarah, then turned back to Christian. "Sarah thinks it would be best for you not to talk to Orpha here. But we will invite Orpha to come to our house this afternoon. You're invited too."

Christian was thrilled. He made his way back to the barn and told the other young men that Orpha didn't want to come outside. "She's helping with the food," he said.

After the women and children had eaten their meal, they called the men inside to take their turn. Christian gulped down his food, eager to leave for Joseph's home.

It seemed like an eternity, but it was only an hour later when he was seated in Joseph and Sarah's little house. Orpha was there, as was Lizzie, another friend of hers.

"I'm so glad you came to visit us today," Sarah said to Orpha. "Was our church service a lot like yours?"

"Pretty much, except that Elder Klein makes it easier for me to stay awake. He is an enthusiastic preacher."

"It was hot and stuffy in the service today," Christian said. "It was hard not to fall asleep."

"I thought the preacher said very interesting things," Orpha said. "He made me think, like our preacher does." She looked directly at Christian. "You should come to visit our church sometime to hear him speak."

Christian paused for a moment. The invitation was unexpected. He sought for words. "Well, I hadn't thought about that. Do you really want me to come?"

"Of course. He tells us we should invite other people."

Christian paused, unsure whether or not to ask the question. Finally, he blurted out: "What will people think of my long hair?"

She paused for a moment. "That might be a bit of a problem if you wanted to join our church. But it would be fine for you to visit. Maybe you should visit our preacher's farm first. Elder Klein lives a little ways north of here beside the Northkill Creek. He's interested in the Indians, so he'd surely be interested in knowing that you lived among them for a while."

"I think I met your elder at the blacksmith shop a few months ago. He seemed friendly enough."

"Yes, he's easy to talk to. I'll tell him that you're interested in meeting him."

Christian hoped that Elder Klein wouldn't try to keep him from seeing Orpha if he didn't attend the church. But after being with Orpha twice, he was willing to risk a run-in with the preacher in order to get to know her a little better.

-15-

In the winter months that followed Joseph's marriage and move to Heidelberg Township, Christian missed seeing him every day. He also envied Joseph, wishing he was fortunate enough to find a young woman whom he liked as much as Joseph liked Sarah.

With Joseph gone from the home farm, he confided more in Anna, who reached out to him. Both she and Barbara showed interest in his affairs, and he was beginning to trust them enough to talk about doubts and uncertainties. He talked less about leaving and began to take at least a measure of interest in the farm.

One sunny day in March, Christian and Anna were contemplating her kitchen garden. Barbara and her children had dropped by for a visit.

"The almanac says this is a good day to plant," Anna said. "As long as we keep things covered from frost."

"My lettuce is up already," said Barbara.

"Grandma! Grandma!" Nine-year-old Mary came running from the creek. "Look what we found!"

Anna reached out to receive the odd-shaped piece in her hand. "That's a sherd of Indian pottery."

"Let's give it to Christian," the child said and ran back to play with the others.

Anna handed it to Christian, who pulled out his knife. He scraped off the caked dirt on the reddish clay piece.

"It's too bad it's broken," he said. "Indians make beautiful little pots." It was proof that the Indians had lived in the Northkill years before the white man came. He'd known it before, but it gripped him in a new way.

The Indians may have built a wigwam on the very spot that his occupied now. Perhaps they had rested in the shade of the same trees and slaked their thirst with water from the same streams. Maybe the trail that ran north from *Dat's* place had been blazed by Indian warriors heading for the gap in the Blue Mountains. Most likely they had been Delawares, venturing from homes that lay farther north and east.

"Thank you," Christian said to Anna. "I'd like to keep it." She nodded and turned back to planning her garden and chatting with Barbara.

He walked slowly toward his wigwam, feeling the edges of the potsherd as he went, trying to picture the woman who had used it, maybe to store bear grease.

Why had the Indians left the Northkill? *Dat* had always said that William Penn had negotiated a treaty and shared the land with Indians, allowing them to hunt in Penn's Woods. But it felt different now. The settlers in the Northkill wanted nothing to do with Indians.

His stomach tightened as he recalled the tense moments in the house when *Mam* had turned away a few hungry warriors who begged for food. At that time of innocence, he'd known next to nothing about Indians and their struggle to survive the white man's presence in the new world. But after sitting around countless campfires where the Natives talked about the white man, the war, and the way they'd been turned out of their native lands, he could never see it that way again.

Christian mused about showing the potsherd to *Dat*. He could wave it in his face and argue, "See, the Indians have been here before. What's wrong with my having a wigwam here?"

He thought better of it, knowing it would only lead to trouble. *Dat* would argue that the white man had paid for the land and that the Indians didn't care about farming anyhow.

I wonder what Joseph will say when he sees this, Christian mused. Joseph had agreed to help *Dat* for the day, so Christian walked toward where Joseph was working. Joseph saw him coming and put down the axe he was using to chop down a tree.

"One of our nieces found this near the creek. I guess Indians must have lived here at one time," he said holding the potsherd out to him.

Joseph took the clay piece from Christian's proffered hand with eagerness. "I'm sure that's true. There's hardly a place in Pennsylvania where Indians didn't live or hunt at one time. Now they've all been displaced—west into the Ohio Territory." He paused. "Did I ever tell you that my Indian mother used to play right here at the Northkill when she was a child? She recognized that hollow tree—the one that was Franey's favorite hiding place."

Christian's eyes brightened. "So she might have played with this little pot?"

"Maybe, while her father was shooting arrows."

"Did you ever shoot arrows when you lived among the Delaware?"

"Not so much, until right at the end of my time with them. A prophet named Neolin tried to get the Delawares to give up their rifles and other trade goods made by the white man. So my friend Miquon and I made a couple of bows and some arrows."

Christians face brightened. "Why don't we make some?"

Joseph shrugged. "Sure. Why not? I know where there is a hickory tree for a bow and I'm sure we can find ash sprouts for arrows."

Christian's face brightened. "If we harvest the wood now, it will dry enough to use by summer."

He walked slowly back to the wigwam, fingering the potsherd in his hand. If he had found this piece in the creek as a child, he would probably have tossed it right back in. It was different now that he had been with the Indians. Making a bow and some arrows would help him feel more at home.

And with Joseph's help, it would be fun.

Anna invited Christian, Joseph, and Sarah to join the family for dinner. Barbara's family also was invited, so the conversation was loud and lively. The two brothers talked about their plans to make bows and arrows. As they spoke, Barbara became quiet. Her face was troubled.

As soon as the children finished eating and ran outside to play, Barbara addressed the matter forthrightly. "Christian. Joseph. I don't want my children to start shooting arrows," she said. "I don't want them to act like crazy Indians, even if they're just pretending."

Christian leaned forward to speak. "The Indians are not the savages that the settlers make them out to be," he said to Barbara. "They do not like to interfere with quarrels they do not own. They are as interested in peace as any of the Amish. The only reason they attacked our family and killed our mother was because savage white men had done them wrong." He clenched his jaws as he spoke.

Barbara shrunk back. Joseph nodded, encouraging Christian.

"The only reason the Indians were drawn into the war was because of the way the white man treated them," Joseph said. "When I living with the Indians, I learned how peaceable and kind they are, how obliging and caring toward one another. You couldn't find better people anywhere. They love their neighbors as themselves, as the Bible tells us to do."

That was too much for Barbara. "Well then. Why did they kill *Mam*? Why did they scalp our brother and sister? What did our family ever do to deserve *that*?" Tears welled in her eyes and her face flushed red.

Christian shook his head, licking his dry lips with an anxious tongue. "We didn't deserve what they did to us," he said. "And they didn't deserve what was done to them."

"What did *we* ever do to them?" Barbara demanded. "All *Mam* did was refuse them a piece of pie! Does that make it right for them to murder people and burn down their house?" Indignation burned bright in her eyes.

Joseph leaned forward to match her fierce gaze. "No, our family didn't attack them. Neither did any members of our church. But we moved onto good land that had been taken from them. Finally, their anger boiled over and they sought revenge."

"What do you mean?" Barbara asked. "We didn't steal their land. We bought it from the Penn brothers, who inherited it from their father. He dealt with the Indians justly by making a treaty and paying for the land. Tell me, what's wrong with that?"

Christian shook his head. "It is true that William Penn bought the land from them. The Delaware people still think highly of him. But when they agreed to sell the land to him, they thought they could keep using it to hunt and fish. They do not live like white men, writing out a deed and fencing off their property so no one else can use it. They share their land with others."

"Why do you take the part of the Indians against your own people?" Barbara asked.

"After living with them, I understand why they are so upset about land," Christian said. "The white man keeps moving the boundaries and driving the Natives farther and farther to the west. The Shawnees believe the white man will not be satisfied until he gets the whole country, all the way to the western ocean."

Joseph nodded agreement. "There is an Indian prophet who predicted that when the whites have killed all of the red men and taken all of their land, then the great turtle who holds this great island on its back will dive deep into the ocean and drown them all as he once did before. And then the Indian shall rise again and take possession of the whole country."

"That's silly." Barbara scowled. "That's not what the Bible says about the way God made the world."

"Okay," Joseph said in a conciliatory tone. "I agree that this land does not rest on the back of a turtle. But the prophet's words show that the Indians believe that the whites will eventually take all of their land. That could easily happen."

"But shouldn't our people, who bought our land in peace, have the right to live here without being attacked?" Barbara insisted.

"Who do you mean by 'our people'—Indians or whites?" Christian asked, trying to look innocent as he spoke.

"Our Amish people, of course," Barbara retorted with a scowl. "You knew who I meant. We always try to live at peace with others. Why did they attack us instead of the people who were fighting them?"

"I've wondered about that too," Christian said slowly. "But my time with the Indians has helped me see things I couldn't see before." He took a deep breath.

Barbara's face relaxed a bit as she heard his reflective tone.

"The Indians attacked our family because we were in a war," Christian said. "They didn't want the war, but the French and the British each tried to win them over to their side. The Delawares and Shawnees joined the French side because they thought it would keep the British from coming into the Ohio Territory. The French provoked them to take revenge against the settlers. We happened to be in their path."

Barbara sighed aloud. "Is that the only reason? Not long before the attack, *Mam* told me that she was afraid the Indians would attack us because they once left a black mark on our front door. *Dat* always told her not to worry about it, but she did. And I wonder if she was right."

Christian spoke up, his voice barely above a whisper. "I never heard anything about that."

"I don't remember that either," Joseph said.

"*Mam* probably didn't tell you because she didn't want you to worry," Barbara said.

"What happened? What kind of mark was it?"

"The Indians had come to our house for food. She didn't give them what they wanted, so when they left, they found a piece of charcoal and made a black X on the front door."

Christian gave Joseph with a knowing look. "That explains why they killed her with a knife instead of a tomahawk."

Joseph nodded his agreement. "I've always wondered about that. Now it makes sense that they were getting revenge."

"Revenge for what?" Barbara asked with tears in her eyes. "Only a savage would kill someone for not giving them food. Mother was probably saving it for Sunday dinner. Or for some poor family who needed it."

"Yeah," Joseph said. "If only she'd known how important it was to share food with them, she'd have hauled a wheelbarrow load of food from the larder and fed them all."

Christian looked at Barbara. "I know this is hard for you to understand, but Indians see hospitality very differently than we do. They always share their food with strangers, no matter how little they have in store."

"So they kill people who don't share their food when they beg for it?"

"No, but that may have been enough to push them over the edge." He thought for a moment. "Maybe they targeted our family after all. Sometimes they attacked specific settlers, if they had offended them for some reason."

The three siblings sat for a time in an uneasy silence, looking down at the floor. Finally Barbara spoke, her voice choked with emotion. "I don't know why God allowed this to happen to our family," she said as she dabbed at her eyes with a handkerchief. "And I don't like the way you're blaming *Mam* for what happened. I'll never understand Indians the way that you do." She paused. "But I'm glad you both came back home." She reached out her hands to grasp theirs.

Christian choked as he held Barbara's hand in his.

Joseph looked sad. "Did you know that Christian and I had our guns loaded on the morning of the Indian attack? If only *Dat* had let us, we may have been able to chase them off. Indians don't usually stand under fire."

"I heard *Dat* talk about that," Barbara said. "He was putting into practice what he taught us—never to shoot at people."

"Looking back on it, I suppose we might have chased the Indians away if we'd have shot at them," Joseph said. "But then they'd have come back to kill the whole family."

"That's what *Dat* thinks would have happened," Barbara said. She let go of their hands and blew her nose, then rose. "The children need me, so I must go," she said. "But I was wondering, did you ever visit the graves where *Mam* and the others are buried?"

They shook their heads no.

"Then we must visit the graves together. And we can talk about some of the good times we had growing up. Would you be willing to do it this Sunday afternoon?"

Christian looked at Joseph. "I'm willing. Would Sarah want to come too?"

"Maybe," Joseph said. "Either way, I'll come. I've always wondered where the graves were."

Barbara looked triumphant. "Good. I'll meet you at the springhouse as soon as we're home from the church service."

They bade goodbye to each other and went their separate ways. As he left, Christian wished he hadn't so quickly agreed to accompany Barbara to the graves. In spite of his many good memories of *Mam* and his siblings, he wasn't ready for this. He couldn't put it in words, but the churning in his stomach warned him to put it off for a time. Although *Mam* had often been present in his dreams, he'd always stuffed down the frightening thoughts that came to mind when he recalled the last moments of her life.

Surely Barbara was trying to evoke pity for his family members who had died, hoping to blunt his devotion to the Indians. He'd already admitted that the Natives had treated the family terribly. Must he hate them too?

She was pushing him into a corner, goading him to crack open the lid of the mental trunk where he'd stuffed the trauma of the Indian attacks. Was she hoping to break the uneasy truce in his heart between the white man and red man, and force him to rethink his very identity? What would he become?

Barbara is not going to keep me from making a bow and some arrows, Christian thought to himself. *Maybe I should tell Barbara I changed my mind about visiting the graves with her.*

-16-

In spite of his hesitancy to visit the graves, Christian decided to brave it out. He met Joseph and Barbara at the springhouse in the early afternoon the following Sunday. After enjoying a cool drink of water, they followed Barbara to a small cleared spot that was surrounded by weeds not far from the house. "This is the place," she said.

Christian gazed at the spot, which gave no hint of its significance apart from the small wooden slabs that protruded from the earth. Each tipped in a different direction. Christian reached down to straighten them. They stood in silence until a crow cawed loudly, breaking the reverence of the moment.

"So . . . they're all buried together?" Christian asked.

Barbara nodded. "We didn't have time to dig three separate graves. The men dug one wide hole and buried them in a hurry, not knowing if the Indians might return. The bishop came and had a little service . . ."

As Christian stood listening, thinking about the family members he had lost, Barbara's voice faded and the ground shimmered under his feet.

A shot rang out.

"Help! I got a bullet in the leg!" It was Jakey. He slammed the door shut against the enemy.

Christian jumped out of bed.

"Indians! In the yard!"

Jakey moaned and held his leg.

"Oh, Jakey! Let me look at you." *Mam* quickly checked and said, panicked, "He's bleeding! Get me some bandages.

Joseph—get me some water." She took the water he brought and began cleaning the wound.

"Is the bullet still in?" *Dat* asked.

"I can't tell for sure."

"I can't see," Franey whined. "Can't we light the lantern?"

"No! We don't want the Indians to see us." *Dat's* voice was emphatic.

Joseph went for the guns. He handed one to Christian, who took it with trembling hands and loaded it in the near darkness. He'd used a gun only a few times, but never to shoot at people.

When he finished ramming in the bullet, he moved toward the window beside Joseph. The moon shone dimly on the forms of a French officer and a group of Indians standing near the bake oven. The Natives wore feathers and war paint.

"Look," Joseph whispered. "There must be a dozen of them."

"Stay back from the windows," *Dat* shouted. He grasped Christian's shoulder and pulled him back. Christian shrugged off *Dat's* hand and stepped to the side of the window.

"Joseph, put your gun down," *Dat* said in the kind of quiet voice he reserved for nonnegotiable matters.

"Why, *Dat*? I can get a good shot off from here."

"You know why. We don't shoot people."

"But *Dat, we can't let them shoot at us!*"

"Joseph, that's enough. Christian, I mean that for you too." *Dat* put his hand on the gun. Christian clung to it for a moment and then surrendered it with a sigh. It was a relief of sorts, knowing that he wouldn't be asked to shoot at the Indians.

A small flame flickered and soon lit up several faces. A warrior moved toward the end of the house with a pair of burning brands in his hands.

A few minutes later, Christian sniffed the air. "I smell smoke! They've set the house on fire." Franey began to wail. "I'm afraid! I'm scared of those Indians!"

"Hush," *Mam* told her. She looked fearfully at *Dat*.

Joseph spoke. "We'll never get out of here alive unless we shoot at them. I could shoot into the air to scare them into the woods."

"Joseph, you heard what I told you."

Christian put his arm around Franey as they crouched in the corner of the cabin. They could hear the flames crackling.

"Joseph, give me the gun."

Terrified, Christian watched flames break through the dry shingles of the roof. Smoke billowed down the stairs. Soon, the flames licked their way through the ceiling. Christian took one of the handkerchiefs *Mam* had soaked in a bucket of water and covered his nose and mouth.

When the ceiling began to sway, *Dat* called out, "Follow me! We're going to the cellar."

Christian trembled as he took his place, last in line behind the three other children and *Mam*. He closed the door behind him and groped his way down the stairs. The root cellar was cool and musty. His nose and throat burned from the thickening smoke, despite the handkerchief he held over his nose. The hungry flames gnawed their way through the floorboards, licking off the edges to expose the fire in the room above. The floor above them shook with a loud thump and then sagged as a shower of sparks fell into the cellar through several gaps in the boards. Christian squeezed his small frame into the rough stone corner with Franey.

Soon *Dat* pried open the lid on a barrel of apple cider and used a wooden dipper to splash cider onto the burning floorboards overhead. Jakey and Joseph joined *Dat* to help, dipping their hands full of cider and tossing it onto the ceiling until the barrel was empty. It seemed to slow down the flames, but the heat and smoke were intense. He tried to cough the smoke out of his lungs.

Dat rolled an empty barrel toward the lone window that faced the back of the house. He flipped the barrel upside down. "We can't hold on any longer. We'll have to crawl out the window." He grabbed a handful of dried peaches from a covered basket in the corner. "Children, I want you to put some peaches in your pockets. You might need them."

Christian stuffed a handful of dried slices into his pocket.

Joseph was the first one to scramble onto the barrel and out the window into the morning sunlight. He poked his head back inside. "I don't see anyone! They must have gone into the woods."

Dat grabbed Christian's arm. "You go next."

He scrambled onto the barrel and crawled out the window on the blackened ground next to the house. He scanned the edge of the woods. No Indians in sight.

Next came Jakey, with some difficulty because of his hurt leg, and after him Franey's petite figure emerged. And then it was *Mam*, struggling to get through the window, which was too small for her portly frame. She disappeared back inside. *Dat* poked his head out.

"Boys! Find me a rock I can use for a hammer."

Christian grabbed a good-sized rock and passed it to *Dat*.

"That'll work." *Dat* took the rock and splintered off the wooden stop on the four sides of the window frame. Soon *Mam*'s ample frame pressed against the sides of the window for the second time. As Joseph tugged on *Mam*'s arms to help her through, Christian spied a movement in the peach orchard. His heart leaped into his throat as he turned to *Dat*, who had just scrambled out of the cellar behind mother.

"*Dat*! An Indian!"

A young warrior stood by the peach trees, picking the ripe fruit. Jacob put his finger to his lips and beckoned the family to follow him around the corner of the house. Just then the warrior spied them and let out a loud whoop. In a few moments, other warriors came running from the woods, yelling and brandishing their weapons.

"Everyone run!" *Dat* shouted.

Christian started off toward the meadow. He didn't get far. Two braves appeared in front of him, hemming him in and then yanking him off his feet. They dragged Christian back toward the house where they'd already captured *Dat* and *Mam*.

Christian saw Jakey stumbling away from the house, hampered by his injured leg. Moments later a warrior struck him with a tomahawk. Jakey screamed. There was a swift motion. Christian couldn't bear to look. The warrior shouted, lifting Jakey's scalp high over his head, still dripping blood.

Christian threw back his head to avoid the tomahawk raised high over his skull. Just then, another warrior shouted something in a strange language. The Indian holding Christian stopped his strike in midair.

His arms were yanked behind his back. Christian cried out as they tied his wrists with hemp.

He turned his head aside in time to see a warrior plunge a knife into *Mam*'s chest.

"Herr Yesus!" Mam screamed. Christian looked up as she fell backward onto the ground. The warriors were laughing now, yelling taunts as they knelt down. He closed his eyes. The next time he looked, he saw one of them holding a bloody scalp.

Christian looked away and felt his stomach lurch. He vomited. Trying to wipe his mouth on his shoulder, he turned his head in time to see three warriors emerged from the woods, leading Joseph with his hands bound behind his back. Christian thought he'd escaped.

A man in a French uniform motioned for the warriors to follow him. Another warrior yanked Christian toward the front of the line that formed, and then kicked him in the back of his legs as they started to march toward the path that led off the farm. The sour taste of vomit was in his mouth as he began his long, torturous journey.

The sound of a crow cawing loudly from a branch above the three graves brought Christian back to the present. His heart beat rapidly and his legs trembled. His breath came in short gasps.

Barbara and Joseph were looking at him oddly. "Are you okay?" asked Barbara.

Christian nodded as he put his hands on his knees and closed his eyes. He longed to think of *Mam* apart from the gruesome scene that marked the end of her life. To think of Jesus apart from *Mam*'s desperate cry—*Herr Yesus!*—just moments before she died. Why hadn't Jesus heard her frantic prayer and spared her life?

Christian straightened up and shook his head to clear his vision. "I need to go now," he said. He wanted to be alone for a while. Maybe later, when he'd had some time to sort through his jumbled feelings, he could ask Joseph and Barbara how they managed to stay calm in the face of memories that brought him such trauma. Perhaps then he could find some of the peace that Joseph seemed to experience.

-17-

In the days that passed after Christian visited the graves, Orpha was never far from his mind. In a way he could not explain, she reminded him of good times with *Mam*, without bringing to mind the pain of *Mam*'s death.

What drew him most was Orpha's infectious laughter, leavened by a streak of serious reflection. Perhaps if he got to know her better, he too could find such joy. Happiness still proved elusive to him, given the way that *Dat* expected him to join a community, forcing him to break the vow he'd made to the Indians. Since Joseph had found his way back into the community through the love of a woman, it might be possible for him as well.

One day near the end of March when Christian spoke with Orpha at Joseph's house, she encouraged him to visit Elder Klein's home. The next day, he gathered the courage to follow her suggestion. *Perhaps I could ask him about the vow,* he thought. Elder Klein seemed like someone who would give good counsel.

At midmorning, he set out on the path that ran beside the Northkill Creek toward the Klein farm. The air was alive with the chirps and calls of birds. A robin pulled a long earthworm from the moist soil near the path. Newly shorn sheep grazed in a meadow strewn with purple and white violets. A cowbell tinkled from the edge of the woods. In the distance, he saw the elder's family home, which doubled as a meeting place for the small Dunker congregation.

On the side of the small farm lane stood a barn with an open door. The whirring and clicking sounds of a machine greeted Christian as he stepped into the doorway. He shouted a "Ho!" and paused to let his eyes adjust to the darkness.

The elder stood behind a large wooden frame, working a wooden pedal up and down with his foot. A rod fastened to the pedal rose and fell on the side of a wooden wheel, lending the energy to spin a lathe, which held a long and slender piece of wood in its grip. The elder guided a sharp chisel on the top of a tool rest, slicing off shavings from the spinning wood.

The older man stopped his work as Christian approached. "Hello! Didn't I meet you at the smithy's shop? What can I do for you?"

Christian was mesmerized by the contraption. "I never saw a machine like this," he said. "What are you making?"

"I'm turning a spindle to match that one." He pointed to a broken spindle in a chair off to the side.

Christian looked on, fascinated. "Do you mind if I watch you work?"

"Not at all."

Christian stepped closer as the elder spun the flywheel with his hand and began to pedal. As soon as the spindle spun rapidly enough, the elder put his tool to work, peeling off layers of wood like *Mam* had peeled the skin from an apple with her paring knife.

Christian studied the machine carefully, noting the metal parts of the mechanism. He observed the way that the elder cradled the chisel in his hands, holding it against the spindle with the skill honed by long use. Christian had seen *Dat* carve wood with a knife, but this was very different. There was nothing like this among the Shawnees.

When Elder Klein finished turning the piece, he took it out of the lathe and brushed off several wood shavings that clung to his long beard. He showed the newly formed piece to Christian and then said, "Aren't you the one who lived among the Indians for a while?"

Christian nodded. "Yes. I spent eight winters with the Shawnees." He paused. "A woman from your church said you know something about missionary work with the Indians."

"What was her name?"

"Orpha Rupp."

The elder's face broke into a smile. "Orpha is a wonderful young woman. I wish our fellowship had more like her."

Christian felt his face grow warm. "She said you knew a Moravian missionary who worked with the Indians."

"She probably meant Christian Frederick Post. He's doing a good work."

Christian paused, not sure how to word the question that plagued his mind. "I don't want to keep you from fixing your chair," he said. "Maybe you can work while we talk." It would be easier to talk if the elder wasn't looking at him.

"Sure," Elder Klein said. "I can listen while I'm working, if that suits you." He turned to remove the broken spindle from the chair. "Did you have a question for me?"

"Yes." Christian paused for a long moment. "I was wondering if it's ever right to break a vow."

The elder looked thoughtful as he stroked the new spindle with his hand. "That's a difficult question to answer. What makes you ask?"

"Oh, nothing in particular," Christian tried to sound nonchalant. "I was wondering if settlers understand vows the same way as Indians."

"I don't know how the Indians make vows, but we Dunkers follow the way of Jesus, who taught us not to swear oaths. We should let our *yes* be *yes* and our *no* be *no*."

"Is it ever right to change your mind about a promise?"

The elder stroked his beard, considering. "It depends. Sometimes people make foolish promises—especially children. They shouldn't be held accountable to keep them."

"Thank you. That's all I wanted to know." Christian hoped the elder wouldn't probe any further. He wasn't ready to give more detail about the vow he'd made to Little Bear.

Christian was about to leave when he remembered the other reason he'd come. "Would it be okay if I visited your church?"

Elder Klein beamed. "Of course. We'd be very glad to have you. In fact, tomorrow would be a very good time—it's Easter

Sunday." He smiled, and Christian had to smile back. Several wood shavings clung tenaciously to the elder's hair, which he was completely unaware of. Who could be afraid of this man?

However, Christian cautioned himself to go slowly. He hadn't expected such an enthusiastic welcome. At least not so soon. Did he really want to visit a church again? And should he trust someone he had known for such a brief time? Then he reminded himself of the reason for going.

"Do you think Orpha will be there?"

"Oh yes, she's there whenever the doors are open. We'll meet at the house right over there," the elder said, pointing through the doorway. He smiled again. "If you come, maybe you can sit on this chair. I hope to have it finished by then."

Christian's mind raced as he considered the elder's invitation. He dimly recalled Easter as the time to celebrate the resurrection of Jesus Christ from the dead. The Indians seldom spoke of resurrection, but now that he'd visited *Mam*'s grave, he wondered if Jesus would raise her body too, and call her through the skies to heaven. He seldom thought of heaven, but wished to go there rather than to the place the Bible called hell. Both places seemed foreign to him now. But what could it hurt to learn more about them from the Dunker church?

It was comforting to know that he'd almost certainly meet Orpha there. But he wished he hadn't been so forward in naming her. If that word got out to others, it would surely lead to teasing and might even push Orpha away.

On the other hand, he doubted that the elder would betray his confidence. The elder's articulate German speech bespoke a cultured upbringing, and Christian would have normally been nervous about talking with such a man. But the sawdust and shavings made the elder seem more approachable.

"Shall we expect you tomorrow?" the elder asked.

"I-I guess so," Christian stammered, bereft of an adequate excuse to refuse the kind invitation.

"Very good. We'll plan to see you. Our church service starts at nine o'clock in the morning."

Christian headed back home on the same path he'd come, deep in thought. Why should he subject himself to gaping stares or a boring worship service? Yet if he got to spend time with Orpha, and she was happy to see him, it could be worth it. He could also learn more about Christ's resurrection from the dead and the Dunker congregation's interest in Indian peoples. For a brief moment, he dreamed that they might embrace his desire to be an Indian without seeking to change him.

I wonder what Joseph would say, Christian thought. *Maybe I'll ask him.*

Now that Joseph had moved away from the home farm, Anna thought Christian seemed quieter. Although he now readily helped Jacob with some tasks, such as pruning branches in the orchard or sharpening tools, he was still reluctant to join in the church fellowship. Anna longed for Christian to follow the same path Joseph had taken, even if it took him longer.

It's because Joseph found a woman he liked, she thought. Nothing would help Christian to adjust to life on the farm more quickly than a helpmeet. But what self-respecting young woman would want to marry Christian now, stuck as he was in his Indian ways? Why couldn't he understand that?

Anna determined not to give him advice, but she prayed about it often and listened for hints that he'd found someone he liked. If only he would find a suitable girl! She'd do her best to encourage a relationship.

On Easter Sunday morning, she saw Christian out in the yard.

"Christian! Do you want to attend worship with us today?"

Christian blushed. "No," he said. "I have other plans this morning."

She ached to ask him for details but thought the better of it. Like his father, he resented probing. Why force him to say he was going fishing?

Several weeks later, she was walking to the home of a sick widow with an herbal remedy in her basket. As she passed a neighbor's home, her eyes were drawn to a young woman who was supervising three children. She glanced at the woman and then stopped to take a longer look.

"You look familiar to me," she said. "Didn't I meet you at Joseph and Sarah's wedding?"

"Yes," the girl said, smiling. "I'm Orpha."

Anna's heart leapt. Orpha had sparked Christian's interest at the wedding. Anna wished he'd take the opportunity to make a better acquaintance.

"My son Christian enjoyed meeting you at the wedding," she said.

Orpha beamed. "I enjoy talking with him. He has visited our church a couple of times."

Anna tried not to look surprised. *Why has Christian said nothing to me about this?* she wondered. "What do you think brings him there?"

Orpha said with a twinkle, "He *says* he likes our preacher. Elder Klein invited him to come on Easter Sunday, and he has come two or three times since then."

"That's good to know," Anna said studying her face. Orpha looked studiously innocent. Anna looked around the farm. "Do you live here?"

"No, I came a few weeks ago as a *Maud* (maid). Mrs. Heisey had a baby, and I'm helping her with the children." As she spoke, three young children came running to her.

"They look like they're having fun," Anna said.

Orpha brushed several wisps of hair from the oldest girl's eyes. "Yes, they love to play together. This is Hannah," she said as she put her hand on top of the oldest girl's head. "And this is Rebecca," she said, pointing to the other girl, "and that's James." The boy bolted away and turned a few somersaults on the ground nearby. "It's a little hard to keep up with him, and I do get tired out by the end of the day. Especially when I do the washing and baking for the family."

"I heard Sarah say that she is a friend of yours," Anna said. "It made me wonder—who are your parents?"

"I live with Reuben and Leah Stump most of the time," Orpha said as she glared at one of the young charges who was pulling another's hair. "James, you stop that." The boy grinned and ran off. "Sometimes he does naughty things to get my attention," Orpha said. "But he's a good boy usually."

"Children naturally look for attention," Anna said. "I have several grandchildren who act like that sometimes." She paused and then asked, "So your name is Orpha Stump?"

A shadow darkened Orpha's face. "No, Reuben and Leah are my foster parents. My parents both died on a ship. When we came from the Old Country."

"Oh my," Anna said, her face showing her dismay. "That is very sad. Were you with them on the trip?"

"Yes, I was ten years old, the same age Hannah is now. Many children on the ship got sick and died. I got sick at the same time as my parents, but I was fortunate enough to live. Elder Klein told me that God must have some special purpose for me in life."

"I'm sure that the preacher is right," Anna said. "God always has a purpose for everything."

"I think God wants me to marry a man who will be a preacher someday."

Anna caught her breath at the boldness of the young woman's remark. Did she realize the responsibility or the heartaches that could mean for her? Becoming a preacher was not one's own choice, but rather God's choice, at least in the Amish church. *Such certainty for one so young!*

"Sarah says you're from the Dunker church. How do you choose your preachers?"

"We elect a man from among our members to serve. Elder George Klein is a godly man, and I want to marry someone like him."

Anna nodded her affirmation. "It's important to make sure you marry the right man. I was widowed for a few years after I lost my first husband. It took me a long time to decide to marry Jacob."

"Did you have children?"

"Our daughter Susanna died when she was a baby, and my husband not long after, but I'm sure that God must have had a reason for that. Now I'm a stepmother to four children and grandmother to thirteen."

"So you're Christian's stepmother?"

Anna nodded.

"I thought you looked too young to be his mother," Orpha said. "He says you are kind."

Anna blushed. "That's very kind of you to say. He lost his mother in an Indian attack, and I don't think I can ever take her place."

"No, but Christian says he appreciates the way that you have treated him and Joseph since they came back home from the Indian villages. You value the many things they learned from the Indians, like healing with herb remedies."

Anna's heart quickened. "Both of them had to make many adjustments since they came back home. It's a little harder for Christian than it was for Joseph."

Orpha followed her three charges with her eye and then turned to look directly at Anna. "Why do you suppose it's so hard for him?"

Thoughts flashed through Anna's mind like swallows darting over a pond at sunset. How often she'd tried to answer that question in her own mind. But why was Orpha asking the question? Might she have an interest in Christian?

"You've talked with him," Anna replied. "What do *you* think makes it so hard for him?"

Orpha didn't hesitate. "He loves the Indian way of life so much. And he's angry for the way they've been mistreated by people who read the Bible and call themselves Christians. He hates when people speak disrespectfully of the Native people."

Anna nodded as she listened. "You seem to understand him. Maybe that's why he likes being with you."

Orpha got a faraway look in her eyes. "I like Christian, and I admire his knowledge of the woods. But he's not for me. I want to marry a godly man who is willing to be a minister if the church calls him." She shook herself and smiled at Anna. "I don't think that will happen with Christian, do you? At least not in the near future."

Anna marveled at Orpha's discernment. *What a thoughtful young woman.*

The sounds of an argument echoed not far off. "The children need my attention," Orpha said. "It was nice to talk."

"Yes," Anna said, chuckling, as she saw the children turn and run toward the creek that lay within sight of the path. "I hope we can talk again sometime."

Anna waved goodbye and resumed her journey toward the widow's home. *I wish Orpha were part of our Amish fellowship,* she thought. *I wonder if she'd come for the sake of a young man.*

-18-

It was mid-May, and Anna knew that Jacob was frustrated that Christian showed such little interest in the burgeoning farmwork. With Joseph at work on the other farm, it put a greater burden on Jacob and John.

In the weeks following her chance meeting with Orpha, Anna looked for the best way to talk to Christian about it. She longed to understand Christian the way that Orpha did—to understand the reason behind his deep loyalty to the Indian way of life.

When is Christian going to tell us that he's visiting the Dunker church? She'd told Jacob about it after her conversation with Orpha, not wanting him to find out from someone else. As she expected, Jacob was upset to learn about Christian's interest in the Dunker sect, but he agreed to say nothing to Christian about it unless he brought it up first.

Anna glanced at the almanac. It said it was a good day to plant cucumbers. She headed for the kitchen garden with a bag of seeds and cleared the leaves and weeds that had accumulated over a season of dormancy out of one of the raised beds. She laid the seeds with care in small furrows she scratched into the soft dirt, then covered them with a pass of her hand. Anna breathed a prayer that they would sprout in due time. If only God would bless the seeds she planted and curse the unwanted weeds.

She found herself wondering what the garden of Eden had looked like. How wonderful it must have been to cultivate that ground before the first weeds came as punishment for disobedience to the Creator.

The deacon said Eve's fall showed that women were more easily beguiled than men, which was why wives needed to submit to their husbands in everything. *If only Eve had not yielded to the tempter!* Anna thought. Weeds were like the troubling thoughts that sprang up unbidden in her mind. How was she to root them out?

As she walked toward the creek to fill the clay jars she used to water her seedbed, she gazed at Christian's wigwam, a daily reminder that Christian clung to his Indian identity. As she stood gazing at the obvious sign of resistance to *Dat*'s authority, Christian emerged and headed toward the creek for his daily bath. Like the Shawnees, Christian bathed in the creek every day, when a weekly bath in a small tub was sufficient for the white settlers. Did the Indians think they could remain pure by washing more often? Hadn't Jesus told his disciples that purity comes from the inside, not from washing one's hands?

Anna resumed her work, pulling the weeds in another part of her garden. A light rain had brought many new weeds to the surface, and she was determined to conquer them before they took over the bed.

She chopped through the smaller weeds with her hoe and pulled out the larger ones by hand. *Where did this one come from?* she asked herself as she yanked at a particularly large weed. *I think I pulled it out once before and the roots grew right back.*

The acrid smell of the weed assaulted her nose. *Maybe that's what Bishop Jake meant when he talked about the root of bitterness last Sunday.* He had quoted from the epistle to the Hebrews, warning that no one should "fail of the grace of God" and that "no root of bitterness" should spring up among the church.

The bishop said that grudges and bitterness against others were like weeds in a garden. The bishop looked at her as he spoke, causing her to wonder if he was referring to the way she talked about Silas Burkholder.

The bishop was right; she felt bitterness of soul every time she thought of Silas. She swallowed the bile that sprang to her throat as she thought about the way that Silas had smeared her reputation in the neighborhood.

As she yanked out weeds, she rehearsed ways to get even with Silas. Her mind flew back to the evening when Silas had come to her house, not long after her husband had passed away. For the hundredth time—or was it the thousandth?—she felt him pin her arms to her sides and press himself against her. She could think of nothing she had done to provoke him, other than give him a friendly smile when he arrived at the door.

She'd taken seriously her mother's warning not to show undue affection to any man except her husband. Did a foot massage to bring healing count as affection? Or rubbing someone's shoulders to loosen their tight muscles? She had done that for a few men—Jacob among them—not long after his family had assisted her with some fallen branches. She could still see the flash of anger in Lizzie's eyes as she massaged Jacob's tired shoulders.

"There are some things you can't change in other people," the bishop said, "and bitterness will only make things worse. The person who forgives does more for himself than for anyone else."

It was true that the bitter stirrings in her heart hadn't done anything to make her feel better. But how could she forgive Silas if he didn't admit he'd been wrong? Even if she forgave him, she knew she didn't want to ever be near him again. Sometimes, thinking about it kept her awake at night.

Anna straightened up. Her back ached. If she could prove her innocence, it would change many things for the good, even the way that Jacob viewed her. Although he said he believed her account of what happened, she felt his reservation, especially when the two of them were around the bishop. She suspected that the bishop had never approved of their marriage, although he never said it. She admired Jacob for marrying her despite his reservations.

She sopped up the tears on her cheeks with the edge of her apron. There appeared to be no way to rid herself of the bitter feelings she had toward Silas. Maybe that's what the weed of bitterness was about—the persistent stain of thoughts that couldn't be washed away with water, not even tears of grief.

But what was she to do?

After Christian returned from a day of fishing with Joseph, he saw Anna walking from the house toward her kitchen garden. When she turned and saw him, she waved him over.

He hesitated for a moment and then headed to the place where Anna stood waiting. She stroked the purple sedum that flourished by the gate as Christian approached. *Mam* said some believed sedum protected the house from lightning. *Dat* said people must always trust God to protect them. He recalled the time that lightning struck the huge oak tree in front of the yard, sending a branch through the upstairs window into Franey's room. *Perhaps we should have planted more sedum that year.*

A hog pushed its snout against the bottom of the garden gate. Anna shooed it away. She swung open the gate and beckoned Christian through. As Anna turned to shut the gate, the hog tried to push its way through. Christian suppressed a smile as she gave it a kick in the snout with her bare foot. *Maybe she could help me stand up to* Dat. The hog squealed and backed far enough away for her to latch the gate. No wonder they needed a fence. That hog could root out all her plants in half a day.

Anna reached down to pluck a basil leaf and teasingly held it under Christian's nose. He laughed and sniffed. The fragrance transported him—back to the Sunday mornings of yesteryear, when *Mam* would tuck a few basil sprigs into her pocket and under her head covering. "It smells good," *Mam* said. From time to time when it felt stuffy in the church service, she'd pull out her handkerchief and let him crush the sprigs with his fingers.

Christian stood gazing at the earthenware crocks that stood next to the cucumber plants. Anna used the same watering technique as *Mam* once had, placing one end of a twisted woolen rag into the crock and extending the other to the root of the plant in the middle of a small hill. On warm days, the water followed the wick out of the crock and onto the ground. How many times had *Mam* made him fill those little crocks with water from the creek? She said it was better than pouring water directly on the plants.

Christian followed Anna to the corner of the garden where the hops grew. *Dat* had rigged up a couple of tall poles, twice as high as Christian could reach, and the hop vines had wrapped their leafy arms around the pole and climbed all the way to the top. With their roots planted in the soil about an arm's stretch apart, the tops were tied together so that the plants formed an upside-down *V. Mam* had always said, "*M'r muss die hoppe roppe eb dar September wind driwwer blost.* (You must pick the hops before the September wind blows over them.)"

He sighed and then startled. These memories of his mother were good ones. And he hadn't thought of the Indian attacks—until this moment. Resolutely, he put those thoughts away and concentrated on the garden.

Each year *Dat* had helped *Mam* take down the tall poles so that the children—mostly he and Franey—could pull the small cones from the plants and put them in baskets for *Mam*. She had steeped the flowers in warm water overnight and then used them as yeast to make her bread dough rise.

Being with Anna in the garden reminded him of the day—before the Indian attack—when their whole family had gone to help trim trees after the terrible storm that had taken down part of a big tree in the Hochstetler yard. "She's a widow," *Mam* had said of Anna. "She needs our help."

The young widow hadn't seemed to mind his many questions, as *Mam* sometimes did. She'd taught him the names of at least ten herb plants in her garden, one for each of his fingers. His time in the Shawnee camp had erased most of their German names from his mind, but walking in Anna's garden still had that familiar feeling.

Anna led him up and down the paths that ran between the raised beds in the garden, pointing out her plants and commenting on many of them. She took the same pride in her garden as did the Shawnee women—a place to work without interference from men.

Anna seemed most proud of her flowers, scattered throughout several of the raised beds. Unlike the rest of the farm, their only purpose was to cheer the heart by delighting the eyes. Anna reached down and plucked the last of the season's bright-red tulips and carried them as a bunch in her hand.

Christian looked on with appreciation. *I'm so glad Anna helps* Dat *understand me. One of these days, I'm going to tell her about Orpha and about my going to the Dunker church.*

Every Sunday morning when there was a church service, Anna asked herself whether to invite Christian to join them. Jacob had lapsed into silence about the matter of Christian's church attendance, resigning himself to wait until Christian brought it up. He said Christian was old enough to make his own decisions about church, regardless of how painful it might be to them.

Given this frame of mind, Anna could not have anticipated the visitor who stopped by on a Sunday afternoon near the end of May. Jacob was dozing in his chair when Anna heard a knock on the door. She opened it to see a man with brown eyes and dark-brown hair. He wore a black suit and carried a black hat in his hand.

"I'm George Klein," he said, "the elder at the Dunker church not far from here."

Anna looked at Jacob, who opened his eyes and leaned forward. "We have a guest," she said. "He says his name is George Klein from the Dunker church."

"Come on in," Jacob said, rising out of his chair. "Our son Christian mentioned your name."

"Yes," the elder said. "Christian has been attending our church. I thought I should pay you a visit."

"I'm glad that you came by," Anna said. "Please sit down. We're concerned about him."

"He is an unusual young man," George commented, finding a seat. "He had a most interesting experience among the Indian people."

Anna nodded. "He's not quite made himself at home in this neighborhood."

"So I hear."

"Tell us about your church," Anna said. "We don't know much about the Dunkers, except that you are plain people like us."

"We came from the Old Country," George said. "We practice nonconformity and nonresistance, much as you Amish do. We have no creed but the New Testament, and we seek to obey Jesus Christ in everything he commanded."

Just then another knock sounded on the door. It was Jake and Catharine Hertzler. Anna welcomed them and introduced them to Elder Klein. She invited the Hertzlers to sit while she prepared some pennyroyal tea.

"As I was saying," George continued, "we Brethren seek to obey Jesus Christ in everything, as instructed in the New Testament."

"I understand that you baptize by dunking," Bishop Jake said. "That's different than we Amish do it."

"Yes, that's why people call us the Dunkers," George said. "We always baptize outdoors in a flowing stream, just as our Lord Jesus was baptized in the Jordan River."

Anna wondered how the bishop might respond. Baptism was their most contentious point of difference with the

Dunkers—so contentious, in fact, that members who left the Amish faith to join the Dunkers were often shunned.

"The Bible doesn't say that Jesus was dunked under the water," Bishop Jake countered in a friendly manner. "He may simply have waded into the water, and then John the Baptist poured water on his head. That's why we baptize by pouring water on the person's head."

"I don't want to argue about this," George said, "but the word *baptize* really means to immerse something in water. The person being baptized kneels down in the water, and we immerse them three times with their face forward, in the name of the Father, the Son, and the Holy Ghost."

"Do you accept people into your church who have been baptized in a different way?" the bishop asked, with an edge in his voice.

"No," George answered, with no malice. "In order to preserve the unity of our church and to promote a common discipline, we require everyone to be baptized in the same way."

"I don't know if you'll get Christian to be baptized in that way," Anna said. "He can be a bit stubborn about such things."

"We welcome him to come and worship with us, even if he hasn't yet made the decision to be baptized."

Anna smiled. "I think he comes mainly to be with one of the young women who is a friend of our daughter-in-law."

"I've been noticing that," George said soberly. "I pray that his attendance may lead him to a more serious commitment. I don't want to be guilty of stealing someone else's sheep, so I wanted to make sure he wasn't a member of your church already."

"No, not yet." Jacob leaned forward to speak. It appeared to Anna that the words that came next were difficult ones for him to speak. "Will you let Christian join your church if he keeps dressing the way he does now? It seems to me that his Indian appearance is very important to him."

George studied the floor for a moment. "I suppose he will need to make a few changes. Maybe Orpha will be a good influence for him." He paused. "I'm trying to understand why he still tries to be like an Indian now that he has been released from captivity."

"That is hard for us to understand as well," Anna said. "But he seems determined to keep the customs of the Indians."

"Maybe he needs a little more time," George said. "He enjoyed his life among the Indians. Apparently he didn't want to come back home, even when the British wanted him to do so."

Jacob nodded. "Yes, he says he loves the Indians, despite what they did to our family. I suppose it's because he was fairly young when he was taken, and grew up liking to do things the way they did."

"We'll try to instruct him in the ways of the gospel," George said. "We know that some of the Indians came to be believers, so Christian can certainly be one too."

By this time, the water was hot. Anna steeped the tea and then served their guests.

"Have you been a preacher long?" Bishop Jake asked politely.

"Since 1750. I was a Lutheran minister before I was baptized into the Dunker church. That was in Amwell, New Jersey. I moved to this area to be with my brothers."

"You came from the Old Country?" the bishop asked.

"Yes, from Zweibruken, in Rhenish Bavaria. I came to this country in '38, and lived in New Jersey until I moved here."

"So you're a farmer-preacher?" Anna asked.

"Yes, and I do some woodworking too. I'm teaching it to my boys."

Anna wished for more conversation about Christian. "Maybe you can help us understand why Christian finds it so hard to adjust back to life here," she said. "It seems he likes Indian life better than the way we settlers live. After what the Indians did to him, it doesn't make sense."

George knit his brow as he looked at Jacob. "Didn't Christian say that you were captive among the Indians too?

Surely that must help you understand something about his situation."

Jacob shook his head. "The entire time I was with them, I made plans to escape. It was different for my boys. They got to like the Indians and found it hard to leave the villages. Christian and his brother Joseph both went back to visit them once, and I expect Christian will want to go again." Jacob sighed. "He hates farmwork."

"Did he learn to be lazy from the Indians?" George asked.

Jacob shook his head. "No, the Indians aren't lazy." He paused, thinking. "They divide the work differently. The men leave the fieldwork to the women." He shook his head. "Now Christian thinks that way too."

George shook his head as well and rose from his chair. "I don't understand the Indians as well as I'd like. Maybe I'll learn more from Christian." He thanked everyone politely, put on his hat, and then moved toward the door.

Anna watched as he walked up the path. It was all so strange; she didn't know how to make sense of it. She was glad that Christian was feeling drawn toward a faith as similar to theirs as the Dunkers' was. But she still couldn't piece it all together. What was drawing him to attend the Dunker church rather than the church in which he had grown up?

-19-

One Sunday after a church service, Christian and Orpha chatted near the creek. "I love this pink yarrow," Orpha said, stroking the flat-topped cluster of pink florets.

"So do I," Christian said. "It looks beautiful, and you can use it for medicine too."

"Really? How?"

"The Indians use it to make a tea to sweat out a cold. Anna made some this summer. I think she understands plants about as well as the Shawnees."

Orpha paused for a moment as a butterfly hovered overhead before fluttering away in an erratic dance of flight. "Reuben and Leah say that some people think Anna practices witchcraft with her herbal remedies. Like Indians do."

"Whoever told them such a thing?"

"A man named Silas Burkholder. My parents know him. He's an upstanding man."

Christian scowled. "That's ridiculous," he said. "I never saw Anna do anything that looked like witchcraft."

"I can't believe it either," she said, as sober as Christian had ever seen her. "But he convinced Reuben and Leah. Because you live there on the farm, they don't like me being around you."

Christian's skin tightened. "I wouldn't believe a word Silas says. If anyone is practicing witchcraft, it's more likely to be Silas than Anna. I wish Reuben understood that."

Orpha cocked her head. "I mentioned it to Joseph and Sarah the other day. They said your sister Barbara knows all about this. Maybe you should talk to her."

Deep in thought, Christian bade her goodbye.

A couple of days later, he walked to Barbara's house, determined to find out what she knew. He had often walked with *Mam* this way when they went to visit Barbara. How things had changed! Now Barbara's daughter Magdalena, who had been about Franey's age, was becoming a young woman. How the two girls would've enjoyed each other's company if Franey had not been killed in the attack.

As he'd hoped, Barbara was at the bake oven, putting fresh dough onto the hearth. Christian sniffed appreciatively. The smell of freshly baked bread was everywhere, and several loaves lay cooling in a basket nearby.

Christian studied the hearth. The interior dome was shaped like a giant boiled egg, cut in half lengthwise and turned upside down.

"You know when to come," she said with a mock frown, brandishing her *Schiesser*, the long-handled wooden paddle the English called a "peel." "I remember you and Joseph used to fight about who would get the first bite of a fresh loaf when *Mam* was baking." She grinned. "Don't you like the way Anna bakes?" she teased.

"Of course I like Anna's bread," Christian said indignantly. He reached down to pick up one of several round rye baskets filled with a large lump of raw dough and handed it to Barbara. "Anna's a good cook. But I'm still getting used to eating white people's food."

"Christian, you can't mean that! You ate *Mam*'s food for eleven years before you tasted Indian food for the first time. From what I hear about it, I don't see how you can stand to eat it."

"Well, I miss it, although Anna tries to cook like the Indians sometimes. She says she does it just for me."

Barbara snorted. "I'm sure she doesn't do it for *Dat*. He hated most of the food in the Seneca village."

Christian leaned closer, interested. "I wouldn't know. I never heard him talk about it."

"I had to draw it out of him. It wasn't until after the Lancaster treaty conference in '62 that he talked about his experience in captivity. That was about the time he got the idea in his head that he wanted to marry Anna."

"So how long have they been married?"

"Since December '62."

"I suppose you were happy to see him get married," Christian ventured.

His sister glared at Christian as she swung open the bake oven door and pulled out more fresh loaves with her long wooden paddle. "I told him *Mam* wouldn't have wanted that, but he didn't seem to care. You know how *Dat* always worries about what people think. This time, he did what he wanted, even though some people at the church did not approve."

Christian's eyebrows rose. "Really?"

Barbara slipped the fresh loaves into the basket with the other finished loaves and handed it to Christian. "A rumor went around our church about her. Silas Burkholder went to her for help not long after she became a widow. She offered him a drink for his ailments, but he wouldn't take it. He said it was a witch's brew that she made from an old Indian remedy in her herb book full of magical arts."

Christian bit his lip. "Do you think it's true?"

"No, but I don't understand Indians like you do."

"Anna understands Indian remedies," Christian said, "but she's the furthest thing from a witch."

"The other part of the rumor was that Anna was a little too familiar with Silas when she massaged his shoulders. She says she never even touched the man, but *Mam* suspected it could be true. About the same time that happened, Anna brought a pie to our house, and then gave *Dat* a foot massage."

"I remember that. I loved her peaches!"

Barbara nodded vigorously. "The way Anna rubbed *Dat*'s feet and neck got her in trouble with *Mam*." Barbara motioned with her hand. "You might as well come into the house and eat a piece of bread."

Christian followed her. "I met Silas at the smithy's place when I went there to get something welded for *Dat*. The way he treated me, I wouldn't believe a word he said about Anna. I think he's out to make trouble."

Barbara snorted. "I guess you can think whatever you want about him. Now if you promise to help me dry some apple slices in the oven after it cools down a little, I'll let you have some fresh rye bread."

"Of course I'll help. I want to see if your bread is as good as *Mam*'s used to be." Christian followed Barbara toward the house. "Anna will never take the place of *Mam*, but I think she's a pretty good stepmother."

Barbara shrugged. "I'm learning to get along with her without complaining too much."

"What's there to complain about? She loves your children."

Barbara frowned. "Sometimes I wish she wouldn't try so hard to take *Mam*'s place in the family. No one can ever do that."

Christian refused to back off. "She was *Dat*'s choice, so we might as well get used to it. I can't think of any other widow in this neighborhood I'd rather have for a stepmother."

Barbara swung open the cabin door and motioned for Christian to put the loaves onto the table. "Do you want some *lattwaerrick* (apple butter) on it?"

Christian's mouth watered. "Of course."

Barbara cut open a loaf and spread it with apple butter. Just then a wail emanated from behind the house. Barbara stood and jammed the remainder of the loaf into his hand. "I have to go see what's wrong with Ruth. Here, take some bread with you to chew on while you're walking home."

Christian refused to budge. "Come on, Barbara. I wanted to hear more about that rumor Silas was spreading around about Anna."

Barbara waved him away. "Come back someday when you're ready to talk about something else besides Anna."

Christian wasn't sure whether to laugh or cry as he said goodbye and headed home. Now he knew why Barbara sometimes seemed cool to Anna. But was it fair? It bothered him that church members spread a rumor that wasn't true. Why should they believe Silas rather than Anna? She was such a sincere member of the church! Back in the Shawnee village, the women were always more believable than the men. In the rare times a man was found guilty of raping a woman there, the village made him pay for it with his life.

If Silas has been telling lies about Anna, I wonder what he's saying about me?

A couple of months after Christian talked with Barbara about the rumor, he saw Anna working in the melon patch. He watched as she stooped to pull a ripe melon from the vine. After a year at home, he had come to love Anna. She was kind.

Plus, she was a good healer. Her special lotion always helped him cope with mosquito bites. And she'd even made a lotion to treat his poison ivy. Using her herbal remedies was like being back among the Shawnees. Her bread was good too, as was her jam—things he'd missed during his stay among the Indians.

It was August, and *Dat*'s fruit trees were ripening fast. Christian walked to the orchard and looked at the top of the corner tree, where a cluster of three pears clung at the end of the topmost branch. His mouth watered. *I've got to get those.* He hoisted himself onto the first branch and kept climbing up until he got almost within reach of his prize. He peeked toward the watermelon patch and saw Anna looking at him. He waved at her and she waved back and then came walking toward him.

"I'm getting my breakfast," he said.

"Will you pick one for me too?" Anna asked.

"Sure." He scrunched out a little farther on the branch, which bowed under his weight.

"Be careful. Those branches are apt to break."

"Don't worry." He hung on to the branch with one hand and stretched to grab the pears, which were dangling beyond the reach of his fingers.

The branch swayed. He heard a crack as it gave way underneath him. He landed heavily on the branch below. The branch creaked and bowed heavily. In the nick of time, he grabbed a different one to keep from falling as that branch broke as well.

A sharp pain shot through his ribs. The end of a dead branch jabbed into the side of his chest. He dangled there for a few moments and then let himself drop the rest of the way to the ground. Ripe pears fell in a shower around him.

Anna rushed over. "Christian! Are you all right?"

"I think so." He rubbed his ribs. Blood oozed from a heavy scratch. He sat for a moment, trying to feel for broken bones. Tenderly, he moved his arms and legs. More confidently, as nothing seemed unduly injured, he got up. "I'll be all right," he said to Anna.

She still looked worried.

He bent down to pick up several pears. "I got enough for both of us to eat for breakfast." He handed one to her.

She laughed as she took it. "Thank you. That's not the way I usually pick pears. Are you sure nothing is broken? Let's get something on that big scratch."

Christian ate two of the pears as Anna mixed a lotion and spread it on his ribs. "I was glad to see you in the orchard," she said. "I was hoping to pick pears today. Maybe you can help me, if you're not feeling too shaken up."

Christian nodded. "Sure, I'll help you." Picking fruit would be much more interesting than cutting hay in the hot sun with *Dat*.

Anna went to a small bookshelf and took out her illustrated herb book. She laid it open on the table. "Look, Christian."

Christian flipped through the pages, pausing to admire some of the botanical drawings. "What a beautiful book. Where did you get it?" he asked.

"My father passed it on to me."

"I love these illustrations." He paused. "May I take it to the garden?"

"Sure. But be sure to take care of it."

Outside, Christian compared the drawings in the book with the plants in her garden. For the first time since his return to the Northkill, he longed to read again, to be able to understand all the information and captions that went with each drawing. *Mam* had always said he was going to be the best reader in the family, but that was before . . .

"I admire the way you use plants to heal people," Christian said. "That's the way the Indians do it. If we knew how to use all the Creator's plants well, we'd stay healthy."

"That's what the author of this book teaches," Anna said. "He explains how to use plants to make all kinds of remedies: teas, spirits, plasters, and so forth."

Christian paused, considering. Should he mention Silas's accusation? Cautiously, he asked, "Is there anything in this book about magic cures?"

"No, not this one. But some herb books tell about *Braucherei* (powwowing). That's witchcraft. I don't believe in that. And I'm not like the healers who claim their remedies come from Indians descended from the Lost Tribes of Israel."

That was reassuring; it put the nix to the rumor about Anna practicing witchcraft. But Christian recalled Black Elk and his appeal to the spirits. "I think the Indian shamans sometimes tried to cure that way."

Anna's face turned dark. "Some people accuse me of using Indian cures, and others call me a witch." She looked at him beseechingly. "It's not true. Rumors like that can be very destructive."

Relief and sympathy washed over Christian as he saw the hurt on Anna's face. How could anyone tell such lies about this woman, who had shown him nothing but kindness? Anger surged through him as he thought about Silas. How could he help clear Anna's reputation? Maybe he would start by telling Orpha what he had learned about the way Anna made her medicines.

Dat was walking in from the barn, so Anna excused herself and left Christian in the garden alone. He browsed through the book contentedly. Perhaps he could pick pears later in the morning and go fishing in the afternoon.

Not long after, Anna waved him into the house. She offered him a slice of bread on a plate with a scrambled egg. He ate both the bread and the egg, something he'd been reluctant to do since returning to the Northkill. He was still getting used to eggs, since the Shawnees never kept chickens.

After he finished eating, Anna gave him a basket for each hand and led the way back to the orchard. The scratch on Christian's bare chest was an angry welt. He was glad for the salve that Anna had put on it.

Christian stopped by the barn to pick up a crude wooden ladder. He followed Anna to the tree he had climbed before breakfast. More cautiously this time, he set the ladder against a large branch. He held a basket in one hand and picked pears with the other. Anna hummed aloud as she plucked the fruit from the lowest branches.

Christian swatted away the scratchy branches that poked against his sore chest. It was going to be a hot day, and he looked forward to fishing in the coolness of the nearby woods. He soon had a basketful. He handed it to Anna, who rewarded him with a big smile. She passed him another empty basket.

When that basket was full, Anna walked to the spring-house and returned with a cup of cold water. He climbed down the ladder and took the cup into his hands. It looked like the same metal cup he'd used as a child. He remembered the times he'd sneaked away from onerous jobs in the fields in order to slake his thirst. Yes, and the time he'd poured a cool

cup of water down Barbara's back. Ha! He remembered the
way she'd whacked his ear for it.

He handed the cup back to Anna and climbed back up the
ladder onto a branch farther up. He broke off a small branch
and hung the basket onto the stub that remained. He shooed
away the flies that buzzed around his head and landed on the
pears, sucking eagerly from the juice where he'd broken their
skin. At least there were no mosquitoes.

Christian stopped several times to eat a pear, and by the
time they had finished picking the fruit on three of the pear
trees in the orchard, he was a little sick in his stomach. Maybe
dried corn would help.

Together, they put away the ladder and brought all the pears
to the house. They spread them onto the floor in a corner of
the room, where they could finish ripening before Anna cut
them up to dry. "Thank you for helping me," Anna said. "I'll
make you some pear kuchen from these." She paused. "Would
you mind carrying a basket of these down to Joseph's house? I
know he really likes pears."

"I'd be glad to do that," Christian replied. "I'll take them
right away."

For the first time, as he embarked on the long walk to
Joseph's house, he felt a twinge of satisfaction about farmwork. Doing something for Anna made him feel like it was his
own work, not *Dat's* work thrust upon him.

Besides, Joseph and Sarah were friends with Orpha, and
they might provide an opportunity for him to get to know her
better.

-20-

I t was some months after Anna's chance meeting with Orpha at the neighbor's house that Christian learned about it. He determined to meet Orpha there sometime, away from the watchful gaze of her foster parents. Twice he walked past the house without seeing her. In mid-September, as he made his way down the rutted path that ran past the Heisey farm, his fortune turned. His heart beat faster as he spied Orpha outside, tossing a stuffed ball with the children.

Christian stopped, pretending a deep interest in two squirrels chasing each other through the trees. He loitered nearby until Orpha looked his way.

"Christian!"

"Oh, hello, Orpha." Christian tried to look nonchalant as he pointed toward the apple trees that stood nearby. "It looks like these apples are ready to pick."

"Yes, they are good for cider. We've picked several bushels." She paused. "I love apples. I never get tired of eating them."

"Would you like me to pick one for you now?" Christian asked.

"Sure. Get one for yourself too."

"Come with me, Orpha," Christian said. "You can show me the one you want." If only she would follow him into the orchard, they might have a few moments together alone.

With a quick look toward the children, who were happily playing with the ball by themselves, Orpha nodded. "Okay, but not for long. I need to keep an eye on those rascals."

They walked toward the orchard, side by side. "I see you have different varieties," Christian said, struggling to make small talk and sounding formal. "Which one do you like best?" Inwardly, he kicked himself.

Orpha pointed to a tree that was heavy with yellow apples. "Those are my favorites. They are really tasty. We have a lot of them this season."

"The biggest ones are at the top," Christian said. He swung into the tree, then climbed up the branches. The branches bowed under his weight. He moved out onto a big branch to get a beautiful yellow apple that lay inches beyond his reach.

"Be careful," Orpha said. "Don't break your neck! That branch doesn't look very strong."

"I've got it," Christian said as he snared a big golden apple. *This is sure to impress Orpha and make her happy.* He picked another one for himself and then made his way down the tree with the two apples in his hand.

"You didn't have to go to all that trouble for me," Orpha said as Christian dropped the last few feet to the ground.

"You choose," he said, holding both apples out toward her.

"Thank you. I'll take this one." She chose the smaller one and rubbed it clean with her apron before taking a bite. The sunlight glowed on several wisps of hair that slipped out from under her head covering.

Christian rubbed the remaining apple against his shirt, then also took a bite. He swallowed and said, "I could help you pick apples this week."

"Don't your parents have an orchard too?"

"Yes, we grow lots of fruit. Several kinds of apples, peaches, and pears. We also make a lot of cider."

"Then I suppose you'll have more than enough to do in your orchard for the next few weeks."

"*Dat* says we should always help our neighbors when we can," Christian said, a bit self-righteously. "People came to help us with the rye harvest. Now I can help you with the fruit."

There was an awkward silence as Orpha finished the last bite of her apple and threw the core on the ground. "I'd have to ask my parents," she said quietly.

"Why should they mind?" Christian tried not to sound too anxious.

"Reuben and Leah are a little strict. They don't like for me to spend time alone with men."

That was what he had expected. But he was irritated nonetheless. "We wouldn't have to be alone. We could pick apples at the same time other people are here."

Orpha avoided his gaze. "I'd have to see what they say."

Christian tried a different approach. "We're going to have an apple *schnitzing* at our house later this month," Christian said. "Would you like to come?"

Orpha paused to consider. "Who else will be there?"

"Some of our neighbors, mostly people who are part of *Dat* and Anna's church. We'll have a lot of fun. I can show you the new bow and arrows that Joseph and I made. We'll bob for apples and do some singing. Then we'll cut up apples to dry."

"Reuben and Leah say we have plenty of things to do in our own church. I'm going to a *schnitzing* at one of the member's houses next Wednesday evening."

"Could I come with you?" Christian asked. It seemed forward of him to ask, but how else was he to get to know her?

Orpha looked at the ground. "I don't feel free to invite you without permission. But Joseph and Sarah will likely be there. Maybe you can ask them if you can come."

Discouraged, Christian relented. "Okay, I can talk to them." He searched anxiously for words to keep Orpha engaged in the conversation. "Do you want another apple? I can pick another one for you."

"No, I think I've had enough."

Just then Mrs. Heisey called. "Orpha! I need you."

"I've got to go," Orpha said. "Thanks again for picking such a beautiful apple for me. And I'd love to watch you shoot arrows sometime."

Christian sighed as he watched her walk toward the house. *She sure is pretty.* If only he could find a way to spend more time with her, to prove that he was worthy of her affection.

He worried she was using Reuben and Leah as an excuse to keep him at arm's length. Maybe he should introduce himself to them and ask them directly.

Women were hard to understand. How was he to know what Orpha was thinking? Did her reluctance to spend time with him have something to do with his doubts about Christian faith or his lack of enthusiasm for the church? Orpha spoke enthusiastically about her personal faith in Jesus Christ, which was hard for him to understand, even when she tried to explain it. He wished he could embrace faith like hers, but his doubts loomed too large to ignore.

If Orpha's foster parents were worried that he'd be a bad influence on her because of the rumor that Anna's herbal remedies were based on witchcraft, it might pay to talk to Anna about that story. If Reuben and Leah simply didn't like the length or style of his hair—well, he wasn't ready to change that. At least not yet.

The next day, Christian walked to Joseph's home to get permission to come to the *schnitzing*. "Of course you can come as our guest," Sarah said as he explained his situation. "That would be a good time for you to see Orpha."

Joseph nodded his agreement. "It will be held at Aaron Benedict's home, a little ways up the creek from George Klein's house."

At the apple *schnitzing* the following Wednesday night, Christian found himself nervous. As a young boy, these events had always been a time for fun and games. He recalled a time when he watched his older brother Jakey flirt with a young woman to whom he was engaged at the time of the Indian attack. *Jakey*. He sobered as he remembered his death.

There were more than a dozen people at the *schnitzing* when Christian arrived. Orpha was not in sight. Christian helped carry the last of several baskets of apples to the place where they would be cut into pieces.

He pulled out the knife from his belt to begin cutting the apples. Orpha arrived shortly after, accompanied by a young man whom Christian had seen at the Dunker Church. He looked to be about Orpha's age, and a bit taller. Christian drew in his breath as he watched the two of them chat with each other. They were obviously good friends. But is that all they were?

He tried not to stare but kept glancing in their direction as the two of them worked next to each other at a table, helping to cut up apples and spread them out on a sheet to dry.

Christian tried to hide his irritation that Orpha was so openly friendly with another young man. Was she completely uninterested in him? Or was she letting him know that she preferred someone else?

Christian studied the young man, trying to determine what might draw her to him. He had to admit that he was quite handsome, with wavy brown hair. He seemed socially at ease, and found ways to make Orpha laugh. Others around him laughed too, and a pang of jealousy mixed with self-pity pricked Christian's heart.

Why didn't Orpha laugh at his jokes in the same way? Back in the Shawnee village, it was easy for him to make people laugh, particularly when he poked fun at the stupidity and ineptness of his own white people. Nobody laughed at those jokes in the Northkill.

Watching Orpha and the young man laugh together reminded him that he had laughed so much more as a young boy than he did now. Was that why Orpha was reluctant to spend time with him? The year since he had returned to the Northkill had been full of so much worry. When might he feel the simple urge to laugh again?

The next time Orpha laughed, Christian caught her eye. She immediately looked away. *She must not want to see me. Or maybe she's embarrassed that I'm watching her spend time with someone else.*

He scowled at Orpha, who looked self-conscious. She laughed less too. Why hadn't she told him that she was planning to come with someone else? What was the best thing to do now? Should he leave the *schnitzing* to save himself and Orpha some embarrassment?

He slipped into the darkness that lay beyond the circles cast by the lantern lights, considering. He was about to walk home when he saw Joseph approaching.

"What's the matter?" Joseph asked.

"Nothing," Christian said, kicking at the ground. "I just needed to get away for a little bit."

"It's about Orpha, isn't it? You aren't happy that she's with another man."

"Of course not. I invited her to come with me and she said she couldn't come, and now she shows up with someone else."

Joseph raised his eyebrows. "She doesn't owe you anything."

Christian pouted. "I wonder what she sees in that man she's with."

"Quit being so bothered about it. Come have some fun. We're going to play some games and do some singing."

Christian shrugged his shoulders and followed Joseph back to where the children were bobbing for apples. He paused for a moment, watching a boy trying to grab an apple with his teeth.

Christian grinned as another boy sneaked from behind and shoved the bobber's head down hard into the water. The boy who was dunked sprang up and swished his hair, sprinkling the people who stood close by. They shrieked and moved back. Christian didn't mind getting wet. It was a warm September night, and the moon was shining brightly.

But as Christian watched the fun, his stomach turned queasy and his legs felt weak. He slipped back into the darkness. His heart began to beat rapidly and his breath came in short gasps. *What is wrong with me?* he thought as he sat cross-legged on the ground. Bobbing for apples was supposed to be fun.

He hadn't felt so strange in years, not since the Indians had attacked their home in the early hours of the morning after the apple *schnitzing.* That night, he had been the boy bobbing for apples, oblivious to the danger that would strike a few hours later.

Christian listened for the sound of an enemy in the woods. An involuntary shudder swept over him as the resonant hoot of a great horned owl pierced the night. Was it an Indian sending a signal?

He took a deep breath and told himself that it was unlikely that any Indians would be nearby now, unless his friends from the Shawnee village had decided to come visit him.

Christian was lost in his thoughts when Joseph appeared again. "I thought you were going to join in the fun. Why are you back here again?"

"I'm not feeling well." Christian wondered whether to tell Joseph about his strange fears. "I was thinking about the last time we had an apple *schnitzing.*"

Joseph nodded. "Well, we haven't *schnitzed* apples since we were taken by the Indians."

"That's when I'm talking about. The Indians were probably watching us from the woods that night, planning their attack."

Joseph shook his head, irritated. "I'm sure there aren't any Indians here now, so come and have a good time. Besides, the Indians are our friends."

Christian followed Joseph back to the *schnitzing,* but his heart wasn't in it. His stomach hurt, and he felt a sense of dread all evening. Although the others laughed and joined in the games; nothing was fun for him. The real reason he'd come to the *schnitzing* wasn't for games, but to see Orpha. To see her with another man was so disappointing that he thought of going to see Summer Rain. She was white, but at least she understood Indians. Certainly better than Orpha did.

-21-

Over the next several days, Christian tried to put Orpha out of his mind. But whenever he thought about Summer Rain or other women he knew, they fell short in comparison. How was he to win Orpha's affection? At times, she seemed delighted to be with him. At other times, she held back. Why?

Maybe Barbara could help him figure out the best way to approach Orpha. Barbara certainly understood women's ways better than he. On the last day of September, he made up his mind to talk to her.

As Christian approached Barbara's house, he saw her working outside in the kitchen garden. She was pulling weeds and throwing them onto a pile outside the garden fence. Christian walked up to the pile and watched her for a few moments.

"Can I help you do some weeding?"

"Of course. I'd be happy to let you pull them all yourself," Barbara told him. "Since it rained last night, they pull pretty easily. They got away from me in the dry weather, when they were hard to pull."

Christian swung open the gate and walked to where Barbara was working.

"You can pull the weeds in the patch over there," she said, pointing to the place where the red-veined beets grew. "Just be sure not to pull any of the beets with the weeds."

Christian laughed. "I know better than that."

Barbara smiled. "Okay. When you finish with that part, I'll get you some apple cider to drink, and then we can talk. I'm sure you didn't come here to pick weeds."

Christian dug into the task, yanking out weeds by the roots and tossing them onto a small pile nearby.

"I like to knock the dirt off the roots before I throw them out," Barbara said. "There's no use wasting good soil."

Christian grimaced. *Why must she be so bossy?* He tried to comply with her wishes, noisily whacking the weeds onto one of the boards that formed the path and tossing them onto the pile. A butterfly flitted around him as a mockingbird went through its repertoire in a nearby tree.

When Christian had pulled all the weeds from among the beets as well as the cabbages, Barbara left to get the cider. He rested for a few moments, watching a blue jay chase away a couple of robins in a tree nearby. A hog wandered up to the weed pile and rooted through it with its snout.

While Barbara was gone, Christian rehearsed how he might get the best advice from her. She loved nothing more than to give advice, if she was in the right mood. Sometimes, she could be callous, dismissing his concerns with a wave of her hand. At other times she listened well and really paid attention to his problems. *Dat* always said, "Medicine and advice are two things more pleasant to give than to receive." It might be painful to hear Barbara's advice, but asking for it was the easiest way to get her attention, and she might be able to help. He needed it.

Barbara returned shortly with some cider, and they stood in the shade of a large oak, drinking it together.

"I thought you might be able to give me some advice," Christian began.

Barbara leaned forward as he spoke.

"I've been getting to know this girl named Orpha Rupp. She lives not far from Joseph's house. I met her at Joseph and Sarah's wedding."

Barbara nodded. "I know who she is. She's part of the Dunker church. So you'd like to marry her?"

Christian grimaced. Barbara was her usual self, jumping ahead of what he was trying to say. "I wouldn't say that, but I'd like to get to know her better."

"That shouldn't be hard to do," Barbara said crisply. "You know where she lives and where she goes to church."

"You make it sound so easy. It's hard to find time alone with her. I don't think her parents like me."

"I'm sure they don't want you dragging her off to Indian country."

"Why should they think I'd do that?"

"Christian, think about the way you dress and wear your hair," his sister said, as if she were trying to be patient with him. "It's obvious that you're not ready to settle down here. Why would any girl want to marry you?"

Christian was silent for a moment. This conversation wasn't going the way he had hoped. "Maybe if I find the right girl who shows an interest in me, I'll want to stay around here."

Barbara shook her head. "It doesn't work that way. First you have to prove that you're going to stay. *Then* some girl might be interested in you."

"Orpha seems to like me, at least a little bit. But when I invited her to come to the *schnitzing* with me this week, she said no."

"I can't blame her. You have to spend more time getting to know her without asking her to do something that everybody can see."

"I already tried that."

Barbara shrugged and held out the pitcher of cider. "Do you want another drink?" Christian nodded and she poured him more.

Christian cleared his throat. "I was hoping you could talk to Orpha," he said. "Maybe you could find out whether or not she really likes me, and how I might get to know her better."

Barbara's lips parted in a soft smile. "I might be able to do that."

"Please don't tell her that I sent you."

"Of course not." She chuckled and added, "Unless she asks."

Christian socked her lightly on the shoulder the way he had done as a boy when she teased him. "You wouldn't dare."

Barbara laughed. "I'll try to find a time and a way that will seem natural to her. Since she is Joseph and Sarah's friend, I'll talk to them first."

Christian sighed with relief. "Thank you."

"Don't be surprised if she says she doesn't want to marry an Indian. Or someone who acts like one."

"Don't ask her about marriage," Christian said. "Ask her about getting to know me better."

"Either way, she'll say the same thing."

"Let me know as soon as you find out," Christian said as he handed her his empty cup. "Thanks, Barbara."

She hugged him briefly and he started back home. Was it good for Barbara to be involved? He hoped so. But it was hard to know.

A week later, Christian went back to Barbara's home, eager to see what she'd heard from Orpha. When he arrived, Barbara's husband, Cristy, was scutching flax inside the barn. A dust-filled shaft of sunlight streamed onto his work, accenting the cobwebs that sagged from the wooden beams.

Christian stood for a few minutes watching Cristy beat the woody stem off the long interior fibers with a wooden scutching knife and a small iron scraper. It was early October, and the harvest would soon be in. Christian knew it was time to get the flax ready for the linen weavers.

Soon Barbara appeared. "You came at a good time," she said with a smile. "Would you rather scutch or heckle?"

"Must I always work when I come to visit you?" Christian asked with a fake pout. "The last time I came here, you asked me to pull weeds."

"That's true, but you gave me work to do as well," Barbara replied. "You sent me to make Orpha Rupp want to marry you. That's not an easy job." She winked as she spoke, so Christian relaxed. She must have at least a little good news.

Christian wasn't eager to work with flax at all, but heckling the fibers appealed to him more than whacking off the stem. "I'll heckle."

Barbara motioned him to the side of the barn, where she'd set up a small table with four heckling combs, arranged from coarse to fine. "I shouldn't need to show you how to do this," she said, pulling a handful of strands through the coarsest comb. "You watched *Dat* and *Mam* do it often enough."

Too often, Christian thought. He gathered up the fibers where Cristy had tossed them onto the ground and began to pull them through the heckling combs as Barbara looked on. "So what did Orpha say?"

"I didn't get to talk to Orpha, but I had a long talk with Sarah."

Christian's face fell. "What does Sarah know about this?"

"Sarah knows a lot. She talks to Orpha often."

"So what did Sarah say?"

Barbara smiled. "You really want to know, don't you?"

Christian straightened up as he held several strands of flax fibers in his hand. "Why else would I be asking?" Barbara could be so exasperating. How did Cristy put up with it?

"Sarah said that Orpha likes you. She talks about you often."

Christian's eyes brightened. What more could he hope for? "Really? So why can't I see her more?"

"Her foster parents don't want her to spend time alone with you."

"What do they have against me?"

"It's not that they don't like you. But they have some goals in mind for Orpha. They don't think she'll reach them if she gets married to you."

"Why would they think that? They hardly know me." Christian yanked a handful of flax fibers through the finest comb, splitting it into the thin strands that would make fine linen. Despite his disappointment about Orpha's foster parents, his head was awhirl with joy. Orpha liked him? She talked about him often?

"You won't change their minds unless you change your ways," Barbara said.

"Why should I try to please them?" Christian asked. "It's Orpha I'm interested in."

At that moment, three of Barbara's children rounded the corner of the barn. "What is Christian doing here?" Mary asked.

"We're talking," Barbara replied. "Now go back to your play."

Mary looked up at Christian's face. "What are you talking about? Can I listen?"

Barbara shook her head.

Mary stuck out her lower lip. "I want to hear what you're talking about."

Barbara gave her a stern look. "No, you go and play. If you don't, I'll make you carry some flax for *Dat*."

Christian suppressed a grin as his niece frowned and stomped away. The young girl was as persistent as her mother. *The apple doesn't fall far from the tree.*

Barbara sighed and turned back to Christian. "You won't be able to marry Orpha without permission from her foster parents. You're going to have to deal with them whether you like it or not."

"We could run away and live somewhere else."

"Don't be ridiculous. Orpha loves her friends at the Dunker church. She wants to live on a farm around here."

Christian looked grim. "I hate farming. I don't want to be like *Dat*. He's so tied down to the farm that he can hardly find time to go hunting and fishing."

Barbara was silent. Then she said, "You're telling me what you *don't* want. I'd like to hear what you *do* want."

Christian was silent. She was right. "I want Orpha to like me," he said softly.

"You have to want something more than that. What do you want to do for a living? What do you want out of life?"

Christian hung his head. "I wish I knew. For a while, I thought I would go back to my Indian village, but I don't think that will work out. So I don't know what to do."

Barbara looked directly into Christian's eyes. "Like I said, you need to figure out what you want to do with your life. You won't get Orpha to marry you until you've proven to Orpha and her foster parents that you're the kind of husband they want you to be."

She returned to heckling with vigor, drawing the fibers through the coarser combs and tossing them to Christian for the finer step.

He worked for a little while, deep in thought. He wouldn't tell Barbara, but it felt good to work with his hands as he was thinking. Barbara would soon spin the fibers he was holding in his hands, and they'd come back from the weaver as linen cloth. Perhaps she'd make Mary a new dress; she'd certainly outgrown the one she was wearing.

"I need to go," he told Barbara when they'd caught up with Cristy's work. "I know the children want your attention, and I've taken too much of your time already."

Christian turned and walked toward the path. It was immensely comforting to know that Orpha liked him. If he couldn't get Orpha to come his way, maybe he could go her way. He could keep attending the Dunker church; Elder Klein seemed friendly enough, and at least he could see Orpha there without raising anyone's suspicions. Maybe he needed to be more patient. And persistent.

-22-

On the strength of Barbara's encouragement to pursue Orpha's affection, Christian decided to attend the Dunker church almost every week. One Sunday as he was ready to leave the church service, a stout man approached him with two boys at his side. The man seemed nervous.

"I'm Simon Gish," he said. He paused, struggling to speak. "These are my sons, Lester and Daniel. I'm glad to see that you've been coming to our church."

Christian nodded. "I appreciate the people here." He looked at the two boys, who stood squirming under their father's gaze.

"My boys have something to say to you," Simon said, looking down at them as he spoke. "I learned they were involved in some mischief that affected you some months back. Boys, you tell Christian what you have to say."

There was a long silence. Finally, the older boy spoke. "Dad said we have to tell you we're sorry for what we did to your wigwam," Lester said, looking down at the floor.

"We were with some other boys," Daniel added, "and we helped them burn it down."

Christian's face hardened. "Why did you do it?" he asked.

Both of the boys tugged to get away, but their father gripped their shoulders with his large hands.

"I don't know," Lester said.

"Me neither," Daniel added.

Christian glared at the boys, who were still looking down. "Is there something wrong with having a wigwam?"

The boys shrugged. "I guess not," Lester said in a quiet voice.

"Do you realize that was my home? A wigwam is an Indian house."

"I didn't think about that," Lester said, pulling hard against his father's grip. "I didn't mean to hurt anybody."

"What would you say if I burned down your house?"

"That's different," Daniel ventured.

"How is it different?"

"Yours was a little Indian shack. Ours is a real house."

Christian took a sharp breath to tamp down his rising anger. "What don't you like about Indian houses?" Christian looked at Simon and then at his sons, who remained silent.

"You said other boys were involved," Christian said, trying not to glare at the boys. "Who were they?"

Simon squeezed the boys' arms hard. "I want you to talk to this man. You did something wrong, and I want you to make it right."

"We promised not to tell," Lester said.

Christian looked around, noticing that Elder Klein stood nearby, observing. He didn't want to prolong the confrontation, but he wasn't about to let the boys off easily.

Christian motioned for Elder Klein to come over, and then looked at Simon. "Have your boys tell Elder Klein what you did. Maybe he can help you make it right."

"I knew about this," Elder Klein said to Christian. "I wondered when the boys were going to talk to you."

"They say other boys were involved. I'd like to know who they were, but the boys won't tell."

Elder Klein looked down at the boys: "I think the boys should talk to their friends this week, and if they're all willing to say they're sorry, we can meet next Sunday to talk about a way for them to make amends." He peered at Simon. "Does that seem like a workable plan?"

After Simon agreed, Elder Klein looked at Christian. "Would you be willing to meet with the boys and their fathers?"

"Yes."

Simon released his grip on his boys, and they quickly ran outside.

"We'll plan to meet after church next Sunday," Klein said. "I'm glad we're getting to the bottom of this."

"I am too," Simon said, and turned to walk away.

"I think they hate Indians," Christian said to Elder Klein. "That's why I wasn't ready to let them off easily."

"Don't be too hard on them," Klein said. "Boys will be boys, and sometimes they do mischievous things without thinking."

"What could be worse than burning down my house? People don't go around burning down other people's houses unless they have something against them."

"That's true. But boys sometimes dare each other to do bad things, without thinking of the way it hurts others."

Christian paused, thinking. "They probably heard their parents saying bad things about Indians, so they didn't think it would hurt to burn down my wigwam."

Elder Klein took a deep breath. "Don't be too quick to accuse. Let's first hear from the boys, and then you can decide what to say. It will be better for you to forgive them than to hold a grudge against them. It could be a good lesson for them to learn."

"I hope so," Christian said. He was grateful to learn that it was boys, and not older men, who had burned down the wigwam. But boys often did things that reflected their parents' attitudes.

The week dragged by, and Christian worried. What if the fathers turned against him and took the part of their sons? What if Elder Klein called it mischief and let them get by with it? What if the other boys refused to come?

He was glad Elder Klein would take charge of the meeting; he could force the boys to show they were sorry. Otherwise, he wasn't about to offer them forgiveness. The boys needed to make up for what they had done.

As he pondered what he might demand of the boys, he thought of Joseph. He had helped to build the wigwam, and he understood Indian ways. Perhaps he could ask Joseph to meet with the group next Sunday. That way he wouldn't feel so alone. The more he thought about it, the more it made sense to invite Joseph to accompany him the next Sunday.

The next Sunday, Christian headed for the Dunker church. His stomach was tied in knots. He found some comfort in knowing that Joseph would join him in the meeting with the boys and their fathers.

Elder Klein came to meet him when he arrived at the door. "I'm sure you're wondering about the meeting this afternoon," he said. Christian nodded.

"I learned that the two other boys were from the Amish church, but all three fathers agreed to meet this afternoon at two o'clock at my home."

"Is it all right if I have Joseph with me?" Christian asked. "He helped me to build the wigwam."

"Yes, it will be fine for Joseph to be there with you. I hope that you don't make it too hard for the boys. All four of them have already gotten a licking from their fathers."

Christian shrank back. The Indians wouldn't have punished their sons that way. They would have found a way to shame them instead of hitting them.

"I must prepare for the service now," Elder Klein said, "but I'll meet you with the others in my living room at two o'clock today."

The worship service crawled by slowly. The elder's sermon was about forgiveness. At the beginning of his sermon, Elder Klein asked the congregation to recite the Lord's Prayer, and then he talked about the phrase "And forgive us our debts, as we forgive our debtors." He told about the way that Jesus forgave his enemies who nailed him to the cross.

Twice while he was listening to the sermon, Christian saw Elder Klein looking directly at him. Was the preacher aiming his sermon specifically at him, trying to convince him to forgive the boys that had burned down his wigwam?

I can forgive them if they show that they're truly sorry and do something to make it right, he thought. He had already rebuilt his wigwam, so he didn't need help with that. *Maybe Joseph will think of something they could do.*

Faithful to his word, Elder Klein led the meeting that afternoon. On one side of the room sat the four boys with the three fathers.

Christian sat opposite them with Joseph at his side. The tone of the meeting was sober, with the boys mostly looking down as Elder Klein addressed them. "Boys," he said, looking at each one in a firm yet tender gaze, "you all know we've come here today because you've done something wrong against this young man, and you desire to make it right. Is that correct?"

Each one nodded solemnly as he looked at them in turn.

"Then I want each one of you to tell this young man that you're sorry," he continued. He paused as he looked at each boy, waiting.

"I'm sorry," each one said in turn, looking down at the floor.

The elder paused for a moment: "Is there anything more that any one of you boys would like to say?" They all shook their heads in turn.

The elder looked at Christian. "Do you have anything to say?"

Christian nodded. "Yes, I think the boys should do something to show they're sorry. Joseph, what do you think?"

Joseph leaned forward. "I was thinking about this on the way to the church service this morning. I remembered that Jakey and I once did something naughty like you boys did. We started a little fire near a neighbor's old outhouse, and threw burning sticks at the side of the outhouse to scare the old man who was using it. When he ran out and hollered at us, we ran away so he wouldn't know who did it. We didn't realize that some old leaves were smoldering on the ground in back of the outhouse. It burned down that night." He looked at Christian. "Don't you remember? You were with us when that happened."

The boys smirked as Joseph recounted the incident.

Christian was irked. "But we didn't mean to burn down that outhouse. And besides, that's a lot different than a wigwam, which was my home."

"But I don't believe that we ever told that man we're sorry," Joseph went on. "Maybe we should do that before we ask these young boys to do it."

Christian was incredulous. He looked around at Elder Klein and the three fathers. All sat stony-faced, waiting for his response. Suddenly he thought of Orpha, suspecting that she'd likely agree with Joseph if she heard about the outhouse.

"So you don't think they should do anything?" he asked Joseph.

"Yes, I've been thinking of something they could do," Joseph said. "I think they should spend a half a day with the two of us, learning about the Indians, so they'd know how much a wigwam means to us. We could teach them how to use a knife and hatchet, shoot some arrows, and play some Indian games."

Joseph looked at the boys. "Would you like to do that?"

All four boys nodded eagerly.

Elder Klein looked at the fathers. "Are you okay with that?"

The three men looked around at one another and then nodded in turn.

"Then we will consider this matter settled," Klein said. "You men can arrange when you want to get together to learn about the Indians."

After a short discussion, they agreed to meet the following Thursday. Christian felt a rush of relief. In spite of his disgust at Joseph for mentioning the outhouse, it provided the chance to teach the boys some helpful things about the Shawnees and Delawares. He would look forward to that.

As the day approached, Christian half-dreaded the event. What if the boys made fun of the Indian games or participated in a halfhearted manner? Joseph would be there. That helped. He could make it a success. If these young boys enjoyed the games as much as his nieces and nephews did at the family gathering, it would be well worth the effort.

Christian woke with the late October sun and washed his face in the creek. He strung his bow and set up a sheaf of rye for a target. After shooting a half-dozen arrows for practice, he felt confident. Now he'd be able to show those boys what he could do. Surely none of the fathers or sons could come close to matching his accuracy with the bow.

Not long after Joseph came by, Simon Gish arrived with his boys, Lester and Daniel. They were followed by the other two fathers with their sons. "Can I join in the fun," Simon asked, "or is this for the boys only?"

Christian looked at Joseph, and raised an eyebrow. Fathers played games with their children back in the Shawnee village.

"Sure, you fathers may take part if you wish," Joseph said. "Christian and I will show you some skills we learned in our Indian villages. We'll play some games too, which you'll really enjoy. But let's start by taking a walk in the woods to see what we can find."

Joseph led the group into the woods, where Christian taught them to identify animal tracks. "Look at this," he said, happening upon the fresh hoofprints of a deer. "Let's see what we can learn about this animal."

He had never felt more alive as he helped the group to estimate the size and weight of the deer, and then led them to follow its trail on and off the path, and even through a creek.

"There it is!" whispered Lester, trembling with excitement as he pointed at a large buck that was nearly hidden behind some brush.

Christian nodded. "If I were back among the Shawnees, I'd take that buck for venison. But today, we'll be satisfied to look at it."

The buck soon bounded away, and the group headed back to the clearing by the creek.

"Now we're going to teach you how to shoot with a bow and arrow," Christian said. "First you watch me, and then I'll let you do it."

In one smooth action, he put an arrow in the bow, drew back the string, and let it fly. The arrow landed in the center of the target.

"Wow," Lester said. "Can I try that now?"

Christian smiled with satisfaction at the expression on the boy's face. "Okay, I'll let you go first." He put the bow into the boy's hands and then stood behind him, guiding the boy's hands with his own. "Let's take it one step at a time." He put an arrow in place and helped the boy to pull back on the string until it was taut. "Keep your eye on the target," he said. He felt proud of the skills he'd learned from the Shawnees.

"Ready? Let it fly."

The arrow sailed over the top of the target, landing on the grass beyond.

"Don't worry," Christian said, seeing the disappointment in Lester's face. "If you practice, you'll soon get better at it. Now run to retrieve the arrow. And bring mine back too."

Comforted by his words, Lester ran to get them.

"Who wants to go next?" Christian asked.

"I will," the other three boys said at once.

Christian smiled at their eagerness. "Daniel, you may shoot now." Christian stood behind the boy and guided his hands through the motions as he had his older brother. Daniel released the arrow with a flair. The boy whooped with joy as the arrow hit the outer edge of the target.

"I did better than you," he boasted to his older brother, who stood with the two retrieved arrows, his face downcast.

"You got lucky," Lester retorted. "I bet you can't do it again."

"Hold it," Christian said. "Let's not argue about who is best until we've all done it several times." With that, he let the other boys try their luck.

After each had shot once, Joseph took the bow and put all six arrows into the center of the target.

Christian's face broke into a grin. The boys were looking at him and Joseph with deep admiration. Joseph was as fast and accurate with the arrow as any Shawnee he knew.

The rest of the morning went by quickly, with several running games and a rock-throwing contest. Even the fathers seemed reluctant to go home.

"Thank you so much for teaching us about Indians," Simon said. "It was a very worthwhile morning." The rest nodded and chorused their thank-yous and goodbyes as they left for their separate homes.

"I'm glad I didn't try to punish them," Christian said to Joseph as they watched their guests disappear from sight.

"I knew this would be better," Joseph replied. "Revenge may be sweet at times, but having fun together with people who've wronged you is even sweeter."

-23-

Throughout the fall and winter, Christian was increasingly drawn to Elder Klein's enthusiasm for his faith, expressed in purposeful yet gentle ways. Despite his doubts, Christian found himself longing for a quiet spirit and focused faith like Elder Klein seemed to have. So he readily accepted the elder's invitation to accompany him to hear Christian Frederick Post speak at the North Heidelberg Moravian church in mid-March. It was not far from Elder Klein's home.

Christian heard the news with interest. Post was a celebrated Moravian missionary who worked among the Indians, and Christian couldn't wait to meet him, thinking he might find a white man who could really understand him.

A slight breeze that Sunday afternoon made Christian glad for the jacket Anna had made for him. He was glad, too, that he'd finally accepted Anna's offer for him to stay in the cabin that Joseph had occupied until his marriage to Sarah. It was much more comfortable than the wigwam in the wintertime. He followed Elder Klein into the meetinghouse, and the two sat together on one of the plain wooden benches close to the front. Christian felt conspicuous.

A sexton opened the door of the woodstove, tossed in a few chunks of firewood, and then slammed the door shut. The heat would soon compensate for the cold air in the room.

Christian had never met a Moravian. "Where do they come from?" he asked Elder Klein. Unlike the moments before the morning worship service, when people sat stone-silent, neighbors and friends conversed eagerly as they waited to hear a guest speaker.

"From Europe," Elder Klein explained, "just like your folks and mine. Count Zinzendorf let them start a community in

Saxony called Herrnhut, which sent missionaries to other countries. Some of them came here to America to evangelize the Indian people. They started the town of Bethlehem, and built missions for the Delaware Indians at Gnadenhütten and Wechquetank, not so far north of here. Both closed because of the war."

Christian nodded. "Joseph told me that most of the Delawares now live in the Ohio Territory."

"That's true. The white settlers didn't believe the Indians in the Moravian churches were true believers. Some of them were massacred by the colonists when the war broke out." He paused. "It's sad."

The excitement in the room grew. More people crowded in. When all the seats in the meetinghouse were taken, people stood. A dozen children crowded into a spot on the floor near the pulpit.

Christian sat impatiently through the songs and prayers that began the worship service. Finally, the deacon introduced Post. "Christian Frederick Post came to Pennsylvania in 1742 to work among the German churches. He learned the Native Indian languages so well that he was appointed to work with Indians," he said. "He started a mission among the Delawares and Shawnees in the Ohio Territory but was forced to quit during Pontiac's War. Most recently, he worked with the Miskito Indians on the coast of the Caribbean Sea."

"Thanks be to God!" someone called out from the back of the room as Post took the pulpit.

Christian leaned forward to listen. He'd never met a white man who tried to start a church among the Indians. What would a Christian Indian look like?

"*Hatito*," Post said, and motioned for the congregation to repeat it. Christian could hardly believe his ears. "*Hatito!*" he almost shouted in return. It was the first time he'd heard a white man who showed interest in the Shawnee language. The man spoke the simple greeting with confidence and grace. *This is a man worth listening to.*

"Some of the most exciting and the most dangerous times of my life have been among the Indians," Post declared in the German tongue. Christian sat forward in his seat. He was sure this was the missionary that Orpha had talked about. He wished she were here with him.

"Perhaps the hardest part about working among the Indians," Post said, "is getting the settlers to agree that it's a good idea. A lot of white folks think that Indians can't be Christians, and they don't like us trying to bring them into our churches."

Christian nodded. *That's the way people around here would respond if someone tried to establish an Indian mission.*

Post told of the time when he'd been thrown in jail for seven weeks because the settlers were trying to stop his mission work. "I was expelled from both the territories of Connecticut and New York because of the settlers' suspicions. They seem to think that God only loves our race, and that the Natives are heathen savages who should not mix with our people. But the Lamb was slain for all people, and the glories of his kingdom demand that we tell the good news of Jesus to them."

A chorus of *amens* rang out from different parts of the room.

"The biggest problem was that I married an Indian woman," Post said. "Although my wife was a Christian convert, they didn't think it was right for us to marry each other. And they didn't think that Indians should be part of the same church with whites."

The room became silent as the missionary spoke. Christian found himself agreeing. *Yes, that would be a problem here,* he thought. *Who knows what would've happened if I'd married Morning Dew and brought her home with me?*

Post sensed the tension in the room and moved on to speak of something else. He recounted the time he had negotiated with the Indian chiefs during their war against the British. "The British sent me to the Western Indians," he said, "to per-suade the chiefs to give up their loyalty to the French army and make peace with the colonists here. It was an impossible mission, but I felt constrained by the Lord to do it. These were the chiefs who ordered the attacks on your neighborhood in Berks County."

Christian held his breath. Did Post know about the attack on his family? Only the slight whimper of a child broke the silence that hung over the room.

"The only reason they sent me," Post said, "was because they knew the Indians respected me. I carried no weapons, and they knew I would never take another's life in the name of God."

Christian listened. *This man has real courage.*

"When I got to the town of Wyoming, Chief Teedyuscung tried to convince me to go back home. He said the Indians would kill me. I told him I would go on this peace mission to the Ohio. Even if I died in the undertaking before completing the mission, my death would be the means of saving hundreds of other lives. So I left from there with several chiefs. We ran into many dangers on the way. The French sent scouts and Indians to kill me, but God protected me."

Christian shook his head in awe as Post told of traveling through Kuskuskies to meet with Chief Shingas, the terror of the frontier for whose head Governor Denny had set a price of two hundred pounds.

Post spoke with fervor. "The most difficult moment on the trip came when we were camped opposite Fort Duquesne on the Allegheny River. The French officers insisted they bring me into the fort, where they would surely have killed me. But since I was there on a mission from the King of England and the governor of Pennsylvania, the Indians protected me.

"There must have been more than three hundred warriors at the fort from several tribes. It was so dangerous that we left during the night and went back to Kuskuskies, where the Indians gave me a peace belt of eight rows of wampum."

Christian held his breath as Post paused for a moment. The congregation was rapt with attention.

"From there, we hastened back over the mountains to Fort Augusta, and then to Philadelphia. It was a great honor for me to bring the peace belt and a message from the Indian chiefs to the governor. It was an even greater honor for me to carry his message of peace and forgiveness back to the chiefs who had wrought the bloody attacks, in return for their forsaking their loyalty to the French. The chiefs accepted the governor's message and agreed to the terms of peace."

Christian looked sideways at Elder Klein, who was leaning forward as he listened to Post's message. Perhaps he could explain where Post found his courage when death lurked on every side.

"I do not regret that I went on this peace mission," Post said, his face somber. "It helped bring the war to an end and saved the lives of many colonists. I assured them by authority of the king that we would leave the lands of the Allegheny and the Ohio as hunting grounds for our Indian friends. I grieve that the British did not keep those promises. That was why Chief Pontiac and his allies conspired to destroy the British forts in 1763."

Post paused to struggle with his emotions. "My heart grieves when I think of the treaties the white man has broken. We came to the Indians in the name of God, and they have been more honest than we. I feel a deep sorrow. As Moravians, we have always shared the gospel so that the Lamb who was slain may receive the glorious reward of his suffering. Because of the wrongs we have done to the Indians, I fear we may never win them back for the glory of the Lamb." Post spoke slowly now, his voice etched with grief.

As Post finished his remarks, the elder in charge of the congregation rose and stood beside him. The elder looked earnestly at the congregation. "No one but God knows what would have happened had our brother not been obedient to God's voice and conducted this peace mission. Perhaps this would now be French territory and we would not have the freedom to worship as Protestants here." His voice broke. He paused to regain his composure and then put his arm around Post as he motioned for the congregation to stand.

"Let us pray for this brave brother," he said. "He shall soon embark for the Miskito Coast to work with the Indians there." With that he stretched out his hands toward the missionary, as did the congregation, and then he prayed fervently for his safety and success.

Christian sheepishly lifted his hands as well. It felt strange, yet right, to extend a hand of blessing toward the missionary. For the first time, he saw one could be a fervent Christian without rejecting the Indian way of life. It was the greatest gift Post could have offered him that night, and he was eager to receive it.

As the service ended, Christian sought a few moments of personal conversation with the missionary, but others crowded in.

"Let's go," Elder Klein said to Christian. The two headed out the door and onto the path toward home.

"Are you glad you came?" Klein asked as they walked toward home, their backs toward the setting sun.

Christian nodded. "He gave me a lot to think about. I wish Joseph had been there."

"Perhaps you can tell Joseph what you heard," the elder suggested.

"I surely will," Christian said. It would take some time to fully comprehend the impact of Post's words. Already he sensed his life would never be the same.

Christian stumbled into bed that night, pondering what had happened. He longed to be as courageous as Christian Frederick Post. What would it be like to walk into the heart of enemy territory at Fort Duquesne without weapons to defend himself? To carry out a peace mission in the face of death?

Since Post had managed to marry an Indian wife, why couldn't he? If only he could be loved by the Indians as well as the white man, as Post was. He was trying, but it seemed impossible.

"Christian Frederick Post." He savored the name on his tongue. Christian was his own name, although he'd been called Stargazer for more than seven years. How often he had contemplated the stars at night during those years, seeking to find a greater power in the heavens than was obvious on earth. He marveled at the change of seasons and the movement of the constellations, gazing in awe at the immensity of it all. He had taken comfort in the knowledge that he was watching the same stars as his family back home. Did the Indians worship the same Creator God as the Amish church of his youth—the All-Powerful One whose outstretched hands moved the sun from one end of the heavens to the others, and set the stars on a course that one could predict over time?

Perhaps Post was a stargazer too. How else could he find his bearings on his long trip through the woods?

Post had come to love the Indian people even though he'd never been taken captive and forced to join a tribe. He said it was because of God's love for them as expressed in his son, Jesus Christ. Because of a call from God, Post was determined to demonstrate God's love to the Natives. To risk his life to tell them about the Christian way. It was more than Christian could grasp.

What is my calling? How can I be faithful to the Creator? These and other questions plagued him like pesky flies as he lay awake, listening to the night sounds through a partially open window.

A screech owl sang its long, tremulous trill from a nearby tree. Christian's thoughts were diverted. Might he get the owl to come closer? Christian trilled in return. No reply.

He was completely quiet. The sound of the gentle ripple of the stream nearby was broken by the sound of a beaver slapping its tail on the surface of the water.

The night sounds were a comfort of sorts, a sign that all was well. But what Christian wanted most was for sleep to come, to shoo away the questions that plagued his mind. Listening to Post had made him wonder what led people to do hard things. What kept them going in the face of trouble or danger?

Christian was nearly twenty-one years of age, at which time he'd be on his own. But he didn't want to work as hard as his *Dat*. He didn't have *Dat*'s drive. Nothing was so important that he'd wear himself out in its pursuit.

But what if Post was right? What if God loved the Indian people so much that he would call people to dedicate their lives to share the good news with them? Was it possible to believe it so strongly that you'd risk your life for their sake? Christian turned over, hoping for sleep to come.

The owl trilled again, much closer this time. Good. He hadn't lost his touch for owl calls after all. He smiled in the dark.

For him to be like Post wasn't really possible. It would take more courage or conviction than he could muster, and perhaps more talent too. *Maybe, if I found something that I really cared about, like Elder Klein does.*

Living among the Indians had cast doubt on the things he'd been taught as a child, sapping his enthusiasm for the church community. Maybe if he hung around with people like Christian Frederick Post he'd feel a new sense of call on his life.

But it made more sense to join the Dunker church, since that's where Orpha was. They seemed as enthusiastic about their faith as the Moravians.

Dat didn't show his emotions like the Dunkers, but he had his convictions too. Why else would he have forbidden Joseph and him to shoot at the Indians? Yes, the Amish had convictions every bit as strong as the Dunkers or the Moravians. But they didn't grip his imagination. What was he to do?

Christian turned over in his bed, hoping that sleep would come soon. He trilled again. After a long pause, the owl trilled in return. *I won't go to sleep if I keep hooting at that owl,* he chided himself.

Something must be wrong with me. I would like to be strong like Post, or Dat, or even Elder Klein. I wonder if they ever felt lost or weak like I do. They seem to have something that I'm missing.

Christian turned over again, deeply tired but unable to fall asleep. A sheep bleated repeatedly from the meadow, a distressed call that reflected the anguish in his own heart. His mind flashed back to a winter evening when the whole family was seated near the hearth fire.

"*Mam,* tell us a Bible story," Christian had said, looking expectantly into his mother's face. A wolf howled in the distance as Christian scrunched up close to *Mam*'s chair with Franey huddled at his side. "And cover us with the quilt."

Mam unfolded the quilt and wrapped it around the two children's shoulders, so that only their heads stuck out. It was a favorite activity on a winter night, especially when the wind howled and the roof creaked. The wolf howled again, and a sheep bleated loudly in response.

"I'm going to check the sheep," *Dat* said, putting on his coat and hat. "I don't like the sound of that wolf." A gust of cold air swished across the floor as *Dat* swung open the door and stepped into the night.

Christian shivered, as much from the sound of the wolf as from the cold draft. Franey snuggled against Christian's side as the two of them pressed tightly against *Mam*'s ample legs.

"A shepherd once had one hundred sheep," *Mam* said, launching into the story. "But one evening, when they came in from the pasture, he counted only ninety-nine."

Christian turned to Franey. "I can count to one hundred," he said with his nose held high. Little Franey could only count to ten, which is how old Christian was.

"Listen to the story," *Mam* said gently. "The shepherd counted his sheep twice to make sure he was counting right. Sure enough, there were only ninety-nine."

The wolf howled again and the window paned rattled in the wind. "I know what happens next," Christian said. "The shepherd went to look for the one that was missing." He knew the story well, but he never tired of hearing *Mam* tell it.

"That's right," *Mam* said, relaying how the loving shepherd called for his lost sheep by name, searching hither and yon by lantern light until he found it, a forlorn lamb caught in a thicket at the edge of a steep cliff.

Now *Mam* came to his favorite part of the story, when the shepherd carried the rescued lamb back home in his arms, tenderly singing a lullaby. When *Mam* had finished singing the lullaby, she ended the story by saying, "That good shepherd was Jesus, who cares for us more than anyone else."

She had hardly said the words when *Dat* entered the house amidst a swish of cold air. "Betsy was outside the pen," he said, "trying to get in. I put her in the barn with the rest of the sheep, where they should all be safe."

Christian turned on his bed and pulled the blanket around him as he recalled that cold winter evening nearly a decade before. He ached to be carried in the arms of the loving shepherd, and to share the safety of the sheepfold with others whom Jesus had called by name.

I've got to talk to somebody about this. He took a deep breath as the owl trilled again. *I'm going to talk to Elder Klein first thing tomorrow. I'm sure he'll understand.*

PART III

-24-

When Christian woke up the next morning, he walked to the creek and splashed water on his face to rub the sleep out of his eyes. After making a breakfast of fried eggs and dried pork, he headed into the woods. The sun spilled light onto the path as he walked. He had no destination in mind, except to take in the comforting sights and sounds of the forest. In this place, more than any other, he could work his way through a jumble of emotions.

The Moravian missionary's speech had plowed a furrow long and deep in Christian's fertile mind. He turned the man's words over and over in his thoughts. He could not dismiss Post's declaration: "I told the governor that I would go on the peace mission to the Ohio, even if I died in the undertaking."

In his mind's eye, he saw the missionary walking into danger with the good shepherd Jesus at his side, confident of his loving care. "I want to be like Christian Frederick Post," he said aloud, knowing that none but the forest was a witness. "I wonder if that means I need to become a Christian."

A Christian. Unlike the many times in the past, his reluctance to the idea melted away in the face of his desire for a personal sense of God's presence. He had long resisted *Dat's* wishes that he join the Amish church, sympathizing deeply with the Native Americans who devoutly worshiped the Creator without a church fellowship.

The inner voices that had often shouted at each other since he'd come back to the Northkill now spoke to each other civilly, conversing in gentle tones that hinted at the coming of a settled peace within his soul.

He stood and raised his hands high, watching the leaves of a tall oak tree wave gently in the breeze. "The wind bloweth where it listeth," he had heard Elder Klein read from Scripture. "Thou hearest the sound thereof, but canst not tell whence it cometh, and whither it goeth: so is every one that is born of the Spirit."

"Great Creator," he prayed as he gazed into the sky. "I believe in Jesus Christ, the Good Shepherd, who laid down his life for the sheep. I want to be born of the Spirit, and belong to his flock."

A deep, inner peace warmed his being as he stood watching the clouds scud across the open spaces between the branches of the trees. *I want to live for the good of others. I want to be like Christian Frederick Post.* His breath came easily now, buoyed by the renewed hope that rose inside him. He headed back to his house. *Orpha will be very happy that I met the missionary she had talked about. After I see Elder Klein, I'll tell her what I've done.*

As he neared his cabin, a few bars of a song, taught to him by his older brother Jakey, came to mind. He hummed the melody under his breath. He hadn't thought of it in nearly ten years—half his lifetime. It was a song about Switzerland, the land of *Mam* and *Dat*'s birth. The music came to him more easily than the words, but he could still recall the first verse:

> *Farewell ye Alps, ye fair and pleasant hill,*
> *My native village in the quiet dell.*
> *Your faithful fields another now will till,*
> *My father's house no more I'll see at will.*
> *May God be with you now, as I must bid farewell.*

The words and music of the song spirited him back to the scene of that joyous social, the apple *schnitzing* the evening before he was captured. He could see *Mam*, standing next to *Dat* and blending her mellow voice with his. A young man yodeled in the manner of the Swiss, his Adam's apple bobbing up and down as he ranged the scale from baritone to falsetto soprano.

The words of the last verse came to him now as he remembered *Dat* tapping his feet in rhythm with the tune:

To all farewell, I now must part from you,
Farewell; for me, there is no other choice.
Led on by Christ, who is my shepherd true,
Through trials sore, into green pastures new,
Then home to his reward, forever to rejoice.

Dat and *Mam* must have sung that song when they left the Old Country. It was a gentle way to leave one's family, a stark contrast to the unceremonious and callous means by which the British had yanked him away from his Shawnee family. Or the way the Shawnees had ripped him from his family home. After his adoption he'd decided not to hold that against them, but the memories of his capture lived on.

Christian whistled the tune as he walked to Elder Klein's house late that morning. The words now spoke of his own farewell, a deliberate goodbye to a way of life he had known for more than nine years. He was on the path with Christ, the true shepherd.

Christian found Elder Klein working in his workshop, making wooden shingles. "Christian! What can I do for you?" the elder asked, laying down his woodworking plane and brushing the shavings off his work apron.

"Do you remember when I asked if it was ever right to break a vow?"

"Yes, I do. Did you want to talk about that?"

Christian nodded. "I'd like to become a Christian and join your church." He paused. "But I might have to break a vow to do that."

"I see," said the Elder. He put aside his work. "Why don't we go inside where Dorothy can get us a drink of water? We can talk more there."

Christian nodded and followed the elder into the house.

"Dorothy, can you get us some cold water from the spring?" the elder asked his wife as they stepped inside.

"Of course," she replied. "I'll bring a cup for both of you." She looked at Christian with a kind expression.

The elder pulled two chairs together and invited Christian to sit down. "Now, tell me what brought this about."

"When I was with the Shawnees," Christian began, "I made a blood pact with my Indian brother, Little Bear. I vowed to always be a brother to him, since he had no other family, and never to take up the white man's ways. I've always tried to keep that vow, because I was afraid that evil spirits would take revenge on me if I broke it."

The elder nodded. "I can understand the problem. That vow has made it hard for you to fit in here."

Christian nodded. "But when I heard the missionary speak last night, I think I can look at the vow in a new way."

The elder smiled. "I'm so glad to hear that. What stood out to you in his testimony?"

"I could tell he lived among the Indians because he knew God loves them as much as the whites. He wasn't trying to take advantage of them," Christian said.

The elder leaned forward. "That means a lot, doesn't it?"

Christian swallowed hard and nodded. "It means being a Christian is more than a white man's religion. Jesus loves the Indians too."

"That's true," the elder said, looking straight into Christian's eyes. "God loves you whether you're an Indian, a white man, or some of both. And you can join our church without taking advantage of the Indians or adopting the bad habits of the whites."

"Good. That settles it for me. What do I need to do to join your church?"

Elder Klein leaned toward Christian. "First of all, we'll ask you to give a testimony to your conversion."

Christian shrank back. "I wouldn't know what to say."

"Tell us how you decided to become a Christian," the elder said. "You can explain what you learned from the Moravian missionary."

"Is that the only requirement?"

"Not quite. You will also be examined by two or more brethren, to make sure that you have embraced the doctrines of defenselessness, nonswearing, and not conforming to the world. If they are pleased with your answers, they can bring a recommendation to the church council, which consists of all the members. And then, if all the members agree to invite you to join the church, you can be baptized and become part of our fellowship."

Elder Klein took a sip of his water while Christian absorbed what he heard. "How does that sound to you?"

Christian thought. Was the church council like the tribal council back in the Shawnee village? There, the warriors decided whether or not to go to war, and the women gathered to decide whether or not a captive would be adopted or put to death. "What if someone objects to my joining the church?" His voice quavered.

"If the objection is serious enough, we would need to postpone the baptism until everyone has approved of your membership." Even though the elder said these words with gentleness and grace, Christian felt an icy hand grip his chest. There were several men who always looked at his long hair with disdain.

Christian cleared his throat. "Will I need to cut my hair like the other men, and start to grow a beard?"

"If that's what the members decided, would you be willing to do so?"

Christian paused. "Maybe." Seeing the expression on the elder's face change slightly, he hastily added, "Probably."

The elder nodded. "Good. The congregation is always concerned about the willingness of a baptismal candidate to submit to the church. It's like submitting to the Lord. The Bible says we are like clay in the hands of God the Potter, who molds us into vessels for his use. The clay doesn't get to decide what kind of vessel it will be. That's up to the Potter."

The elder went on. "Submitting to baptism shows our willingness to die to ourselves and our own desires. So ... if you're not willing to give up something like your scalp lock, you're probably not ready to be baptized."

The elder's quiet words pierced Christian's heart. Was he prepared to give up his Indian identity in order to join the Brethren, when he'd butted heads with *Dat* over the same question ever since he'd returned to the Northkill?

Christian gazed into the elder's face. Maybe this man was more like *Dat* than he had first thought. Why would he do for this elder what he was not willing to do for *Dat*?

"I can plan for a meeting with a couple of men this Sunday," the elder said. "Do you want me to do that?"

Christian took a deep breath, hoping the elder couldn't hear the desperate pounding of his heart. He nodded and said simply, "Yes."

"Don't worry too much about this. When the congregation hears about all you've gone through, they'll likely want you to join the church." Elder Klein gripped his shoulder and looked into his eyes. "Will you be ready to give a testimony next Sunday after the church service? After that, we can plan for a members meeting to consider your request to join."

Christian nodded again. "I'll do it," he said. The two talked a bit longer, and then Christian took his leave. If only he didn't need to speak in front of the whole church. He couldn't recall that the Amish church had ever required such a thing.

Perhaps he should ask Joseph or Sarah if they had given a testimony when they joined the church shortly before getting married. Better yet, he could ask Orpha. Since she was both a church member and a friend, she might be willing to help him plan what to say.

Christian knocked on the door of Orpha's home, eager to tell her about his newfound faith. He was disappointed when

Reuben answered the door. He was a burly man with heavy eyebrows, and his expression was forbidding.

"What do you want?" Reuben asked. His words sounded more like an interrogation than a welcome.

"Um . . . I was hoping to speak to Orpha," Christian said. "Would she be available?"

"I know she's outside somewhere. She might not want to be bothered."

"I have something very important to tell her. I'm sure she would want to know." Christian stood his ground.

"Well then, you can go around the house and speak to her in the garden. But don't take too much of her time."

Christian turned and walked around the corner of the house. How could Reuben be so rude? No Indian would speak that way, even to a stranger.

His face brightened when he saw Orpha in the garden. She stood and straightened her petticoat. "Christian! How good to see you! Is anything wrong?"

"What are you planting?" he asked, stalling for time. It was too early in the season for most plants.

"Some lettuce and onions. I'll put a little straw over them to keep the frost away." She brushed away several strands of hair from her face. "What brings you here in the middle of the day?"

"I've decided to join your church, but I need help with what to say."

Orpha clapped her hands. "That's wonderful! What led you to do that?"

"I've been thinking about it for a long time. But last night, I went with Elder Klein to hear a Moravian missionary named Christian Frederick Post. I decided to become a Christian."

She broke into a wide smile. "I'm so pleased. What did your family say?"

Christian paused for a moment before speaking. "I haven't told them yet, because I don't think they're going to like it. *Dat* wants very much for me to join his church."

"You need to follow your convictions," Orpha said confidently. "And you must explain how you made your decision to them."

"I told Elder Klein this morning. He said I'd have to give a testimony in order to be baptized and join the church." He paused. "I don't know what to say."

"Reuben and Leah have been members much longer. They'll know what you should say."

"Oh." Christian tried to appear calm, but he felt afraid. How could he please Orpha's foster parents? What if they accused him of professing faith in order to win Orpha's hand?

"Why don't you tell Reuben about your decision? I think he'll like that." Orpha gathered her gardening things and motioned for him to follow her.

At the house, Orpha found her foster parents and brought them into the kitchen. The four sat down together. Christian took his place beside Orpha, across from Reuben and Leah.

Orpha looked at Christian. "Tell Reuben and Leah what you told me. I'm sure they'll want to hear it."

Christian cleared his throat and leaned forward. "I've decided to be baptized and join your church."

Reuben's expression didn't change. "I'm glad to hear it," he said, glancing at Orpha. "Did Orpha talk you into this?"

"No, no, she had nothing to do with it," Christian said, hoping that his voice wasn't too emphatic. "I've been talking with Elder Klein, and he took me to a meeting with the Moravians last night. That's when I made my decision."

Reuben looked skeptical. Leah was expressionless.

"You'll need to give a testimony at church." Reuben's voice was flat.

A lump rose in Christian's throat. "That's what Elder Klein told me. I've never heard anybody give a testimony, so I don't know what to say."

"The main thing we want to know is that you are truly converted, and willing to count the cost of being a church member."

"What do you mean, 'count the cost'?"

Reuben leaned forward. "Jesus taught that we need to count the cost of being a disciple. You have to be willing to suffer for your beliefs, especially when it divides families."

Christian took a deep breath. There was no doubt that *Dat* would be unhappy. Anna might be more sympathetic.

Leah saw the confusion on his face and spoke up. "When you give your testimony, the important thing is to tell how you decided to believe in Jesus Christ."

Orpha stroked Christian's hand under the table. He squeezed hers in return.

"Ever since I was with the Indians, I've compared what I learned there with the things I heard as a child. I know that God in heaven is the Great Creator, and that he cares for the whole world, even the plants and animals. He loves the Indians as much as the white man. And I know that God sent Jesus Christ into the world to save everyone from their sins— both the white man and the Indians."

He paused and looked at Reuben, hoping he was saying the right kind of things.

Reuben nodded. "That's good. If you say that to the church, and give a little more detail about your experience, you'll have a good testimony."

Christian nodded and scooted back his chair. "I must be going. I don't want to keep you from your work."

"That's not a problem," Reuben said. Although he still wasn't friendly, Christian thought his voice seemed warmer. "We must never be too busy to talk about the ways of the Lord."

Christian stood and prepared to leave. "I hope your garden grows well," he said to Orpha as he turned toward the door. Orpha followed him outside and closed the door behind her.

"I'm proud of your decision," she said. "I think Reuben appreciated your courage."

Christian's heart soared. That was better than he could have hoped for. With Orpha and her foster parents on his side, he was ready to go ahead with the baptism.

No matter what *Dat* or the rest of his family would say.

-25-

Anna often dreamed of the day when people looked to her for advice, rather than seeing her as the one who needed it. But she could hardly have envisioned that it would occur on the threshold of spring, nearly two years after Christian's return.

She had finished her morning chores and was checking the almanac for gardening advice when she heard a knock on the door. She was surprised to find Catharine Hertzler there.

"Catharine! So good to see you." Her friendliness turned to concern when she saw Catharine's face. "Are you okay?"

"I have some pain in my back," Catharine said. "And I was hoping that you might be able to help me."

"Have a seat in this chair," Anna said, deeply pleased that the bishop's wife would look to her for help. It was an opportunity to compensate Catharine for the many times Anna had reached out to her.

Catharine moved slowly and carefully, wincing as she sank into the chair. "I hope you can do something for me."

"Let's start with a warm cup of sassafras tea," Anna said, tossing a few sprigs into a cup and adding hot water from the kettle over the fire. "Also, take some deep breaths and try to relax. I suppose that your muscles are rather tight, and this might help."

In a few moments, Anna put a warm cup of tea into Catharine's hands and listened patiently as she told about her symptoms.

"I think it might be helpful for me to rub your feet," Anna said in response. "The nerves in your feet will show where there is tightness in your body."

Catharine nodded and took off her shoes and woolen stockings.

Anna gently washed Catharine's feet with a warm cloth and pulled out a small jar of lotion that she had made from herbs. She spread the lotion on her hands and began to gently rub Catharine's feet. "Let me know if I press too hard," she said.

Catharine leaned back in the chair and closed her eyes. "Do many people come to have their feet rubbed these days?" she asked.

Anna felt herself tense. What had prompted Catharine's question? Ever since Silas Burkholder's accusation, people had been less inclined to come to her for a foot massage. She had never summoned the courage to talk to Catharine about it.

"Yes, some people come, but not many. Of course, Jacob likes his feet rubbed often. He likes for me to really press in on the muscles." Without realizing it, she pressed her thumb hard into the center of Catharine's foot.

"Ouch," Catharine said, catching her breath. "It's a little sore there."

"I'm sorry, I'll try to be gentler," Anna replied. She continued rubbing and a thought occurred to her. *I wish people would be gentler when they press on the sore spots in my life. Words can hurt.*

"I've come to make an apology," Catharine said, as though reading Anna's mind. Her eyes glistened as she spoke. "A few years ago, Silas Burkholder came around to Jake, telling him that he had come to you for a foot rub. He said you tried to draw him in to something more."

Anna drew in her breath. Nothing pained her more than that false accusation.

"Last week," Catharine continued with a sober face, "two women from our neighborhood told me that Silas had grabbed them and tried to kiss them. They had a hard time getting away. I wonder if that's what he did to you as well."

Anna nodded. Her eyes welled with tears. "Silas was upset because I wouldn't massage his feet or shoulders, as he asked me to. When I told him to leave, he grabbed me and held me tight. When I tried to push him away, he threatened me." Her voice shook as she relived those moments. "I finally got away and ran toward the neighbor's place." She paused, holding Catharine's foot in her hand.

"I'm so sorry we believed him," Catharine said. "He always seemed like an upstanding man."

Anna wiped the tears from her cheeks, then blew her nose. Catharine put her hand on Anna's shoulder. "I'm sorry we didn't really listen to your side of the story."

Her apology prompted more tears. Anna wept softly with her head on Catharine's shoulder. Finally, she stepped back and looked into Catharine's glistening eyes. "Thank you. It means so much to know that you believe me."

Catharine nodded and hugged Anna again. Anna took a deep breath. "You have brought such healing to me today, and now I will see if I can bring healing for you. I must finish rubbing your feet."

Catharine smiled warmly and sat back in the chair. Anna bent down as before. For her, rubbing Catharine's feet was reminiscent of Mary Magdalene washing the feet of Jesus. It was a lowly task in Jesus' day, relegated to the servants of lower rank. But Anna didn't mind touching people's feet. It was a simple way to touch a person's body with healing love. She added a bit of lotion to her hand and gently rubbed Catharine's feet, massaging the places where the muscles had hardened into knots.

"Thank you so much for what you have done for me today," Catharine said when Anna finished. "I feel better already."

"You have done even more for me," Anna said. "And I shall never forget it." She saw Catharine to the door and watched as her friend walked away from the house. *She believes me!* The sky seemed clearer now, with light wisps of clouds drifting across the sky. The daffodils at the edge of her garden heralded a change of season—the coming of spring and a time of new joy.

A few minutes later, Jacob came in. *Should I tell him what has happened?* Anna wondered. *Will he understand how important this is to me?*

She recalled a moment several years earlier when she and Jacob were still getting to know one another. They had stood, together, watching the stars on a clear night. For Anna, it had been a time of vulnerability after Ulrich's death and the loss of her child. Being with Jacob—a widower who had lost his wife and two children in the Indian attack—had opened up the possibilities for both of them to find healing in their love for each other.

She thrived on Jacob's companionship in the daily struggle to earn a living from the soil. Being married to Jacob had restored the sense of security she'd lost with Ulrich's death. But more than that, she felt that the two of them were coming to understand each other—to sympathize with the pain each had endured. Jacob's loss loomed large in comparison with her own—the murder of his wife and two children and the destruction of the house and outbuildings on the farm, not to mention the sons who were wrested from him for years and reoriented to a completely different way of life before returning home. She could never fully comprehend his pain.

She felt his sympathy for the loss of her own spouse, a young man in his prime jerked away by an accident he could not have avoided. He empathized with her loss of a baby girl who had failed to thrive, and even more, with her seeming inability to conceive another child—one that would be welcomed into the loving arms of them both.

However, she knew that Jacob struggled to comprehend the depth of the harm that Silas had caused her, first by his unwelcomed physical advances and then by the falsehoods he'd spread about her as a cover-up. Their love for each other carried them through times of misunderstanding. But she hoped for even more healing.

Jacob struggled to understand Christian's pain in the same way he struggled to understand hers. Thus she decided not to mention Catharine's apology, though she longed for the time when the whole family could understand each other more fully.

A couple of days later, Christian saw Anna with a pail of milk, heading from the barn to the house. He paused for a moment, considering. Should he tell her about his decision to join the Dunkers? Yes, it would be good to let her know. She'd find out sooner or later anyhow. It would be best if she heard it directly from him rather than someone else.

But what if she or *Dat* tried to put a stop to the baptism? What if they voiced an objection to one of the Dunker members, who could then keep him from joining? He stopped.

But maybe Anna could help him figure out a way to speak to *Dat*, he thought. Was it worth the risk? Yes.

"Anna!"

She turned and smiled, then put down the wooden pail. Seeing his expression, she turned serious. "Is anything wrong?"

"Nothing is wrong," Christian said. "But I have something to tell you. I've decided to become a Christian and join the Dunkers."

"How did you come to that decision?" Anna looked sympathetic. "You haven't shown much interest in the church since you came to the Northkill."

"I've been doing a lot of thinking," Christian said, feeling freer now to share since she didn't look angry.

"That's good," Anna nodded, her face mostly serious but showing the hint of a smile. "Have you been talking with George Klein?"

Christian nodded. "He took me to the Moravian church a few nights ago to hear a missionary named Christian

Frederick Post tell about his work with the Indians. I like him. He understands me."

"In what way?" Anna asked, showing genuine interest.

"He was married to an Indian woman and helped bring peace to the frontier. The French might have won the war if it hadn't been for him."

"I hadn't heard of him before," Anna said. "But it sounds as though he's a wonderful man."

"He helped me see that I can join the church and still care about my Indian people back in the Ohio Territory," Christian said.

Anna's face softened into a smile. "I'm so glad you want to join a church. I'm sure that *Dat* will be glad too. We have been praying for you. Every day."

"Thank you," Christian said. She hadn't mentioned the Dunkers. She probably wasn't happy about that part of his decision.

"Will you come to my baptism?" It seemed a little risky to ask, but the words slipped out. There was little chance that *Dat* would come, but Anna might consent to be there.

Anna looked down in silence for a moment. "Thanks for inviting me," she said. "I'll need to talk to *Dat* about it. I don't want to promise I'll come without talking to him."

Christian's heart leapt. For now, that was all he needed to hear. No use pressing the issue, since it put her at odds with *Dat*.

-26-

Anna walked slowly toward Catharine's house, worried about what Jacob would say if he knew about her mission. She needed Catharine's support for her plan to attend Christian's baptism. She didn't want to raise Jacob's ire or fail to be submissive to him. Catharine might be able to help her find a way through these issues.

The sun was up, and slight breeze stirred the air. *Such a beautiful day!* She reveled in the wildlife around her. A cardinal poured out its song as she walked, filling the air with its sound. A rabbit scampered on the path ahead, darting back and forth before hopping into the weeds.

A dog barked when she arrived at Catharine's house, announcing her arrival. Catharine came to the door, curious.

"Anna! So good to see you." Anna noticed Catharine was moving more freely and with less pain.

"How are you feeling?"

Catharine twirled around. "See? I am so much better, thanks to you!" She gave Anna a hug. Catharine continued, "Come with me to the creek. I was about to start doing laundry."

"Good," Anna said. "I have something to ask you—and I prefer that we be alone."

She helped Catharine carry the tub of hot water to the edge of the creek. Catharine shaved small bits of lye soap into the hot water, and Anna stirred it with a wooden paddle until bubbles rose to the surface. And then, as Catharine sorted the clothes, Anna began her tale.

"I came to tell you that Christian has decided to be baptized in the Dunker church," Anna said. "I'd like to attend his baptism, but I haven't talked to Jacob about it. I'm afraid if I ask him about it, he'll say no. What do you think I should do?"

Catharine looked curious. "Why do you want to be there?"

"Because Christian has made an important decision, and I want to support him."

Thoughtfully, Catharine reached for a shirt and began scrubbing it. "Even if he joins the Dunker church instead of ours?"

"Yes."

"Are you sure the Dunkers won't be a bad influence on Christian?"

Anna thought for a moment. She looked away and saw Jake in the distance. He was working in the field, spreading cow manure.

"I know people say that. I wonder why."

"They teach that anyone is lost who baptizes differently than they do," Catharine said as she scrubbed the collar on one of her husband's shirts, then rinsed it in the hot water.

"Elder Klein didn't tell us that when he was at our home."

"Maybe not, but Jake says that's what their church teaches."

Anna frowned and took the clean shirt from Catharine. She handed her a dirty one. "Is that the main problem with Dunkers?"

"Yes, but there are others. They use voting to choose their ministers and decide on their church standards. And they are Pietists, so they're more likely to vote using their feelings than by the standards which are upheld by the ministers in our church."

"I see."

"And their men wear mustaches, like the men in the military. They may eventually lose their opposition to war."

Yes, Anna's father had said he would never wear a mustache for that reason.

Catharine stopped scrubbing and looked at Anna with sadness in her eyes. "I'm afraid our members might look down on Christian if he left us to join the Dunkers."

Anna pressed her lips together. *It's so unfair!* She was quiet for a moment. "Even if he had never joined our church?"

"We've already lost several families to the Dunkers. We can't act as though it doesn't matter." Catharine stepped to the edge of the creek to rinse another shirt. "If you go to the baptism, people will think you approve of what he's doing."

"That's why I wanted to talk to you," Anna said, taking a shirt from Catharine to wring the water out. "I don't want to disobey our church's rules; I want to show Christian that I care about him. I know he'll be happy if I come to his baptism."

Together, they finished rinsing the clothing and wrung out the water by twisting it into thick ropes. After flapping each piece of clothing to chase away the wrinkles, they spread it out on nearby branches and bushes to dry.

"So you want to go to the baptism to make Christian happy, even if it makes Jacob or the bishop unhappy?" Catharine asked.

"No, I want everyone to be happy."

"That's not always possible."

"I know. That's why I came to talk to you. If you think it's all right for me to go, I can tell Jacob so, and he might not mind if I go."

Catharine shook her head. "I wouldn't advise you to do something that neither my husband nor Jacob would do."

Anna hung her head. "I was afraid you would say that. I guess I'll go home now." She fought back tears as she turned to leave.

"Wait," Catharine said. Slowly, she added, "Maybe there's another way to work at this."

Anna turned to look at Catharine. There was a small smile on her face as she poured the laundry water onto the ground.

"What's that?"

"Anna, I can see why you want to go to Christian's baptism. If I were in your shoes, I would want to go myself."

"You would? I thought you said I shouldn't go if Jacob doesn't want me to."

"Our husbands don't always understand us women. When I really want Jake to understand what I'm thinking, I have to figure out a way to make it as important to him as it is to me."

"How do you do that?"

"I often pray that God will help me. It doesn't always work, but sometimes it does. I'll pray that it works for you when you talk to Jacob this time."

"Can I tell Jacob that I talked to you about the baptism?"

"No, I'd rather you didn't. Think about what's important to Jacob, and God will show you what to say."

Anna twisted her skirt nervously. What would she say? She still didn't have a clue. How would God tell her the right words? She didn't know.

"Take courage," Catharine said. "I'll be praying for you."

"Thank you," Anna said. She certainly hadn't gotten the answer she had hoped for. Yet, as always, Catharine's answer had forced her to think. She wondered if Catharine spoke to her husband that way.

"Take courage," Catharine had said. It took courage all right. She couldn't remember the last time someone had said that to her.

Anna's head hurt as she left for home. How could she make her wish for Christian as important to Jacob as it was to her? Maybe she should ask Jacob what he would do, and then ask him if he wanted to know what she would like to do.

It seemed simple enough, but rather risky. *What if he says no, and forbids me to go?* she mused. *I'm going to take a chance. Catharine will be praying for me.*

Christian walked toward Joseph's home, hoping to win his approval—better yet, his support—for his decision to join the Dunkers. Joseph might even be able to help get *Dat* to approve it.

Joseph grinned as Christian approached the field where he was digging a small channel to carry water from the stream into the meadow. "It looks like our baby is going to be born any day now," he said.

"That's a little scary, isn't it?" Christian asked. "How does it feel to soon be a dad?"

"Sarah and I are looking forward to having a family."

"That's good," Christian said, although having babies was the farthest thing from his mind. Politely he said, "I'm looking forward to being an uncle again."

Joseph wiped his forehead and put down his shovel. "You didn't come all the way out here to ask me about how I'm doing. What's on your mind?"

"I came to ask what you'd think about me joining the Dunkers."

Joseph smirked. "Barbara told me you've been attending that church. She said that's the only way you're able to see Orpha Rupp."

Hotly, Christian said, "That's not the real reason. I decided the Dunker church is the best place for me, regardless of what happens with Orpha."

Joseph shook his head with an impish grin. "That's not the way Barbara made it sound."

Christian scowled, then confessed, "Okay, so that's part of it. Orpha's a nice girl. But the main reason is that—"

"Let's say *another* reason," Joseph interrupted.

"Didn't the Delawares teach you not to interrupt other people when they're talking?"

"Okay, go ahead. What were you going to say about the reason you wanted to join the Dunkers?"

"I decided to make a change in my life. I'm ready to get baptized and join the church, like you did more than a year ago. Elder Klein helped me to see that I don't have to give up my love for Indians in order to become a Christian."

Joseph quit smiling and looked more serious. "Of course you don't. Look at me. I joined the church and I still love the Indians. But now I'm married and getting ready to raise a family. If you did that—joined our church—it would make *Dat* happy. You'd get land to farm too."

Christian reflected on how much Joseph had changed now that he'd found Sarah. Being married and starting a family was changing Joseph's purpose in life. It made him willing to do hard work—like digging irrigation channels to make the meadow flourish for his livestock.

"The important thing is that the Dunkers are more like the Moravians, who care about the Indians. They send missionaries to help them." He paused. "Maybe someday I'll do that."

Joseph's eyes widened. "You've always had your own way of doing things, so I'm not surprised."

"Do you think it's a bad idea to join the Dunkers?"

Joseph picked up his shovel and began digging. "No, not at all. If you're convicted to do it, you should go ahead, regardless of what *Dat* says. I'm happy that I joined the Amish church and took up farmwork."

"Really? I thought you'd rather hunt and fish."

"I get tired of farmwork," Joseph admitted, "but it's better than living from hand to mouth the way the Indians often do. And I'm happy to be married to Sarah rather than to an Indian woman."

Christian paused to watch for a few moments. "I guess I agree with you. At one time, I would have liked to get married to Morning Dew, but I think Orpha will make a better wife for me."

Joseph poked Christian's chest as he spoke. "Reuben won't allow you to marry her unless you cut your hair and comb it the way the Dunkers do."

"How do you know that?"

"Because he's my neighbor. I know how he thinks."

"So you think that if I cut my hair and dress the way the Dunkers do, Reuben will let me marry Orpha?"

"First you need to dress and act like a Dunker. Then get baptized. Later, you can ask Orpha to marry you. If you ask him too quickly, he'll say no, and it might be hard for you to change his mind later."

"Is that how it was for you to marry Sarah? Were you worried that her *Dat* would say no?"

"Yes, sort of. But I started dressing like the Amish and joined the church, and then I asked him if I could marry Sarah. By that time, he believed that I was a sincere member and ready to take up a farm."

He thought for a moment. "And now they're very happy that we're going to have a baby. They want us to take over the farm before long so they can move to Conestoga."

Christian pondered Joseph's words. How had his brother gotten so far ahead of him in life? He felt a twinge of envy.

"I'm going to be baptized next Sunday," he said. "Will you come to watch me be baptized? We'll be outside. It will be done in the creek."

"It depends on when the baby comes. I don't want to leave Sarah by herself."

"Please come," Christian said. "You won't have to leave Sarah for long."

He turned and walked back toward home. If only Joseph could help *Dat* to understand. And if he didn't . . . Well, that would make things a lot harder.

Christian stood outside the Klein home. His testimony had gone well. As he thought back over his time in front of the Dunker council meeting, he couldn't think of anything he had left out or wished he hadn't said.

So far, so good. He was impatient to hear about the church's response to his request for membership.

Elder Klein came outside and invited him in. Most of the others had gone.

"You can sit down," the elder said, pulling up a chair. Christian sat down hard. "I suppose you're wondering what the people said. We don't quote people, but I can tell you a couple of things that were mentioned." Christian nodded nervously.

"As always, people wanted to make sure you had a genuine conversion. I assured them that you were sincere, and that you care about the salvation of the Indian people."

Christian relaxed a little. At least the elder stood with him. Or so it seemed.

Klein paused. "There was one brother who felt that you made the decision to join our church because you were interested in one of our young women."

"That was Reuben Stump, wasn't it?" The words burst out, spilling Christian's biggest worry. When he saw the expression on the elder's face change, he wished he'd kept his tongue.

"I think the brother who spoke expressed the concern of several others."

Christian frowned but said nothing.

"Don't be too quick to judge the members," the elder said gently. "Everyone was willing to give you the benefit of the doubt, and you must do the same for them."

"Did anyone think I should wear my hair differently?" That was the other question he was worried about.

Elder Klein's visage changed. "Most wish you'd wear your hair like the rest of us."

Christian sighed. "Should I wait to be baptized until people change their minds?"

The elder took a deep breath. "Is your long hair more important to you than baptism and church membership?"

Christian squirmed in his chair. "Can't I be a Christian without wearing my hair the same way as everyone else?"

"I'm sure you can. But the Spirit of Christ leads us to unity of faith and practice, even if outsiders think it petty or trifling. Would you like to put off the baptism for a little while?"

Christian's mind raced. What would Orpha say if he delayed? Or Reuben and Leah? Joseph had already told him they wouldn't give him permission to marry Orpha if he didn't cut his hair. And maybe if he cut his hair, *Dat* and Anna would come to the baptism as well.

He looked at the elder, who sat quietly in his chair.

"I'll get my hair cut," Christian said, looking down.

"Then we'll do the baptism Sunday after next. It will take place outside after the regular worship service. You may invite members of your family to attend. It might be a little cold but we'll pray for sunshine."

"Thank you." Christian rose and left with his mind in a quandary. Had he done the right thing? How would he explain his decision to Little Bear, who would surely see short hair as capitulation to the white man's way? Why had he given in to the elder's desires, after vigorously resisting *Dat*'s wishes for so long?

Despite the questions that dogged him all the way home, his heart was at peace. He didn't have to explain his decision to anyone. *I'll ask Anna to cut my hair tomorrow. After that, my family will be more likely to come to the baptism.*

-27-

Several days after Christian learned that the Dunkers were ready to receive him as a member, he found Barbara at the door of his cabin. What might she want?

"Can I come in?"

"Of course. What brings you here?"

"This place is a mess," Barbara said, ignoring his question as she looked around the inside of his cabin.

"It's home to me." Why must his big sister act like a boss? She didn't keep her own home nearly as clean as Anna's.

Barbara put her hands on her hips. "Sarah told me that you're planning to join the Dunkers. I wanted you to know that *Dat* is pretty upset about it."

Christian shrugged his shoulders. "He didn't say anything to me."

Barbara knit her eyebrows. "Why should he? You already know what he wants you to do."

Stubbornly, Christian told her, "I'm old enough to make up my own mind."

"You know the Dunkers don't believe you're saved unless they dunk you three times in a flowing stream," Barbara said. "It's pretty cold outside right now."

"I don't mind. I bathe in the creek when it's cold."

"*Mam* would be disappointed in you," Barbara said in a scolding tone.

"How do you know how *Mam* would feel?"

"She told me things she wouldn't say to you."

Christian snorted. "What difference does it make, now that she's gone?"

Barbara thought for a moment. "I probably shouldn't tell you this, but *Mam* told me that she thought you'd be a minister someday."

Christian's knees buckled and he sank into a chair as the weight of his mother's words pressed down on his shoulders. He closed his eyes to block out Barbara and said, partly to himself, "What made *Mam* say that?"

"We were talking about Bishop Jake, and she said that of all her boys, you would be the most likely to be a preacher."

"So maybe I'll be a minister among the Dunkers. What difference does it make—Amish or Dunkers?"

"Christian! You know it would make all the difference in the world to *Mam*. This is about who we are, not about what church we attend. We are Amish Mennonite people. *Dat's* father left the Reformed church in the Old Country to join the Anabaptists."

Christian took a step toward Barbara, trying to dismiss *Mam's* words from his mind. "If our *Dawdi* (grandfather) left the Reformed church, and *Dat* left the Old Country, why can't I leave the Amish?"

Barbara sighed. "Why must you turn up your nose at *Dat*? He's tried hard to help you get started on the farm. He wants you to be successful."

"Why should I be beholden to him?"

"*Dat* could withhold your inheritance."

Christian caught his breath. He hadn't thought of that. That might make a big difference to Orpha, who wanted to marry a farmer. "So you think that *Dat* might take away my inheritance on the farm if I join the Dunkers?" He tried to sound incredulous, but now that she had raised the issue, he worried that it might be true.

Barbara nodded vigorously. "Yes, that's how he talked to me when I wanted to marry Cristy."

"That was more than ten years ago. Did he say anything to you about it recently?"

"No, he didn't need to. Cristy left the Dunkers to join our church."

"So *Dat* didn't actually talk to you about my inheritance?"

"No, but I know he wants you to join the Amish church as much now as he wanted me to stay Amish when I was getting married."

"What difference does it make if I get inheritance on the farm or not? Maybe Orpha will get one from her family." Christian was desperate, looking for a way out.

"Don't be stupid. She's an orphan."

"Are you saying I shouldn't get married to Orpha?"

"No, I'm saying she should join our church."

"Well, I don't like you telling me what to do. I've made up my mind that I'm going to join the Dunkers no matter what you say. Or what *Dat* says."

Barbara turned to leave. "Someday you'll be sorry." With that, she stomped out the door.

Christian walked out behind her. "That's my problem, not yours. If I need any help from you, I'll ask."

His legs were weak as he turned to walk back inside the cabin. He hadn't even thought about inheritance of land. He could hardly blame himself; the Shawnees had no such concept. All that a man might pass on to his children were a few personal items like clothing and hunting tools. It was different when a family had land. If *Dat* deeded part of his land to him, all the hard work he'd done on the farm as a child would count for something. Clearly, Barbara was looking forward to her share.

Had *Dat* gotten an inheritance from Grandpa Hochstetler? If he had, Christian had never heard about it. *Dat* had left the Alsace in '38, when John and Barbara were little children. Maybe Grandpa Hochstetler had been as unhappy with *Dat* leaving the Old Country as *Dat* would be to have him join the Dunkers.

Dare he ask him about that?

He wished *Mam* were alive, so he could talk to her about his dilemma. She'd talk *Dat* into giving him his rightful inheritance, if it was true that he wanted to withhold it. Once when *Mam* was writing a letter to her parents—the Detweilers— she had commented that they were reluctant to see her come to the new country because they knew they'd never see her again. How was that any different than his wanting to stay with the Indians? Or join the Dunkers?

If he succeeded in marrying to Orpha, at least his Amish family would get to see him often and spend time with his children.

Even if Barbara was right and *Dat* didn't let Christian farm his land anymore, he might be able to find a place to farm nearby. That's what Orpha wanted. Or maybe they could move farther west, where there was plenty of wild land to settle. That would give him opportunity to hunt and fish at will, and still do enough farming to make Orpha happy.

That is, if she consented to marry him. What if he joined the Dunker church and Orpha said no? What if *Dat* wouldn't let him farm the land? He pushed the dreadful thought from his mind.

But he was nearly certain that Orpha would say yes. She had to. Maybe Anna could persuade *Dat* to treat him differently than he had Barbara.

The next morning, he headed for the farm to talk to Anna. He nodded to *Dat,* who was repairing the gate on the corral fence.

He walked toward the springhouse as Anna emerged, carrying a large *rome-hoffa* (cream-crock) that had been cooling in the water. *She must be planning to make butter today.*

"I'll carry that for you," he said.

Anna smiled as he took the crock from her hands and led the way toward the house.

He set the crock on the kitchen table and watched as Anna spooned off the cream into another container with her large creaming spoon. The fat globules of cream stayed in the spoon as the skim milk ran through the tiny holes in the concave surface.

"I've decided to cut my hair," he said.

She tipped the spoon as she turned quickly to face him, spilling a bit of cream on the table.

"How did you decide to do that?" she asked, wiping up the cream with the edge of her apron.

"It seemed like the right time. Joseph cut his some time ago."

"That's good," she said as she poured the cream into a wooden churn. She put on the lid and asked, "Do you want to help me make butter?"

"Sure," he said, gripping the dasher and thrusting it up and down. He'd done it many times for *Mam* as a boy. *Should I ask Anna to cut my hair now?*

"*Dat* said he's planting flax today," Anna said. "I asked him to plant some extra so we'll have enough linen to make a pair of trousers for you. The ones you're wearing are pretty worn out."

Christian nodded. "Thanks for patching these for me. I know *Mam* never enjoyed patching very much."

"I don't mind," she said. "I think of my stitches as tiny prayers. That helps."

Christian stopped churning to look at her. "Does that mean you pray for me while you're patching my clothes?"

She nodded as she rinsed out the cream container. "Yes, of course."

"Well, that's very kind of you." He started churning again, startled by the lump that rose in his throat.

He churned in silence for a few moments, stirring up the courage to say something about his hair. Anna was stirring the hearth fire when he forced out the words. "Would you mind cutting my hair for me? I'm afraid it won't look very nice if I do it myself. I know you always cut *Dat's* hair."

Anna smiled. "Yes, I'll be glad to cut it as soon as we're finished making butter."

That settles it, he thought. *There's no going back now.* If he ever met Little Bear again, he'd have to tell him what the vow meant to him now. So many things had changed since he'd left the Shawnees.

Before long he heard the welcome sound of buttermilk splashing inside the churn. A few drops splattered through the dasher hole.

"It's almost finished," Anna said, taking the dasher from him. She gave a few more thrusts before emptying the churn and putting the butter into a pan to wash and salt it.

Christian fiddled with his long hair as he waited for Anna, glad that *Dat* wasn't there to witness her cutting it. *I can always grow it out if I don't like it.*

Anna left her butter and took up a pair of scissors. He followed her beckoning and sat on a kitchen chair. In a few moments, she was finished. Long strands of hair lay on the floor. "We'll put it in the garden to keep the rabbits away," she said.

"Oh no, we can't do that."

"Why not?"

"The Shawnees always burn their hair."

Anna looked puzzled as Christian scooped the hair from the floor and thrust it into the hearth. It flashed into flame for a brief moment, filling the cabin with its sulfurous odor. He hesitated, wondering if he should explain that for the Shawnees, possessing another's hair was like owning their soul. Whether it was dangling from a scalp or clumped in a container, you wouldn't want your hair to fall into enemy hands. *Anna might understand. She keeps her hair covered. No one sees it but* Dat.

Christian mumbled a thank-you and left Anna to finish her butter. Low-lying clouds sailed overhead, and the cool spring air chilled the newly shorn nape of his neck as he headed for the flax field. If Anna was going to make him a new pair of linen trousers, the least he could do was help *Dat* plant the extra flax seed.

❖

It was nearly bedtime. Anna pondered the best way to talk to Jacob about Christian's plan to join the Dunker church. She'd need to decide soon whether to attend the upcoming baptism. It might be easier to talk about now that Christian had cut his hair. It meant things were changing for the better. Jacob had only mentioned it in passing when he came in for dinner, but she was sure it meant a lot to him. He wasn't one to say much about such things.

If only Jacob would mention the baptism, it would be easier for her to say what she was thinking. At least, that's the way it had always been with Ulrich. Things always worked out best when the men thought they were the first ones to think of something. From what she knew of Lizzie, that's the way that Lizzie and Jacob had communicated as well.

She looked over at Jacob, who was sitting in a chair, nearly asleep. She mentally practiced an opening: "Have you thought more about going to Christian's baptism?" And then she thought the better of it. Things always worked best when Jacob volunteered his thoughts rather than answering her questions.

Maybe she could say, "I saw Catharine the other day, and we talked a little bit about the baptism." No, Catharine didn't want to be drawn into the conversation. That might get her in trouble with Jake, which wouldn't help anything in the long run.

And then she recalled Catharine's suggestion. What if she prayed? God would show her something. Well, she had prayed about it, in a way—if prayer was thinking about something long and hard while wishing God would do something about it. But so far she hadn't come up with anything that had much chance of working. *Maybe over a cup of tea . . .*

She lowered a dipper into the hot water in the kettle, and put it into a cup with a few sprigs of mint. *Dear God,* she beseeched in her spirit, as she breathed in the smell of fresh mint, *please give me the words to say.*

"Jacob," she said, "I have some tea for you."

He shook himself and rubbed his eyes. Sipping the hot drink, he said conversationally, "We made good progress in the field today. Christian helped with the flax and we got it all planted. "

"So Christian helped today?"

"Yes, he seems more interested in the farm lately."

"I wonder what changed his mind."

"I don't know, but he seems to have his eye on Orpha Rupp." Jacob's eyes twinkled. "I imagine he's thinking about marriage."

"Have you talked to him about it?"

"No," said Jacob. "He'll bring it up when he thinks it's the right time."

Anna nodded. *Like father, like son.* "That's probably true," she said as casually as she could manage. "We don't want people prying things out of us that we'd rather keep to ourselves."

Jacob looked up from his cup of tea and gazed into her eyes. "Yes," he said, with a tenderness of spirit that let Anna know he really meant it. It was like a little bridge that might carry them to greater understanding with each other. Boldly, she plunged in.

"I've been talking to Christian lately," she said, "and he's been telling me things that I wish I had known long ago."

"I've noticed that he talks to you quite easily," said Jacob. "Maybe he sees you more like his mother these days. He always talked to Lizzie more than me, and I'm sure he misses her a lot."

Anna's heart pounded as she considered what to say next. She mustn't spoil this wonderful moment by saying the wrong thing. "Tell me what Christian liked the most about Lizzie."

"Lizzie always defended him when the older boys got too rowdy. He was the youngest, and they sometimes made fun of him. She even stood up for him one day when I used the switch on him. I might have been a little too rough on him, and she told me it was enough, right there in Christian's hearing."

Anna lifted her eyebrows.

"I told her in no uncertain terms it was my business to discipline my boys, and she shouldn't stand in the way. It got between us, and it was only a month later—" Jacob's voice broke. He covered his emotions by drinking the rest of the tea. He brought his voice under control and continued.

"It was only a month later when Lizzie was killed. I doubt that Christian would remember that, with all that he's gone through in so many years since then." They were both silent for a while.

"More?" she asked as Jacob set his cup back on the table. He nodded. She brewed a fresh cup. Both were silent, thinking.

"Maybe you should ask him," Anna said.

"What good would that do?"

"It could help you understand each other. Catharine says that when we don't talk things out with each other, we act them out in the way we treat each other. I know that was true between me and Ulrich. If I felt like I needed to say something to him, but kept it inside, he could tell something was wrong."

Jacob cocked his head. "There's something I've been meaning to tell you for a long time. Maybe this is the time to say it."

Anna braced herself for a hard word. Men could be insensitive when they talked about their feelings.

"We've only been married a few years," Jacob said, "and the longer we're married, the more I think you're like Lizzie. The bishop told me it's not good to compare you with Lizzie, but I can't help it. One of the things I like about you is that you speak your own mind and you're not afraid to say what you think, even if I disagree. And I've come to see that it's a good thing that you stick up for Christian sometimes, the way Lizzie did."

Anna's heart sang. "That's a kind thing to say."

Jacob reached out and laid his hand on hers across the table. "I think if Lizzie were here today, she'd do the same thing for Christian that you've been doing. You know. Listening to him. Treating him kindly. Accepting him as he is. It's something that's hard for me." Jacob spoke in soft tones.

Anna sat motionless.

"I'm very disappointed that Christian is not going to join the Amish church. For all the years that he was gone, I prayed that God would bring him back so that he could join the church and carry on our faith." His voice broke. "And now, it looks as though he's going to join the Dunkers instead. I'm afraid that the people in our church will think I didn't do my duty."

Anna shook her head. "I don't think there's a man in our church who could do better than you in this situation," she said tenderly. "I've seen how much you care about it."

"I feel so helpless," Jacob replied. "I don't know what else I can do."

It was the moment that Anna had been longing for. She gathered her courage and said, "I'm glad Christian is joining a church after living with the Indians for years. I wish he would join the Amish, but I want to support the decision he's made, and even attend his baptism if—"

"I thought you might want to go," Jacob said.

Anna sat in amazement. "You'll be all right with it, then?"

A sadness settled into Jacob's eyes. "Please don't ask me to bless something the church frowns upon. But if you decide to go, I won't stand in your way."

A flood of relief washed over her. Catharine had given her good advice. By listening carefully to what was most important to Jacob, she had made progress toward her own goal. To see Jacob and Christian fully reconciled to each other would be even more satisfying.

-28-

As the appointed day for his baptism neared, Christian worried he might not be doing the right thing. By casting his lot with the Dunkers, he was threatening to break his ties to both the Indians and the Amish. His adoptive brother, Little Bear, would accuse him of breaking his vow, no matter how carefully he tried to explain his reasons. And his birth family, especially *Dat*, might censure him for rejecting the community of faith that he had known since childhood.

Why had he given in so easily to Elder Klein's request that he cut his hair? Now he'd given up a lot, with little to show for it. Although Orpha was happy that he was joining her church, she'd not made any commitment to be his lifelong companion. And even if she had, her foster parents would have to agree to their marriage. Maybe he should tell Elder Klein that he needed more time to decide.

And then he recalled Post's resolute courage in the face of danger, his willingness to complete a mission without the guarantee of success. If he hadn't taken a risk, his life wouldn't have meant much to himself or anyone else. That's because he had done it in response to God's call, not because of what people would think. Christian gathered up his courage. He would go through with it.

On the day of the baptism, Christian sat through the worship service in Elder Klein's home. He was still unsure whether his family planned to attend. He surveyed the room. None of them were present for the preaching service. Perhaps they would come to the baptism itself, which would be done outside.

He tried to concentrate as Elder Klein opened the Bible and read a few verses from the sixth chapter of Romans.

"Therefore, we are buried with him by baptism into death: that like as Christ was raised up from the dead by the glory of the Father, even so we also should walk in newness of life." Then he laid his Bible on the table and said, "When we submit to the sacred ordinance of baptism, we are submitting to Jesus himself. We die to ourselves and our sinful temptations in order to live for God."

Yes, Christian mused, *something died inside me when I decided to leave some of my old ways of thinking in order to become a follower of Jesus in the Dunker way. But now I feel so much more alive.*

When the sermon was over, Elder Klein invited the congregation to come outside. The creek where the baptism would take place flowed through Elder Klein's farm, so it was only a short distance. It was made deeper and wider now for the baptism, dammed by rocks and logs downstream. Elder Klein led the way to the creek and then waited for people to arrive at the water's edge.

Christian stood there beside the elder, anxiously surveying the group. There were three dozen people or so. Orpha was there, with two friends at her side. She smiled when he looked in her direction. There was Aaron Benedict, a man who always looked askance at Christian's hair. There too were Reuben and Leah Stump, who had tried to keep him away from Orpha.

Where was Joseph? Or Anna? Or *Dat*?

At a signal from the elder, Aaron waded into the stream with a large stick in his hand. He walked to a place in the middle of the water and tapped on the bottom with his stick. He nodded, satisfied at the depth, and waded back to the bank.

The elder knelt on the grassy edge of the creek. Christian knelt beside him. Elder Klein raised his voice in earnest prayer for Christian, thanking God for his commitment and praying that he might indeed be worthy of God's call.

What can I do to be worthy? Christian wondered quietly to himself as the elder prayed. *Maybe Barbara is right that I'm joining the church because of Orpha. How can I be sure I'm doing this for the right reasons? Will God be angry with me if I'm not sincere enough to be baptized?*

Christian was so deep in thought he didn't notice that the elder had finished praying and was now standing beside him. Christian blushed and jumped to his feet. Everyone chuckled. He saw Orpha watching him. She smiled encouragingly.

The elder turned to walk into the creek, motioning for Christian to follow. There was no stopping now. If he was doing the wrong thing—or the right thing for the wrong reason—that was the way it would be.

They moved to the center of the creek. With his arm on Christian's shoulder, the elder invited Christian to turn and face downstream.

"It is now time to baptize our brother, who has made his confession," the elder said. A hush fell. The elder turned to face the congregation standing on the shore. The only sound that broke the silence was the cooing of a dove in a tree that hung over the water.

The elder began to recite the questions he'd rehearsed with Christian in private: "Dost thou believe that Jesus Christ is the Son of God, and that he has brought from heaven a saving gospel? If so, you may answer 'yea.'"

"Yea."

"Dost thou willingly renounce Satan, with all his pernicious ways, and all the simple pleasures of the world?"

"Yea," he replied. *I hope it doesn't mean pleasures such as fishing and hunting.*

"Dost thou covenant with God, in Christ Jesus, to be faithful unto death?"

"Yea."

"Upon this confession of faith, which thou hast made before God and these witnesses, thou shalt, for the remission of sins, be baptized in the name of the Father, and of the Son, and of the Holy Ghost."

Elder Klein said in a low voice: "Please kneel." Christian knelt down, wincing as his kneecap hit the sharp edge of a rock. He scooted sideways a few inches, submersed in water to his armpits, facing the congregation gathered at the creek side.

The elder put his left hand on Christian's forehead and the other on the nape of his neck. "I am going to put you under three times forward," he said. "You may hold your nose if you wish."

Christian nodded to show he was ready.

"I now baptize you in the name of the Father," the elder said as he thrust Christian forward and down into the water with a practiced motion.

Although Christian thought he was ready, he stiffened as the elder pushed him under the surface. The memories rushed back. He remembered his time as a new captive in the Shawnee village.

He had flailed his arms as three young women forced his head under the water of the nearby creek. He resisted with all his might, but one of the young women dove under the water and swept his feet out from under him. He struggled as though he was drowning, thrashing at the water and swinging at the young women. But they laughed at his antics and another young woman waded into the water to subdue him.

After they held him under the surface for a few moments, they pulled him up and let him breathe. He gasped for air, puzzled by what they were doing. They shoved him under again, this time scrubbing his back vigorously with small stones from the creek bottom.

I'm going to die.

But they pulled him up again. Two of them held his arms while the third scrubbed his chest, his back, and arms. A few sharp stones scratched his skin, marking him with red streaks on his arms and shoulders. It was the only way, they claimed, to cleanse him of all of his white ways and bring him into the tribe.

The memory faded as Elder Klein pulled him back to the surface. And then he intoned, "In the name of the Son" and plunged him back under. This time Christian did not resist.

"And in the name of the Holy Ghost," the elder said, and lowered him under the surface for the third time.

This time, when the elder pulled Christian's head out of the water, he put his hand on his forehead and prayed a prayer of blessing on him. And then he lifted him to his feet and said, "Rise to newness of life." He raised his voice loudly so that the congregation could hear it clearly.

He pulled Christian near and greeted him with a "holy kiss," a ceremonial salutation inspired by scriptural instruction. Not associated with romance, it was practiced only between persons of the same gender. They kissed, lightly touching each other's lips. Then he led the way to the bank. As Christian stepped out of the water, a man Christian did not know extended a hand of fellowship. He kissed him and said, "God bless you, brother."

"Brother?" It was the first time Christian had been addressed that way since he'd been with the Shawnees. He now belonged to the Christian fellowship, the communion of saints who sought to be God's faithful ones.

That's when he noticed Barbara, cradling little Ruth in her arms. Anna was there too, holding on to her granddaughter Elizabeth's hand. And there was Orpha, who met his eyes with a wide smile.

Dorothy, the elder's wife, handed him a towel. Christian dried his face and hair. As Christian looked around at the crowd of people, he saw *Dat* standing on the far side beside Joseph. Had they been there all along?

Christian caught *Dat*'s eye for a moment but could not read his face. Several men stepped up. "God bless you, Brother Christian," each one said before greeting him with a kiss.

The congregation began to disperse. Christian went to *Dat*, who was standing with Anna, Joseph, and Barbara. "Thanks for coming," he said. "This means a lot to me."

"I'm glad you chose to be baptized," *Dat* said, reaching out to shake Christian's hand.

Anna hugged him, as did Joseph and Barbara. At that moment, the April sun broke through a cloud. He turned his face skyward and basked in the rays of the sun. To Christian, they seemed to convey the warmth of God's love. Christian sought nothing more—words could too readily spoil the sacredness of the moment.

Later on, there would be ample time to talk about the implications of his new life as a Dunker.

In the weeks that passed after the baptism, Christian lived with new energy and purpose, extending even to farmwork. *Dat* was helping Joseph at the Heidelberg property. Christian decided to try his hand at the spring plowing.

"Come, Blitz, let's go," Christian said. "We have work to do." He stroked the aging gelding's nose and led him out of the corral. He'd never plowed without *Dat*'s guidance before, but he was determined to prove he could do it. The fastest way to show *Dat* that he'd really changed was to take up hard work on the farm.

It took him longer to get the harness on Blitz than it would have for *Dat*, but he managed it by himself. He hitched the plow onto the harness and headed for the field.

The tip of the blade dug into the soil, making the plow skew this way and that. "How does *Dat* do this?" he asked out loud, with only Blitz to hear. "What am I doing wrong?" he mumbled to himself.

And then he remembered. "Whoa," he said. Blitz seemed more than happy to stop. He stood still while Christian returned to the barn to find the plow slide. He lifted the plow and inserted it into a groove in the long piece of wood made to carry the weight of the plow on the way to the field. He was proud that he'd remembered and it imparted confidence that he'd catch on to this task in due time.

In a few minutes, he got to the edge of the field and put the point of the plow into the soil. Blitz dug in, pulling with a familiar gait.

Who would have thought this moment would be possible? He still remembered how Blitz had run from the corral on the fateful morning of the attack on the farm. The gelding had barely escaped the Indian warriors. They grabbed for his halter as he hurtled through the corral gate.

Now here they were, horse and grown boy together more than nine years later. It seemed wrong to tear up large portions of soil with the plow, but Christian was changing his mind about the need for it.

"Giddup, Blitz," he said, as much to show he was in charge as to hurry the gelding's pace. Blitz was more familiar with plowing than he.

Wham! The tip of the plow hit a rock buried below the surface. Christian forced the point back into the soil and tried to guide it in a straight line. It was virtually impossible, since a web of hidden roots impeded his path. Christian's admiration for *Dat's* strength and skill grew as he wrestled with the handles. He had to admit that *Dat's* life hadn't been easy.

"Whoa," he said, pulling on the reins. Blitz stopped in his tracks and looked back at Christian as though asking what was happening.

Christian pulled out his handkerchief and wiped the sweat from his brow. The early May sun beat down. Christian took off his hat. The wind felt cool on his perspiring brow. It was a new feeling, since he'd quit shaving the hair around the edges of his scalp.

Christian had made several rounds when Anna approached the field. "I thought you might want some cold bee balm," she said. "I cooled it in the springhouse."

He reached out to take the tea. "Thank you."

"It looks like you're doing a good job."

Christian sighed. "I don't know about that. My muscles are so tired that I'm not plowing as deep as I'd like."

"I didn't think you liked to plow."

Christian shrugged. "It's really hard work, but it needs to be done." He paused. "I've decided that I can be a farmer after all."

"That's good." Anna smiled encouragingly.

Christian grinned. "As long as I have some time to go hunting and fishing, I'll be happy. I don't want to work all the time, but I want to make a living for myself."

Anna smiled and lifted her jar. "More tea?" Christian nodded and held out his cup.

"I suppose that Orpha will be happy to see you plowing."

"How did you guess?"

"She seems to be the kind that would make a good farmer's wife."

Christian smiled. "I know she'd rather be a farmer's wife than a hunter's wife. If I can prove to her that I'm a good provider, she might marry me." He paused. "But don't say anything to *Dat* about that."

"Why shouldn't *Dat* know?"

Christian fingered the reins as he stared at the ground.

"If he wasn't happy with my joining the Dunkers, he probably won't be happy with my marrying one of those girls."

"Don't be too sure. If you want, I'll invite you both for supper. *Dat* might like Orpha more than you think."

Christian looked into Anna's eyes for a moment. Did she really believe that?

"Well, I better get back to plowing," he said, his voice husky with emotion.

Anna was becoming a true mother to him. He missed his *Mam*, and he knew that Anna could never replace her. But Anna's care for him felt like a salve, healing wounds he had tried to ignore.

"Giddup," he said to Blitz as he blinked back tears and thrust the plow into the soil.

-29-

"Christian, would you mind going to market with me?" Anna asked. Jacob was in Heidelberg, lending Joseph a hand with some farmwork. "I need a few things, but don't care to go by myself." Anna always felt a little uneasy at market. She didn't like large crowds, and she was also afraid she'd meet Silas Burkholder.

"Sure, I'll go with you," Christian said. "Let me hitch Blitz to the wagon."

My, how Christian has changed since he joined the Dunkers, Anna mused. *He's becoming so thoughtful of others.*

It was a beautiful spring day, and Anna drank in the sights along the way as Christian drove the wagon. The flax fields were bursting with purple flowers. Sheep grazed in the lush meadows. The wheat and spelt were growing well and looked as though they might soon come into head.

They had just pulled up to the hitching post when Christian turned eagerly to Anna. "Look, there's Orpha! Do you mind buying a few things by yourself? I'd like to spend some time with her."

Anna smiled. "No, I don't mind," she said. "As long as you get back to the wagon by noon." Anna took a basket from the back of the wagon and Christian hurried off to catch up with Orpha.

Anna walked from one stand to another, picking up the items on her list: salt, two small containers of seasoning, two needles, and some thread. An hour passed quickly. Anna came to the farrier's stand, which stood a little distance from the others. Since childhood, she'd been intrigued by horses. She enjoyed watching the farrier work with the horses' hooves, whether trimming, grooming, or shoeing. It was important to keep one's feet in good condition—whether human or beast. She smiled at the comparison.

Suddenly, she found Silas Burkholder in front of her. "Did you come to watch the farrier rasp my horse's hooves?" he asked.

Anna moved back a step. "No," she said, startled by his impudence. "I have no interest in your horse."

"You should," he said. "He gets his hooves trimmed just like you trim people's toenails when you massage their feet."

A young man standing close by laughed aloud. "You can trim my toenails anytime," he said, lifting up a bare foot. "I'm tired of trimming them myself."

Anna shuddered to see his overly long nails, badly split and caked with dirt. *I need to get out of here*, she thought, panic rising within her.

Silas leered and blocked her path as she turned to retrace her steps. "I have something to say to you," he said. "Listen."

Her heart pounded as she peered at the small knot of men who were standing nearby. There were no other women within earshot. *Where's Christian? How am I going to get away from here?*

"Please move away," she told Silas firmly. "I need to go now."

He laughed. "I don't let witches tell me what to do." He reached out and gripped her arm.

She pulled back. "Please let me go!"

The man with the ugly toenails crossed his arms. "You won't get away from Silas," he said. "You might as well do what he asks." He laughed.

Just then, Anna heard a shout. "Hey! Let go of her."

Before she had time to turn around, Christian rushed past her. He grabbed Silas and slammed him to the ground, then straddled him.

Anna watched as Christian smashed Silas's face into the dirt. "Christian! Stop!"

"Let go of me, you varmint!" Silas yelled, spitting dirt out of his mouth.

"You're the varmint," Christian said. He yanked Silas's arms up hard behind his back.

Anna trembled with fear. Would the other men hurt Christian? But they were cowards, she thought, looking around. They watched, but they didn't join in.

"Stop that!" Silas yelled as Christian held his arms locked behind him. "I didn't do anything wrong."

"You know better than that. You mistreated Anna years ago. You lied to cover it up. Now you're going to pay for your sins." Christian's muscles bulged as he jerked Silas sideways— within inches of a fresh pile of horse dung.

Anna covered her face with her hands. Christian wouldn't submit Silas to such treatment, would he? "Christian! That's enough!"

"I'm no sinner," Silas howled.

"You're an abuser and a liar," Christian said. He grunted as he yanked Silas off the ground and dangled his face a few inches above the fresh manure. "Now tell me that you're never going to get close to Anna again."

"I don't make promises to savages."

Anna looked around at the half-dozen men who stood nearby. She was relieved that no one else showed interest in joining the fight.

"I'm going to count to ten," Christian said. "If you say 'I'm sorry, Anna' before I get to ten, I'll let you go. If not—"

"Indians are too stupid to count."

Several in the crowd tittered.

"You're next," Christian said to the closest, his face flushed red with exertion. The young man sobered and backed away a few steps.

The farrier—who had stopped his work to watch the fight—looked amused. "You'd better do what the young feller says, Silas. Looks like you picked the wrong fight this time."

Christian started to count. "One, two, three, four, five, six, seven—"

"I'm sorry," Silas said, barely loud enough for Anna to hear it.

"Say it to Anna," Christian said, "and say it loud enough that everyone can hear you." He resumed his count: "Eight, nine—"

"I'm sorry, Anna," Silas said just as Christian finished the count.

Christian jerked Silas to his feet and swung him around. His eyes blazed. "You're lucky I decided to become a Christian and join the Dunker church," he said. "If I'd have dealt with you like a Shawnee, you'd have a hatchet in your brain."

Silas brushed himself off. He was breathing hard. He refused to look at anyone.

Anna wanted nothing more than to leave. "Christian," she said, "I'd like to go now."

"Not till I say one more thing to Silas."

Christian pulled the tomahawk from his belt and waved it in Silas' face. "If you ever bother Anna again or call her a witch, you'll regret it. Do you understand?"

Silas shrunk back. "Yes," he mumbled.

Christian looked around at the men, his face as hard as flint. "The same applies to you all. Good day."

Anna's hand trembled as she held onto Christian's arm. They walked away. "You surprised me," she said. "I thought you were with Orpha."

"Reuben and Leah took her home. That's why I came looking for you."

"Thanks for dealing with Silas. I hope that's the last time he bothers me."

"If he ever bothers you again, I'll make sure he's sorry."

Anna fell silent. *I can't imagine Jacob dealing with Silas this way*, Anna thought. *Christian still has a lot of Shawnee in him.*

"Did you find everything you needed?" Christian asked.

"No," she said, "but I'd like to go home now. I need to get away from here." She was deep in thought as they reached the wagon. They were both silent most of the way home. She wondered what would have happened to her if Christian hadn't shown up.

The news of Christian's actions was going to spread fast. What would Jacob think if he heard of Christian's fight with Silas? She'd tell Jacob about it as soon as he came back home.

"I've put a little rosemary with salt on this slice of bread for you," she said to Jacob the morning after he arrived back home after two days of work at the Heidelberg property. "The Sauer almanac says this is supposed to be good for the eyes—if you eat it in the morning."

"Thank you. If Sauer said it, I believe it." Jacob took the bread from her hand and took a bite. "It tastes good too."

"Christian was plowing this week," she said. "I thought he didn't like to plow."

Jacob took another bite of the rosemary. "That's right. He's always said he doesn't like to plow, but he did it this time without my asking him."

Anna spooned some mush from the kettle onto Jacob's plate. "What do you think changed his mind?" She wondered whether he was willing to admit that the Dunkers were having a positive effect on his son.

"I think he has marriage on his mind. He's finally come to see that if he wants to be married and have a family, he's going to have to take some responsibility around here."

Anna added mush to her plate and sat down at the table across from Jacob.

Together they bowed their heads in silence. Under her breath, Anna repeated the prayer she had been taught as a child.

"It's good to see that Christian is taking more interest in the farm," Anna said as they began their meal.

Jacob nodded. "He might become a farmer yet. Until this week, I wondered if that would ever happen."

"The other day, Joseph told me one reason it took so long for Christian to decide," Anna said.

"Why was that?"

"When he was with the Indians, he vowed never to follow white man's ways—meaning he wouldn't dress like the whites or farm land taken from the Indians. He didn't want to break that vow."

Jacob's mouth dropped open. "Really?"

Anna sat down at the table. "It wasn't until he met that Moravian missionary that he felt free to leave his Indian ways. Or join the church."

"If only it were our church instead of the Dunkers."

"But that's not what he decided. We have to live with the way it is."

Jacob shrugged his shoulders. "It doesn't mean I have to like it."

Anna paused for a moment, then took a deep breath. "Do you remember what you told me a couple of months ago—that you like the way I speak my own mind?"

"Of course."

"Well, I have something I'd like to say to you now."

"Should I finish my breakfast first?" There was a hint of a smile on Jacob's face.

"Yes, go ahead and finish your breakfast and then we'll talk afterwards." She scraped the last few crumbs of mush onto Jacob's plate and then sat quietly, waiting for Jacob to speak.

He finished his breakfast in silence and then he moved to the rocking chair.

Anna took a chair opposite him. "Barbara told me that you might remove Christian from your will."

"I don't have a will."

"Are you going to write one?"

"I have no plans."

"Will you give Christian an equal inheritance with the other children?"

Jacob stroked his beard as he rocked in his chair. "I haven't decided yet. I know there are a couple of men in our church who don't think I should. I remember that Stephen Sweitzer didn't share the inheritance with his son who refused to join the Amish."

"Their sons weren't taken by the Indians," Anna said, her voice rising. "They have no idea what Christian has gone through." She paused. "Don't let them tell you what is best. Do what you think is right."

"Why should I give Christian an inheritance like the rest, if he joins the Dunkers?"

"Because it's the right thing to do. Christian is trying to prove that he's made a change in his life. It shows how much he admires you. He wants to please you."

Jacob paused. Again he stroked his beard, as though to let the words soak in.

"Is that all you have to say about it?"

"No. I have been praying about something else I want to share with you."

Jacob cocked his head inquiringly.

"The other day, Christian went to market with me. I happened to meet Silas Burkholder, and he started bothering me. I thought I wasn't going to get away."

Jacob's eye narrowed. "That man! He'd better stay away from you! Please don't go to the market by yourself."

"I was lucky Christian was with me. He was so upset that he threw Silas down and sat on him."

"Really? Silas is a big man."

"The Indians must have taught him how to fight. He had Silas under his thumb. Maybe you can ask him about it. And I wish you'd talk with him about the inheritance."

Jacob thought for a moment. "I don't mind talking about what happened with Silas, but I don't want to say anything to him about the inheritance."

"It doesn't need to happen right away. But I'd like to see it happen before the snow blows this fall."

"I'm not ready to make a decision about my will. I'm not sick or old, so I should have plenty of time to decide. Let's see if Christian's changes really last. If he gets married and has children—and keeps working hard on the farm—I might be willing to give him an equal inheritance."

"Even if he stays in the Dunker church?"

"Maybe. But it's too early for me to decide."

Anna choked back a retort. It would do no good to push Jacob toward a decision he didn't want to make. She sighed. "You're right." She rose from her chair and cleared the table. Jacob took his hat from the peg by the door and walked into the sunlight.

Anna watched him move toward the barn. Had she said too much? But Christian needed an equal portion of the inheritance. Wasn't there a better way of resolving their differences than withholding his share?

Anna made her way to the garden. She thought about the time when Jacob had given his testimony at a church meal and passed around the wampum bracelet given to him by Scar Face as a sign of reconciliation. Her heart beat faster as she considered the effect it had had on her when Jacob told about his Indian captivity, his escape back to the Northkill, and his longing for his sons to be released.

She'd been so absorbed by his words that she had continued holding the wampum bracelet, long after he was done speaking. When she returned it to him after the gathering, it had emboldened him to ask for her hand in marriage.

Perhaps if Christian could give a similar account in a family gathering—or in a church service—Jacob would see how much God had done in his son's life without worrying about whether he joined the Amish church. She dreamed that it would happen.

She knelt down on a path that ran through the garden. "*Herr Gott*," she prayed, "please soften Jacob's heart toward Christian." She paused and added, "Not my will but thine be done."

When she opened her eyes, she could smell sage. She had crushed a few leaves with her knees. She stroked the leaves gently with her hands and held a few sprigs to her face, breathing deeply of their fragrance. Perhaps someday the fragrance of the Creator's love would draw Jacob and his sons into a bond they'd never experienced before.

-30-

In the five months following his baptism, Christian found a way to talk to Orpha nearly every Sunday. In spite of her foster parents' worries, they found time to be together alone, often on long walks. He was convinced that if he were to ask her to marry him, she would say yes. But there was one more way she asked him to show his devotion to the church—to participate in the fall love feast, a semiannual event he'd missed in the spring.

"What kind of feast is it?" he asked. "What kind of food do you serve?"

"We eat soup with bread. But the love feast is more than food. It's a weekend of services from Saturday morning to Sunday noon."

It sounded like a long time to be in church, but that didn't matter as long as he could be with Orpha. "When will this take place?" he asked her.

"Two weeks from now."

"I'll plan to be there," he said.

True to his word, a fortnight later Christian went to Elder Klein's home for the service. The house was crowded with more people than Christian could remember seeing at any previous church service. There were new faces. All the available places to sit were taken. Many of the children sat on the floor. Elder Klein reveled in the event. "In this love feast," he said, "we celebrate our purity, unity, and regeneration as saints of the Lord."

After the Saturday service, the women served the food. It was a simple meal, not a feast as Christian had envisioned. But the people seemed glad to be together. They lingered over the food, providing a sense of celebration.

There was not enough room for everyone to be served at the same time, so Christian waited for his turn at the table. By the time he was served, he was quite ready for the fare. First there was the soup flavored with mutton and served with wheat bread, and a choice of butter or *lattwaerrick* for a spread. But oh, the pies! So many choices—custard, gooseberry, cherry, peach, currant, and apple. Christian chose apple pie with a cup of coffee, a drink he'd not tasted before. As he relished his pie, he listened quietly to the conversations. Orpha was her usual joyful self, absorbed in conversations with several young women her age.

When everyone had finished eating, Elder Klein preached. He exhorted the congregation to consider the sincerity of their faith, as the apostle Paul had taught the church in Corinth: "Let a man examine himself . . . for he that eateth and drinketh unworthily, eateth and drinketh damnation to himself, not discerning the Lord's body."

The words settled heavily on Christian shoulders. Was he worthy to participate in such a solemn gathering? He still had many questions about Christian faith and the beliefs of the Dunkers. Would the congregation reject him if he wasn't sure of everything?

He was relieved for a break in the long service, a time to take a short walk outside. It was a cloudy day, made drearier by a sharp breeze.

When he went back inside, a man read from the Gospel of John—recounting the story of Jesus washing the feet of his twelve disciples after celebrating the Jewish Passover meal with them. Jesus told them, "If I then, your Lord and Master, have washed your feet; ye also ought to wash one another's feet."

"We will do as the Lord commanded us," Elder Klein explained. Two men fetched water from the creek, each carrying a wooden basin—one for use by men and the other for women. The elder's wife added hot water from the pot that hung over her fireplace.

The first person to have his feet washed sat on a chair and put his feet into the basin. The elder designated someone to wash and dry the first group of men's feet. It was different than the Amish way, Christian observed, where they washed each other's feet in pairs.

Each time when the designated man finished washing and drying another's feet, the two of them stood and greeted each other with a holy kiss.

By the time Christian's turn came, the elder had designated Aaron Benedict to wash and dry. Christian panicked. Aaron was the one whom he imagined had objected to his baptism. What if he sat down to have his feet washed, and Aaron refused to do it?

There was no escape. Klein's gentle smile persuaded him to take his place on the chair in front of the tub where Aaron stood with stolid expression. He looked friendly enough as he motioned for Christian to come forward. After his feet were washed and dried, Christian rose from his chair. Aaron gripped Christian's trembling hand in his, and pulled him close. "God bless you," he said as he kissed him gently. "Welcome to our church."

"God bless you too," Christian mumbled, his heart beating hard. He stumbled back to his seat, aware that many eyes were on him. Nevertheless, it hadn't turned out as bad as he had feared.

Christian sat quietly as the rest of the men and women finished their foot washing. What would the Shawnees say if they had witnessed this ritual? It could only confirm the strangeness of the whites!

That evening, they celebrated the Lord's Supper. It was a somber time to remember the new meaning that Jesus had given to the Jewish Passover meal. The group ate another simple meal served with beef, and sopped their bread in a savory broth. The members ate mostly in silence, reflecting on Elder Klein's invitation to meditate in preparation for sharing the ordinance of communion. After everyone had eaten, they sang a number of hymns while the women cleared the tables and Elder Klein's wife, Dorothy, brought out the bread and wine.

Elder Klein read a Scripture and spoke about Christ's suffering on the cross. He urged them to clear their hearts of malice or unforgiveness toward others in the fellowship, lest their unity be broken. Just before the sharing of communion, the elder invited the members to follow him in "passing the peace," forming a chain of unity. The elder greeted the brother next to him with a kiss, who passed the greeting around the circle. Sister Dorothy passed the peace in the circle of sisters. It was like the solemn peace circle among the Shawnees, Christian thought, minus the peace pipe.

As a symbol of unity, the congregation shared a common loaf of bread and drank from a common cup, divided between men and women. After Elder Klein led a closing prayer, the congregation sang a final hymn and rose from the tables to go home.

Christian lingered, hoping to speak to Orpha alone. He caught her gaze as she was leaving with Reuben and Leah. She shook her head slightly. *No,* he thought, crestfallen. *Oh well. Maybe tomorrow.*

The next morning, Christian came back for the final service of the love feast weekend. Elder Klein was at his best in the Sunday sermon, exhorting the congregation to be constant in their devotion to the "faith which was once delivered unto the saints." He declared that all those who clung closely to the teaching of the Brethren and submitted to the authority of the congregation were indeed saints of God.

Am I a saint? Christian knew he'd never qualify to have his name listed in the almanac with those of Saint Peter or Saint John. Orpha seemed far more saintly than he, perhaps too holy to marry him.

Only a short time before, he'd rejected the true meaning of his name. But now that he'd been baptized and shared in the love feast, he was a Christian and a full member of the

Dunker church. A warm sense of belonging enveloped his being, not unlike the time he was adopted by the Indians, but
in response to a very different vow. Now he felt accountable
for his commitment not only to the congregation, but also to
Creator God, as part of a larger family.

He was confident that the steps he'd taken would be
enough to convince Orpha of the sincerity of his Christian
commitment. But would they be enough to persuade Orpha's
foster parents to let him have her hand? He'd been dreaming
of it for months.

It was time to take a risk and find out.

Nearly a week passed before Christian summoned the
courage to talk to Orpha's foster parents. Reuben could be so
intimidating. At least Leah had a friendly smile.

The apples were ripe in *Dat*'s orchard. As Christian picked
them and placed them into a basket, he practiced what he
might say to the Stumps. He could not bear the thought of
their withholding permission for the marriage. They had to
say yes.

Early on Saturday morning, Christian walked to the Stump
home. He knocked, then stood nervously, with his hat in his
hand.

He heard the sound of heavy footsteps and then the door
swung open wide. Reuben stood there, his large frame block-
ing the doorway.

"Christian! Reuben, don't leave the lad standing there.
Invite him in," Leah said from the kitchen hearth.

"Yes, come in." Reuben moved slowly out of the doorway
and gestured toward a chair.

Christian sat.

"How can we help you?" Reuben asked, towering over him.

Christian started to speak, but a sudden tickle in his throat
made him cough instead. He couldn't seem to get the tickle
out of his throat.

Leah put her hand on Reuben's shoulder. "Let's all sit down at the table, and we can have a cup of tea before Christian tells us what brought him here."

"That's fine by me," Reuben replied.

Christian fiddled with his hat and then laid it on the table.

Leah frowned. "Reuben, please take Christian's hat."

Christian handed his hat to Reuben, who hung it on a peg next to the door.

"It's so nice to have cooler weather," Leah said. "I think September is my favorite month of the year. What name do the Indians give it?"

"The Shawnees call it the Harvest Moon. It's when they start to gather in their crops."

"Do Indians raise crops?" Reuben asked. "I thought they mostly hunt wild animals."

Christian tried not to show his irritation at the man's ignorance. "Yes, they have many crops—corn, pumpkins, squash, beans, and wild rice."

Christian drummed his fingers on the table as the small talk went on, waiting for the right moment to ask the question that had prompted his mission.

He had nearly finished his tea when Reuben asked again, "What is it that brings you here today?"

Christian cleared his throat, searching for the right words to say. "I guess you know that I've been spending some time with Orpha," he said.

"Yes, that would be hard not to notice," Reuben replied. "I figured you might be coming to talk about her."

Leah gave Reuben a hard look. "Why don't you let him finish what he wants to say?"

Christian looked down at his hands. "Well, I . . ." He fumbled for words. "I thought . . ." He paused. Had he come too soon? Perhaps if he'd waited a few more weeks, they'd be more likely to say yes to his request.

"If you're wanting to marry Orpha, go ahead and ask," Reuben said. Clearly he wasn't a man to mince words.

Christian blushed. "You're right. I'd like to ask Orpha to marry me, but I was told I needed to ask you first."

"Yes, she'll need our permission. Young women don't decide to get married on their own."

Christian looked helpless. "What do I need to do?"

"You're doing the right thing by coming here," Reuben said, sitting back in his chair a bit. "We took Orpha into our home when she was a little girl. We never had any children of our own, so she's like a daughter to us. We want to make sure she marries well."

"I guess you know that I'm committed to your church," Christian said, with new confidence.

"Yes, that's been good to see. What are you going to do for a living?"

"I'm planning to farm part of my father's land. He has enough for all of us."

Reuben considered this for a few moments. "Do you plan to stay around here? I don't want you carrying Orpha off to the Indians."

"Yes, I'm going to stay here and farm."

"Orpha likes you a lot," Leah said with a smile, "and I think you'd make a good couple."

Reuben glared at her. "Not so fast. I have another question."

Christian took a long, deep breath as he rubbed his thumbs together. What more did Reuben need to know?

"How many children do you want to have?"

Christian was taken aback. What business was it of Reuben's to ask this kind of question?

"Reuben, why must you discuss that now?" Leah asked.

"Because I want lots of grandchildren. This is our only chance."

Christian was at a loss for words. How could he even bring up the subject to Orpha before she agreed to marry him?

"I guess we'll have as many as the Lord gives us," Christian said hesitatingly. Why would Reuben mention children if he wasn't about to say yes?

"That's a good answer," Leah said, reaching across the table to put her hand on Reuben's arm. "Now tell the young man he can marry Orpha."

"You heard that," Reuben said. "Is that good enough for you?"

Christian straightened in his chair, realizing this was the moment he had hoped for. "Yes, of course. Thank you. That's what I came for." He reached out and shook Reuben's hand and scooted back his chair. "I guess I'll be going. I hope to talk to Orpha yet today."

"Good luck," Reuben said, fetching Christian's hat for him.

"Thank you." Christian left in haste, nearly tripping over the threshold of the door and then walking as fast as he possible on the path that led from the Stump home.

It was late afternoon when Christian reached the Heisey house where Orpha was again serving as a *Maud* because of another new baby.

"Hello, Christian," Orpha called from the apple orchard. She was standing on a small ladder, picking apples and placing them in a basket.

His heart pounded. No one else was in sight.

"How are the apples?" he asked.

"Not as nice as the ones on Reuben and Leah's farm. But here's one that looks pretty good," she said, handing him a ripe red apple that looked nearly perfect. Her cheeks were rosy from exertion and the slight chill of the mid-September breeze.

"May I help you pick?"

"Sure, why not? The folks here will be surprised I picked them so fast." She handed him an empty basket and he scrambled up the tree.

He set the basket between two limbs and began filling it with apples.

"Anna's going to have an apple *schnitzing* at *Dat's* house next Tuesday evening," he said. "I was hoping you could come. There'll be lots of people there. It should be lots of fun." He paused as he stretched to reach for an apple. "Have you ever bobbed for apples?"

"Oh yes," Orpha said. "But I'm afraid I'm getting a little too old for that. We usually let the younger ones get wet."

"I'll never forget how we bobbed for apples on the night before the Indians attacked our house. They might even have been watching us without us knowing it."

Orpha shivered. "Don't talk that way or I won't come."

Christian started to laugh and then turned sober. "Remember, I'm an Indian now. Or at least I was until I got baptized. They won't hurt you as long as you're with me."

Orpha looked into the tree where Christian was picking. "That's good. I'll be glad to come to the *schnitzing*. I like Anna—and I think she likes me too."

Christian picked a couple more apples and tossed them into the basket before climbing down the tree. This was the moment he had been planning for.

He handed the basket to Orpha. "I'm glad you're coming to the *schnitzing*. Anna thinks we make a good couple."

"Did she say that?" Orpha looked hopeful and dubious at the same time.

"Okay. She didn't say it, but I know it's true."

A smile played around Orpha's lips. "Is that supposed to make a difference to me?" Clearly, Orpha was teasing. That was a really good sign.

"No, it doesn't matter what Anna thinks. What do you think? Don't we make a good couple?" He flashed his most winsome smile.

Orpha gazed into Christian's eyes. "There's nobody I'd rather spend time with than you."

"Oh, Orpha, I would love to spend the rest of my life with you."

He opened his arms and she leaned into them. He pulled her into an embrace.

She relaxed in his arms for a moment and then pulled back. "You know that Reuben might not approve."

"I've already talked to him. He gave me permission to marry you. I mean, to ask you."

Orpha's cheeks glowed pink. "Did he say yes? I can't believe it!"

"He said yes," Christian answered, scanning her face. "But will you?"

"Yes!" Orpha said, her face radiant. "You know, I could never have imagined I'd marry someone like you—someone with your story."

He smiled coyly. "What story is that?"

"You know: the life you've led until now. Not many people in our community have experienced what you did. But I think it's made you stronger, somehow. More able to love others."

Christian held her tight for a few moments and then asked, "So can we tell the folks at the apple *schnitzing* that we're getting married?"

"Yes!" Her face was radiant. "This will be the best *schnitzing* ever."

"I'll go home and tell Anna right away," Christian said. "She might need a little time to get used to the idea."

"And I'll go tell Reuben and Leah," Orpha said. Christian released her and she gathered two baskets of apples. She smiled at him. "They'll need to help me make wedding plans."

Christian collected the three remaining baskets and followed her toward the Heisey house. He felt a lightness in his spirit as he rehearsed in his mind what had just happened. He could hardly believe it. He was going to marry Orpha! She had said yes, and so had her foster parents. Now, if only *Dat* could be convinced that marrying Orpha was a good thing, everything would turn out right.

He headed back to the farm to tell Anna, confident that she'd find the best way to talk to *Dat* about it.

-31-

Anna was pleased to hear about the engagement. She invited Christian and Orpha for a meal, as well as Joseph and Sarah. They set a date for just over a week later.

Christian and Orpha arrived first. "Come in," Anna said, noting the broad smile on Orpha's face. It promised to be a pleasant evening.

"I like the way your hair looks," Anna said to Christian. In the five months since she had cut off his scalp lock, he'd let the rest of the hair on his scalp grow, so that it was nearly of uniform length. Jacob looked on with approval but said nothing.

Joseph came to the door a few minutes later. Sarah was right behind him, carrying their infant daughter. She had been born during the spring, and Joseph had taken eagerly to fatherhood. It felt like such a long time ago that he had shown up at their door that December night when they had hardly recognized him. Anna was thrilled to watch Joseph love and care for his new young family and to reflect on God's provision for him through the years.

Jacob sat at the one end of the table and Anna at the other. The two other couples sat on opposite sides of the table, with the infant nestled in a basket on the floor nearby. After all were settled in their places, Jacob bowed his head for silent prayer. The rest followed suit.

Anna silently thanked God for the food, ending with a few words of petition for the evening: *Lord God, let this be an evening when we truly show our love to each other. Let us forgive each other as needed.*

Anna served a fresh cabbage salad laced with raw cucumbers, carrots, onions, and a touch of her favorite caraway seed. The main dish was a stew reflecting the bounty of the season, with cooked potatoes, turnips, and endives, flavored with chives.

"How's the plowing going this week?" Jacob asked, looking at Christian. Anna drew in her breath. It was the kind of question that could set Christian on edge. This would be a test to see if things had really changed between father and son. Was that what Jacob intended?

"It's going good," Christian said, nodding. "Blitz is getting a little old, but he can still work."

Jacob gave a broad smile. "I think he likes you. You handle him really well."

Anna's heart leapt. How kind of Jacob to speak to Christian that way!

Christian grinned. "Maybe he remembers the times I fed him apples from the orchard when I was a little boy. It's a wonder he didn't get a stomachache." He laughed. "I know I used to get stomachaches from eating too many tart apples."

Dat smiled. "I think you used to eat too many peaches too. *Mam* always had to remind you that you'd had enough."

"I remember the time when I brought your family some peach pie," Anna said. "I know you were pretty eager to eat it that time."

Christian's face turned sober. "I always liked peaches," he said. "But ever since the raid on our farm, I can't look at our peach orchard without thinking of the time when the Indians attacked."

"I was thinking of that myself," Jacob said. "When I looked at the calendar this morning, I realized it was ten years ago today that it happened."

Anna's muscles tensed. She had been hoping Jacob and his sons could finally talk about their experiences. But now that it seemed that they would, she was worried. She glanced at Christian, whose face was hard to read. Everyone was quiet for a moment.

"Ten years!" Joseph said softly. He shook his head. "I can remember it as though it happened last week. I'm still surprised that you thought of asking us to carry dried peaches in our pockets. That's how we escaped the gauntlet."

Anna looked at Jacob. "I don't believe you ever told me about that."

Jacob scratched his head as though he was thinking. "I might've forgotten to mention it to you. Christian and Joseph, remember when the house was burning and we were crawling out of the basement, I told you to stuff some dried peaches in your pockets. We carried them with us on the trail, and when we got to the Indian village, we gave them to the chief. He liked them so much that he spared all three of us from running the gauntlet."

Christian nodded, as did Joseph, who added, "That saved us a lot of misery, *Dat*."

Orpha knit her brow. "What's a gauntlet? It sounds terrible."

Christian nodded. "It's awful. I've seen people get hurt badly . . ." His voice trailed off, and Joseph took up the story.

"The whole village comes out with weapons," Joseph said. "They bring hatchets, knives, switches, clubs—and then line up in two rows opposite each other. They make the victim run between the rows and everyone swings their weapons at them."

Anna shrunk back as Joseph explained. "It's a way to test the captive's bravery. The people who act like cowards or beg for mercy get hurt worse than anyone else."

"*Dat* did the smart thing by making the chief happy," Christian said. "He sure loved those peaches."

Anna rose from the table and fetched her freshly baked pie. "Now that we're talking about peaches, it's about time to eat some peach pie." She set the pie on the table and cut it into wedges, distributing a piece to each one.

Her face beamed as Christian eagerly dug into his piece. "This is even better than I remembered," he said.

They finished their pie and had sat talking for a little while when Joseph bade them farewell and left with his family.

Christian leaned toward Jacob. "*Dat*," he said, "I think I'm going to really enjoy working on the farm. Now that I've decided to join the church and get married to Orpha, I want to do my best to be a good provider." Anna's limbs felt lighter as Christian spoke. Surely this would make Jacob very happy.

Christian went on. "*Dat*, I'm sorry it took me so long to decide to do this. You've been very patient."

It was the moment that Anna had been praying for. Now it was Jacob's turn to offer a word of forgiveness. His face turned sober. "I'm afraid I haven't been patient enough. As we talked about peaches tonight, I was reminded of something very special that happened when I went to the treaty conference at Lancaster to receive you and Joseph back from the Indians. That's when I met Scar Face, the man who killed our little Franey."

"Oh no," said Orpha, closing her eyes. "That must have been awful!"

"It was one of the hardest things I ever did," said Jacob weakly. He cleared his throat. "But I gave that man a basket of peaches. And he gave me a wampum bracelet in return. I know that wampum means a lot to you, so I'm going to give it to you."

Anna watched in amazement as Jacob went to the bedroom and pulled it from the wooden chest.

"I never felt free to wear this bracelet," he said as he returned. "But if you want, you may wear it as a sign of peace between the Indian and the white man inside your heart. It will also remind you . . ." Jacob paused. "It can remind you of my love for you."

"Thanks, *Dat*," Christian said, his voice breaking with emotion.

Jacob continued. "And now that you're getting married, I'm going to give you a tract of land to farm on your own."

Anna saw Christian look at Orpha, whose face glowed with delight. With that, Christian and Jacob started talking about the plot that he would be farming. Anna motioned to

Orpha to join her in the kitchen. The two of them washed the dishes and then warmed themselves by standing near the fire.

"I'm so glad you're going to be part of our family," Anna said to Orpha. "I think that you and Christian are going to get along very well with each other."

"And I'm looking forward to having you as a mother-in-law. I know that Christian is very fond of you."

Anna drank in her words. "Thank you," she said. She held out her arms to Orpha, who stepped into her embrace. The two of them hugged and then Anna asked, "Have you set the date when you're getting married?"

"Not yet. But I hope it won't be long."

"Whenever it is, I'll be available to do anything that you need."

Christian came from the living room, eager to take Orpha for a walk. "Thank you for everything, *Mam*," he said as they moved toward the door.

Anna's eyes flew open. Had Christian really called her *Mam*? Her faced glowed with joy as Christian escorted Orpha out. She turned to Jacob. "Aren't you glad that they found each other?"

"Yes, Anna," her husband said. "I think she's bringing out the best in him, the way you do in me." Anna beamed and kissed Jacob lightly on the lips.

"I like your father and Anna," Orpha said as she and Christian left the house. "I think they care a lot about you, both in their own way."

"I know they do," Christian said, "but it's taken me a while to understand that. You helped me see it." He reached out to take her hand.

She clasped his fingers as they walked. "Where are we going?"

"Nowhere special. It's a beautiful evening."

They soon passed the graves near the house and Christian commented, "Did I ever tell you that several of my family are buried here?"

"No. You haven't said much about them. I don't think you even told me their names."

Christian considered this. "I guess I still think like an Indian. We don't usually say the names of departed loved ones out loud."

Orpha looked quizzical. "Why not?"

"We worry that it will make their spirits restless, thinking we are calling them back."

Orpha laughed despite herself. "That's strange."

"Many Indian ways seem strange to white people." Christian paused, as though deciding whether to break the taboo in favor of his fiancée. He looked down at the graves. And then he heard a voice that sounded a lot like *Mam's*. *Of course you should say our names. How else will people remember us?* It was true. How would his children or their children know the story if he didn't tell them? How would Orpha know who he truly was unless she knew this part of him?

Christian pointed at the graves one by one. "Barbara told me that mother is buried right here," he said first. "Her name was Lizzie. On this side of her is Jakey, who was nineteen when he died." His voice was low as he spoke.

He stepped a few feet to the left. "And then on this side is Veronica. We always called her Franey. She was six when she died." His voice turned husky.

"I wonder how the Indians decided to kill those three and let the rest live," Orpha said.

"I've often wondered that myself, especially with Franey. The Shawnees captured a lot of little girls her age. But I do know why they spared me."

"I imagine it had to do with your beautiful blue eyes."

Christian's mouth dropped open. "How did you know?"

"I guessed."

"It's true. A warrior was bringing a tomahawk down over my head, but he stopped in midair when he saw my blue eyes. White captives with blue eyes are worth twice as much in ransom as others."

Orpha put her arm around Christian's waist. "You're worth more than twice as much to me as any other young man I know. I love your blue eyes. And your strong arms. And . . ." She paused.

Christian put his arm around her shoulder. "Were you starting to say something?"

"It sounds strange to say it, but I love that you've been among the Indians."

"Really?"

"Yes, it makes you different from the other men I know. You know so much more about the woods, about hunting and fishing and so many other things."

Christian sighed. "Most of the people around here think it was a terrible thing. They despise the Indians. You know how hard it was for me to come back to this way of living."

Orpha nodded. "It was terribly wrong for the Indians to kill your mama and siblings and to take you captive. But white people did terrible things to the Indians too. At least that's what the Moravian missionaries say. I think Elder Klein agrees with them."

They continued walking, deep in thought. Eventually Orpha turned to Christian. "Remember when the elder preached last Sunday, he mentioned that sometimes terrible things happen to us, but God uses it for good?" she asked. "Like the time that the patriarch Joseph's brothers sold him into slavery in Egypt. They intended it for evil but God made it turn out for good."

Christian nodded. "*Dat* sometimes quotes the Bible verse that says, 'And we know that all things work together for good to them that love God, to them who are the called according to his purpose.' I suppose that's the kind of thing he was talking about."

Orpha's eyes glistened. Christian took her hand and they continued down the road.

After what seemed like a long time, Orpha broke the silence. "Thanks for showing me the graves of your loved ones. You must miss them very much."

He nodded and blinked back tears. "The same way you miss your parents."

They were silent for a moment. "I've often wondered why God allowed them to die but let me live. It doesn't seem fair," Orpha said.

Christian nodded. "Maybe God was thinking of how much I'd need you. You are worth more to me than any other girl I've ever met."

Orpha smiled through her tears but resisted him when he tried to draw her close. "I was going to say it was terrible that white people brought smallpox and other diseases to the Indians. A lot of children were left as orphans too."

They walked for a time before Orpha spoke again. "I think my parents got typhus on the ship because they were trying to help other sick people. At least they died for a good reason. It's been hard for me to live in a foster home. But God has been good to me." Her eyes twinkled. "Especially now that I've found you, I can claim that verse that your father likes: 'All things work together for good.'"

Christian gazed at the grandeur of a large oak. "That's because Creator God sees the whole forest, like we do when we climb the top of the ridge. From here we can only see the trees."

Orpha looked thoughtful as Christian continued, "Elder Klein says all are called by God to carry out his purpose in the world. That's why I like the Moravian people, especially Christian Frederick Post. Remember the Moravian motto I told you about? 'May the Lamb that was slain receive the reward of his suffering!'"

"I don't know what that means," Orpha said.

"I think it means they try to do everything to bring glory to Jesus, the Lamb of God who died for our sins."

"That sounds like the right thing to do."

Christian took a deep breath. "I want to be that kind of person, even if it means . . ." He paused in midsentence.

Orpha looked into his eyes. "If it means what?"

"Well, even if it means that maybe someday, if God calls me, I would be a minister, like Elder Klein or Christian Frederick Post."

"Oh?"

Christian tried to read Orpha's immediate response, but she remained silent for a moment before speaking. "If that happens, I'll be right by your side," she said.

They walked again. "Let's go sit by the creek," said Christian.

Together, they found a shady place where they could dangle their bare feet in the cool water. They held hands as they listened to the sounds of the woods all around. A chipmunk chattered on the far side of the creek. Several minnows played chase in an eddy at the edge of the stream.

Orpha leaned forward and looked into the water. "What's that?" She pointed toward a stone with a sharp edge that lay on the creek bed.

Christian reached into the water and pulled it out. "Look at this! It's a perfect arrowhead. Probably made by a Delaware. I'll make an arrow with it."

"I hope you always keep your bow and arrows and teach our boys to use them too, if God gives us children."

He stood to his feet and reached for Orpha's hand. As she stood, he pulled her close and kissed her, long and hard.

She closed her eyes and returned it, then drew back and smiled. Christian was so happy he felt as if he could fly. Holding her close, he said, "I hope that we have girls too—and that they are as beautiful as you."

With that, Christian took Orpha's hand. His heart welled with gratitude. Life was turning out much better than he had anticipated upon his return to the Northkill two years earlier.

Now that his eyes were trained to detect telltale clues of the divine in the forest of life, he could reflect on the traces of God's presence on the loneliest paths he'd traveled.

With Orpha at his side, he was confident that God would lead the way into an even better future. A future filled with hope.

Epilogue

January 1776

It was snowing outside when Anna hung the new almanac on the wall, marking the advent of a new year. All signs pointed to a time of great change, both in their home and in the commonwealth.

Jacob was doing poorly and could no longer stand cold weather. Anna feared that he wouldn't live to see the onset of spring. She often wished he would write a will. She'd spoken to him about it more than once, but for some reason he wasn't minded to do so. He spoke lovingly of his four children and twenty-four grandchildren, grateful that all seemed to be thriving. He wished to see their families more often. But their move to a farm they'd purchased from Christian and Orpha in Lebanon Township in Lancaster County some nine months earlier meant that only Christian and Orpha lived close by.

Christian was a Dunker minister now, appointed to care for a small flock in the area. Many who'd once attended the Little Northkill congregation had moved farther west, seeking better soil for farming. Orpha served ably as a minister's wife but was busy with their two sons, Abraham and Adam.

Joseph and Sarah now farmed the land once owned by Sarah's parents, who'd moved to Salisbury Township in Lancaster County. Joseph didn't devote all of his energy to farming, as Jacob once had, but took time to hunt and fish for sport as well as to provide food for the family. He said that part of him would always be Indian.

Barbara lived as a widow with a few children still left at home, having lost Cristy after several years of poor health. In his written will, he'd assured her place in the house and farm for as long as she lived.

John and Katie farmed all the acreage on the plots where Jacob had first settled, but they spoke about someday moving farther west, following the trail of others who had once been part of the congregation. The Berks County colony was shrinking in size, although Bishop Jake Hertzler had committed to stay there until he died. Whether for better land or to escape the bad memories of the Indian attack, folks seemed eager to leave the area.

Perhaps it was the mood of the day too. There was unrest throughout Penn's Woods. The British investment in the long and bitter war with the French and Indians had nearly drowned them in debt, so they sought to recoup it through taxes from the thirteen colonies. Some five years earlier, an angry demonstration against the governor in Massachusetts Bay prompted a massacre in Boston, leading colonists across New England to complain bitterly against the king. Angry colonists ousted the Quaker majority in Pennsylvania's General Assembly, and some entertained the prospect of declaring independence from the crown. Jacob was not in favor of the idea, having pledged his allegiance to the king upon his arrival on the *Charming Nancy*.

One morning right after the full moon in January, Jacob complained that he was unable to get out of bed. Anna stooped over his frame and wiped the sweat off his pallid brow with a wet cloth. His chest swelled and shrank as he labored to pull oxygen into his starving lungs. Bright sunlight streamed through the east window and shone onto Jacob's thin face.

"Does the light hurt your eyes?" Anna asked him gently. He nodded and turned his head slightly.

She stepped to the window and draped a linen sheet over the panes. "Is that better?"

He nodded ever so slightly. Anna settled into a rocking chair near the bed and hummed softly as she kept watch.

A few minutes later, Christian swung open the door and stepped inside.

"How's *Dat*?" he asked quietly as he hung his hat on the peg beside the door.

"He's not well. You can talk to him."

Christian stepped to the bed and laid his hand on his father's arm. "How are you doing, *Dat*?"

Jacob opened his eyes. "Christian?" He spoke so faintly that Anna could barely hear him.

"Yes, *Dat*."

"I think that my time is coming soon," Jacob said softly. "Can you call the other children to come home? I want to say something to everyone."

"Yes, I'll let them all know." He turned to Anna. "*Dat* has something he wants to tell us children. I'll saddle the horse and ride to John's house; he can tell Barbara and Joseph to come right away. I'll let Bishop Jake know too."

He wrapped his overcoat around him, took his hat from the peg, and nodded at Anna as he strode out the door.

Anna rose from her chair and laid her hand on Jacob's arm. "I guess you never got around to writing a will." She forced out the words.

"Why bother?" The muscles in his forearm tightened against her fingers.

"To make sure everything is distributed the way you want it."

His eyes were on her now. "I'm not worried about that. Are you?"

"I guess not."

"Good." He closed his eyes.

She dipped the washcloth in the bowl of water and squeezed out the excess before wiping his brow. "Bishop Jake and the children should be here by this evening or tomorrow morning."

A few moments after Anna lit a lamp to cheer the shadowed room, she heard a knock on the door. It was Bishop Jake.

"I hadn't expected to see you so soon," she said, taking his coat and hat.

"I happened to be at John's home when Christian got there," he said. "John will come soon, along with Joseph and Barbara. I rode a horse, but the rest are coming in a wagon. They hope to get here before dark."

The bishop stepped to the side of Jacob's bed and gazed at the silent figure. "I think he wore himself out," he said in a voice barely above a whisper. "Maybe he'll be rested by the time everyone gets here."

The floor clock chimed six times moments before all four of Jacob's children arrived at the door. Anna welcomed them in and bade them hang their winter garments on the hooks on the wall. Everyone was quiet, sensing the solemnity of the moment.

"I want to sit up," Jacob said.

Anna and Barbara stepped forward and took Jacob's arms, helping him sit up with two pillows propped behind him. Joseph and Christian stood on opposite sides of the bed and John stood at the foot.

"Jake, I want you to read Psalm 91, my favorite passage from the Bible," Jacob said softly.

Anna pulled the leather-covered volume off the shelf and handed it to the bishop, who turned to the passage Jacob had requested.

"Do you want me to read the whole psalm?"

"Yes. My favorite verses are at the beginning of the chapter, but I want to hear them all."

Jake began reading, his voice rising and falling with the German phrases. "He that dwelleth in the secret place of the Most High shall abide under the shadow of the Almighty. I will say of the Lord, He is my refuge and my fortress: my God; in him will I trust."

A tear welled up in Jacob's eye and trickled down the side of his cheek. Anna reached over and dabbed it with a cloth.

Anna watched her husband's face as Jake kept reading. More tears came as the bishop read the last few verses of the chapter: "He shall call upon me, and I will answer him: I will be with him in trouble; I will deliver him, and honour him. With long life will I satisfy him, and shew him my salvation."

Jacob breathed deeply now, as though gathering the strength to speak. "God has been good to me," he said, looking at the bishop. "He has allowed me to have children and grandchildren. He has preserved my life through various trials. Now it is time for me to go to my heavenly home."

"Yes, you've lived a good life," Jake said gently.

Jacob slowly shook his head. "I'm afraid that I have not done enough to repay the Lord for all his goodness to me."

The bishop encased Jacob's calloused right hand in his own. "The Lord grants us his salvation without recompense."

"I wish I had been more thankful for all that others have done for me." Jacob's voice was stronger now.

The bishop looked directly into Jacob's eyes. "You are a man of few words, but I have always sensed your appreciation for all those around you."

"I could have thanked my companion and my children more. At times I have spoken more sharply than I should." He met Anna's gaze as he spoke.

Anna dropped her eyes but held his hand in hers.

"The Bible says we all fall short of the glory of God," Jake said. "We can be grateful for God's patient forgiveness."

"Thanks be to God," Jacob said as he looked around the circle of people. He kept his eyes open but was quiet for a time, as though pondering what else he might say.

After Anna reached over and wiped his forehead, he looked at his oldest son and said, "John, I want you to see to it that Anna is cared for and has a place to live in peace for the rest of her life. She has been a kind and faithful companion to me."

His voice was faint, and Anna leaned in with the others to make sure she caught each precious word. "I did not write a will," Jacob continued, "knowing that some would criticize the way I intend to divide my estate. But please take these words as my final wishes; I want each of you children to get an equal share of this farm when I die."

Anna was caught in surprise and joy. *So that's the way Jacob managed to work things out.*

Jacob paused as though to gather his strength before he continued: "I want each of you to walk in the way of truth. Don't be taken in by the cares of this world. Put your trust in God. May you and your families have many joys, with enough sorrows to keep you humble before God." He looked at each one as he spoke their names. John. Barbara. Joseph. Christian. And then, his energy spent, Jacob sank back onto the pillows and closed his eyes.

The family looked on in hushed silence. When Jacob let out a gasp, Anna gently squeezed his arm. She pulled up a chair and sat next to the bed, holding his hand in hers.

After a brief prayer, Bishop Jake dismissed himself into the wintry darkness and the rest passed the time in whispered conversation. Anna lit two lanterns. The shadows from the flames danced on the wall.

After a while, Christian rose and added some wood to the fire in the stove. Barbara stirred a pot of stew at the hearth. Anna sat in silence, listening to the ticking of the large floor clock and a slight rattle in Jacob's throat.

Barbara was the first to notice that the rattle in Jacob's throat had stopped. "Is *Dat* still breathing?" she asked.

Anna laid her forefinger on Jacob's wrist. She shook her head. "He's gone," she said quietly.

The room was silent for a time as everyone gathered around the bed. And then Christian fetched the family Bible and read the Twenty-Third Psalm. He read the last verse twice: "Surely goodness and mercy shall follow me all the days of my life: and I will dwell in the house of the Lord for ever."

"That verse has been true for *Dat*," he said, "and I hope it will be true for all of us when we come to the end of our time on earth."

"Yes," Anna said. "May it be so."

Historical Note

Christian and Barbara Rupp Hochstetler (Barbara was named Orpha in this novel to avoid confusion with Christian's sister, Barbara) followed a different spiritual path than the rest of Jacob Hochstetler's children in that they did not join the Amish church. We do not know many details of their married life, except for the public record of their taxes and land purchases and Christian's place on the list of ordained Brethren ministers.

On April 7, 1772, Christian and Barbara Hochstetler (later Hostetler) bought a farm in Lebanon Township, which at that time was part of Lancaster County, Pennsylvania. Less than three years later, on March 2, 1775, they sold that land to Christian's father, Jacob, who died without a will less than a year later. On February 17, 1776, Jacob's four heirs—daughter Barbara and sons John, Joseph, and Christian—signed papers dividing the proceeds among them. In that same year, Christian was taxed on "wild land" (undeveloped land) in Bedford County, Pennsylvania (now Somerset County).[1]

Nearly a decade later, on January 17, 1785, Christian took out warrants on two pieces of land in Brother's Valley Township totaling some 421 acres, where the Dunkers were moving into the frontier. Christian and Barbara eventually established a farm there, located two-and-a-half miles west of the present Salisbury, Pennsylvania. It is said that Christian helped to "lay the foundations of this church" in Somerset County.[2]

Christian and Barbara had seven children over a span of twenty-three years, beginning with the birth of their son Abraham in 1770, followed by Adam (1775), Barbara (1778),

---

1. William F. Hochstetler, "History of the Hochstetler Family," *Descendants of Jacob Hochstetler*, ed. Harvey Hostetler (privately printed, 2015), 57.
2. Ibid.

Anna (1787), Christian Jr. (1788), Elizabeth (year unknown), and Jonas (1793). Adam became an influential preacher among the Brethren and beyond, as did Abraham's son Joseph, who was widely known as "the Boy Preacher."[3]

On December 6, 1795, Christian and Barbara sold their farm in Somerset County to move farther west into the frontier, near Mt. Eaton in Shelby County, Kentucky. There they joined with other relatives and church friends to establish a Brethren church and helped to erect a church building.[4] Christian and his sons purchased fifteen hundred acres of land and established farms. Here the Hostetlers became part of the Brethren Association, a group that was at odds with the older and larger Brethren group in the East, which convened a large annual meeting.

Sometime later, Christian and Barbara left Kentucky to move onto a 340-acre farm in a Brethren community in Montgomery County, Ohio. It is said that they left Kentucky for Ohio, at least in part, because the influx of English-speaking settlers was crowding out the use of the German language.[5]

Christian died in 1814. His final will and testament, as well as the inventory of his estate, still exist. The first part of his will says:

> In the name of God, Amen. Whereas I, Christian Hostetler of Randolph Township, Montgomery County of the state of Ohio, being weak in body but thanks be to God in perfect mind and senses do hereby make and constitute this my last will and testament this second day of April, One thousand eight hundred and fourteen in form and manner as follows. 1st I do commit my soul to God that gave it me. 2nd my body to dust from whence it came to be buried in a decent manner by my friends and as touching this worldly stuff that

---

3. David B. Eller, "Hostetler, Joseph," *Brethren Encyclopedia*, vol. 1, ed. Donald F. Durnbaugh (Philadelphia: The Brethren Encyclopedia, Inc., 1983), 631.
4. Hochstetler, "History of the Hochstetler Family," 59.
5. Ibid.

it hath pleased God to bless me with in this life to be divided in manner as follows, to wit. 1st I give and bequeath to my beloved wife Barbara Hostetler one hundred acres of land convenient around the house and spring where we now live and all and singular the household stuff, working tools, and stock of all kinds that I now own to have and to hold during her natural life or during her widowhood when she dies or when shall marry again then all the above property and land to be divided amongst my children.

Christian's son Adam moved from Kentucky to Ohio in 1824 and emerged as a leader of the Hostetler Brethren (also known as Kentucky Dunkards), an independent group. Adam and his colleague Peter Hon were disfellowshiped by the original Brethren for "allowing members to own slaves, relaxing standards for plain dress, using the single mode of feetwashing, expressing sympathy for frontier revivalism, and possibly of espousing the doctrine of universal restoration."[6] Nonetheless, their association prospered, growing to include fifteen congregations in southern Indiana, Ohio, and Kentucky.

By 1828, however, the association was dissolved and merged into the larger Restoration Movement, joining the fellowship called Disciples of Christ. Christian's grandson Joseph was a key figure in this transition, having embraced the reformist views of Alexander Campbell. Joseph traveled widely in defense of the Disciples movement. "By the fall of 1844, he had baptized more than 3,000 persons," an entry in the *Brethren Encyclopedia* suggests. "His success at farming, the practice of medicine, and land investments made him wealthy."[7]

Thus, in contrast to the tens of thousands of Jacob's descendants who remained part of the Anabaptist tradition, most of Christian and Barbara's identified with other Christian traditions.

---

6. David B. Eller, "Hostetler Brethren," *Brethren Encyclopedia*, vol. 1, ed. Donald F. Durnbaugh (Philadelphia: The Brethren Encyclopedia, Inc., 1983), 631–32.
7. Eller, "Hostetler, Joseph," 631.

Acknowledgments

Christian's Hope, like all my books, is the product of much research and many invigorating conversations with people who accompanied me on various stages of the writing journey. A number of individuals deserve my sincere, written acknowledgment.

Thank you to Jeff Bach, director of the Young Center for Anabaptist and Pietist Studies at Elizabethtown College, who put me on the trail of discovery regarding Elder George Klein and the Dunker church. Thank you to Joel Alderfer of the Mennonite Heritage Center in Harleysville, Pennsylvania, who helped me locate copies of the Sauer Almanac and other colonial materials.

Thank you to Becky Gochnauer, director of the 1719 Hans Herr House, who helped me make vital connections with the Native American community. I admire the work her organization has done to construct and interpret an authentic replica of a Native American longhouse. Furthermore, I admire the conciliatory spirit in which Becky and her team interpret the history of the Mennonites in the colonial context, including the colonists' role in the displacement of Native Americans in Pennsylvania.

Thank you to C. Daniel Crews, Moravian historian, who provided feedback regarding the accuracy of the book's depiction of the history, theology, and ethos of mid-eighteenth-century Moravians serving in America.

Thank you to Cindy Crosby, who served as a fiction editor and coach from the conception of the plot to the submission of the manuscript. Thank you to Herald Press editors Amy Gingerich and Valerie Weaver-Zercher, who guided my work toward publication. The marketing staff at Herald Press, particularly Jerilyn Schrock, also deserve my gratitude for their enthusiastic promotion of this book.

Thank you to Goschenhoppen historians Jacquelyn Daley and Robert Wood, who willingly shared their expert knowledge of colonial customs near the time and place where Christian Hochstetler's family lived.

Thank you to Dr. Peter Pugliese, a local physician, and his daughter Patti, custodians of the Klein cemetery. They not only welcomed me onto their property but into their hearts as well.

Thank you to Gerald and Marlene Kaufman, retired professional family counselors and aficionados of the Hochstetler family story. They served as advisors regarding the family dynamics described in these pages and gave helpful feedback to an early draft of the manuscript.

Thank you to readers Robert Alley, Laney Buckwalter, Becky Gochnauer, James D. Hershberger, Beth Hostetler Mark, Rachel Miller, Ruth Py, Rusty Sherrick, and Miriam Stutzman, who offered feedback to an early draft. Rusty, Laney, and Ruth are descendants of Native Americans; they serve as reenactors and interpreters of Native American history and culture. Together with Becky, they served as my advisory group on matters related to the Native American tradition.

Thank you to writing group members Gloria Yoder Diener and Shirley Hershey Showalter, who provided insightful feedback to this book from development of the plot to its completed form. Particular thanks to Gloria, who provided feedback on the first draft of the entire manuscript.

Thank you to the producers and staff of TLC's *Who Do You Think You Are?* They extended to me the privilege of sharing with Hollywood star Katey Sagal about Jacob Hochstetler, our mutual seventh great-grandfather. The show accurately portrayed Hochstetler's Amish legacy, with particular attention to the peace tradition that guided his response to an Indian attack on the family homestead.

Thank you to Patricia Shelly, moderator of Mennonite Church USA, who supported me in this significant diversion from my daily work as executive director. Together we hope that the book will promote the vision of our beloved church: "God calls us to be followers of Jesus Christ and, by the power of the Holy Spirit, to grow as communities of grace, joy, and peace, so that God's healing and hope flow through us to the world."

Thank you to my wife, Bonita, for her loving forbearance of my frequent preoccupation with the research and writing of this book.

Above all, I give thanks to God, the Great Creator, whose visage was unveiled in the face of Jesus Christ, the incarnate one whose reconciling love transforms human relationships, making peace possible even between disparate peoples. *Soli Deo Gloria.*

The Author

Ervin R. Stutzman was born into an Amish home in Kalona, Iowa, and spent his boyhood years in Hutchinson, Kansas. He serves as executive director for Mennonite Church USA. He holds master's degrees from the University of Cincinnati and Eastern Mennonite Seminary, and received his PhD from Temple University.

Stutzman is the author of *Jacob's Choice* and *Joseph's Dilemma*, books 1 and 2 of the Return to Northkill series; *Tobias of the Amish*, a story of his father's life and community; *Emma, A Widow Among the Amish*, the story of his mother; and several other books and articles.

Ervin married Bonita L. Haldeman of Manheim, Pennsylvania. They live in Harrisonburg, Virginia, where they are members of the Park View Mennonite Church. Ervin and Bonita enjoy spending time with their three adult children and four grandchildren.

Read all the books in the Return to Northkill series by Ervin R. Stutzman

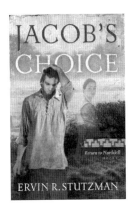

JACOB'S CHOICE
Return to Northkill, BOOK 1

PB. 9780836196818. $14.99 USD
HC. 9781513801681. $28.99 USD

Jacob Hochstetler is a peace-loving Amish settler beside the Northkill Creek in Pennsylvania when warriors, goaded by the hostilities of the French and Indian War, attack his family. Taken captive, Jacob finds his beliefs about love and nonresistance severely tested. After enduring a hard winter as a prisoner, Jacob makes a harrowing escape. Based on actual events, *Jacob's Choice* tells the story of one man's pursuit of restoration that leads to a complicated romance, an unrelenting search for his sons, and an astounding act of reconciliation.

Expanded Edition
HC. 9780836198751. $29.99 USD

The expanded edition of *Jacob's Choice* includes the novel itself along with maps, photographs, family tree charts, and other historical documents to help readers enter the story and era of the Hochstetler family.

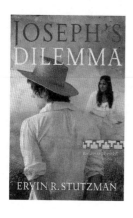

JOSEPH'S DILEMMA
Return to Northkill, BOOK 2

PB. 9780836199093. $14.99 USD
HC. 9781513801698. $28.99 USD

Amish teen Joseph Hochstetler is taken into captivity by Native Americans during the French and Indian War. Joseph finds himself pressed between his unfolding romance with a young Indian woman and the tug of his heritage. Based on actual events, *Joseph's Dilemma* traces the wrenching dilemma of a young man caught between his Amish past, his love for a woman, and an unknown future. When no decision seems like the right one, can the providence of God open up a new way?

CHRISTIAN'S HOPE
Return to Northkill, BOOK 3

PB. 9780836199420. $14.99 USD
HC. 9781513801285. $28.99 USD

When Christian Hochstetler returns after seven years of life with the Delaware Indians, he finds that many things have shifted. His father, Jacob, wants him to settle back into a predictable Amish life of farming, and Christian's friendship with Orpha Rupp also beckons him to stay. Yet Christian feels restless, and when he meets an outgoing preacher from another church in the area with a new take on the gospel message, Christian stands ready for a change. Will Christian choose to remain Amish, or will he depart from the faith of his childhood?

Discussion questions for all books in the series available at HeraldPress.com/StudyGuides.